The 9th Place

OTHER TITLES by NIVEN DALLAS

DALLAS TRUE STORY COLLECTIONS

Book one: We've Got to get Out
Book two: The Good The Bad & The Truth
Book three: A Man Without Love
Book four: A Brick or the Key

REALISTIC FICTION

The 9th Place
World Order Conspiracy

The 9th Place

By Niven Dallas

The 9th Place

Copyright © Niven Dallas 2011

All Rights Reserved

All the characters in this book are fictitious; any resemblance to actual persons living or dead is purely coincidental.

Cover design and artwork by Niven Dallas

Cover photo shows an enhanced image, believed to be that of a small, ten thousand year old meteorite crater. This very rare IIAB iron meteorite strike discovered 1989 in almost the exact centre of the Great Sandy Desert Western Australia. For the purpose of this fictional novel, this small meteorite crater now identified by the author as the 9th Place.

Front and back cover photos by Shutterstock.

First Published   25th April 2013
E-Book ISBN   978-0-9875833-6-9
Trade Paperback ISBN   978-0-9875833-4-5
Hard Cover ISBN   978-0-9875833-5-2

Authors Note

This deep and fast-moving thriller is a work of fiction; however, the story written around many world proven facts, real places, and events. A novel constructed with thought and care, to entertain and stimulate the readers mind.

I must state at this early time this story is not about religion, or denouncing, or accepting the existence of any God. A God may well exist; I leave this matter of existence to the many elevated experts on our planet with a far greater knowledge than I do.

My story offers a fresh look at our human development, and evolution, using current knowledge, many existing facts, and some well-placed fiction. Yes, this novel differs from the normally accepted religious view, yet still leaves room for a reason as to why religion exists.

Is there another example we should all consider. Possibly some new view, awaiting discovery that in the near future may become the truth.

The questions raised are. Why did humans become the most developed species on earth? Why do we kill in conflict more of our own species than any other species? Why over the last five-thousand years, have we humans used religion to convince one another that a supreme creator, or as it would seem, a number of Gods do indeed exist somewhere. Also that these Gods give us their favour and support in our wars and killings.

This story resolves a few of the many questions asked by the inquiring few. Why did the human race need to create religion? Why do we humans need conflict and war?

Are you ready to consider, maybe there is another power that demands compliance to the rules of existence. Rules you have come to know all too well, but do not fully understand. Made and enforced by a universal Entity… an Entity that is not a God.

I have attempted to offer another possibility for our very existence on this planet we call earth. This by binding together a number of strange unexplained known events, and a few philosophies, now recorded in our history. Then offering my explanation of what may have happened, and indeed, may be still happening. Thus creating a new concept and a believable, thrilling, and realistic story; answering. Why are we here? Is there a purpose to life? Are we alone? Then the final question answered… Why do we exist?

Dedication

I have decided to dedicate this novel to all the inquisitive people who enjoy a good realistic "could happen" story, and have a mind to ask the questions. Why are we here, and are we alone. What is the meaning of life? Then the most important question of all... Why do we exist?

I also thank my proofreader's, especially my daughter Tracy for finding most of my grammatical errors and arguing over almost every word, demanding the technical parts made easier to understand for the non-technical reader.

Lastly, to my very tolerant and understanding wife Lesley. My lovely lady who endured years of a hermit husband while writing this complex thriller novel; plus other novels, also my collection of DALLAS true short stories. Writing is a lonely business.

Table of Contents

Albert Einstein

"If people are good only because they fear punishment, and hope for reward, then we are a sorry lot indeed."

"It was, of course, a lie what you read about my religious convictions, a lie which is being systematically repeated. I do not believe in a personal God and I have never denied this but have expressed it clearly."

"I believe in Spinoza's God who reveals himself in the orderly harmony of what exists, not in a God who concerns himself with fates and actions of human beings."

(Albert Einstein.)

Charles Darwin

"Intelligence is based on how efficient a species became at doing the things they need to survive."

"I see no good reasons why the views given in this volume should shock the religious views of anyone."

"The question of whether there exists a Creator and Ruler of the Universe has been answered in the affirmative by some of the highest intellects that have ever existed."

(Charles Darwin.)

Dear reader,
After reading this novel, and with my story fresh in your mind, I ask that you should again read the above quotes. You may agree with me, that these two brilliant minds could have been thinking of the Entity.

"Omnia causa fiunt." (Everything happens for a reason.)

Prologue

My name is Tom, Tom Harold... Professor Thomas Harold. If you want to know the truth, then I will tell you the truth.

As a young scientist, I too sought and demanded the truth. Then after a long academic career, it soon became obvious on my retirement from teaching at Princeton, the truth found me. The challenge before you now, is really quite simple... Will you read my story carefully; with an open enquiring mind, then consider the information to accept any of this manuscript as the truth.

I will begin with saying that a God may well exist. My story might in fact add some new depth and understanding on that subject. This truth may help you as it did me, in providing a way of explaining how the role of a God in our lives has come to have some genuine meaning for many people. Nevertheless, those people should ask, for what purpose and for what reason do they believe in a personal God?

No matter what you believe: or which religion you may follow, the story you are about to read will unfold as a simple, but vast universal plan. Such a simple plan that not only answers most questions to why we exist. However, I must also say, a plan that explains the very reason for us humans ever existing on this planet... in this solar system... at this very time.

You will soon come to understand the all-powerful Entity does not consider its self as a God; no, on the contrary, the Entity has a mission. An enormous universal mission, and for us humans, who at that particular time, it had formed another plan. A plan, which just happened to include the future of our small planet Earth.

To understand this Entities universal mission, would also include finding answers to the age-old questions, "Why are we here," "What is the meaning of life," and "Why do we exist."

We know and understand everything has a life cycle, a beginning, and an end, both here on earth and within the boundless limits of the universe. Nevertheless, you must also except that all event-cycles are defined by time. You will soon learn and come to understand, that all time in this universe belongs to the Entity.

The rules are simple. Everything must remain in perfect order and balance. The time-life-cycle of an object or species must end their cycle in the correct order. This well-planned time-cycle will end, only after the conclusion of a predetermined and useful life-mission. The Entity you are about to read about is the keeper of that time; including all time-cycles, of all objects, and all life within this known and unknown universe.

Many warnings and timely advice provided over thousands of earth-years remained mostly ignored. These warnings advised earlier humans to change their future direction. We have all read about these warnings in the old scriptures, in our religious teachings. Now it would appear most have misinterpreted the warnings as a threat from a God. Many had convinced others that they were the chosen ones, the prophets of a God.

The true message eventually lost and misconstrued over time to develop into yet another religion. However, I was soon to find the all-powerful Entity had its own set of universal rules and evolving problems. We humans had become such a problem, eventually becoming a threat to the continued balance, and ultimately the very existence of our own small solar system.

You must understand that the seeding of suitable planets with life is a long and tedious occupation. A committed business, taking many hundreds of billions of earth-years to develop from single cell to multi cell life. The Entity had come up with some new ways to speed things up a bit.

The only problem being, this planet Earth was well on the way to bringing down its own cycle of destruction. This path of self-destruction being well underway, long before the Earth could reach any useful seeding stage... unless it received a little help. Help from those that had caused the problem... we humans.

I will start my story from where I thought, for me, there was a beginning. Then continue through, to where I know there is no known end...

Chapter One

Urgent Meeting in the Lion's Den

It was another bitterly cold February morning. Tom was feeling his age, exhausted after his regular forty-minute morning run. The hot shower was a welcome event, but did little to wash away the strange sensation he felt deep inside, this odd sense that something was about to happen, and soon.

He put the strange feeling in the back of his mind while he carefully applied the final touch-up and trim to his well-manicured goatee beard, and then moved back from the mirror to admire his effort. Not bad, not bad at all, except for the steel-grey colour, then again his neat goatee did match his still full head of hair.

He had been tempted when Annie was alive to consider a colour tint then thought why bother; after all, he was a sixty-eight year old African-American Professor of Anthropology, and his students expected him to have grey hair. He glanced at the clock. It was now 6:45am, time to consider other matters of far more importance, such as breakfast.

A phone began to ring; it was his latest cell phone. Tom had managed to get by all these years without a cell phone. He hated his cell phone, managing to lose three of these annoying things in the past

1

eighteen months. Nevertheless, as Professor of Evolutionary Anthropology at Princeton, he was required to carry a phone. Now he had another problem, where was the annoying little critter hiding.

The phone kept on ringing, while trying to locate the position before again accused of ignoring it. However, his aches and pains gained from the morning jog were slowing him down. Tom accepted this as a price he had to pay in keeping the fat off. As an Anthropologist, he knew all too well the possible damage caused by overstressed and overworked old joints. He had seen the damage many times in his large collection of Egyptian pyramid builders bone relics.

Maybe he should give up on the running part, and start power walking as many others had in his morning group. Although much younger, they had wisely started to take things easy.

The ringing appeared to be coming from his mini bar; of course, the first place he would visit on arriving home from work. The demanding cell phone eventually found, neatly parked behind a bottle of his favourite single malt whisky.

'Hello Tom Harold here, what can I do for you on this fine cold winter's morning?'

'Good morning Professor Harold, it's Alice, the Vice Chancellor would like to have an urgent meeting with you this afternoon in his office at four o'clock, would that be okay with you?'

Tom knew all too well that this was not just a polite request. This was a direct order from Vice Chancellor George, known as the Lion for the way he defended his territory and position. The man had a PhD in behavioural psychology and used the qualification at every opportunity. Why the hell would he get his secretary to call him at home at ten-to-seven in the morning, he would be at the University in less than an hour.

This was George's childish way of installing a level of psychological doubt in him, putting George at the advantage of having stressed Tom all day, wondering why the urgent meeting. Well two can play that silly childish game.

'Alice, I do hope that you can claim this as extra time in having to start work so early. I'll be at Princeton in less than an hour; couldn't this have waited until then?'

He paused for a brief moment thinking… this early phone call obviously carefully planned. Should he comply, or should he have some denial fun with George? Then softly capitulating, accepting his fun was limited.

'Then I guess your boss George has told you to make the call at this time. The fact is Alice; I have an important meeting with my corporate sponsors at that same time. What about a reschedule of this urgent meeting to seven o'clock tonight at one of the local bars, say J.B. Winberie's in Palmer Square. Would that nice pub suit him, what do you think?'

This brought about fits of giggles and laughter from Alice. She knew well that Tom and George had a personality clash, and barely talked to each other. To have a social meeting and a drink in a bar with Vice Chancellor George, was just as unlikely as Tom having found a sponsor to fund his unusual research project.

Alice liked Tom and kept him informed as to what George was doing. Alice would have liked to become more involved with Tom, but the timing was not quite right. Tom needed more time, as he was still coming to terms over the loss of his wife to breast cancer almost two years ago.

'All right then Tom, I will pass on your suggestion when the Vice Chancellor arrives, and no doubt you will hear his explosive reaction from across the campus. You certainly know how to push his alpha-male buttons to stir him up.'

Tom replied almost to himself.

'Alice what the hell has that cunning old Lion George cooked up for me this time. As you know, I have been avoiding George for quite some time. I have a strong suspicion that the man is about to try something on. I refuse to be an easy meal, to be eaten-up by George and his stupid Princeton politics and bureaucratic university crap.'

There was a short silence. Tom could hear Alice's gentle breathing, and then she replied in a hushed voice as if someone might be listening.

'Remember Tom you never heard this from me. The Vice Chancellor has been talking to one of the bright young lecturers and has, all but offered her your faculty chair. I know it is unfair Tom, but I would assume this will be what George wants to talk about.'

Tom digested this not so surprising news. The bright young lecturer was an easy guess, it would almost certainly be that nice-looking thirty-four year-old Dr Lucy Baxter; but then again she is also a good Anthropologist, one of Tom's best students. Tom then

3

reconsidered the situation, hell I can't avoid the Lion forever. I guess now would be the ideal time for a talk with George.

'Tell George I will be pleased to attend his urgent meeting promptly at four this afternoon... in his Lion's den.'

The day went as planned. Two short one-hour morning lectures on Evolutionary Anthropology, and a well-attended afternoon lecture on the Anthropology of Religion, based on Ludwig Feuerbach 1841 on anthropological principles of religion.

Tom sat in the outer reception office chatting away with Alice; it was now long past four. He did not mind the waiting; he rather liked Alice, then thinking, maybe one day he would find the courage to ask her out to dinner. Then his mind quickly diverted back to George. To make him wait, he knew was just another one of George's psychological mind games.

As he was quietly contemplating this ridiculous situation, the office door suddenly opened. In the doorway appeared the Vice Chancellor wearing his well-practised business smile.

'Sorry to keep you waiting Tom, as you well know managing the day-to-day business of this large university can be quite demanding.'

Tom followed Professor George Gamble into his large well-furnished office. Tom had little patience or time for this long presiding Vice Chancellor. A man who had in his fourteen years in the chair, managed to convince the entire panel of Deans to rubber-stamp and grant his every wish.

The two men looked at each other across the large oak desk. The seconds passed in silence. Tom could sense that George was trying to work out a soft opening for his latest demand... and then he suddenly launched into action.

'Tom, I don't suppose you would reconsider the grant committee's suggestion, being for you to present another subject for your research?'

George had been down this path many times before, although Tom had always stood his ground. The main reason for Tom seeking a lecturer's post at Princeton University so many years ago was the faculty was non-sectarian. As such, he could continue his research into the "beginning of life" theory without fear of religious interference.

Unfortunately, Vice Chancellor George had never been a supporter of Tom's line of research into the connection of early religious beliefs and anthropological evolution.

Over the past months, this made painfully clear; Tom did however understand that George only had limited research grant funds available. In addition, that his great master plan was to link all of the existing research projects together, to fall within the same or connecting fields. Tom's research work was well outside the universities current research areas.

There was however a major problem. Tom had developed a powerful personality following in his thirty years of service, being highly respected as Princeton's most senior lecturer in Evolutionary Anthropology. He had published seven successful books and many hundreds of research and technical papers on his unusual subject. Yet he had never until recently been offered a faculty chair, or for that matter, a position as an Associate Professor.

Vice Chancellor George had eventually, if not reluctantly offered Tom a faculty chair. This position made available by the sudden, odd, and unfortunate death of the sitting Professor of Evolutionary Anthropology. The man had apparently died from a mysterious virus, thought contracted while on a recent field research trip in South America. However, much to Tom's surprise this unexpected offer of a faculty chair also came with a number of special conditions firmly attached.

After almost thirty long hard years at Princeton, Tom graciously accepted the chair as Professor of Evolutionary Anthropology. One condition being, Tom not offered any form of research grant. He had to agree to totally funding his own research, and finding his own sponsor. The second condition was that should Tom be unsuccessful in attracting external research funding, he would then agree to step aside and give up his chair to another candidate.

The time limit imposed by the Vice Chancellor was eighteen months, and this time had now expired. This was what Tom had suspected was the real reason for the meeting. George was about to offer him an ultimatum. Accept a Princeton research grant for research into a subject of the grant committee's choosing, or resign his position as Professor of Evolutionary Anthropology at Princeton University.

Tom looked George in the eye and surveyed his face for any hint of weakness; this was one hell of a cool guy. George ruled his domain with the singular drive of a dictator, being more feared than respected. George would rather lose his best Professor of Evolutionary

Anthropology than back down and lose face, and Tom knew this. As such, this would be a game for keeps.

Today there will be a winner and a loser. Two long minutes of silence elapsed, George never flinched or broke eye contact with Tom, with George considered a good player at his weekly poker game. Tom then spoke slow and softly as he carefully played his hand.

'George, as you well know, my life's-work has been researching the possible connection between early religious beliefs and anthropological evolution. Over these many years, I have provided the world with some sound theories in that a connection may well exist. At this late stage in my academic life, I consider that I must continue with my research work.'

Tom paused as he considered a little flexibility in his argument.

'I do fully understand what you are trying to achieve with the University's limited research funding. I can also see that our research interests are worlds apart; as such, I will honour our agreement established some eighteen months ago and resign my faculty chair.'

George held his poker face, showing no surprise at Tom's decision, knowing he still had some high cards to play. After all, his job was to get what was best for Princeton University, and as usual always thought his way was best.

'Tom, would you please reconsider your decision, as we do not want you to leave us. Your previous position as a senior lecturer of Evolutionary Anthropology is still available; not forgetting the title of Professor will remain with you for life.'

There was no doubting it. George confidently thought he had all the angles covered. In Tom's mind, George had gambled that he would stay… and lost. This man was so sure of himself that he would win this round against the sixty-eight year-old African-American academic. However, George had miscalculated the game, and his opponent.

Tom cared little for academic titles being firstly a man of principle, learning, and passion. George was about to find out, that principle, passion, and age trumps bureaucratic bullshit every time. Tom raised himself from the nice comfortable leather chair, then looking down at George's hopeful face.

'George, my resignation from Princeton University will be on your desk by eight thirty tomorrow morning, as promised.'

Walking back to his lecture rooms Tom sighed with relief. His odd feeling this morning, something was about to happen had come true; he now had no job, and no income. Well now it was over, he had been dreading this moment for months. There was no way he could have generated sufficient financial interest in his research project. Then again, he was never a moneyman.

Few people could understand the depth of his field of research let alone wish to fund it. Nowadays everything revolved around potential profits. If there was no hope or possibility of a research project producing a commercial product that could return a profit, then funding was almost impossible.

Reflecting on those matters, Tom took to mentally calculating his own present financial position. He still had the family home worth about four hundred thousand dollars. It was now far too big for his needs since Annie had died two years ago. He now lived alone as his son and daughter were both in their late thirties, and married with families of their own.

Then he had about four hundred and twenty thousand dollars in his superannuation fund and about nine thousand six hundred dollars cash in his bank account.

His other small income came from his book royalties. Unlike a good thriller novel, his book royalty cheques had all but dried-up. In just a few months, he could no longer expect any further income from that source.

Tom looked around the large lecture room thinking, would he miss all of this; it had been his life for so long. He then accepted the reality; it would not be a luxury retirement, but modest and liveable. Securing another lecturing position at his age would be difficult enough, however finding a University that was none secular so he could continue his research would be all but impossible.

He was spinning a few potential income ideas through his mind, thinking he could still pound the lecture circuits to earn some pocket money. While he was pondering his financial options, his new cell phone rang out loudly.

Chapter Two

The Universal Wide Web

'Professor Harold this is Elaine, the Clinical Nurse Manager at the Mercy Hospice New Jersey, we have a Professor Benjamin Lock here who has asked me to get in touch with you. I am afraid the Professor at ninety-four is not in very good health, I am sorry to advise he is dying from complications of advanced lung cancer. The Professor would like to see you most urgently.'

Tom was shocked at this bad news, thinking, was this his odd feeling this morning, something was about to happen. Therefore, he concluded it was not his resigning from Princeton.

He had been corresponding with Ben regularly for many years. Ben had never mentioned anything about lung cancer, or that he was ill. Ben's written arguments and theories were as usual well-presented and concise. In recent phone conversations, Ben had been his normal sharp and bright-minded self, displaying no sign of a man who was not well. However, this did explain why in recent years Ben had always declined any face-to-face meetings. Then realising his delayed reply had struck him speechless...

'I will be on my way shortly Nurse Elaine, tell Ben I will be there within two hours depending on the traffic.'

It was a miserable cold day, the rain thundered down on the car all the way to the Mercy Hospice. The Hospice was a converted grand old house, dominated by big old trees, branches waving like huge arms in the wind. Were the trees waving a welcome or were they waving him away, Tom could not decide. The small front car park was full, so Tom had to walk some distance in the heavy rain to the once-grand entrance. Stepping through the front door was like stepping into another world,

The inside was a stark difference from the dreary looking outside. From what he could see, the entry had been much modernised; a full makeover as they say, bright and business-like. Tom was standing at the glass reception desk thinking, it's a wonder they ever get any patients wanting to stay here after seeing the grim appearance of the outside. Then again remembering, this was after all a Hospice; a place where people came to die. Just then, a cheery voice interrupted his gloomy thoughts...

'You must be Professor Thomas Harold, we spoke on the phone; come this way, Professor Benjamin is in the day room. I must say we've never had so many Professors at our little Hospice before.'

Tom thought a good thing too, as this was after all not the best place for anybody to end up, being a Professor or not.

'Professor Harold, you must understand that Professor Lock is very ill indeed, he is a terminal lung cancer patient. We do not expect him to last long, a day maybe two at most. The Professor is very frail and connected to a round the clock monitoring system; he also needs the continuous use of an oxygen cannula to assist with his breathing.

He refuses to take any type of medication that may slow down his mind, and has firmly dictated to me what kind, and how much pain reducing drugs are administered to him.' Then the Nurse added with a wink and a smile. 'He's a very naughty boy, come this way Professor Harold,'

Tom followed the plump jolly clinical manager down a long hallway, who then promptly stopped outside a closed door.

'You know Professor Harold, Professor Lock insisted that he be put in a wheel chair to see you, he is a very stubborn man indeed; follow me through here please.'

Amusing, so Ben was a naughty boy, and stubborn. I guess that is one-way of describing a ninety-four-year-old cranky retired Professor of Physics with a bent on Condensed-Matter Physics. Who was running out, or better described as, has run out of time to prove his theory on the beginning of all life, when in reality he was at the end of his own life.

Ben was not looking well at all, but then what did he expect to see as he hesitated at the door, the nurse breezed ahead in a powerful business-like stride.

'Look who we have here Professor, an old friend has come to visit you, well isn't that nice.'

Ben's face screwed up at CNM Elaine's patronising childlike introduction, and then weakly waving his hand in a gesture for her to go.

'That will be all for now Elaine,' dismissing the CNM to leave the room immediately, then catching sight of Tom in the doorway, raised his voice as best he could to attract Tom's attention.

'Well don't just stand there with that pitiful look on your face man; get over here, we can't have a conversation at this distance anymore. I'm a sick old man you know,' followed by much coughing and spluttering.

Ben may be sick and dying, but there was nothing wrong with his cranky temperament, as it all sounded quite normal. Tom walked the few steps briskly to comply with Ben's order. The old friends shook hands, Tom realising just how weak Ben was by the limp almost non-existent handgrip. Then Ben's upper lip curled around the oxygen cannula in a wicked smile with a sparkle in his eye.

'I don't suppose you'd have a fag on you would you Tom? I've been busting for a fag since that damn woman Elaine found my hidden stash last week' as he looked up with a pleading face, which rapidly changed to anger. 'I mean to say Tom, it doesn't take a goddamn Physicist to work out, that a few more fags now aren't going to make any difference to me at my terminal stage in life. In fact, I could prove smoking actually extend my life by giving me some reason to live a bit longer...'

Ben was up to his old tricks again. He had a scientific theory on just about everything, including his own time of death, and his heavy smoking habit, but Tom liked the reference to the "Physicist" part, since Ben was himself a Physicist.

'Sorry Ben, you should have asked that nice hospice manager Elaine for me to bring along some cigarettes for you, when you first asked her to call me.'

Just the thought of that suggestion raised another cheesy smile on Ben's grey face, followed by a fit of coughing.

'Anyway Ben, you know I gave up smoking over ten years ago and that was only a pipe. You also know I've never smoked cigarettes, the nicotine sticks.'

That was close, as he was just about to say cancer sticks. Then Ben gave him his what-the-hell look, and deciding quickly to get down to business.

'Tom, we have known each other for over thirty-five years, and I still remember our first meeting all that time ago. It was to discuss our common interest in the beginning of all life, and if religion and genetic evolution, were in some way linked. Our individual research paths have crossed a number of scientific boundaries over the years, now having evolved in much the same way as the very subjects we are both studying.'

Ben was of course correct; he was in fact referring to the popular "big bang" theory, and the seeding of suitable planets within our solar system and beyond, with the basic particles of life matter. The topic and questions most argued about by Tom and Ben were.

Is there a plan to this continuing evolutional change to all life forms on the planet Earth? Could this be a part of a greater universal plan, controlled by some form of advanced intelligence? If there were such a form of universal intelligence, was it known to exist in the distant past, and just accepted; feared, then worshipped as an all-powerful God.'

These and other related subject matters were debated first at arranged meetings, and then in recent years by long letters and phone calls. They discussed the views and teachings of the old philosophers on these matters, in particular Spinoza's philosophy in 1656. Baruch Spinoza believed that everything that happens occurs through the operation of necessity. He did not believe that a God ruled over the universe, but he did believe in cause and effect, as such, any existence of a God is the natural world and has no personality.

Ben continued with his interesting new variation to their well-explored view. Tom now suspected this was the very reason for this meeting, he was running out of time... Alternatively, did Ben have some new evidence to share with him?

'As we have discussed many times before, such theories have some merit Tom, especially with the emerging proof of previous advanced ancient civilisations. Our present civilisation may have progressed to the mobile phone and the jet airliner. However, we remain mystified by many ancient world wonders.

A good example is the ancient City of Sacsayhuaman, built by the Incas in Peru. How huge hundred ton blocks of granite and limestone could be shaped so accurately, and fitted with such precision, that even today it is not possible to insert a piece of paper between the blocks.

One would wonder did ancient man have some form of advanced technical help with building this huge city over 4800 years ago. The stone building blocks on this site, each calculated to weigh between fifty to over 300 tonnes. How did they move such a staggering weight, with only a wooden lift structure and a simple weaved rope?

Surviving Inca writings claim a god named Viracocha passed on the necessary building knowledge. Interestingly, Viracocha described as a very tall, pale-skinned man with white hair. Now just where the hell do you think he came from?'

Ben paused in his delivery, it was his way of making sure that nothing previously discussed had been left out of the debate, and that all parties understood the debate to that point. However, unlike many previous discussions, his verbal effort significantly laboured, gasping with a shortness of breath.

Tom had always thought Ben's revision style, was most likely the very same way that Albert Einstein and his debating club would have revised their theories. A time when Ben was a member of that elite club of boozy chain-smoking geniuses... so many years ago.

Tom knew from Ben's many references, that the "Einstein Club" had debated this very same subject many times. Their conclusion was a link or connection must exist, awaiting discovery. A link connecting all the ancient wonders and civilisations from the past to our current time. The missing link to explain the future development of our species and all humanity.

Ben's eyes took on a new sparkle; he could see that he now had Tom's full attention. Tom sensed that he might be correct in his assumption that in the face of death Ben wanted to share some special knowledge with him. Ben most certainly had something on his mind, and now he sensed Ben was about to tell him.

'As we have discussed and debated many times before, is there a force or power yet to be discovered. A power that has intelligence; yet free in time and space, with no mass or particle matter.

13

I would propose that this intelligence somehow connected, yet in many places at the same time. I am suggesting to you, that this form of power does indeed exist, and not only on this planet, but throughout our known galaxy and beyond, to the entire unknown universe.

I further suggest that this power is most certainly not a God, well not in the way that we of the human race has decided how a God should act.'

Ben stopped to take a much-needed deep sniff of oxygen; it was becoming obvious that Ben was tiring fast; however, resting was not on Ben's mind, then launching into his theory.

'Tom, in consideration of the known facts and researched probabilities, granted at this time without factual evidence. Most research scientists would simply eliminate all of the absolute impossibilities, and end up with a similar hypothesis to my theory.'

Ben stared into Tom's eyes looking for any flicker of a challenge to his statement, or the dreaded look of utter disbelief. Ben then continued.

'You accept an electrical force does indeed exist, it cannot be seen, but can most certainly be felt. We understand this as a power on earth that can easily kill, yet used by our understanding for the good of all who use this force. We also know that gravitational forces exist; yet again, are invisible. However, we can also feel gravity; explained on this planet as the weight of a mass.

Then we have the interesting grey area of biological physics. With change's to gravitational waves and fields, having a marked effect on all biological life forms; bird and insect navigation, animal migration, and with we humans in our mood swings'

Tom, I know we have discussed these matters many times before, however now is the time you must look over our work again, and in detail.

'All these forces and many more exist in profusion throughout the universe. All are dependent on one thing "matter." We know there are other known forms of radiation that is not made of light or matter, known as neutrino radiation. As previously discussed, neutrinos are particles that travel at the speed of light similar to electromagnetic radiation.

These particles being smaller than quarks can slip right past ordinary matter particles, and escape. Billions of these neutrino particles are flowing through your body and all other matter every nanosecond. The Arnold Somerfield Tachyon particle and field theory

14

is close to my own theory, except that I believe a field or force exists within the space between the matter particles, and not as antimatter. Now bear with me awhile young man.'

Tom found it amusing that Ben talked to him like a little boy, then again there was in truth some twenty-six years of generation gap between them, and after all physics was not his area of expertise. Ben continued.

'Photons have been proved to travel faster than light, admittedly on our world only in a waveguide, but still, convincing proof there is a force in existence that is faster than the speed of light. Then again, you will also have to accept Dr Lene Hau's fine work in using a controlled cloud of ultra-cold atoms that can bring light photons to a complete stop.

We must consider this new proven ability. Think of the huge possibilities; light photons that can remain stationary. Now if you consider the current research into the existence of a radiated force that can travel through any matter many times faster than light... Then you would have the means to support a gigantic and endless form of intelligence... throughout the universe.

On the other hand, light controlled by this force, varied in speed from beyond the speed of light down to zero, this would provide a means of modulation over an inconceivable bandwidth for data and information. So then, consider if that same force were also a form of higher intelligence, then you are a long way to understanding the workings, method, and reason for the meaning of the entire universe.

There was a long silence as Ben gave Tom time to digest this new theory. Tom was thinking hard to find fault, deciding it was only a theory, and what connection did this theory have to his research into the connection of religion and evolution. Tom did not have long to wait for his unasked question to be answered.

'I believe that humans have, since time began known of this force, but never fully understood the link with time, light, life force, and intelligence. In their ignorance, early humans have created a simple way of accepting this unseen force, by calling it a God.

Religion by definition is having a strong belief in a supernatural power that both creates and controls human destiny. A belief fashioned by humans; however, I suspect this belief was encouraged by others of an advanced intelligence who knew the truth. Ancient people then worshipped and feared all of what was unknown, or understood, worshipping this superior intelligence as Gods.

Consider this; what if all of this mysterious faster-than-light universal intelligent force was just a massive intergalactic broadband Internet, a sort of universal intelligence with a specific plan?'

Tom thought about this new theory on the birth of religion.

'Are you suggesting something similar to a "Universal Wide Web," I must admit this theory, or idea would fit all the pieces together.'

'It's more than an idea Tom; it is a sound theory, with a large percentage of it already proven scientific fact.'

Tom was well aware of Ben's theory from his many publications; he needed more time to absorb this new variation as to how religion first created. The old man appeared to be tiring fast. He suggested that he should rest for a while. Ben reached out from his wheelchair and grasped Tom's arm with surprising force, then spoke in a clear unwavering voice.

'My time is near Tom, we will surely never meet again in this life. I have something for you. I ask you as my most trusted friend and student to please carry-on the research needed to resolve this most remarkable scientific mystery.'

Tom was a little startled at this sudden revelation, to what was Ben referring? Tom had copies of all Ben's research work. He was well aware of the vast number of theories and unexplained phenomena that Ben had documented and researched over the past sixty years. Tom had found all of this research most interesting, however, needing a great deal of further research.

Much of Ben's research was at most still just unproven scientific mysteries. Tom knew Ben well; there was something that Ben had not shared with him, something important that he now feels compelled to tell him all about.

Looking down a Ben's serious expression, Tom could not mistake the onset of a tear in the corner of Ben's eye, deciding there was something more to all of this, and then adding...

'Well Ben you have certainly got me all interested, and now I am downright suspicious, just what new evidence have you got for me?

16

Chapter Three

The Gadichi man's bone

With childish fascination, Tom watched as Ben reached under the large heavy blanket covering his legs and produced a standard 30-centimetre long plastic field-sample tube. He then slowly removed the air-seal screw top and withdrew an object covered in thin paper. Ben gently un-wrapped the acid free paper and handed Tom a bone section.

Tom was shocked into silence as he inspected the bone. It was obviously part of a human right upper femur including the head, or hip joint. The lower femur joint was missing, neatly cut-off, not broken as would be expected. Ben inhaled a lungful of oxygen continuing with renewed energy, eager to provide the detail.

'What you are now holding is the undeniable proof, and the missing link to a past civilisation with an advanced intelligence; and might I add, far more advanced technology than we have in our world today.'

As Tom turned the bone over in his shaking hands for a closer examination. He noted the femoral head was made of a dark-grey metal, forming the ball joint, shaped, as would the natural joint. The metal fused into the bone fragment with such detail, the metal prosthesis and the bone were as one. Ben continued his breathless story, between oxygen sniffs.

'X-ray and metallurgical tests show the prosthesis does not intrude into the medullary canal. In addition, the metal internal structure

17

honeycombed, in much the same way as a natural bone. The ingenious design offering excellent lightweight strength, yet still allowing the bone marrow to migrate the full extent of the limb, thus following the same bone structure as the natural human anatomy. This technique is unknown to our medical science; as such, is far more advanced than our present orthopaedic medical technology.'

Ben took another hefty gasp from his oxygen and continued.

'As for the metal material, test's show the elements are mostly known. But some of the elements that make up the complex alloy metal and how they are fuse together are not fully understood at this time.'

Tom was amazed at this object and whispered. 'This human bone is very old, how did you come by this odd specimen?'

'I received the relic by mail just over three months ago; however, I must admit I did know of its existence for quite some time. Tom; you must forgive me for not telling you of this important find, at the time I was sure that it was part of some elaborate hoax.'

Tom was thinking the same thing, although Ben did say he had some tests done. Tom had an avalanche of questions building in his mind, with Ben, sensing his doubt; he coughed and spluttered then, started slowly talking again.

'About four years ago, I received some photos by post of the relic you are holding. A few days after receiving the photos, a man telephoned telling me he was the one who had sent the photos. The man then told me an interesting, but completely unbelievable story, of how he came by the bone.'

Ben could see he now had Tom's full attention again, with Tom eagerly prompting the slow and halting Ben to continue.

'Well go on Ben, what was this man's story then?'

Ben gave Tom a fierce glance at this prompt, took a whiff of his oxygen, and went on.

'Bluey was his name, I don't know why he was called Bluey, I never got his real name, but he was an Australian with a thick hard to understand Aussie accent, kept calling me "mate." Said he was a gold prospector, and had travelled around the outback areas of Western Australia for many years looking for gold.

Tom, I think the Australian outback is their word for a remote or desert area. Anyway, Bluey said he did all right, and had made a good living as a gold prospector, and was now retired with his wife Marge in a place called Kalgoorlie.

He said he needed to be near a bloody hospital since he now has a bloody bad ticker, (smiling at his attempt at an Australian accent.) 'He also told me that this bone once belonged to a Gadichi man called Munyo. As I understand things, this Munyo Gadichi man is much like an African Witch doctor; interestingly, as you know they also use bones to read the future and cast spells.

Apparently, the bone was part of the old dying Gadichi man's charm tool-kit, a local indigenous man who he had met on his many gold prospecting travels in the Australian outback.

Bluey knew off, and believed in the local Indian ways and had the Gadichi man cast a reading into his future, and this is where the story has a little twist. The old Witch doctor foretold that Bluey would find much gold, apparently providing him with a rough paper-bark map to find a special desert location.

However, there was a clear-cut condition to Bluey getting his hands-on the gold map. The old Witch doctor saying, there was a far more important thing that he must do first. He must agree to return a magic bone back to its resting-place, as the "Mooroopna" (ghost spirits) were now angry and wanted their bone back. Bluey had agreed to the deal and was then given another rough paper-bark map, showing the location where to return the bone.'

Tom's eyes were like saucers his imagination was running wild. This was a great story if nothing else; on the other hand, it was now time to poke some holes in this very unscientific story,

'Ben, how the hell did this Bluey guy, in such a remote part of Australia, get to know of you halfway around the world in New Jersey America?'

'Oh well, now that's a strange story on its own,' replied Ben with a short sniff, 'When Bluey got the Witch doctors gold map, he headed into the nearest town to get some supplies. He then decided to carefully wrap the bone in some paper, and found a cardboard box to store the bone in for safety. Bluey then went on another gold prospecting trip this time using the Gadichi man's gold map.

Seemingly, the Witch doctor was right as Bluey eventually found one of the largest gold nuggets ever discovered in Australia. Bluey's luck and fortunes had suddenly changed. He then registered a prospector's claim over the land where the gold nugget found, then sold the gold claim to a large gold-mining company. I suppose you could say that Bluey's financial worries were over, he could now live in comfort and enjoy a good life, but unfortunately this was not to be.' Ben paused for yet another intake of life sustaining oxygen.

Tom eagerly prompted Ben again.

'Well don't just stop there Ben, what the hell happened next?'

The fire started to rise in old Ben's tired eyes as Tom realised that he had gone that fraction too far… Ben had now taken on a firmer voice.

'Now hold on there a minute young Tom, I need a bit of a rest, don't you forget that I'm a dying old man. If you want to hear this entire story before I die then you'll just have to be goddamn patient with me,' then with a twinkle in his eye. 'Are you sure you don't happen to have just one fag around somewhere?'

'No, I'm sorry Ben I don't; but I would very much like to hear the rest of this fascinating story.'

Ben gave out a wheezy sigh of defeat and slowly continued.

'As time went by Bluey was enjoying his life of leisure, when one day he had a massive heart attack and almost died. In hospital, he had time to consider again the deal he had agreed to with Munyo the Gadichi man, and the promise he had made in returning the bone to its rightful home.

When Bluey got out of hospital, he retrieved the old cardboard box with the bone. While he was uncovering the old bone, he noticed he had wrapped it in a few pages of the "Time magazine." Remember that article Time did on me Tom, about "Condensed-Matter Physics; well that was the same few pages in which Bluey had apparently wrapped the bone relic? Bluey then decided to get in contact with me, as the bone was a bit strange and thought that I may be interested.

I asked Bluey to send me the bone for scientific examination, he said he would, but then I never heard directly from Bluey again after that one phone call and receiving the photos.

Three years later, Bluey's wife Marge sent me the bone and the tree bark map drawn by the old witch doctor for its return. It also included a small note advising me that Bluey had since died from another heart attack, and that he had wanted me to have this bone relic. Bluey had only one last request, asking that the Gadichi man's bone returned to the place on the bark map.

Well there you have it Tom. You now have the complete story of how I came to be in possession of this astonishing bone relic.'

Ben fell silent, waiting for Tom to ask the most obvious question; however, Tom remained caught in deep thought, not realizing Ben had stopped talking. So many odd coincidences it was a very spooky story, then he snapped out of his mesmerised state.

'Ben you said that you had some tests carried out, did you by chance managed to get the bone relic dated and DNA tested?'

'I thought you would never ask I did indeed. I had the bone carbon-14 dated to 11,410 years old. As you know, C14 at that end of the scale is a little inaccurate give or take a thousand years, so I had the remains tested by electron spin. This confirmed a date of 10,480 years old.

Still not convinced the remains could be that old, I had the tests carried out all over again and for good measure had them uranium-thorium dated, that test came back at 10,400 years. The DNA test will take a further five weeks. All these tests are expensive you know, I can only call on a few favour's these days.' Ben paused for gasp to allow the fresh intake of oxygen to take effect; he then went on in a breathless voice.

'A remarkable outcome I'm sure you would agree. The entire test results, including the metallurgical tests are right here for you to examine.'

Tom was speechless; 10,400 years old, but then only for a short moment as he had so many questions to ask Ben, who was obviously enjoying the sensational moment and Tom's, expected response.

'Are you saying that these remains, this human femur with its metal prosthetic hip ball are over ten-thousand years old? How the hell did you manage to keep a lid on this major anthropological find? After all the testing labs must know the significance of these results, and the fact that you are now sitting on an important world changing discovery?'

'With great difficulty Tom, and might I add, with many a well construed lie. As for the various tests, I alone prepared all the bone scraping samples, slides, and tests. Nobody at this time has seen the complete bone relic. The DNA and other tests being all carried out at a number of different, but well-respected laboratories around the world. I think our large anthropological earthmoving secret is safe for the time being.

Well young man the ball is now firmly in your court, no pun intended of course,' followed by another one of Ben's cheesy smiles.

'What have you decided will be your first move Tom? I foresee an urgent trip to Australia, and very soon.'

Tom was down on one knee alongside Ben's wheelchair. The old friends looked at each other eye to eye, they realised that this may well be the last time that they would have together. Tom answered Ben's question like a student to a teacher.

'I will start my research at the very beginning. At the known relic site of the positive find, as any good Anthropologist would do. I will use the Gadichi man's map to the find this relic site in Western Australia... Who knows what other interesting things I may discover at this remarkable place?'

Ben had given Tom an Anthropologist's dream, the kind of dream that both scientists had always wanted and longed for. Hard-core, confirmed genetic and technical proof, that this our known world had previously been occupied some 10,400 years ago, by a far more advanced civilisation, with a higher intelligence than the present human race. Tom stood up as Ben handed Tom the laboratory sample tube, and Bluey's old cardboard box containing the strange anthropological treasures, Ben added.

'All the lab research notes and analysis results, along with Bluey's maps are in that box. In addition, there are documents on my own thoughts and conclusions, along with a letter of introduction for you to an old friend of mine, a Professor John Laney. John is the Curator and Director for the University of Western Australia (UWA) Museum of Anthropology in Perth.'

Then Ben added with a crafty wise smile.

'John Laney knows nothing about this significant find in his own backyard. I would suggest to you Tom that you should keep it so.'

Tears came fast to Tom's eyes as he accepted this significant anthropological treasure from his dying friend. Tom shook Ben's thin hand. He could feel the old man trembling at his touch, and then his old friend smiled again, this time with the warmth of a long friendship.

'I'm all excited about what you will uncover in the coming months, but I thought that you of all people would have brought your old dying friend a few last fags.'

Tom half-turned to walk away as what more could be said, he then paused in deep thought again; this time about his old friend Ben, realising that Ben remained a dedicated scientist to the end. Ben was getting excited about an anthropological field project that he most certainly would not live to hear the results off. Then looking away to hide his building tears, Tom placed his hand on Ben's frail shoulder.

'Ben, I thank you for this exceptional opportunity, you must think of me in this important new venture, and wish me luck for what I may find. For some strange reason, fate or circumstances have cleared the way for me, providing all the time I will ever need to pursue this great opportunity. Just hours, before I came to visit you, I had resigned my position as Professor of Anthropology at Princeton University. Now I have a much greater mission to achieve in unravelling this astounding world mystery.

Ben, I will be on my way to Australia within the week. Good-bye my old friend, you will always be in my heart and mind.'

As their eyes met for the last time, Ben nodded firmly in reply.

Tom walked away; tears flowing freely now, out through the door without looking back. Ben and Tom both knew there was considerable and important work ahead. What new scientific world-changing wonders will he find, waiting undiscovered in the vast Australian desert?

Outside the wind was blowing hard with the rain still thundering down. Tom had a deep and distinct feeling; his world, as he knew it was about to change. This strange unusual weather was no matter now; it did not matter at all.

Chapter Four

Life delivered by meteorite

The unrelated lecture question was being asked by the smart arsed fourth year student with his arm in a plaster cast. In Doctor Emma Archers mind, this was a proven principle of simple quantum and classical mechanics.

Kinetic energy, is zero to the mass at rest in a constant moving object, he would know that. Then she realised his motive for the question, it was simply to engage her in a light bantering come-on conversation. Emma had little time or tolerance for all of this alpha male drivel. With a coy look, sharply replied...

'Let me give you a wee example to ponder sir. If a mass did not stabilise to zero kinetic energy, then all the people standing in an accelerating bus would end up crushed. Sending all the standing passengers down to the back-end of the bus throughout the journey. As another example, your pint of beer would continue to slop out of the glass all over your face instead of reaching zero energy when you brought it up to your mouth to drink.'

They both stared at each other in silence He with a childish smirk on his face, and Emma with her best coy scholarly pose, while the class hung on to their every word... he then smugly replied in his upper-class crisp English accent.

'I do say Doctor Archer; we should put this fantastic pint-of-beer theory of yours to the test down at the local pub. It is after all almost four o'clock. As for the bus, well madam, we can motor ourselves over there in splendid style in my new red BMW Z4 sports car.'

The lecture room filled with laughter at this half-baked come-on. Emma was not interested. She had booked a basement mini lecture theatre. Randall knew that, as they were both due down there in twenty minutes to meet up with their fellow research colleagues. In her quaint Scottish accent, Emma sweetly responded.

'Mister Randall, you know that I have to be somewhere soon, however, I do believe that you already have a personal experience with the effects of kinetic energy.'

The smug look on Randall's face slipped a little as Emma delivered her stinging reply.

Why lad, it was only this-time last week, after consuming a considerable number of pints of beer at the local pub. Your previous sports car came to a stop quite suddenly, by the intervention of a rather solid power pole on the Oxford bypass road. Your wee car stopped, and you... well you did not stop at all, did you?'

Emma continued by lecturing Randall like a small schoolboy.

'Now, for your homework this weekend, I want you to calculate the mass, and speed of your car, and the kinetic energy released when your car hit the power pole. I want you to then calculate your body mass converted to kinetic energy when you were catapulted from your now stationary wee sports car, since you were not wearing your seatbelt... tut tut.

Just for the hell of it, you can also calculate the distance that you travelled through the air. Before hitting the ground, also the compound mass weight at impact, which I believe was what broke your arm. That should keep you out of the pub for a while. As for the rest of you, please do have a very nice weekend.'

The room burst into a loud applause as Emma smiling waved them goodbye, leaving the large lecture theatre by slipping out into the narrow service corridor.

Emma was quite pleased with the defeated glum look on the student's face; it was well worth the effort in bringing him down a little.

On the other hand, Randall was most certainly not a dimwit and had proved his worth many times over, especially with his odd views on how he looked at chaos theory.

26

Randall, or rather, his wealthy parents had funded many of the chaos group's research expenses. Emma knew he would be on his way down to the basement mini lecture theatre, to join her and the other members of the chaos group. Emma was looking forward to Randall's research paper about his newly found clustered gravity wave theory.

Bartholomew Randall had been a fourth year student for three years. He was stuck in a fourth year treadmill time warp. He could not pass his fourth year exams, or so everybody led to believe.

Nobody was game enough to use Randall's first name, not even Bart, as he disliked the Simpsons. In fact, he disliked television, and sport, and most things physical. He loved only Doctor Emma, his fast computer, Quantum physics, and beer in that order.

Randal was an accomplished pretend nerd. Who at the ripe old age of twenty-nine, had a childish schoolboy crush on the good-looking thirty-four-year-old Doctor Emma Archer. Alas, he was only one of around 600 other horny male students who attended the prestigious University of Oxford in England.

Emma had her own theories about Randall. That was, he purposely botched his end of year exams so he could stay in Oxford University to be close to her, and the chaos group. A further reason was being involved with the groups many odd and captivating research projects. Then of course, there was also the free access to all the well-equipped science laboratories, and the access to the all-important particle accelerator.

Emma had made things very clear that she was not romantically interested in Randall. For Emma, Randall was a good friend concluding that his boyish immature attitude lacked any serious relationship meaning.

He was really just a charming, good-looking, wealthy six foot three inch young man, acting like a spoiled boy. Emma had pointed out many times she only wanted access to his brilliant mind, his money, and his odd view on matters regarding the chaos theory. Randall did not appear to notice Emma's repeated rejections, as he continued trying to win her attention with silly provoking questions during her lectures, such as today's academic sparing match.

Emma was going through her notes while waiting for the others to arrive. The old white haired Professor already there, back to her, busy marking up the discussion points on a large lecture whiteboard. Professor Reg was always first to arrive at the chaos group meetings,

27

in fact Emma amusingly considered he may not have left the lab from their last meeting held there two days ago.

Professor Reginald Davey at eighty-one years old, was retired from a long life of University lecturing in Astrophysics; however, he would not go home. Professor Reg, his wife Sally, and their grandson Tim lived in a small rented two-bedroom gatehouse flat in the tradesperson's entry to the University cloisters. Such was his lifelong dedication to science; nobody could ever remember having seen him leave the lecture rooms to go home.

The Oxford University research labs were Professor. Reginald's whole life; some say that Professor Reg only resigned his teaching position just to give himself more time in the research labs to complete his life's-work.

Reg took no salary, considered by all as the Godfather, and the bookings-caretaker of the extensive University lecture theatres and research laboratories. Nothing ever moved or happened down in the University lower basement research labs or "the dungeons" as these lower facilities became known, without the full knowledge and approval of Professor Reg.

The next to arrive at the chaos meeting was Lee Wong, fondly known to her close friends as Chirpy. The sixty-two-year old Professor of Quantum Field Theory was a very small Chinese woman with straight black hair, and thick black horn-rimmed glasses. She spoke with a quick-sharp Cantonese accent (hence the nickname,) well known for having a razor-sharp mind and an equally razor-sharp tongue. Everybody watched very carefully, what he or she said to Chirpy, as this four foot nine inch Professor's razor-sharp tongue could cut a full-grown man down to her size in seconds for saying anything that resembled rubbish.

The final member of the Chaos group of six was Jan, the forty-five-year-old Oxford Principal Caretaker, and part-time lab assistant. Jan had been working at Oxford University for nearly twenty years as a caretaker recently promoted to a part-time lab assistant only three years ago.

This promotion allowed Jan to change from his normal caretaker brown coat to a white lab coat. He was extremely proud of his new uniform and now only seen in an impeccably pressed white lab coat with three pens spaced neatly along the breast top pocket.

Not many people at Oxford knew Jan's real name was Rupert Somerfield, as everybody within the University knew him only as Jan.

28

Jan had originally intended to become a University graduate, studying condensed matter physics. Unfortunately, Jan suffered from a small stutter that became a large stutter when excited, and regrettably, also somewhat dyslexic.

Both of these problems were causing him much grief in studying at the same pace as his year. To subsidise his university fees, Jan had taken the job as a university caretaker, then later opted out as a full-time student. However, he continued to attend all the lectures, on every subject and discipline that he could find time to attend. Jan's dyslexic out-of-the-box style of thinking had resolved many technical and scientific anomalies, and had pointed the group in a new direction into further understanding many challenging chaos matters.

The chaos group regarded themselves as a kind of think tank. They choose to take a direct scientific theory down a fast radical path rather than along the more orthodox and proven method that was the accepted steps for normal research.

There was you could say really a seventh member of the chaos group, young Tim the seventeen year old grandson of Professor Reg. Tim is a very special person, being a prodigious savant with a deep and retentive memory for star constellation positions and names. He could accurately calculate the mathematical orbits of meteors, asteroids, and planets all in his head.

With the help of his close friend Randall, in recent months young Tim had developed an obsessive interest in computers... mainly hacking into them.

Tim was a quiet boy who said very little, but when he did speak, he was well worth listening to him. Although most of what Tim said was complex and difficult to follow, requiring the full attention of the chaos group to understand him. Tim was a human Encyclopaedia on the known universe, and sometimes the unknown.

Tim would spend most of his abundant leisure time competing against the University's super-fast computer, on many occasions correcting mathematical formula errors. Two days-a-week Tim also enjoyed time at the Jodrell Bank radio telescope array, special entry courtesy of his famous grandfather Professor Reg having full access to the entire Jodrell Bank facility.

The Oxford chaos group also had access to a number of other special privileges, first being they were answerable to nobody as they funded all their own research programmes. Second, because they were not a part of the normal University research grants funding committee, nor were they required to provide any research or reporting requirements.

Another advantage was the group had full access to the University's research labs and extensive research equipment, since Jan had control over the supply and maintenance of all the equipment and materials stock.

The most significant advantage was old Professor Reg still remained in charge of all the University's research labs and lecture theatre rooms, maintaining the booking schedules. Professor Reg would always find odd slots of vacant lab or theatre time that they could use for their various chaos experiments.

The chaos group was almost invisible to the normal everyday activities of Oxford University. The Dean and the Chancellor of Oxford knew all about the chaos group, and there activities. They had simply accepted the group as a small independent research facility, knowing about most of their research projects. This odd situation accepted as a favour to the long-term respected Professor Reg and his wife Doctor Sally who still held a part-time Oxford position as lecturer in Oceanic and Planetary Physics.

As long as the chaos group's research times and programmes did not interfere with the normal running of the University business, they could continue to use the Universities extensive facilities.

Professor Reg was busy with his back to the chaos group, writing on the lecture board. Being a little deaf, he had not heard or seen the others sitting in the student chairs above, they were now waiting on the last member of the chaos group to arrive. Just then, the dual doors on lecture theatre number nine suddenly burst open. Randall stumbled through using his plastered arm as a battering ram to gain access through the self-closing swing doors while holding a half carton of beer with his one good arm… then announcing in a loud voice.

'Sorry about the small delay my fellow scientists, but I just had to pop next door to get some refreshments. I must say chaps, I have been sitting through a very long boring lecture for the last two hours and I am now as dry as the planet Mars.'

Emma gave Randall a long vicious look that would have made any normal fourth year student cringe, however, the look went completely un-noticed by Randall. Drinking, and for that matter smoking in a lecture room was strictly forbidden; then again this was not a normal lecture session.

Randall proceeded to hand out the beers to the eager hands. When he got to Tim who was sitting on the lectern high chair facing the seated chaos group, digging into the carton he produced a can of coke flipping the top open for him. Tim slowly reached out and accepted the can in his usual silence then looked out into the middle of nowhere, a clear sign that he was about say something.

'Mars has ice water at the poles far beneath the surface material, and in some deep craters, not a dry planet, has never been a dry planet.'

'Thanks for that information Timothy old chap I will remember not to use Mars as my dry example next time.'

Everybody started to gulp down their beer as Professor Reg began his opening comments on the last meeting. The old man turned and smiled at his audience. Then placed his smouldering pipe into a large heavy glass ashtray in front of him, adjusted the angle of his polka dot bow tie, then with a gentle cough for attention continued with his opening comments.

'Ladies and gentlemen, we have come far in our research. We know the exciting small discoveries that we have achieved to date, would normally warrant the publishing of our results at the very least in a technical paper. However, we have all agreed to withhold from releasing any of our research data until we have completed all of our targeted research.

I remind you, this being our important group research. An extensive research, covering how, and why, our early planet earth initially seeded with the basic building blocks of life from outer space.

We now believe we know how life first came to be on this planet, but still need to know why. As you are aware, planet earth is to date the only known planet in our solar system that supports life. This will be our new focus... why only us?'

Professor Reg paused and took a long satisfying drink from his can of beer; he then picked up his pipe and pointed the mouthpiece toward Chirpy.

'Chirpy will bring you up-to-date on her recent findings.'

Professor Reg then left the lectern, taking his large glass ashtray with him. Chirpy strutted down to the lectern holding a bundle of papers in one hand and a plastic milk crate in the other, Doctor Emma Archer followed close behind holding Chirpy's glass of red wine.

Nobody dared to laugh as Chirpy placed the plastic milk crate down behind the lectern and stood on it. The elevation did little to increase Chirpy's visual image, as even with this assisted elevation, her head was just barely visible above the lectern, then in her chirpy high-pitched voice.

'I will commence with an offer; those of you who have quenched your thirst on Randall's workman's beer can now take part in a nice glass of red wine, having brought two excellent bottles in my carry-bag.' Then casting her eye at Randall, 'the sooner we get Randall off the labourer's ale and into appreciating good red wine, then the sooner this young man will grow up. With such a mature change, he might pass his end of year exams and finally gain his degree.'

All clapped in acceptance of this suggestion except Randall, who leapt to his feet launching into a rebuttal to Chirpy's attack on his preferred alcoholic drink.

'I do believe that we have an agreement then, I supply the beer, and you Chirpy will supply the wine? I do mean to say madam, we have been at this for some three years now; nobody ever mentioned to me his or her preference for wine. I would like to say....'

'Sit down Sir.' Chirpy's sharp tongue cut through Randall's ramblings.

'Mister Randall, your dribbling on about anything other than scientific matters is as usual, just childish crap. We have much more serious and significant matters to discuss here today other than your workman's beer.'

Randall promptly sat down with a stunned look, thinking now what have I done. It was after all Chirpy who brought-up the booze matter first.

Chirpy used her right index finger to push back her thick black glasses tightly onto her face then read from her bundle of notes.

'As you are all aware, for a number of years meteors have been randomly sampled just before they enter the earth's atmosphere. The samples were from all the common meteor showers, with Perseids and Orionids being the only two showers to prove some evidence of bacteria-morphs.

Why was it that out of the five known common meteor showers that arrive in our atmosphere each year, only two showers have provided a confirmed existence of bacteria, and that being dead bacteria. While the other three meteor showers have no indication of any basic single-cell life, past or present... I must confess we have no idea why at this stage.'

Chirpy then waved her bundle of notes above her head like a flag.

'From this research, we can conclude that no new basic life from outer space is heading our way. Who knows, maybe Earth is adequately seeded with life. Another possibility is there are no more live organic forms in our solar system or possibly the galaxy. Well chaos group, I have some interesting news for you today.'

Chirpy paused for effect, took a sip of her wine, and surveyed her small audience for retained maximum attention.

'My friends, this line of research has proved most interesting. I have the feeling we have been deliberately bypassed. As you all know, it is now a proven fact that all meteors, asteroids, and comets are interstellar coming from outside of our solar system. Therefore the question would be. Why are we being bombarded and targeted on an annual basis, at this particular time in our history, with only baron or dead meteors and small asteroids?'

Chirpy paused to consult her notes and then continued.

'Now we have another strange, yet connecting mystery. I have just managed to get my hands-on an unauthorised copy of NASA's findings of the latest space mission to the asteroid belt. As you are all aware, the plan was to land a small sample probe on a large asteroid called Vista. This mission was a great scientific success, and fully reported in all the worlds press.

Even so, matters not reported, this important mission also carried out the sampling of many two-hundred metre wide asteroids, and thousands small meteorites. The main purpose was to prove if any basic life forms existed, and here are the findings.'

Chirpy then waved another large folder of documents above her head for effect.

'And what would you know my dear chaos group of friends; the results were a conclusive twenty-two percent positive in finding live single cell bacteria across the full range of samples.'

There was an aura of tense hush not a word spoken as the six brilliant minds in the lecture theatre were all in deep thought about this significant information. Jan was the first to speak in his slight stutter.

'Co-could you spare another bbeer please Randall?'

Randall replied in his crisp manner.

'You know the rules better than I do Jan, you must only speak from the lectern old boy, please do take another beer on your way down there.'

Jan shuffled to his feet and made his way down to the lectern smiling at Chirpy as they passed. Jan did not like speaking let alone public speaking but knew that Randall was only trying to get him to put his thoughts into the discussion. He knew that they were all his friends and would not laugh at his stuttering London accent. They were all very used to him now… and his brand of humour.

'Fi-friends Romans and countrymen, l-lend me your bleeding ears.

Randall cut into Jan's stuttering light-hearted speech.

'Oh for Christ sake Jan do get on with it old chap, we all know you like to crap on when you're holding the floor, however this is all becoming very exciting stuff. Now let us all hear what is on your mind old boy?'

'W-well, the way I see things are the chaotic ra-random tracks of m-meteors now have some form of calculated o-order. Some parts of our solar s-system is being delivered with life, and other areas a-are not. This is n no longer a chaos th-theory; no, it's a full-on order of a planned e-event.'

Everybody had turned his or her attention to Tim. He had lifted his head from staring at the floor and was looking out into nowhere up over the heads of all who were watching him. There was no point in following his gaze, as they all knew that nothing was there… Tim was about to speak.

'We must discover where the space objects carrying Archaea and Eucarya came from. These single cell building blocks of life have come from somewhere. Most importantly, we must find where they are going. Jupiter does not attract them all.'

Jan took a long drink from his can and came back to life with a jolt.

'Just h-how would y-you do that Tim, the b-bleeding lot are all in o-orbit w whizzing around the sun in the asteroid belt o-out past Mars. We're bleeding lucky that j-Jupiter cop's most of em, cause if it didn't….'

At Jan's comment, Tim lifted his head and spoke again, addressing nobody in particular.

'This is not chaos or disorder. Change is only the wing movement of a butterfly. Just one tiny shift in a gravity wave will send life on its way to seed a planet in another galaxy; which planet, who directs the seed of life, and where does it originate from? I need to find the answer.'

Now everybody was staring at Tim in deep thought. Tim had a point; how, why, and when were all these asteroids and meteors thrown out of orbit from the asteroid belt into deep space, never to be seen again going? Jan also had a good point; there was now some sort of recognised order to this newly discovered phenomenon.

Next up to the lectern was Randall who promptly started to write out a long complicated equation on the whiteboard, then announced with a grin.

'That, my fellow scientists is the secret formula for my home-brewed beer. I am sure we can sell it to United Breweries. With this,' waving his good arm at the board, 'we could make millions to fund our chaos group research for many years.'

Professor Reg, Jan, and Emma burst out laughing. However, Chirpy could not see the humour in any of this, and stood up screeching in her chirpy high-pitched voice.

'That equation is a mathematical constant relating to electromagnetic, strong, weak, and gravitational. Mr Randall, you are starting to piss me off and make me angry. Would you please get on with what you have to say about this new sum of yours?'

Randall's face swiftly switched from the beaming smile of a confident idiot to the serious look of a scolded naughty schoolboy. Remembering it was not a wise move to piss-off Chirpy.

'Yes well, as you all know I have been working on gravity waves and gravity earth surface clusters. Over the last few months, I have been playing around with quantum bits and low frequency electromagnetic waves using superconducting quantum interference devices, squids for short. My friends, you also know the new physics lab has a very nice superconducting loop with two Josephson junctions. Well to reduce the length of my story, I managed to borrow the thing with the help of Jan and....'

Jan froze in horror, quickly bursting in before Randall made him into an intellectual criminal.

'For c-Christ s sake don't dob m-me in chum. Tell them what you bleeding f-found, not how you b-broke into the bloody interferometer lab.'

With a quick pause and a swig of his beer, Randall continued with his research findings.

'Please do accept my apologies old chap. Well, in a nutshell so to speak, I have found a true correlation between normal electromagnetic waves at low frequencies, when subjected to super-low temperatures and the existence of surface gravity waves. What's more interesting chaps, is that they are strongest at certain places on the earth's surface. This equation proves my point.'

Randall took another drink from his beer and looked up at his captivated audience. Noticing the confused looks, he continued with his lecture, offering a simple explanation.

'We know that the moon has great influence on our gravity, hence the change in our ocean's tides, and we also know that the Polar Regions have a lower gravity than the equator. Now I believe that we have proved that gravity waves can gather in various spots, areas and clusters around the world, and for some reason in varying strengths and values.

My current research interest is; are these gravity wave clusters in a specific place for a particular reason. Have they moved position over a period in our time; and is this phenomenon, found only on our planet earth. Could these strange gravity wave clusters have some connection with Chirpy's dead incoming rocks from outer space?' then a silly grin spread over his face.

'Changes of gravity are known to affect the human and animal personality. You never know my fellow scientists I may have stumbled across the very reason why dogs howl at the full moon and sometimes bite the postmen.'

Randall came up to his seat and sat down in silence drinking his beer, still wearing a silly grin on his face. He was seriously considering lighting up another cigarette, and then he thought no, that would really piss-off Chirpy.

Emma could see that what Randall had found was significant, little was known about these odd gravity waves, other than Einstein's 1915 theory that they must exist. Prior to this theory, the only other proof to the existence of gravity as a force was that of physical weight and Newton's law of motion.

Einstein was mainly interested in quantum gravity waves, ripples in space, and curved time. However, what Randall had now provided was some small fragment of evidence that these gravity waves may also exist as localised on the surface of this planet earth.

A wild picture was starting to form in Emma's head. If these gravity wave positions could somehow be detected and plotted, and if some scale or value eventually applied. The possibilities were endless; many of the answers to why unexplained things happen on our world might be resolved, and many unexplained chaos theories could now have a factual answer.

Randall may have been joking; however, there was some truth in his silly observation in the known fact that the moon cycle has an effect on all life forms on earth. If proven this theory may well provide an answer as to why some humans and animals had some form of personality change with a full moon event.

It may also follow that a person, or animal, or any life form within a high gravity wave zone, may experience life differently. This could influence health, wellbeing, or a more powerful change to their instinct or personality. Besides, it may offer the decisive answer as to how bees find their way, birds and fish migrate, and how ants and crickets can predict a weather change.

Taking a sip of her wine, an interesting thought came to her. Could it be that ancient humans might have had prior knowledge of this strange gravity phenomenon? If they did, and in some way had located these high gravity wave spots, they most certainly would have considered these locations as sacred places.

Then again, these locations would have been the best places to build temples to their Gods. Besides, how would they have known that these gravity spots existed, as we have only just stumbled across the phenomenon ourselves? It was all starting to drift way outside the limits of acceptable and debatable scientific reason; nevertheless, she thought, there may well be a link worth researching.

All were absorbed in the discussion, jotting down their notes. Just then, there was a sharp tapping noise and they all looked down to the lectern. Professor Reg had taken up the speaker's position with Tim sitting next to him on the high stool.

Professor Reg continued to tap his pipe until he had the complete attention of the group. Scanning his small audience, he ultimately locked eyes with Chirpy's disapproving smokers glare. He continued to speak as he casually emptied out the last contents of his old pipe into a glass ashtray that now sat mysteriously back on the lectern.

'Fellow researchers, we have come a long way to understanding how life was first brought to this planet. We now need to pursue the reason why the delivery of life turned off, and as Tim has suggested by whom or for what reason.

Randall has indeed provided us with an interesting new angle, and insight into the Einstein theory on gravity wave phenomena. Most importantly, what have we learnt from this new wave cluster information; simply that we may now be closer to understanding the reason why dogs howl at a full moon, ha ha ha he.'

Professor Reg burst into shaking laughter at his own joke, then noticing he was the only one laughing. The others just stared down at him in silence. Realising he was alone in his joyful moment; he abruptly stopped, then in defending his outburst of laughter.

'Well I cannot for the life of me see how comets, asteroids, and meteorites seeding our planet Earth with early life, and clustered gravity waves changing the mental moods of humans and animals have anything in common. Then again I am but a simple 81-year old Astrophysicist.'

Professor Reg paused, looking around the small lecture theatre over the top of his reading glasses while busily refilling his blackened pipe from a plastic zip pouch.

Emma sensing the change of mood suddenly stood-up and walked down to the lectern. Then in her quaint Scottish accent…

'My turn next, you have all had a wee go except me. Friends, I do think I may be able to cast some light on a connection with these two differing events.'

With a big smile, Emma opened her folder of documents on the lectern stand as the old Professor slowly made his way back to his seat, madly sucking some life back into his favourite pipe.

'First, let me remind us all what we aim to achieve at our meetings, and our current research profile. We are a group of friends enjoying a social drink while studying the many strange un-answered questions about quantum mechanics, and in particular chaos systems and dynamics.

As we know chaotic random behaviour as observed in many fields of science, has always displayed as complex disorder. These random variations usually found in natural electrical and magnetic fields to the changing forces of gravity.

In nature, chaotic systems normally present as utter disorder, found in weather and climate patterns, and in the oscillations and the movement of ocean waves. These confused chaotic systems and movements appear to be random. Yet, we now know that all these systems follow a distinct set of underlying patterns.

Professor Reg and Chirpy have discovered some form of interesting order in the previously known random incoming of comets, asteroids, and meteorites. Jan and Randall have detected unusual wee gravity wave values, found in clusters in some areas of our planet earth. Both of these research subjects are matters much within quantum mechanics, and our chaos research field.

We have all agreed that everything in our solar system and on our world has evolved for a purpose, all things and events ultimately linked in some way or another. I have this feeling. Call it Scottish female intuition if you will. I know this is not much of a scientific conclusion, but it's the best I can come up with at this time, that both of these minor discoveries are somehow linked.'

There was a solo clapping from Randall's hand slapping on his thigh gradually joined by the others. Randall then rested back with his feet up on the chair in front and his plastered left arm resting gently on the adjoining chair.

Being an eccentric, and ignoring the standard protocol, he made his comment speaking directly to the group from this uncomfortable position.

'You know, Jan and I have had that very same strange feeling, and we are only chaps, without the help of any female intuition. This Scottish female intuition stuff might be worth researching... Who knows if the birds and bees are possibly in some form of collusion, using gravity waves as well as magnetic forces to manipulate human love? This may well have a dramatic consequence for our human existence, including the birth-rate.'

Chirpy, Sally and Emma gave Randall a chilling look that would have caused any normal male to freeze into a solid block of quivering silence.

Emma could see that her report ending was a little irrational and scientifically flawed... Randall was making fun of her. Thinking in future, she might keep her theories to herself for now. Randall continued.

'I agree chaps, this is all very exciting stuff and I do have some great ideas on how to plot any further possible gravity clusters that may reside around this planet. Nonetheless, we will need to borrow someone's rather expensive multimillion pound laser interferometer equipment...'

Chirpy butted into Randall's aloof speech.

'Least said is best. Do not tell us about your illegal exploits within these University grounds. We would much prefer to just hear your results than what you get up to in the dead of night around these research labs.' Then turning to Professor Reg, 'Professor Reg, you would not condone any of this meddling with the University's expensive research equipment; would you?'

'No of course not,' replied Professor Reg with wink at Randall that everybody had seen except Chirpy.

Emma was still a little miffed at Randall's feminist remarks. She gathered her papers shuffling them into a neat pile, and asked the group if there were any further matters for discussion at this meeting. There was a short maintained silence suggesting there were no further matters pending.

'In closing this meeting I would like to advise you all that I will be on a short lecture tour in India over the next two weeks. Another important thing worth mentioning is I have heard that a number of people in this University have become exceedingly interested in what we are researching.

The Chairman of Physics, Professor Roger Davis is now asking for rough copies of our private research work. He is claiming pressured into providing details on what we are all working on, he now wants to keep the interested party happy, and off his back as it were. Should we now include Professor Davis in our research information?'

Nobody was listening to Emma as all were now looking at Tim. Tim was staring up at the back of the lecture theatre with a blank look on his face, and then he spoke in a low haunting voice.

'This sender or transmitter of life is of no use without a receiver to receive life. At the start of our solar system, we were receiving this life. Where is the sender, this transmitter? Is the transmitter still broadcasting, do receivers still function somewhere?

The entire chaos group remained silent nobody had an answer.

Chapter Five

Some Order in chaos

It had been three weeks since that last mind-bending meeting of the chaos group. In the following first few days, there were the many emails, phone calls, and improvised meetings at the University regarding the newly discovered information. Then suddenly all communication between the chaos group and Emma in India abruptly stopped.

Emma had returned today from her two-week overseas lecture trip, becoming more than a little concerned at the current University gossip. This was mainly about Professor Reg, that on a recent visit to Jodrell Bank he had realigned and re-targeted a joint American and Russian space probe called Planck, as they say, for gathering private information.

In another story, a severely reprimanded Jan stood down by the University events coordinating board. Apparently, he had run up to test-shot condition the multi-million pound LIGO, (Laser Interferometer Gravitational Wave Observatory) clearly without authority and offering no explanation or to the reasons why.

Everybody in the chaos group had for some reason gone to ground. Nobody was answering his or her mobile phones or emails; everything was in lock-down, what was going on? Professor Reg was still at Jodrell Bank, no doubt attempting to explain his manipulation of an expensive international asset and not contactable, as he did not believe in mobile phones.

Randall's only email was very short and to the point, he would explain everything when he got back to Oxford in about four days. He had just left the island of Bermuda and on his way to the Great Pyramid of Giza in Egypt. Nobody could say why Randall had gone to these places. By Emma's reckoning today was Randall's fourth day... he should be back from his strange travels today.

Jan had suddenly taken leave for a week without pay, stating that he was going to visit a sick friend who just happens to be a NASA geophysicist. The only contact from Jan was a brief SMS saying, (see you tonight J.) Emma was beginning to wonder just what she had come back to, as it appears that her friendly social group was now in their own state of chaos.

Emma lent against the balcony rail and looked down into the front quad, her mind going over the strange incidents. She had to take a two-hour lecture on quantum mechanics in ten minutes. Nervously she looked around then opened her high stress temptation packet of cigarettes.

She was fumbling for a light, knowing that it was a grievous offence to smoke on the University campus grounds. Suddenly a small hand snatched the cigarette from her mouth, and a sharp crisp voice demanded that Emma follow. A startled look down confirmed that Chirpy was now in control of the situation.

Emma quickly followed the small woman at a fast walking pace into a nearby reading room. Chirpy was looking up displaying one of her Chinese expressionless faces with not a hint of what was going on inside her head. Emma had always thought that Chirpy would have made the ideal spy, or Gulag interrogator.

'Cigarettes will stunt your growth Doctor Archer; did you know that I used to smoke four packets a day? Why do you think I remained at the size of a ten-year-old? Well I will tell you, as that was the age when I started smoking. I was lucky indeed, in that all my development continued above the level of the cigarette, hence my brain continued to develop unaffected.

Emma, as all the others had in the chaos group, was never quite sure if Chirpy was purposely being funny in some of the things that she said. Just like all the others, she tried carefully not to laugh at such odd comical comments.

'What the hell's going on Chirpy? Three days after I left for India, nobody in the group would return any of my calls or emails. I have been away only two weeks, and now it is obvious that something significant has happened to cause this lock-down.

I know we had all agreed we would use this style of communication shutdown, but only in the highest of risk situations, including a possible breach of secrecy. Another thing, what is going on with Professor Reg, Randall, and Jan? You're the only one of the group I have seen since I got back from India.'

Chirpy looked up into Emma's confused face and detected a small level of fear.

'Things are not as bad as you suspect Emma. We must move to protect our information; it is now apparently very valuable to many other interested parties. These people are possibly the same people within this University that you had mentioned at our last meeting.

All I know is whoever they are they have powerful friends. We will have a meeting tonight at this location to discuss the developing situation,' handing Emma a small piece of paper. 'The group has come up with some very interesting data that needs to be discussed urgently but not on campus,' then looking around the room, 'these walls have eyes and ears.

Randall and Tim have removed all our research notes and data from the University's computer server. You should do as all the others have and keep all your information on your personal laptop, and take it everywhere with you. Do not plug your laptop into the University's computer router system and do not use Wi-Fi or Bluetooth. We will exchange all our information in future by using only a direct USB lap-link or USB memory sticks for total security.'

Emma stared down at Chirpy with a new heightened level of concern.

'You have me worried Chirpy, we are only carrying out some basic private research, why all the cloak-and-dagger secrecy stuff? Do you think someone is trying to pinch our research data and take the credit for our recent chaos work?'

Chirpy pursed her lips in a look of deep thought.

'Emma, our new data is turning up some interesting and frightening possibilities, one's that will need some urgent answers which your second qualification in Mathematical science research may be of some use. There are now some very complicated equations, and exceptionally large time-shift numbers and sums to compute, also some rather unusual geological profiling to work out. I must go; I have a lecture to give in a few minutes.'

Chirpy put her finger to her lips in a gesture of silence and was gone.

Suddenly, the University erupted into a busy mass of students scurrying across the quad to their next lecture; it must be ten minutes to the hour. Emma jumped back into reality. Confirmed by her Omega watch that she was going be late for her next tuition lecture, and she still had to get over to the Martin Wood complex lecture theatre before the session bell.

Emma power-walked across the campus quad thinking about this secrecy stuff, it all sounded a bit over the top, and as for the quantum mathematics. Well, the entire group were more than capable of crunching a few equations.

She was intrigue about all this, and then remembering Chirpy's note still held in her hand, the crumpled piece of paper had an address written in Chirpy's neat handwriting. She recognised this was Professor Reg and Sally's little flat.

Flat one.
The old Gatehouse. 20 Parks Road, Oxford.
(On the corner of Keble Road and Parks Road)
Speak to no one and be there at nine sharp tonight.

The lecture was in full swing, but the chaos meeting was still on her mind. Just then, Emma heard the Oxford clock bell-tower strike four o'clock, signalling the end of this lecture session yet her present lecture was still in full debate.

It was a good attendance, proving once again that her lectures on string theory were highly regarded by students and many of the Oxford academic staff. Scanning the sea of faces Emma could not see Jan, Randall, or Tim in the theatre. Most times at least one would be present to add some colour to the proceedings by asking a series of various awkward questions, maybe tonight's meeting will provide the answer.

Just off to the right a woman in her forties stood up with a hand raised, Emma motioned her to speak.

'Doctor Pam Holder... Doctor Archer, the passing of time and new technology has proved Einstein's hundred year-old theories that gravity waves do in fact exist in space; as such, they are no longer a theory. My question to you is, in your string theory lecture you believe that some evidence shows that gravitons may exist on the surface of

44

earth. Just how accurate is this theory; is it as close as Einstein's theory was to the existence of gravity waves in space?'

Emma was a little suspicious of this American woman; she was obviously not a student, maybe a visiting academic. She could not recollect ever seeing her around on the various Oxford campuses.

'Doctor Holder, I believe that gravitons do exist here as explained earlier in my lecture. Not only that, I also believe by my research that gravity waves and gravitons may well exist together in clusters.'

The strange Doctor was not going away and had further questions.

'Doctor Archer, the LISA (Laser Interferometer Space Antenna) and the LHC (Large Hadron collider) have proved beyond doubt Einstein's theories on gravity waves in that they do indeed exist. Will this same equipment also prove that your surface gravitons exist? And that they may, as suspected, be in some way related with gravity waves?'

'Doctor Holder, as you are no doubt aware the Large Hadron Collider will not reach its maximum potential power until the middle of December 2012. By which time the collider will have built up enough energy to smash the atom strings containing this required information.

This atomic particle collision experiment, will I hope prove Einstein's theory one-way or the other. Until then we will all have to wait some eleven months to find out if the fourth force "subatomic gravitons" do exist along with gravity waves; or as I have said previously, possibly a duality.'

The strange Doctor politely thanked Emma and sat down. Immediately a man in his sixties stood up, without addressing normal lecture protocol and in a loud, clear voice asking Emma a question.

'My name is Professor James Herman of Harvard University, Cambridge Massachusetts. Doctor Archer, other than that proved recently using the LIGO, and early low power tests using the LHC. Do you really think gravity waves exist freely on the surface of our planet earth? And more to the point, should they actually exist; what do you think would be keeping them there?'

This man was also an American; obviously more used to giving answers than asking them, Emma also had the feeling that the Doctor Holder was an associate of this man. What was going on?

'Professor Herman; again, as I have said earlier in my lecture, gravity waves have no mass as such will pass through all matter which includes the earth, and might I add, will also pass through you. We

45

aim to prove shortly in our research, that gravity waves can affect a mass and all matter, and yet still pass right through them.

The more interesting areas we wish to prove in the coming experiments using the Large Hadron Collider would be the effect of time. In particular, that time and light curves might be affected by gravity and dark matter, as predicted by Einstein. Firstly, we would need to prove the existence of the zero mass Higgs boson particle, known as the God particle or the fourth force. These important experiments will open a new window into how this universe of ours works in this dimension… and possibly the next.'

Emma was experiencing the sound of loud alarm bells. This Professor was asking questions close to what her chaos group were researching. Was this a coincidence?

'Professor Herman, if random gravity waves were found, "roaming" as you say free on the surface of our planet. Then yes, something would have to be causing the waves to remain anchored to the surface or in a particular area or spot. However, I think that this theory would be a highly unlikely scenario at this time.'

The questions asked were close to the chaos group's unpublished line of research. Then a thought occurred to her, who are these two people, who are they representing, and how many others might there be in this large lecture theatre? Emma was a little frightened.

Were they here just to delve into her research group's work? Were they the same people that Chirpy was referring to as powerful people, and possibly dangerous people? Emma knew that she must quickly bring this unusual lecture session to an end.

'Ladies and gentlemen I notice the time is now four thirty well past our lecture end time. Unfortunately my work does not finish when the lecture ends as I still have to write-up my notes and then set-up my next lecture for tomorrow at 9:30am. Think of me please, as I will still be working long after most of you have finished for the day and enjoying your second or third drink at the Royal Oak.

That did it. That broke the spell of the tentative class as the students rose from their seats in one sudden rushed movement at the thought of a drink down at the local pub. Applauding Emma's excellent lecture, as they all made a fast move for the exits. Emma thought time to leave, and grabbed her notes, then disappeared out the side exit into the corridor but felt the many eyes on her back following her rapid departure out the door.

Back in her University office, Emma began to write-up her lecture notes, a few students and staff stopped by to say hello. Everything was going as normal when a student came in and sat at the desk for a chat.

Emma quickly noticed her visitor chair opposite her desk had moved position. This chair was heavy, and positioned for a good reason. Mainly so as the person sitting in it could not see her computer screen, or read what she had open on her desk. While she was away, this chair being obviously moved... but why?

When the student left Emma decided to go home, it was then that she noticed a brown mark showing past the edge of her desk. The computer screen base normally positioned to cover the mark. it had also been moved. The mark caused by a cigarette burn by Randall's careless cigarette last year. Then she remembered what Chirpy had said that Randall had removed all her computer data from the University main server system that was most likely reason why things on her desk required moving around.

Emma was about to call Randall when to her surprise Randall appeared in her office doorway with a big boyish grin on his face.

'Don't just stand there you silly boy, come on in, and tell me what's going on around this place, and why you're not answering any of my calls.'

Randall waltzed into the office and sat down on the moved chair handing Emma a magnifying glass and a phone SIM card.

'Take a close look my dear; tell me what you think of this just newly released integrated circuit.'

Emma was studying the SIM card under the magnifying glass; she could clearly read the miniature writing in one corner.

Replace this card with the one in your phone then
wait for me to text you, and cover the screen. Do not
discuss our Chaos group project in your office... full of bugs.

Randall brought out his phone and began texting at a furious speed, at the same time talking to Emma.

'You know my dear, only Mater has the right by seniority to call me a boy. This description being a reflection of my earlier years in short pants. Might I say that at my somewhat mature stage in life that this title is now dishonourable... do you not think?'

Emma looked up from her miniature reading and replied blatantly with a smile.

'As long as you remember Randall that only my now deceased Grandmother had the right to call me "dear."

Emma quickly changed over the SIM card in her phone handing the old one back to Randall.

'Yes I think we could find a use for this new chip, we should get it checked out in the electronics lab sometime next week.

Just then, Emma's phone vibrated, proving the new SIM card was working well. She read the text with her hand over the screen.

"Emma your office is well and truly bugged with cameras
over your shoulder watching your computer screen
and one over the entry door watching your desk and a
microphone in this chair listening to my beer farts.
Life is most interesting in the field of spying. You will
need to let me sweep your flat, as I believe that all our abodes
may well be bugged except Professor Reg. I must say they are
very good quality bugs. We should say and do nothing to
arouse any suspicion and carry on in our normal sweet
way. Be careful you are not followed tonight.
This is exciting stuff... Fellow spy BR"

Emma and Randall exchanged small talk for the next ten minutes, during this time Emma slipped Randall a key to her flat. They wound up their careful chat with Randall deciding to go down to the pub offering to take Emma out for pub dinner and a drink, asking four times without a hint of success.

'Another time Randall, I still have around two hours of work to finish here and I have a busy day yet to be planned for tomorrow.'

Randall stood up and walked to the door, then turning with a big grin,

'You know what they say, "all work and no play makes for a miserable day" one day I will win the key to your heart.'

Emma thought about that last comment as Randall left; well he does not have the key to my heart but he now has the key to my flat. An embarrassing thought slowly materialised in her mind. Was this another one of Randall's silly games, will he ever grow up, should she get the locks changed? However, Randall did sound genuine about the bugs.

This was all new to Emma; she was having problems adjusting to the thought of covert movements and was worried about the cameras in her office, and now possibly in her home. Then with a thought of horror, they may have put a camera in her bedroom?

Emma then decided it best to remain in her office for now, giving Randall time to check out her flat for any listening devices. She could eat something later.

Emma spent the next two hours going through her student submission papers. Pleased to read that her teachings, theories, and views had inspired many of her students to write some interesting conclusions on her lecture material.

Just then, a loud booming bell interrupted her pleasant task. The first loud toll of the Oxford University Tom bell brought the sudden realisation that she would be late for her meeting with the chaos group. The Tom bell tower commissioned by Sir Christopher Wren in 1682 will toll one-hundred times to remind all students about the first hundred students who formed the Oxford University in 1167. The last bell will strike after one-hundred and one tolls ending at exactly 9:05pm Oxford time, the very time that Emma should be at her chaos meeting.

At around five seconds between each toll Emma had calculated it would take a little over eight minutes to the last toll. Her sums confirmed that she had exactly three and a half minutes to get to the chaos meeting on time.

Emma already knew the fastest way to the old gatehouse. This smaller entry gate was actually the old tradesman's entrance to the 1870 Keble College, as the main grand entrances were facing Parks Road and Keble Road.

Professor Reg and his wife Sally, along with their grandson Tim, lived in what she had understood was a small two bedroom Gatekeeper's house. This small flat was part of the narrow cloisters lane entry, which avoided passing through the main Victorian Gothic style single heavy arch entry-gate to the Keble Liddon quad.

From the front, the old gatehouse entry was set well back into a dark corner, obscured by a massive old oak tree. The small outer gate always kept closed, but never locked. Those that knew would use this access to cut-off the corner to get to the physics departments and the Martin Wood lecture theatre both of which were just across the road.

No doubt, Professor Reg could see the advantage of this position in his later years as everywhere for him was an easy walk to all areas of the campus and both the East and West physics lab sites.

One dim light burnt over the centre of the old narrow arch giving little light and was quite spooky in a Dickens period sort of way. The heavy steel entry gate was set well back into the arched cloisters wall. This was the beginning of a dark thirty-metre long tunnel, opening on to the campus quad.

Halfway along the entry tunnel was a single low wattage light in a protected metal cage bolted to the roof. Direct below the light set into each side of the wall was a solid old wooden door, one was fitted with a large steel knocker. Alongside this door was a highly polished brass plate glinting in the lowlight, which simply read.

Flat one. 20, Parks Road
Reginald & Sally Davey

Then another small plastic sign above the doors heavy knocker read.

Knock hard as we are both a little deaf.

Professor Reg and his wife had lived here for many years, although never once been invited to their flat. She had put this down to the possibility the flat was small and having very little space to entertain. Emma did as the sign advised, and slammed the heavy iron doorknocker hard twice. She was immediately alarmed at how loud it was echoing through the stone cloister tunnel. Looking around Emma was sure that she must have attracted someone's attention, and she was correct. Suddenly the door opened to a smiling Doctor Sally.

'Well hello Emma it's nice to see you again my dear, all the others have arrived and are downstairs waiting for you. The den is full of Reginald and Randall's smoke, and Chirpy is busy giving them both a stern lecture on the health hazards of smoking, come along, follow me.'

Dr Sally was an energetic seventy-six-year old looking only sixty, being six years younger than Professor Reg. She was now retired from full-time university work but still held a small part-time position in the Oceanic and Planetary Physics lab; being well published and respected in her field.

The entry passage was surprisingly long and well lit showing modern decor and paintings. What's more it was warm, Emma figured the flat, which was built in 1870 must be heated by some modern means.

Sally disappeared down a steep narrow stairway as Emma followed trying to keep-up. At the lower level the area opened into a much wider corridor with various quite large open rooms on each side, Emma heard them first as Chirpy's voice rose above the rumble of male voices.

'Are you gentlemen aware, that continued smoking makes you most unattractive to your fellow humans and also very ugly?

Then Randall's upper crust English accent cut into Chirpy's Chinese health speech....

'Madam, I really must protest. We are all scientists in this room, as such would never make such a bold statement. Most certainly not one that could not be substantiated by irrefutable and conclusive proof.'

Emma had reached the open door; at first glance, she was amazed at the size of the room. It was well lit and as big as the small lecture rooms in the University, well appointed to hold a lecture. Chirpy had her back to the door, then jumping to her feet and launched into a vicious an attack on Randall and his poor understanding of the harmful effects of smoking.

'Mister Randall, believe me, I can indeed offer you irrefutable and conclusive proof. Frankly, I can offer you my life's research on this very important subject. My research and personal experience supports the convincing proof to the great disadvantages of smoking, so do listen clearly to what I am about to say.'

Professor Reg was busy refilling his pipe while looking Chirpy in the eye over the top of his reading glasses; he held his gaze with a faint smile on his face. Randall was sitting in a large leather chair looking at Chirpy with smart cocky look on his face and a well-lit cigarette dripping casually from the corner of his mouth. His left arm firmly encased in plaster resting carefully on a small side table. Chirpy began her story.

'My whole life has been a sadly missed natural mating disaster all caused by smoking. I do have mirrors in home and all I see is an ugly little four-foot nine-inch woman; yet as a child, I was most beautiful. That is, I was beautiful before I started smoking.

51

I am the living proof and the unquestionable scientific conclusion that smoking can retard your growth, make you ugly, and ruin your life as a possible future mate.

Can you just try to imagine how it feels, for a mature woman to go into the child's clothing section in a department store to buy clothes, as that is the only place that has my size? Then to find only brightly coloured party dresses or school uniforms. I now have all my outer clothes tailor-made at great expense, in an attempt to look like a normal mature woman.

Since I stopped smoking four years ago, I have grown a further two centimetres in height. As for attracting male company, Jan has taken me out to dinner three times now.' Jan nodded his head enthusiastically in acknowledgement to this claim. Then in a blistering voice concluded with…

'These are the irrefutable and decisive scientific facts that cannot be denied.'

There was a hushed guilty mood in the room. You could have heard a pin drop, with Professor Reg staring uncomfortably at the bowl of his smouldering pipe, while Randall looked transfixed at the top of his beer can parked in his left hand, well out of reach of his mouth.

Chirpy had opened up her heart; she had bared her soul and fears to this very special group of friends. In her quaint but comic manner, she had reached them all. Emma turned to Sally who had tears in her eyes while quickly brushing her own away; they both had walked into this special tender decisive moment. Chirpy had finally found male company and who knows… perhaps love.

Chapter Six

Clustered gravity waves

'Sorry I am a bit late I think the Tom bell might have been fast again, just joking' nobody laughed at her corny joke, and then quickly changing the subject, 'I am impressed at the size of your lodgings. Who would ever believe there was so much room behind that spooky old front door? Professor Reg and Sally, I think you guys have been holding out on us, this is a great place to live.'

That broke the mood of sadness and gloom in the room then everybody turned on Emma with smart remarks for being late. Emma with a big smile beamed it around the room and found a nice leather chair to sit on. Then holding up her hand for permission to speak, asked the first important question of the meeting.

'I have only been away just two weeks, what's happened here while I was gone, and what's all this silly spying stuff about,' then staring ferociously at Randall. 'Randall, did you find any of those bug things in my flat, and just what were you researching in Bermuda and Egypt. I understand you were also visiting the great pyramids of Giza?'

Randall drew a deep breath to answer Emma's entire torrent of questions, however, Professor Reg appeared to have not heard a word, or even noticed Emma's demanding questions. Professor Reg tapped his pipe on the arm of his chair for attention, signalling his intention to speak.

'If I may bring you all up-to-date on the latest developments and what we have discovered in the last few days, then we can start from there.'

Professor Reg paused and lit up his newly filled pipe. Chirpy cringed giving him the evil eye... This effort was a total waste of time, as Professor Reg never even noticed her display of venomous disapproval.

'Over the last two weeks Randall has fed all of our known gravity wave data into the HGSC (Harvard and Gates Super Computer.) As you know this university has access to this computer via a broadband satellite link three times a week. While accessing the HGSC Tim did a bit of tinkering...'

Chirpy could not contain herself and butted in with a screech.

'You mean that Tim and Randall hacked into the world's largest and fastest computer, containing some of the world's most sensitive government and research-company data. You should all be ashamed of yourselves.

You know that it is a US Federal crime to access protected government data. Are you also aware, if you were found tinkering, our piss-weak British government would simply just hand you lot over to the US federal marshals to be convicted of terrorism. You would both most likely end-up in the American Guantanamo interrogation centre?'

Randall coughed on his cigarette while grinning at this outburst, then cleared his throat. He had ignored Chirpy's dire warning on smoking and most other things.

'Professor Reg, may I just jump in for a moment in a response to Chirpy, in Tim's defence. Chirpy, things are not quite, as they would seem. While I was loading up our important data into the HGSC, Tim filled in some free time sniffing around in the non-volatile and random memory; as anyone would do, I suppose, well given the opportunity.

Tim actually came across some very interesting mathematical data not uploaded and cleared off by the previous user. This data interestingly enough was on a similar research topic as our own gravity wave chaos stuff, and might I add we also learnt a thing or two, gaining some important data that we did not previously have.'

Emma had the answer to one of her questions, or so she thought, bursting into Randall's defence speech.

'This would explain why the Americans are interested in our chaos group research. I had two Harvard people asking probing questions about this subject at my last lecture only this afternoon. They must know something about what we are researching.'

Suddenly Tim spoke and everybody went quiet turning to listen.

'The computer back-trace was Chinese. The source of the last HGSC online client being in China. They know about the gravity phenomena in some parts of the world, but do not know why. No mention is made of gravity clusters or surface locations in their equations.'

Emma was dumfounded at Tim's blunt statement; was Tim correct, were the Chinese researching the very same gravity phenomena? It was of no use talking direct to Tim, as he would only speak when prompted by a mind-bending technical challenge, and then only in his own good time. The only person that could get close to a direct response from Tim was Randall, but Emma had not finished speaking yet.

'If Tim is right and by past experience he usually is right, although I would like to see Tim's HGSC data. We must have stumbled across something significant to have the Chinese and the Yanks sniffing around our innocent little after-hours drink and chaos project.'

Everybody watched in silence as Tim walked over to Chirpy and handed her a thumb-drive USB memory stick, Chirpy nodded her thanks and plugged the thumb-drive into the side of her laptop computer. As Chirpy went about working on Tim's new data, Randall spoke.

'I must say chap's, this is no longer a few innocent scientists probing the mysteries of quantum mechanics and chaos theories, lubricated with a few beers and wine;' glancing over at Chirpy for acknowledging her wine, 'we are most definitely on to something worthwhile here, and I would suggest something rather big.

Playing around with other people's expensive computer stuff has without doubt attracted more than a few interested parties around the world of late. It appears obvious to me that our every move might have surveillance. By all accounts, big brother may be watching. We must be very careful. Emma you were about to say something prior to Tim's last revelation?'

Snapping out of her deep thoughts, Emma responded.

'Well yes, a number of things Randall. Firstly, what is the current status on these surveillance bugs, who has been infected, where are they, and who owns the wee beasts?'

Randall was now in his best-elevated element... the centre of attention. Switching to a suitably serious face, he continued with his amateur spy report.

'Well as far as I can ascertain, your office is the only place fitted with two cameras and one mini microphone bug. Professor Reg and I have no University office, and Jan shares an office with about twenty others so no bugs found there. However, this may not be the case with our places of rest.'

All were watching and waiting. Randall smiled while scanning the attentive faces, and then slowly lit another cigarette blowing a perfect smoke ring for maximum effect. He neatly parked his burning fag in the fingers of his left hand, captivated by a plaster cast arm. Then casually taking a long drink with his free right hand, he continued with his spy report.

'I do suspect that Chirpy, Emma, Jan, and I may all have one bug in our homes. I would suggest it may well be installed in the bedroom.' There was a gaping of mouths and a low sigh of surprise from all, except Tim. 'Chaps, I now believe we have yet another important problem to solve.'

Emma was not convinced, now recovered from Randall's suspenseful claim, she enquired suspiciously. 'And what problem would that be, I dare to ask?'

'Simply because I am sure that the Russians are also on to us.'

A further hush descended on the group, all looked at Randall for some hint of truth in his statement. Jan could not believe in Randall's outrageous claim.

'Randall, y-you're bonkers and paranoid about p-people spying on us. We might h-have got the Yanks all upset by u-using there bleeding HGSC, but what proof h-have you got about the ruddy Russians?'

Randall cocked his head to one side with a knowing look and a sly grin, and then slowly provided an answer.

'Well, since you have asked, I will now tell you chaps. This spying matter is now more than obvious to me. You see my fellow scientists, the British secret service would have put the bug in the kitchen, as they know well, that is the place where most ordinary British people spend their time when at home.

Now as for the American CIA, they would have put a bug in every room because, well, they can afford to do so. The Chinese are smart people, they would have put the bug in the dining room, as they know that this is where the conversation flows most in a normal family house. As for the Russians, well the FSO are only interested in real secrets and as such know quite well, they are always discussed in bed.'

Without warning, a large heavy file bounced off the side of Randall's head and spilt out all over the floor. Everyone burst out laughing then turned to see the four foot nine inch Chirpy standing on her chair, fists clenched resting on her hips, with a furious look on her face.

'What rubbish goes through that childish mind of yours? Can you for just one moment try to be an adult? Randall, you must know, or at the least understand the value of this gravity cluster discovery. This is now an important scientific matter. Making silly jokes and all this laughing will not resolve the problems that still need urgent answers.'

Randall quickly recovered his bent composure, rubbing his soar head.

'I say madam violence is not an answer either. You must surely see that I still have a previous injury and in no way able to defend myself.'

The six foot three Randall started waving his well-autographed plaster cast left arm for all to take note.

'Yes I must admit that I do tend to see the humourist side to life's little trials and tribulations, however my dialogue is always tainted with a considerable amount of fact and the truth.'

Jan burst into flowing stutters.

'Are y-you telling us the truth... the bloody Russians a-are also bleeding sniffing around our chaos g-group?'

'Well not quite old boy, however those little damn listening bugs in Emma's office are without doubt Russian made.'

Chirpy sat down with a look of amazement on her face, Sally was first to recover with a question all wanted answered.

'Let me try and get my seventy-six-year old academic brain around all of this. Are you are telling this group that the British MI6, the American CIA, the Chinese CSS, and the Russian FSO. Are all interested in our little after hours get together we have jokingly called the Chaos Group.

A better description would be having a few after-hours drinks and a brainstorming session. All this interest because we have accidentally stumbled across a way to identify life-bearing, and dead meteorites in showers heading towards earth, and some yet to figure out connection with earthbound gravity waves?'

Randall still holding his painful head replied to Sally with a glum look.

'Well, the short answer is yes. You know, there may also be other matters that concern them in what we are playing around with here. Although I must say, this is all I can see at the moment that might attract their attention and interest.'

Randall looked around the room, realising that his story was not believable, and then moved to convince them with the known facts.

'The mini cameras are Chinese, and the mini microphones are Russian but without doubt installed and owned by the Chinese. However, in truth, only Emma installed, and infected with any covert spying gear. I can only assume that is because Emma is the leader of our little chaos group and eventually all our research data will end up in Emma's hands.

I for one believe, there is some yet unknown, good reason why in recent times we have attracted two, possibly three, spying types with what our group is researching. Others will surely follow. I do indeed have more riveting data and information to share with you all. Meanwhile it would appear that my tarnished image needs some repair. For further conformation on my somewhat unconvincing report, maybe we should listen to what Professor Reg has been trying to say all evening.'

'Thank you Randall,' while tapping the bowl of his pipe into another large glass ashtray.

'Not one of you has given thought to how we had determined the existence of clustered gravity waves on earth.

You have all accepted the preliminary data provided by Sally, Jan, and myself that we have the scientific evidence, which of course we do have. I will now attempt to explain, why we are all in trouble, if not in danger from the authorities.

Jan, without any authority, has spun up the LIGO (Laser Interferometer Gravitational Wave Observatory) from the rest stand-by mode. He then carried out three unauthorised test shots for our chaos group.

Our strict University event's committee have taken a very dim view of this episode. Yet to decide on what disciplinary action they will take to Jan's so-called LIGO tinkering. This chaos group's data gathering may well have cost him his job.

As for myself, well I provided to Jan all of the input data for the LIGO. This critical data acquired with my unauthorised manipulation of the Russian and American joint project deep space probe "Planck" at Jodrell Bank.

I simply sent a set of new steering coordinates to the space probe turning the LISA (Laser Interferometer Space Antenna) probe around to face back towards earth. Instead of looking for gravity waves in deep space, the Planck probe scanned the earth for Eigen vibrations and gravity waves, and found them. Three test shots gave us a complete scan of the globe providing a mass of information, all of which is currently undergoing detailed process.

As for my tinkering with expensive international space assets at Jodrell Bank, I think that I have managed to convince them I had suffered some sort of senior's moment, possibly as an 81-year-old senile Astrophysicist. My terrible mistake was in loading up some wrong steering data into the Planck deep space probe. The Jodrell Bank management were not happy and have since suspended my rights of access to the facility, nevertheless Tim is still very much welcome there.'

Chirpy had quietened down a bit from her furious attack on Randall, opening up with a staccato of questions.

'Professor Reg, with all this data of ours being collected from both the LIGO and the Planck probe, the data would have been sent to a number of world scientific organisations who share the vast operating expenses of this probe. These people are involved with all of the test results streaming from this equipment. It can be only a matter of time before someone takes a close look at the Planck data then everyone will know what we have been up to.'

'You are of course correct about the Planck data Chirpy; and yes, it is beamed back from deep space and available to all who have the means to decode it. However, Jan with the help of Randall and Tim, have locked out our LIGO data, which we now hold in a safe location.'

Professor Reg looked over his half lens spectacles and said with a knowing smile...

'Without both sets of data, an observer would see nothing of interest except that the planet earth may have some random gravity waves. Not such a great discovery these days as this is now a proven theory in deep space. However, I do believe that we now have some other very interesting information to tell you all, please tell us your recent findings Randall.'

Randall gallantly stood up to address the attentive group, discharging another huge cloud of cigarette smoke in what became a poorly constructed and failed smoke ring.

'My fellow scientists, for some reason we are being watched. By Jove, I do think we may have stumbled across some answers to a few of the earth's bizarre scientific anomalies. Jan and I have plotted a number of the newly identified world surface gravity wave clusters that for some unknown reason form themselves into recognisable rings.

This rather strange gravity ring phenomena discovered using LIGO and the Planck deep space probe has provided some rather odd mysteries. We have determined that the gravity cluster rings only found near some of the world's most significant and ancient landmarks. At this time we have only located and plotted three such sites however, we have uncovered far more additional mysteries than we have solved to date.'

Professor Reg took over from Randall.

'The first cluster site being plotted close to the Great Pyramids of Giza. Sally has mapped the exact position of three distinct and separate gravity clusters, one being direct over Giza and two others at random distance but within eighty kilometres of the site. All three clusters are of differing size and strength, the weakest being the cluster ring actually over Giza.'

Jan could not hold back, then in his stuttering excitement burst into the conversation.

'I thought this was a strange ph-phenomenon thing, so I figured t-that the strangest known place on earth w-was the Bermuda t triangle well you tell them R-Randall.'

'Well yes, this area proved very strange indeed. Again, we detected three distinct gravity cluster rings all were of differing size and strength, and all overwater. This time I chose the weakest cluster ring to start my research; finding it to be positioned directly over the Bermuda triangles only known, confirmed seabed Mayan Pyramid. This huge pyramid structure is now resting at a depth of some two miles below the surface.

The two other nearby clusters proved to be in locations of no significant importance just the same as Giza. Conversely the cluster positions were not in the same relative positions in fact they were much further apart.'

Sally added some further information,

'On hearing of Randall's report, Jan and I decided to check-out other significant ancient locations around the world starting with our very own Stonehenge. This believed to be world's oldest known man-made stone structure, recently re-dated to some 10,800 years old.

Our findings were conclusive that three gravity cluster rings did in fact exist, one small cluster ring directly over the Stonehenge site and two others close by, this time within one-hundred and fifty kilometres. Again these clusters were at random distances and strengths.'

Chirpy abruptly raised her hand stopping the debate in its tracks.

'This data I have just received from Tim is most interesting. I will in due course translate all the text from Chinese to English but for now, I will explain what the Chinese appear to know.

I must point out the previous information given to us by Tim must be from his own mathematical conclusions of the large number of equations within this file. The reason being as there is no English text that I can see thus far. A remarkable feat I am sure you would all agree.

The Chinese are aware of the variation of gravity strengths on the surface of the planet, having determined ten significant places or areas on earth. So far as can be understood, the Chinese have not made the connection between the odd gravity phenomena, and any ancient sites.

They think it has all to do with some new American global defence system. They are currently working on that possibility having expressed their deepest concerns in a recent diplomatic dispatch to the Americans.'

Professor Reg removed the pipe from his mouth waving it around in the air.to attract the groups attention

'Have any of you considered that the Chinese may actually have a point, this whole gravity thing could well be just a part of some massive American defence experiment? No wonder the Yanks are sniffing around Oxford and our chaos research project, we have obviously stumbled across one of their top secret military experiments.'

Chirpy responded as only Chirpy would.

'Not quite so Professor Reg, I am now reading one of Randall's hacked HGSC files. The Americans know all about the Chinese interest in this gravity phenomenon as it was the Chinese who actually fronted the Yanks about it.

No Professor, the Americans became interested in us only when they did a HGSC sweep for similar material and came up with us. Now both the Yanks and the Chinese are looking into our backyard to see what we are playing with. This would tell me with certainty that this gravity cluster phenomena has nothing to do with the Americans or Chinese playing around with some experimental gravity force.

Have any of you considered that these gravity ring clusters could be just a natural phenomenon, possibly similar to the Northern Lights, the Aurora Borealis? We may have accidentally created a big problem for ourselves. Now we have the suspicious, crisis conscious, nosey superpowers sniffing around our small research project.'

The chaos group were not at all convinced at Chirpy's conclusion, and suspected that she was just stimulating questions and some chaos group thoughts on the subject, and she succeeded, getting a thrusting reaction from Jan.

'How c-could you come to that con-conclusion Chirpy? We have reliably t-tied these gravity c-clusters to three ancient s-sites, and the Ch-Chinese have found ten sites.

We need the Chinese p-plotted gravity positions, and try to link them to our own p-positions. Another thing, w-we can't use that b-bloody HGSC gear again as they are right on to us. If they bloody well catch us a-at it, we'll all end up in the b-bleeding clink.'

Randall stubbed his cigarette out in an ashtray, placed perilously close to Chirpy's low down nose. She hissed and glared at him in utter distaste. Randall was completely unaware of his offensive action and proceeded to talk in his crisp English accent.

'Thank you Jan, I totally agree with you old chap. Well my fellow scientists, it would appear that we have caused somewhat of a stir within the ranks of the superpowers. Which is always a good sign, as it certainly confirms that we are indeed on to something important, and worthwhile? I must apologise to Chirpy....'

Chirpy interjected,

'I sincerely hope it's going to be for stubbing out your filthy cigarette butt right under my nose?'

'No Chirpy I was going to apologise to you for leaving my HGSC hacked files on Tim's thumb drive, as I know you do not agree with the way I collect my important research information.'

Randall moved the dirty, full ashtray over to the other armrest and lit another cigarette, puffing a large, this-time perfect smoke ring into the air just above Chirpy's head, making Chirpy look like an angry angel. He then continued.

'We have been very busy chaps, I have already plotted the ten Chinese gravity sites; this was the very reason that got me started on investigating ancient locations. I just had to go and test a few of the sites out to confirm my suspicions.

Remember that Earth has had known magnetic and gravity variations on many parts of the planet's surface for over three hundred years. What the Chinese have since discovered, is simply there are a number of world sites that measure a far greater concentration of gravity in certain places; in fact ten in all.

As far as I can learn from this data, they do not know about the existence of the gravity ring clusters and therefore do not see the three close related cluster ring sites as we do. They only see one location or area of interest.'

Then pulling his laptop computer closer Randall tapped a few keys and satisfied he had brought up the right file went on.

'I have plotted the ten Chinese earth gravity sites. However, by adding our own gravity wave data, I have come up with the following Earth surface positions. Please take note; and interestingly, also the known natural or man-made, and calculated event age.'

1. The North Pole.
2. The South Pole.
3. Stonehenge (England UK) 10,500
4. Antipodes Island (near New Zealand)
5. The Bermuda Triangle (Mayan pyramid site) 10,400
6. The North-West Cape (North Western Australia)
7. The Great Pyramid of Giza Khufu (Egypt) 10,532
8. Mangaia Island (in the Southern Cook Islands group)
9. Veevers Crater (Western Australia) 10,400
10. North Atlantic Ocean (near the Bermuda Triangle)

'It is worth noting that all the cluster sites we have plotted thus far have separate cluster rings. One over the target and two others close by. In addition, the gravity cluster rings closer to the poles have the shorter distance between them than those that are close to the equator.

Tim and I have recovered a great deal of information from the HGSC. It will take us some time to analyse all the data and even longer now as we will no longer be borrowing our American friend's HGSC super-fast computer. From what we have analysed to date, the Chinese, and the Americans do not know anything about the gravity waves, or for that matter the cluster rings.'

Emma sprang to her feet in response,

'Unfortunately that is no longer the case. This afternoon two strange American academics from Harvard University attended my lecture. I was about to tell you about this when Tim spoke.

They asked the question. "Did I believe if gravity waves existed on the earth's surface and if so, was there any possible relation with the theory of gravitons?"

If the Chinese have not made this important connection yet, then they soon will, as the Harvard Americans most certainly have. My opinion is that we are rapidly running out of time to find the answers to all this strange, newly discovered phenomena.'

A long silence fell over the chaos group. Only the big pendulum clock on the far wall made a sound, as all in the room were thinking and digesting this latest bad news. Then Professor Reg asked a most relevant question.

'You know, something is bothering me about these so-called ten Chinese gravity sites. As I see things, two of these sites are simply the earth's poles, and three are well-known man-made ancient building sites. Two others are just small volcanic islands, one of which I am certain is not even inhabited. On the other hand, the other three sites are the odd ones. As they do not have any significance at all, one being just a position in the North Atlantic Ocean, which Randall has identified as a Mayan pyramid site.

The other is just a small dent in the earth's crust, caused by a small meteorite. The last site is a well-known, but low-key secret radio telescope in Western Australia, which we have in the past used to send and recover data from deep space. Sally my dear, you are the expert on Oceanic and Planetary Physics, what do you make of all this?'

'Well Reginald, I have been doing some research while you people have all been chatting away, what I can tell you is that we have some interesting data emerging. The worlds poles are obviously antipodal however, the next best-known opposite land mass on our world's surface is Antipodes Island. As we all know this island is almost directly on the opposite side of the world to the United Kingdom, hence the name given by a British ship the Reliance in 1810.

However, the closest actual point to being the correct antipodes to this tiny eight by five-kilometre island is actually Stonehenge; the age recently amended to 10,420 years old. So now we have two sets of almost antipodal sites that have our ten odd gravity cluster rings plotted to them.'

Everybody was fascinated at this strange anomaly, Emma asked.

'If Professor Reg is correct and there are three odd gravity sites then I suggest we should investigate them all. However, Randall has just come back from Bermuda, and what data do we have on that area?'

Sally continued.

'As Randall has told us, he brought back from his trip data confirming three gravity clusters lay within the so-called Bermuda triangle, the smallest cluster being direct over the top of a 10,440-year old submerged Mayan pyramid. Now the antipodes to this position is the secret, earth, deep-space radio telescope site called The North-West Cape, situated in a remote part of Western Australia. I might point out; that the Chinese had both of these sites plotted as high gravity areas.

The location in Western Australia is special, known to be one of the quietest low-noise background areas on the surface of our planet; chosen for that very reason. Now we have three sets of antipodal sites with our newly found gravity ring clusters.'

Sally took a drink from her glass of water, then shuffling through her file choose a single sheet of paper, then added more to the deepening mystery.

'The last place Randall visited was the great pyramids of Egypt; again he noted the largest pyramid, being Giza, had the smallest gravity cluster ring. The antipodes to this position is very close to Mangaia Island in the southern Cook Islands, and not all that far from Antipodes Island. Both islands being within 2500 kilometres from the largest land mass, New Zealand. That would now make it four antipodal sites with our gravity cluster rings'

Everybody was stunned then Jan croaked in his stammering voice,

65

'And the ninth gravity cluster place, w-what's this Veevers crater place all about as t-that's in Australia too! What the hell's so s-special about this bleeding place?'

Sally rummaged through her papers and pulled out one lone sheet.

'This site is recorded as the remains of a small meteorite impact crater of some 190,000 tons of material. The impact site dated at 10,400 years ago. The crater impact situated in the State of Western Australia within the Great Sandy Desert, only discovered in 1989 by a Government Geological survey team who were working in the area.

The meteorite crater named after a government survey worker who found the crater, a John Veevers. As meteorite craters go it is really quite small, being only around two hundred and seventy metres across and some eight metres deep. The odd thing about this crater being the walls and the rim of the crater are almost perfect, leading to the conclusion that the impact was a direct vertical hit, a most unusual meteorite event.'

Emma just had to say something.

'Meteorites always enter the earth's atmosphere at an angle. To offer any chance of a meteorite reaching the earth's surface, and to survive our atmosphere, the meteorite or small asteroid must start out being quite large. Our atmosphere slows them down and air friction burns them up on entry. We can see them enter our outer atmosphere as beautiful long-tailed shooting stars; very few ever reach the surface of our planet.

A direct vertical hit on our planet would be all but impossible. Meteorite flight paths are attracted, and directed by the increasing pull of our gravity and the fact our earth is always in motion, rotating.'

Jan still wanted more answers to this rapidly deepening mystery.

'And just what's this V-Veevers crater place the opposite of on our mother bleeding E-Earth then?'

Jan was staring at Sally, eyes bulging in expectation,

'The antipodes of the Veevers impact crater in Australia is a position in the North Atlantic Ocean within 1500 kilometres of the Bermuda triangle, complete with our three gravity cluster rings.'

The group gave out a small gasp, and then Sally went on and summed up all of the available technical data.

'Friends, this last ring-set make the fifth antipodal alignment of ten gravity cluster ring sites that all tie-in with the Chinese identified gravity sites.'

Yet another silence descended over the chaos group as they attempted to digest all of this new and frightening information. They had all formed the same opinion; it was now obvious, none of these strange and unusual antipodal circumstances created by the natural progression of the earth's evolutionary events... They were all man-made

The chaos group's theory then turned into a firm conclusion, some form of external intelligence must have caused these events. So far, four of the ten identified gravity cluster-ring locations found dated around a similar period of between 10,200 to 10,400 years ago... why?

Chirpy added yet another strange observation.

'I have just added up all the gravity cluster-site density figures. That is, all three site cluster rings at each location. They all add up to the same value except for one, the Veevers crater site. That site has exactly double the value of all the other sites. What do you make of that, because it really has me lost?'

Randall was stroking his chin like an old man with a puzzled look on his face, and then his expression changed as some useful information gradually formed inside his head.

'By-Jove chaps a prime site; I think this Veevers crater or ninth site may well be some sort of key to all this. I think we should....

Just then, Tim started speaking. Everybody had completely forgotten about Tim, and now he had something to say. Suddenly all the excitement and squabbling stopped to listen.

'Yes I can see the answer may be found at the ninth position on earth. The five antenna elements must be out of alignment, as the earth's mantle has since moved and the pole axis tilted. We are no longer receiving the signals for life. Then again, we no longer need this life as other new life planets do.'

The whole chaos group stared at Tim in silent awe but Tim just looked aimlessly at the ceiling of his grandfather's nice den with a blank look on his face. Tim the savant had finished speaking; he would add nothing to what he had said, no matter how much the vigorous prompting by others.

Tim, with his remarkable ability to put information together, had fully analysed the data and circumstances, having arrived at the most likely and logical answer. Then Randall suddenly came alive as Tim's vision-like information slowly unfolded in his mind.

Randall jumped in with praise and acknowledgment.

'Well done Timothy old chap, what an excellent deduction, and I do agree with you. Well do you not see my fellow scientists that could well be the correct answer? Over the past 10,400 years, the earth's tectonic plates would have all moved in different directions and by different distances. The original site of the single gravity cluster-ring imprint must have split into two. Then later the earth tilted on its axis a bit causing yet another split creating the three separate gravity cluster-rings; the exact situation we see today.

We should do a detailed plot of the earth's tectonic plate movement for each location and a backwards time-shift calculation over a period of the last 10,400 years. Then making a correction for the last time the earth had a pole shift. My guess is that all the gravity clusters for each location will stack up and form as one single and large gravity wave cluster ring.

Should Tim's five-antenna element theory proved correct. Then we would have all the current evidence that a powerful man-made gravity phenomenon existed on this planet earth around 10,400 years ago. However, we will need to find out why. Why was this powerful gravity force required, and for what use; and then most importantly… created by whom?'

Jan wanted to get in a last word on this matter.

'We will n-need to get access to a really f-fast computer to do those big sums. If Tim and Randall are c-correct about all of this, then we will e-end up with five elements r-right through the c-centre of the earth just as Tim has s-suggested. What is this h-huge gravity system all about then; its g-got me stumped?'

There was a clear methodical tapping of Professor Reg's pipe on his large glass ashtray, bringing everyone to his attention. 'We must be careful what we do and say from here on.

We must use Randall's untraceable SIM phone cards and stay off the University computer system. I think the best way to handle this situation is to carry on and try to act normally. Just do not say anything about this research project in the areas that have these Chinese and Russian bugs.

We should meet again in five days, which should give us enough time to crunch most of the tectonic plate movement numbers and work out our next plan. Friends, this is all very exciting stuff for me to be involved with, considering my late and advancing years.

By this time next week, we may have the true answer as to why the ancients built their magnificent buildings in such special places. Also, we would have the exact reasons why these ancient nations gained accurate consideration of the earth's seasons, and the orientation to the true poles and star constellations.'

Then a thin lonely voice came from Emma adding her thoughts in little more than a whisper,

'Have you people had some thoughts on all of Tim's theories yet? Assuming Tim is correct with this earth receiver theory, what then should we decide about his other theory on the seeding of our planet with early life? What if these two theories were in some way linked?

We should consider the possibility of evidence to the early seeding of our planet, and a receiver that is now no longer working. No longer, God forbid, attracting large catastrophic life-bearing meteorites and asteroids to our planet.

Could these five gravity cluster rods or elements that run through the centre of our planet in fact form some sort of gigantic antenna for a receiver: a receiver of life?'

70

Chapter Seven

The ninth place on Earth

It was only six days since the special chaos meeting in Professor Reg's underground den. Meanwhile Emma had the feeling that her every move was being watched. Randall took great delight in carrying on like some sort of amateur James Bond spy, texting silly little notes to everybody.

It did little for her self-confidence knowing that her University office, and possibly her bedroom bugged. Although she was not, altogether sure that Randall was telling the truth about the bedroom bug part.

The interest in the chaos group's research was not just a feeling; it was real, as the Chairperson of Physics Professor Roger Davis was still insisting on copies of all their private research work. She had also noticed that a number of new old/mature faces were around the campus, or was that just her imagination. New students arrived from around the world almost every day.

Emma was working on the antipodal positions of the ten locations that make-up the five rods or gravity ring elements. She had assumed that Tim was correct and that they would all match-up, however, her world computer model had no equal or antipodal balance as she had expected.

None of the rods appeared in any particular set place or pattern. Various calculations meticulously performed considering the differing angles and distances, but nothing made sense. A pulsing vibration advised her mobile phone was calling out to be answered, stepping out of her office she took the call, it was Professor Reg.

'Emma, could you spare the time to call in at my lodgings after your last lecture today. We Chirpy, Sally, and I have come up with some interesting data that you should see as soon as possible.'

'I will be there promptly at five. Professor Reg, I must ask, have you seen anything of Jan or Randall. At least one of them usually attend my lectures to poke fun at me, and generally give me a hard time. I haven't seen any of them since our last meeting.'

Professor Reg replied in a serious low voice.

'The boys have been very busy working deep in the dungeons including might I say young Tim. All will be explained tonight.'

Professor Reg hung-up and was gone but then Emma had had another quantum chaos thought, what about all the other significant ancient world sites. Were any of them in some strategic or antipodal position, one such place would surely be Easter Island. A quick professional Google world search provided a good quality picture of the antipodal position to Easter Island.

The position was India Rajasthan, in the middle of nowhere in the Thar Desert. The nearest city was Jaisalmer over 250 kilometres to the southeast of the site. Further research confirmed no ancient buildings or known events recorded about this remote desert area. Emma knew there were no gravity ring clusters at the locations, however; it was worth a look to eliminate these areas from the ancient sites with known gravity rings. She could find nothing of significance at both locations and the many other researched positions that she had recorded for the group to ponder over.

The office phone rang making Emma jump.

'Hello Emma this is Roger Walker,'

Emma was startled; thinking, the Chairman of Physics was sounding more than a little cheerful today, I wonder what he wants.

'Sorry to bother you Emma, could you be so kind and pop over to my office for a ten minute chat. Also would you please bring along with you all the promised research papers on your chaos group's work, I will see you shortly then.'

Before she could reply, the phone suddenly went dead with a sharp click. The call was clear and to the point. Professor Roger Walker was not going to give-up easily, on obtaining the information he had requested earlier about the chaos group's research activities. Emma was about to call him back, then thinking Professor Walker was her boss, this sounded more of an order than a request.

Well she might as well call in, as she would be walking past his office on the way home out of the quad. A few minutes later Emma was sitting in the Chairman of Physics plush reception office. She was waiting for him to call her in, wondering as she looked around if he had any mini cameras or bug's installed to listen and watch over his daily activities.

The door opened to a polite smiling Professor Walker, a short balding man in his late sixties wearing half lens reading glasses captivated by a gold lanyard attached to his waistcoat pocket. He looked every bit of the old-style boys club University lecturer. His image was complete wearing a bright red bow tie with white dots. However, his eyes betrayed another man within.

'Thank you for coming over at such short notice Emma, please come in. I do hope this is not an inconvenience in any way.'

Emma had noticed that the cold grey eyes did not reflect his pleasant manner. Much as she tried, she could never find anything to like about this man. He had never earned her trust, and he was very much aware of this. Yet again, Professor Walker was trying to gain her confidence, and Emma was resisting with the feeling that this man had an alternative agenda. She was suspicious, and ready to defend her chaos group's data. Thinking, best to get in first.

'I will have some information prepared for you by tomorrow Professor Walker. Can I ask you just who is requesting this information, as you are aware this is after all a privately funded research project?'

There was a small awkward frustrated delay, then Professor Walker responded but not in his usual polite way, but with a sudden sharp change. A change to a curt demanding no-nonsense voice that caught Emma by surprise.

'Doctor Archer, the University has been most tolerant in allowing your private research group to use the facilities of this University. We have now suffered considerable ridicule and public embarrassment caused by two, or possibly three members of your research group who have realigned, and operated expensive university research equipment for their own purpose.

I am referring to Mr Rupert Somerfield the Principal caretaker here at Oxford. Somerfield, who is I believe a member of your research group, and his messing around with the Universities expensive multi-million-pound LIGO. The events co-ordination committee have recently decided that his silly action was just part of some over enthusiasm, regarding his personal interest in quantum theory, having today closed any further discussion on the matter.

I on the other hand, suspect that he had another motive for his so-called careless actions. Then we have Professor Davey. Now just what would possess a man of his academic standing and respect in our scientific community, to cause such a problem? This man managed to upload a complete set of new steering instructions to the costly American and Russian Planck deep space LISA probe.

Professor Davey has somehow managed to convince the Jodrell Bank committee that he had suffered some sort of senior's moment, and it was all just a terrible mistake. I have known Professor Reginald Davey for over fifteen years. Never in all that time has this 81-year old man suffered anything more debilitating than age related diminished hearing and vision, his mind is as sharp as ever, and works just fine. Professor Reginald Davey never makes mistakes.'

The Chairman's beady eyes glazed with suspicion as he continued with his stern lecture.

'I suspect there is something more to all of this. I would also like to know how that money-spoilt young student Bartholomew Randall got hold of the access codes to go on line to the HGSC (Harvard Gates Super Computer) in America. At this time, we still cannot read his up and downloads with our University access code. We have changed all the access lockout codes; nonetheless this was no deterrent to him, as only this morning he was at it again.'

Emma's eyes narrowed in readied defence of her chaos group. She was right; the Chairman of Physics was on to them. However, he had unwittingly shown his hand, he was obviously watching them all very closely, but why… What else did this man know about her group?

Emma searched his face for clues then seeing none decided to adopt another tactic. To stir him up a bit more, sort of shake the tin, and see what falls out. Emma had learnt over the years from watching politicians. When attacked with a truthful and unwanted line of questioning, one should viciously attack back with a convincing verbal diversion.

'Have you finished with your unfounded attack on my research group Professor Walker? I will now revise my generous offer to you. I have now decided not to provide you with any of our private research data or information, or for that matter... to any of your staff.'

The Chairperson of Physics stood-up, eyes bulging in disbelief, trying to stare down Emma's steady rebellious look. In the short pause, Emma had reaffirmed her view of this man; she could see nothing about the Chairperson she liked. It was obvious this man was not used to being challenged, or refused in any way, especially by a woman.

'Doctor Archer you must realise that you will leave me no option but to with-draw your research groups free complementary access to the University's lecture theatres and research laboratories.

This University has full rights to any research results and data gained or discovered while using the University's extensive facilities.'

The Chancellors eyes had changed, they were now bulging with frustration when Emma delivered her well-timed blow.

'Professor Walker, may I remind you that this Oxford University has for many years, supported secret, and covert research on behalf of various Government agencies on such matters of defence projects. It is not a new or unknown practice.

Many of the so-called agencies using the University's facilities are just private companies working on viable commercial profit returning projects, who will always protect their secrets. I could say without a single doubt in my mind that you would not know everything that was going on behind all those research lab doors. Many of those doors have "Do not enter without authority," some known to have armed security guards.

Professor Walker I would like to know who is pushing you for our so-called research results. As you know my chaos group is nothing more than a few academics enjoying an after work drink and a chat about Quantum mechanics.'

The response was swift; as the Chairman thrust his question to the bone.

'That, as you well know Dr Archer is not the complete truth. We know you have located areas on the surface of this planet that produce higher than normal gravity readings. We now need to know what your findings are.'

'Just who are the "we" Professor Walker, who are you involved with in this... investigation. We the chaos group have a right to know who wants our information.'

Professor Walker looked a bit silly at being caught-out admitting that he was part of, or providing information to someone. He seemed to humble a little and quieten down. As Emma had suspected, a powerful party was manipulating Professor Walker to get this information, and Emma intended to find out who. Professor Walker let out a long sigh...

'Let's start over again Emma, yes I am being pressured to get all your research results. The Americans and the Chinese are both interested in what you and your group are researching. They have come across some of your data but cannot piece it all together to make sense of it.

On the other hand, they do have enough of your data to spark a keen interest in your activities. Both have threatened to withdraw many millions of pounds of research grants from this University, also to reduce their new student enrolment. The financial loss to this University would be enormous. I must report to them with something. Emma I need your cooperation on this important matter.'

Emma had broken the man, or so she thought; now she had him in a position to use him. In another life, Emma thought maybe she would make a good interrogator; she and Chirpy would make an excellent team.

'You can give them these notes for a start Professor Walker,' thrusting her lecture notes into the Chairman's hands.

'The notes contain my current thoughts and variations on Einstein's theory on gravitational waves. As you are aware, the recent LIGO tests have all but confirmed Albert Einstein's gravity waves in space-time theory to be correct. The next obvious step would be to create an earthbound example of a cosmic star collision in the new LHC to study the birth of gravity waves, and such events as cosmic string theory.

You would no doubt also be aware that this University had a LHC (Large Hadron Collider) experiment in progress to determine if this situation may have existed. We did have expensive and valuable time booked for using the new LHC, and then the damn thing broke down again.

The collider repairs are only just completed, and as to date, only a few small experiments are in the system, now scheduled for testing

76

with the repaired machine. I would suggest, that you tell your nosey Americans and Chinese of that fact. In addition, this newly repaired LHC will only crunch our atomic matter when the thing winds up to full operating power. By my latest information, that will not be until around the middle of December 2012, thirteen months from now.'

Emma could see in the cold grey calculating eyes, she was telling the righteous Chairman of Physics everything he already knew, and then she noticed a flicker of change in them.

'Emma these nosey people as you call them are not fools. I will of course give them this information,' waving Emma's lecture notes in front of her.

'However, they will see this offer as I do, as only a delaying strategy. They know all about the gravity spot phenomena and there being some ten locations in all. They also know that your research group have recently visited three of those locations.

This matter has also attracted my own curiosity. I can smell a possible scientific anomaly in the air much the same as I believe the Americans and the Chinese can. However, at this time my first concern is to avoid any potential financial loss to this University. This information will only buy me a little time; these superpowers will most certainly want more.'

This conversation was becoming a little tricky. Professor Walker was playing a game of verbal chess with her. He had offered some of his information in a captive netting sweep to try find out just how much Emma knew about all this. He was fishing, and his hook was alarmingly close, but the bait was all wrong as she was about to take his King and checkmate the game.

'Ten gravity spots... locations? What is this all about Professor Walker? We are researching the possibility of gravity waves here on the surface of the planet earth and a possible link to a string theory of gravitons.

The variation of gravity in certain locations or spots on the earth's surface first discovered more than 100 years ago. Because of this known variation of gravity, as you well know, we have adopted the Standard Gravity Scale. This is the G force scale that provides an average gravity presence over the entire surface of the earth. The local gravity variable is of little interest to us.'

Professor Walker now seated comfortably in his leather chair, fingers laced holding Emma's eye. He was weighing up the information impact; was she bluffing, did she really have no idea about these ten interesting spot gravity areas on the earth's surface?

'Now let me try to get this into perspective Professor Walker. You are saying that we; being my private research group, have attracted the attention of the international superpowers. All because we have stumbled across various strange gravity phenomena that so far we have not noticed. Now they think that we may have the answers to some scientific puzzle, a puzzle about which we have no idea. Have I got that correct, that's just about it isn't it?'

The look on Professor Walkers face would have been worth a thousand pounds, no double that. Emma was delighted; she had convinced the Oxford Chairperson of Physics she was innocent. He was hesitant, having nowhere to go on this conversation and had tumbled into a virtual verbal cul-de-sac… then as an added kick in the shins… Emma continued.

'It has occurred to me Professor Walker that these people of yours think we know something. We should keep them hoping for some results, that will buy us some time.

I will remind you, Rupert Somerfield, the senior caretaker with his staff of around twelve maintain, clean, and restock all the University research lab's. Then we have Professor Davey who freely gives his time to control all the lecture theatres and lab availability schedules for the entire Oxford University. If you deny them access to the very things they do every day as their job, just who do you think will run those important University functions?'

Professor Walker did not look that convinced at Emma's observation but the flicker of doubt was there in his eyes, so just like any good negotiator he would provide a workable compromise... to his advantage.

'Emma, I will leave the situation as it is for now, however, this will be subject to you keeping me updated on any developments to your research project. I am not convinced that these happenings will not have some eventual and useful scientific purpose.

Then we still have the Mr Randall problem to resolve. I want to know how and why he hacked into the HGSC, and for what project, was he using the HGSC. You will provide me with a copy of all his computer request inputs, and the actual download data. Do we have a business understanding Emma?'

'I have no idea what this is all about, however we have nothing to hide. As such I will help you in this silly matter, yes we do have an understanding Professor Walker. Then you and I should have an understanding that all your questions for any further information concerning my chaos group research formally requested directly through me? Regarding Randall, since I have no idea what this HGSC thing is all about; I will ask Randall to provide the information you want, if he is indeed the guilty party... and to me only. You will hear from me shortly.'

Emma quickly got up from the leather chair, and politely shook hands with the Chairperson displaying one of her best beaming smiles, then briskly left the Chairperson's office.

All sorts of things were going through Emma's head, on the way to her flat. Had the Chairperson revealed all that he actually knew; did the Chairperson know more? Emma was thinking that was a close thing, as the man was very good at verbal chess.

Emma stopped and sat down on a park bench to think. How did they know Randall had hacked into the world's fastest computer? At the last meeting, Jan had pointed out to Randall and Tim that they would have to find some other way to crunch all the tectonic plate movements, and the pole shift data for the ten gravity ring locations. Would he be so stupid and hack into the HGSC again?

Randall must have gone mad to use the HGSC; he knew someone was watching him. Then again, she also knew that Randall was not mad but extremely cunning and smart, he must have had a good reason. His modus-operandi was to act stupid on purpose to lead people to believe he was just a silly rich playboy, well he had even convinced her on most occasions.

The door lock on Emma's flat turned much easier than usual and a quick glance at the key confirmed her suspicion... someone had oiled the lock. Thinking she was getting good at this spy business, so what is next? Emma took out the kitchen rubbish then placed the wheelie bin under her bathroom window.

She showered with the radio turned-up loud leaving the radio on, got dressed and slipped out of the bathroom window. Then headed out through the back alleyway to Professor Reg's cloisters flat, thinking smugly, that should keep them busy for a while.

My God she thought, what have things come to, I am actually enjoying this silly spy game. It was just turning five o'clock as Emma slammed the heavy knocker on the Gatehouse door, as instructed twice. This time a smiling Professor Reg answered the door, his smouldering pipe clutched firmly in hand.

'We are still waiting on the others my dear. Would you like a nice cup of tea while we wait,' pointing his pipe up to the roof and his finger to his lips in a gesture of quiet.

Professor Reg signalled Emma to follow and without another word, they went down the narrow stairway to his nicely furnished dungeon den. Professor Reg held his finger to his lips in another gesture of silence. Then reaching in behind some books he then swung open a rack of books to reveal an old arched door following the Keble Victorian Gothic style.

Emma's eyes widened with childlike surprise as Professor Reg again held his finger to his lips for silence. The old door opened without a sound, Emma noticing the well-lubricated massive 18th century hinges. Professor Reg switched on a torch which lit-up the small room about three metres by three metres fitted with old wooden shelves supporting various bits of dusty old Keble College equipment, this was just an old storeroom.

Professor Reg held back a dirty cover sheet revealing yet another door except this one was made of solid steel, and much more modern along the lines of a bomb shelter door, Emma's guess soon confirmed. The door opened with little effort revealing a string of small lights illuminating a steep stairway.

'Come along Emma we have much to discuss tonight,' then noticing the look on Emma's face as she caught sight of the flat panel display on the back of the steel door. 'Just a bit of Randall security, we can see my den and the gatehouse entry from here. The Americans and Chinese are not the only ones who have hidden video cameras you know.'

Professor Reg led the way down the steep set of concrete stairs chuckling at his joke with a sound that echoed off the hard concrete walls like a cackling medieval Warlock. At the base of the stairs was a concrete room with a number of steel doors set into heavy steel frames and one large and long tunnel that disappeared without end.

'Professor Reg, my guess would be that this was an old world-war two air-raid bomb shelter. I had read somewhere that they existed in Oxford but never knew the shelters were still in use, or for that matter were in such good condition. Who else knows about this underground bunker?'

'Well Emma, the Ministry of Defence for a start as they obviously built them. My father was very much involved with the early design and layout of these emergency bunkers under Oxford.

My dad was required to help design these as the most effective way to protect scientific research laboratories. In those days, important research must continue around the clock, including during the bombing raids. In the late sixties father was again called back to upgrade and refit these same facilities as a nuclear shelter. I inherited possibly the only complete set of plans to this place from my father; I know everything that's down here.'

With his hand on the steel door lever Emma interrupted Professor Reg, as she still needed more information.

'Professor Reg, if the MoD knows all about this place then so will the Keble College administration, and possibly our nosey Americans and Chinese.'

'Yes they do know these facilities exist. However, their records will show the facilities decommissioned and stripped out in the seventies, then sealed. Only the MoD having the means to access the bunkers through special sealed locks. I have since locked all the external blast-proof doors from the inside. We can get out at any of the twenty-eight blast doors but nobody can get into the underground system without some extensive cutting work.

The tunnels and rooms were extend to just about all of the Oxford University main surface buildings, with one well hidden blast door and my humble home above having the only direct access... very neat eh!'

Emma needed to know more, this was fascinating history.

'Professor Reg just why were these facilities decommissioned?'

'In 1941 these facilities were being used by over eighty scientists including my father, and might I say Albert Einstein. The race was on to purify uranium 235 and manufacture large amounts of heavy water. The theory of an atomic bomb was about to become a reality, then being only a matter of months away.

About the same time, Germany had developed the powerful bunker buster bomb the V1's and V2's and could easily penetrate these underground bomb shelters. Nobody was safe anymore, and most important, neither was the all-important and critical research work carried out down here.

For security and safety reasons, the whole research project secretly moved to America, forming the now famous Manhattan

Project headed by the renowned physicist Doctor Oppenheimer, the rest is now history.

As for the nuclear shelter part, well this was all government propaganda and conspiracy in trying to make important people in the late sixties feel-good during the Iron Curtain nuclear cold war threat. The idea was that the so-called indispensable people that ran our country would have somewhere to hide in the event of an all-out nuclear war.

You would be surprised at the number of massive underground town-size atomic fall-out shelters built around that time. This Oxford shelter is one of the smallest that I have visited over the years, and it never was quite finished.

As you would know being a scientist, this underground facility would not protect anyone from radiation, and all those silly enough to hide inside it during a nuclear attack, and so eventually, it was decommissioned. Might I add that I was instrumental in pushing the government of the day to admit that this was nothing more than an expensive hiding-hole, in truth it was just a costly sham.'

The smiling 81-year-old Professor Reg had no difficulty in swinging open one of the four heavy steel doors, which opened up into a massive well-lit concrete room full of various types of benches loaded with scientific equipment. Emma could hear Randall's crisp English accent coming from an adjoining room, viciously responded to by Chirpy's high-pitched voice... They were both at it again bickering over health issues. Professor Reg announced their arrival with a cheerful and pleasant offer, with a hope of defusing the room tension.

'Emma and I are ready for a cup of tea, is there any left or should we wait for Sally, Tim, and Jan to arrive first?

Randall greeted Emma with a gracious.

'How very nice to see you again my dear, and on time too, would you like a beer while the tea brews,' eyebrows raised and curling his little finger.

Chirpy's greeting was a little more direct exposing her frustration at Randall, and her near-to-the-limit of Randall's annoying behaviour. Chirpy snapped back to anyone who would listen.

'Well at last we now have another intelligent female down here. Ten more minutes of this man,' pointing direct at Randall, 'and I would have considered kicking him in his shins, that being the only painful area that I could possibly reach.'

Everyone laughed at this amusing comment except the bemused Chirpy.

A clanking noise filled the room, followed by the opening of another heavy metal door then Sally, Tim and Jan tumbled into the room, with Jan stuttering.

'Sorry that we're a b-bit late. We had to all lay low for a while, so w-we could get through the b-bleeding bunker door in the number seven physics research lab on the w-west site. Other than h-here, it's the only way into this bloody place now.'

Everybody found a place to sit-down. Tim followed Sally close by her side holding her hand like a child and looking around as if this was the first time he had been in this room. Emma knew that this was the savant way.

Emma could feel her anger was rising. It would appear by all accounts that she was the only person that was new to this room, and she wanted to know why. Nevertheless, she was a bit slow as Chirpy got in first with a sharp squeaky attack on Professor Reg.

'Now that we are all here I want to have my say about being kept in the dark about this place,' then ramming her thick black glasses back hard on her nose. 'Professor Reg, you have some explaining to do as I do not like being treated like a scientific mushroom.'

The Professor was busy filling his pipe, and without looking at, or directly talking to anybody in particular, started to tell a story.

'Emma and Chirpy are the only members of our group that did not know about these nuclear bomb shelters. I make no apology for this. I had considered that these two ladies were the most vulnerable of our group, and the ones most likely to lose all career creditability with this University should they be found involved in our illegal chaos group activities.

I was in point, trying to keep you two ladies away from any perceived future problems. However, at this present stage in our research, and the large amount of interest generated by other people, I thought it more advantageous to have our meetings down here away from any possible spying.'

Professor Reg gave a little chuckle between many sucking attempts to relight his dead pipe.

'Randall had found out about these shelters from Tim two years ago when they started to become good friends. I of course knew all about these shelters, as my father helped to design and build them for the British Ministry of Defence.

This bunker facility being originally constructed to offer protection to all of the Oxford University administrative and teaching personnel during the Second World War. The main entry blast doors for Keble College are down in the Chapel Crypt basement and another is in the Library basement connected via a long tunnel under the Liddon quad.

Where we are now sitting is directly under the Keble Chapel basement. Other tunnels branch out to all parts of the City of Oxford connecting all the various University's and Government buildings. This blast door entry beneath our Gatehouse flat is not on the official MoD plans as my father had it built especially for his own purpose. I do hope this has answered some of your questions ladies?'

Sally had said nothing since entering the bunker, knowing the history well; she stood up to add her valuable point of view on the secrecy matter.

'This gravity cluster phenomenon is rapidly developing into something well beyond our small chaos group's research capabilities. The new data now before us, gives us a better understanding of how early life first arrived on this planet.

How the ancients were very much involved with a planned path to our present development, and indeed to our eventual and present future. Reginald and I are nearing the end of our long academic careers, and indeed our lives. We have purchased a small unit in Spain. Our plan is to retire there within the next three years; Tim will of course come with us.

We have no fear of the eventual outcome to all this. As for Jan and Randall, well Randall as we all know is well looked after financially and appears to be more interested in solving scientific puzzles and mysteries than gaining any academic qualifications.'

Randall felt for some reason that he should respond, and did.

'Please excuse my interjection, although I must say Sally, you do have my employment profile spot on. Regarding Jan, you should all know that I have guaranteed to him that in the event he should lose his long-standing employment with Oxford University. I will provide him a job at double the salary in one of Papa's many companies, which I will eventually own anyway. As for Tim, I pledge he will always be my friend and well looked after in the event he should require such in the future.'

Professor Reg pointed his pipe at Randall, giving out a sigh of relief.

'Thank you for resolving that major concern Randall, this now brings us to the reason why Emma and Chirpy were excluded from our secret research facility, and left in the mushroom dark.

These two ladies are the only members of our group that would suffer the highest consequences should all of these events turn ugly. Both are still very much involved with their academic careers, and have the most to lose. We will need to know how you both feel about all of this, and these possible future risks before we can proceed.'

The old man looked around the room at the concerned faces. This situation reminded him of the wartime meetings his father attended so long ago... he slowly continued.

What will be revealed this day will without doubt, change your views on the present-day teachings of modern science regarding the beginning of our planet's life. This knowledge may also be very dangerous to all of who possess it...

We must accept that in the miniscule knowledge we have of the universe we are all still only illiterate children. Remember the response by the Catholic Church. For simply suggesting the earth was not the centre of the universe, the church found Galileo guilty of heresy and imprisoned him for life.

Then in times that are more recent, author Salmon Rushdie was sentence to death by an Islamic court, proclaiming a "Fatwa" for suggesting in a fiction novel that the prophet Mohammed, being an Arab had a resident "harem of prostitutes," which after all was normal for a wealthy Arab at that time. There are many powerful people out there, who for their own reasons, do not want the truth told.'

Emma responded, with an obvious level of concern in her voice.

'This all sounds more than a little frightening; I can only assume that you have found something important to report. No doubt, about recent things discovered over these last five days; however, you must all hear this first.

I have just left the Chairperson of Physics Professor Walker's office. This man is convinced that we are all up to something. To suit my purpose, I let him believe that he has turned me into spying for him to find out what is going on in our chaos group.

Professor Walker has agreed not to interfere with any of our research projects on the strict condition that I provide him with full details of our progress for his acknowledged American and Chinese partners.

I must admit I was most concerned that he named Professor Reg, Jan, and Randall as people that have brought the University into disgrace, however, Professor Walker did let slip, that both Professor Reg and Jan had now been cleared of any misconduct; by both the Oxford events committee, and the Jodrell Bank administration.

The Chairperson also expressed his own personal interest, as he was of the opinion that we were on to something very worthwhile. I am now certain that he and his friends have no idea about the extent of our discovery, so I suggest that we just string them all along for a while.'

Randall seeking attention started waving both of his arms, his left arm no longer in a plaster cast.

'What about me Emma,' Randall was delighted that the University Chairperson had found him to be of importance. 'You said that he mentioned me?'

'The Chairperson Professor Walker has instructed me to provide him with your entire upload and downloaded data that you and Tim hacked from using the HGSC. We will need to give him something to keep him and his friends happy. He knows that you have hacked into the HGSC again… only this morning.

I have given Professor Walker a copy of my recent lecture notes advising him that this was the basis of our research project. As you know that is almost the truth, I will from now on continue to send the Chairperson of Physics a copy of my nice neat lecture notes.'

This raised a chuckle from the group including Chirpy, who pointed out.

'Well it looks like the powerful people of this University think we have something useful, and I doubt they will accept a bunch of lecture notes as research data for long. We should give them some real data, what about giving them Tim's computer research into the origins of our galaxy. That should keep them busy for the next few years.

As for my personal academic risk in all of this, I for one am fully committed to researching a final resolve to this mystery. For the advancement of science, whatever the outcome may be to me or my academic career.'

All of the group stood up and clapped Chirpy's gallant speech. The group could easily hear Emma's Scottish voice over the applause, 'I am with you Chirpy, whatever-the-cost. Let's just get on and do this.'

Randall reluctantly levered himself out of his comfortable leather chair to deliver his opening chaos speech.

'Ladies and gentlemen, my fellow scientists, let us begin.' Randall as a matter of breeding added his mandatory grandiose opening to the proceedings.

'I suppose now is the right time to explain why I hacked into the HGSC again, especially after promising to be a good boy, and now having let the Americans and Chinese know all about my... our efforts.'

Jan butted in with his stutter. 'Yeah a and you got young Tim m mixed-up in your e evil computer hacking deeds, shame on you Randall... o old boy.'

'Yes indeed, I have implicated young Tim in my evil deeds, but only as part of my brilliant master plan, which I am convinced you will all agree with me, will work beautifully.'

There was a small pause allowing Randall to draw breathe for his intended lofty speech. Just then, Tim spoke his mind, quite softly in such a large room, making him scarcely audible. Professor Reg cried out in deaf despair, 'what, what did young Tim say?'

For the first time ever Tim looked direct at Professor Reg and repeated what he had said, this time they were all were leaning forward listening hard.

'It is the fastest known computer; we had to use the fastest. The next fastest computer would have taken over six months to produce our result. We finished the analysis in just four days and now we have an answer to this important question... and much more, so much more.'

All were still looking at Tim, then realised that was a waste of time as Tim had finished talking until who knows when. So all eyes became firmly glued back on Randall... then noticing he was the focus of attention again.

'Ah well yes, as Tim has told us we did the mighty deed in four long days with the involuntary help of our American cousins and their HGSC. Tim had worked out how to get around the University's lock-codes and passwords to gain access to the beast. Then I came up with a cunning plan to use the HGSC in full view of the Yanks... so to speak.'

A familiar sharp voice rang out.

"Well don't drag it out young man, how the hell did you use the world's fastest computer, right under the nose and close scrutiny of the Americans who own the damn thing?' Chirpy was clearly showing her impatience at Randall's pompous manner.

'All very simple really, we didn't hide anything. We just uploaded our world tectonic plate migration request data imbedded in Tim's Sagittarius Dwarf Galaxy research data. Tim figured it all-out. The program he wrote splits the requests into hundreds of millions of tiny requests and reassembles the processed data back on the download.

Everybody can see the data transfer up and down however; they can only see what we want them to see. In this instance Tim's Sagittarius Dwarf Galaxy, research stuff. Therefore, Chirpy's good idea was also our choice, sending them all of Tim's data was a rather good one. In fact, we used the data exactly as suggested to satisfy the interest of our nosey superpower spies.

Tim and I have given this new computer program a name... "The invisible story," rather neat don't you think. In the process, we will be educating both the Americans and the Chinese all about our solar system. The demonstrated fact that we are not actually a part of the Milky Way as was first thought, accepted, and taught, since that first sighting by Galileo 1615.

I am convinced that in the future, these snooping superpowers will eventually thank Tim for his magnificent contribution to Astrophysics... I will of course give Emma a copy of our HGSC data transfer, all of which should satisfy their suspicions. It will simply match-up to what they already know about our data.

This fooling around and tinkering has allowed us to use their super-fast computer right under their noses, simply by hiding our research data imbedded in interesting real data on Astrophysics.'

Randall beamed a wide smile, taking a deep powerful draw on his cigarette, and blew one of his best, and most perfect smoke rings ever... an effort that remained suspended at ceiling height for some long seconds. For a moment, all of the chaos group were distracted watching this exhibition waiting in wonder, including Chirpy.

Professor Reg broke the short spell of curiosity as the moment passed, and the group became excited to hear about the HGSC mathematical results.

'As you are all aware, to calculate a start position of a targeted object on the face of this planet, going back 10,400 years ago, is not an easy task. The matter being further complicated by the fact the earth's crust is made-up of some fifteen tectonic plates, all of which are continuously on the move, drifting in different directions and all at differing speeds.

The ten surface gravity ring positions were plotted to the fifteen tectonic plates that make-up the earth's crust. Some of the gravity ring locations were on the same tectonic plate, making those calculations a little easier. We wrote-up a set of equations to include the factual distances that the tectonic plates had moved, which was between 16 and 75 millimetres each year.

Then we plotted the exact direction each plate was moving and had the HGSC crunch all the equations backwards for each of the gravity ring positions over a period of 10,400 years. We then created a computer display model of the earth, before and after. Reproducing images to show one of the three gravity cluster rings had aligned perfectly over the top of the target site ring. However, none of the ten plotted locations were exact antipodal to each other.'

Professor Reg flicked a few switches and a powerful LCD projector came to life providing a bright beam of light and a low hum. The image was showing a slowly revolving computer generated earth model. The model was displaying all the existing and new site locations, re-plotted after all-time, distance, and direction corrections computed.

'As you will note the sets of gravity cluster rings have all moved however, they are still not all aligned as expected. They do not offer much in the way of useful information. Except that now two of the three rings clearly overlap each over the fixed surface earth positions, which had moved with the tectonic plate movement. The other or third gravity cluster ring has remained in its same relative position at each of the ten sites.

We know as a scientific fact that around 800 million years ago the earth experienced a violent and sudden differential core rotation creating a pole axis shift of 67 degrees to almost its present position. I say almost. As the earth's axis and poles have gradually moved by precession to some five degrees of tilt, over the same 10,400 years creating a pole wobble, thereby creating our much-recognised four distinct yearly seasons. Now we will add the pole shift and wobble data to our computer earth model.'

There was a low gasp of awe, as all the gravity cluster rings started gradually aligning at each of the ten surface locations, by neatly stacking on top of each other.

The digital date-recession clock in the corner of the screen stopped at minus 10, 400 years. The room froze with silence. All eyes glued to the large projector screen, Randall took a deep drag on his cigarette, puffed a random cloud of smoke, and spoke again.

'Now I think you chaps will all find this part most interesting... this is the world model retarded a further 100 years to 10,500 years, note there was no change. Now we see the world at 14,500 years, the earliest that the HGSC has managed to calculate back with the last data that I downloaded only this morning.

As you can see there was still no change, everything remains in perfect alignment. Now we will look forward in time to 10,100 years as you can see the gravity cluster rings all separate at each site, rather strange don't you think? My opinion is this gravity ring system was man-made.'

Jan interjected in an excited burst of obvious information.

'What t that means is that this gravity ring s system was in place and w working okay up-to 10,400 y years ago, then it went out of alignment. But all the b bits are still there, a as Tim said it's not working now.'

Randall lit another cigarette and announced in his crisp English voice.

'My scientific friends we are all aware that the earth is not a perfect sphere, in fact it is pulled out of round by the gravity of the moon and the sun. In truth, we continually suffer two quite large fluid bumps caused by this gravity pull. Then added to all this we also have the fact the earth has a greater diameter than a perfect sphere at the equator due to centrifugal forces.

Now consider this friends, just how difficult it would be to calculate the exact antipodal of any position on the earth's surface with all those wild variations. If you thought this computer image of gravity ring stacking was strange and wonderful,' spreading his arms at the projector screen for maximum affect, 'then take a look at this my fellow scientists.'

With the push of a key on his laptop computer, five rods of different colours extended through the earth image. The rods then connected all ten gravity sites into five elements of exact antipodal positions on the earth's surface.

The computer model then started revolving revealing the rods were not quite proportioned, or for that matter in any identifiable balanced pattern, however they did meet exactly in the centre of planet Earth.

The whole group just stared at the bright projector screen silently absorbing all this strange and yet magnificent data on what had happened on earth before, and from 10,400 years ago. They all had the same thought, why was this strange phenomenon created, and by whom, and for what purpose.

Emma was starting to consider what Tim had said a few weeks ago about receivers, antennas, and such; reminding the group.

'Tim has previously put forward a theory that these five antipodal gravity rods through the earth may actually form some sort of receiving antenna. Is there any way we can analyse this, who of us knows anything about the structure of receiving antennas?'

'Well I do,' the quick response came from Professor Reg.

'Much of my early career was in Radio Astronomy. I spent many months, designing and constructing huge radio frequency antenna arrays. I must admit the very same thought had occurred to me, these rods correctly placed and spaced could easily form an antenna array.

However, the RF (radio frequency) spectrum exists with the use of electromagnetic waves. As for this' pointing at the large screen with his pipe. 'This antenna array, if indeed it is an antenna, was obviously not designed for RF waves, perhaps... Gravity waves if indeed such a form of communication actually exists?'

Jan burst in with a flood of stuttering evidence.

'But n-now they do exist. The new LISA (Laser Interferometer Space Antenna) h-has just recently c-confirmed the Eigen vibration wave theory. All of this agreeing with Einstein's proof of gravity t-time space curvature, b-bending of the light photons by g-gravity waves.

We h-have just discovered further p-prove that gravity wave c-clusters do exist on earth. Gravity waves are no longer a theory, they are now a fact, and I a-agree, all of this lot is s some sort of m manufactured system. Not a natural event.'

Chirpy's high-pitched voice cut through the group's deep thoughts like a knife. All turned to see a stern faced Chirpy glaring through her thick black glasses.

'Thank you chaos group, this new information has been most interesting. I would like to go over these discussions, and revise a few things, just in case I have missed something, as at my height things could quite easily go over my head.'

Everyone in the room refrained from laughing, knowing when Chirpy had moved into challenge mode... someone was about be shot down in flames. When Chirpy had any doubts about the evidence put to her, she quickly reacted. Having a keen nose for bullshit, accepting only sound logical theory or proven facts.

'The HGSC calculations provided by Randall and Tim have confirmed that 10,400 years ago... real-time, this planet earth had a form of antipodal gravity rings in place. This as indicated by the computer model currently displayed on the screen. I see no proof of a so-called manufactured antenna system.

The five nicely coloured rods or lines Randal has used to connect the ten antipodal gravity ring sites are his idea... his alone, and does not confirm the existence of any ancient or past antenna. As I observe, and from my understanding, they are just five lines drawn through a computerised graphic of a three-dimensional world sphere.

Tim has mentioned about receiving life from outer space, and to receive there must have been a transmitter. We are all assuming here that we need some sort of antenna to attract life. I see no proof, or data, supporting this theory. However, what we do know is our planets gravity attracts objects from outer space, be that in the way of an asteroid with basic life, or possibly a meteorite shower.

Nevertheless, I do concede to a consistency in these findings worth further discussion. My notes show that some months back we discussed in my research about meteorites and small asteroids. Those containing basic single cell building blocks of life... bacteria. This I have discovered ceased at about this same time of 10,400 years ago.

Further research has now confirmed that we now only receive inbound meteorites containing dead or bacteria morphs. This would indicate to me that Tim was right. When this gravity ring phenomena or world antenna system or whatever it is, went out of alignment some 10,400 years ago, we stopped receiving new life from outer space. Would that be a clearer observation to these discussions?'

Sally was thinking deeply about this and had decided to share her thoughts.

'I for one would totally agree with you Chirpy,' adding a little more on this interesting subject. 'At about this very same period, man and the human race underwent a sudden change, from the standard run-of-the-mill Homo sapiens, to smart Homo sapiens.

One could well ask why the development of our species had made this sudden leap, and at this very same time-period of our planet earth's history. Did we have a little helping hand? We must also understand and accept the fact that all of the significant ancient sites within the stated ten gravity ring sites are dated around the same time period... 10,400 years.'

At a short pause by Sally, Randall spoke out in an excited voice. In doing so, redeemed most of his loss-of-face to Chirpy's antenna attack.

'Now this is interesting chaps. We must discuss this last piece of shattering news, steeped in absolute riveting scientific mystery.

Tim has already mentioned the ninth site or antipodal location is the answer... well he may be correct again. The ninth site, Veevers crater in North-Western Australia, is the only site having gravity rings that did not stack up in the same way as all the others. At this site, the three rings formed two locations, one gravity ring over the strange Veevers meteorite crater, and the other at exactly one and a half kilometres, or one statute mile away.'

Randall slowly rotated the earth image and zoomed into the ninth site... adding in a scholarly voice...

'As Sally has previously advised, the gravity level recorded at this particular site is also exactly twice that of the others. Just as Tim has said, the answer must be there... at the ninth site, or place. I would suggest that someone should go to this strange location and find out what is so significant about this area. Our detailed area maps and a professional Google map search show only a large desert with no special features. The nearest road being over seventy kilometres away, and that is just a primitive dirt track.

I would suggest that Emma should go on a fully funded field research trip to this special ninth location in Australia.'

Professor Reg switched off the LCD projector and addressed the excited group.

'Randall is right. Emma being our elected leader you should be the one to go and field research this strange anomaly, and as soon as possible. I must confess to you Emma, that we have already discussed this field project in detail.

The chaos group have all agreed that you should go to Western Australia, preferably before the superpower spies, or whoever they are, learn too much. Randall and Jan think they have found a safe way to get you into Australia without our nosey spying superpowers knowledge. Randal will explain.

'I do hope you will agree with us Emma as this is our "Pièce de résistance" we are all very proud of our amateur spy efforts. I have borrowed some of my family inheritance and deposited $US100,000 into two newly named gold card credit accounts, and you will take a further $US 20,000 in cash. We have arranged a good quality residential Australian passport for you in the name of Robyn Mills, a sort of borrowed passport from an old Australian girlfriend of mine.

You can still depart on leave for your normal scheduled lecture tour by flying to Moscow with your own passport, and then catch the Orient Express for twelve days of delightful train journey to Beijing. From there, you would then use the Robyn Mills passport to fly directly to Singapore and then on to Perth Western Australia. From Perth, you would then find your way to this Veevers crater site.

Everything is arranged ready for you to go, so what do you think Emma... will you go and find our gold at the end of our rainbow?'

Emma looked around at all the hopeful faces turned waiting to hear her answer. She had suspected that this had been a previously planned mission, and could clearly see that they all wanted her to go and find an explanation to this odd mystery.

A mission to provide some form of conclusive proof, proof that may well change the way we have come to believe about the evolution of our species. This odd and remote place may ultimately hold the answer to the way our planet earth had developed to this present stage.

With a sparkle in her eye and a wide smile, Emma was quick to announce her decision.

'Chaos group I will accept this important field mission. In three week's I will leave on what was to be my normal planned holiday and lecture tour to Moscow. Friends wish me good-luck, as this may well

94

be a world-changing discovery, providing answers to the old questions... Why do we exist, and where do we come from?

96

Chapter Eight

They are watching

'Tony, you know you'll get your money eventually, but mate. I can tell you this, if you ground both my aircraft, how the bloody hell can I earn the money to pay you?'

Tony thought about this truthful and tricky point for a brief moment.

'Doc, to date you still owes me over twenty-nine grand for keeping that bleeding old 1975 Jet-ranger chopper airworthy, and for the recent three yearly major inspections on your bloody old Cessna 402 aircraft.'

Tony made a fast grab at a passing annoying fly and wiped his success on his oil-stained footy shorts, then continued.

'Now I know what you're going to say mate, I can keep the bleeding logbooks until you pay me, but I've had the bleeding logbooks for five long bloody years mate. Listen mate, I got a family to feed, and they can't eat bloody aircraft logbooks.

We've all got our money troubles mate. Why the hell don't you just go back to bleeding teaching at the uni, they're always asking for you to come back lecturing... so you must be good at it right. You'd be a hell-of-a-lot better off at teaching than operating this crappy air charter company in this god-forsaken hole on the edge of this shitty hot desert.'

The fit looking 42-year-old Doctor of Geophysics, David Sharp liked flying. It went well with his neatly trimmed aviator's style moustache and boyish good looks. Doc Dave reached into the cooler esky parked beside his fold-up-chair, flipped the top off two ice-cold beers, and handed one to Tony, the owner of Sandfire Aircraft Maintenance.

Tony was a good mate, but he had his own urgent financial business problems, one of which was Doc Dave. Then he had a moaning wife and three demanding kids, all living in a small transportable home next to the Sandfire airstrip service hangar.

Things had not been too good lately. The Agricultural Department had cut back on their aerial-spray poisonous weed programme, and the main roads had all but finished their highway upgrade. Then to make it worse, the two local offshore oilrigs had started using more boats and fewer helicopters to shift the crews around. It was bad, his business of remote aircraft servicing was not going well at all.

Apart from Doc Dave and a few local cattle-station aircraft that used the Sandfire strip, everything was at a standstill. Tony wiped his dripping brow, and then became briefly distracted by a pair of copulating blowflies in the dead calm of the depressing desert heat. Doc Dave took this opportunity to explain a few things.

'Tony, teaching I admit does have its advantages as I do enjoy being involved with the University, the main problem is I like my fieldwork. I can't stand being cooped-up in a lecture room all day, and another thing, a teaching salary would not come near to paying off my increasing debts.'

Tony removed his salt stained akubra hat and fanned his sweaty face then took another long drink from his beer, gazing out over the airstrip to nowhere.

'You're still chasing bloody ghosts and fame Doc. Nobody wants to hear of your theory on the mines out there waiting for you to find them. Nobody wants to hear about all the strange things that are happening out in the Great Sandy Desert.

You'll just have to admit it to yourself mate, you're flat broke... fucked. You have the bleeding Medusa touch in the fine art of doing business. Mate, everything you've ever been involved in, or with, turns out to be a complete heap of shit.

Believe me Doc; you would be far better off teaching and earning a good steady income. Just accept things as they are and go bankrupted nice and graciously.' Tony then paused to study the setting sun through what remained in his glass beer stubby... 'It's not so bad Doc; I've been bankrupted three bloody times now.'

Doc Dave turned his head to stare at Tony. This acceptance of pending financial doom and capitulation was not on his list of choices, as he snapped back.

'Well, I have been divorced three times now, and those disasters didn't go away. Tony, if I were to declare myself bankrupted tomorrow you would follow within a month, and Max would be out of a job, with little hope of any future flying employment.

The consulting jobs and the small amount of air charter work we get, plus the University field research work that I do bring in, is just enough to keep the bank foreclosure hounds at bay. I can tell you this, even in these sad times, my present business income is more than I would ever earn in a teaching job. I also have to give consideration, and accept the future survival responsibilities to a few people that are my closest friends… those people are you and Max.'

Tony and Doc Dave looked out over the dusty gravel airfield. There was not a hint of a breeze as both sat in silence in the 43-degree heat with just the buzz of the occasional brave fly passing by. They were both watching the shimmering heat coming off the small bitumen hardstand, as it danced around the five dusty aircraft covered in a thin layer of fine red desert sand.

The Jet-ranger helicopter had around seventy hours flying time left until the next hundred hourly service, when it was due for a main rotor gearbox overhaul. Tony might, with CAA (Civil Aviation Authority) get a twenty-five hour extension, failing this, Doc Dave was up for an eighteen thousand dollar time expired overhaul cost.

The Cessna 402 was in far better shape, but Tony had just delivered a crushing blow, the aircraft needed an exhaust turbo booster replaced on the port engine. This was the very point of Tony and the Doc's conversation this day, there was an option.

As luck would have it, a turbo was available on the old grounded Cessna 402 repossessed by a finance company from a defunct mining company over a year ago, and still parked alongside Doc Dave's aircraft. Should he borrow the part from this aircraft to keep his aircraft flying... who would know...? Tony explained the delicate problem.

'Everybody would eventually know mate. The changeover needs an entry in your bleeding engine logbook, complete with the changed turbo part number.

The finance company that now owns this old bird will one day sell it to some bloke who will check and find out the engine logbook accessories times and serial numbers don't add-up. Then you will end-up in jail and I will lose my bloody aircraft engineer's license, great idea Doc.' But Doc had an answer ready...

'And if we were to put the turbocharger back on the engine before the new owner picks-up the aircraft he would never know about it Tony... would he?'

Tony thought about this cunning sly move while looking at the large red ball of the sun rapidly falling in the western sky... and his beer was empty.

'Okay mate, as long as you don't put more than twenty hours on the bleeding turbo. To save your arse I will do it this one and only time.'

Doc Dave lived quite well, owning two modern air-conditioned caravans based on the remote Sandfire airstrip. He also owned a 4X4 Toyota 7-ton refuelling tanker truck for the aircraft, plus two old mini-Mokes for checking the airstrip and the all-important drive across to the nearby Sandfire pub.

His pride and joy was a near new Mercedes 4X4 Unimog vehicle, set-up for extended desert exploration trips.

The neighbouring Sandfire roadhouse generator supplied all the airfield power and a few cartoons of beer. This was in exchange for flying the owner, old Garfield and some of his staff in and out of Port Hedland or Broome, the two nearest towns, both around three hundred and seventy kilometres away.

Doc Dave also had a sort of employee, a 52-year-old overweight Jewish bush pilot, complete with a big black frizzled beard. A man who dreamt of one day becoming an airline captain. Max spent most of his time carrying out hacked illegal satellite EMR ground analysis models for his boss Doc Dave's mining contracts, flying what little air charter there was about, and drinking beer and scotch.

The rest of his time went on writing to the airlines seeking a job and sleeping in his nice cold air-conditioned caravan away from the forty plus degree heat outside, and all the maddening blowflies.

Max was happy with his lot; he had a good number of friends scattered around the many north-west towns he frequently flew in and out of, a few of them were obliging friendly ladies. It suited Max to jump in an aircraft to find peace and sanctuary in his bush hideaway.

One might say Max was a controlled loner he always chose his friends very carefully and kept them well away from his hidey-hole in the bush.

The one thing that Dave and Max had in common, apart from the flying, drinking, and womanising was a keen interest in satellite electronics. Both loved new electronic technology. Max was never happier than when he was hacking into some new government satellite system or an entertainment satellite.

His caravan was full of the latest satellite and radio communications equipment for listening to the stars, and other people's private business. Max was a keen modern "radio ham" always in touch with everyone on his free satellite phone and the latest world developments. He was never short of anyone to talk to around the world, hiding in his air-conditioned caravan on the edge of the West Australian Great Sandy Desert.

Doc Dave's caravan was a comfortable twenty metres distance away from Max's caravan. Separated by a large concrete and shaded alfresco area, unfortunately not quite far enough to lose the sound of Max's snoring after a heavy nights drinking.

Lately the Doc's caravan was vacant for weeks on end. Reason being that Doc Dave was busy most days working, travelling great distances around the remote desert in his Mercedes Unimog. He was carrying out many small subcontract Geophysical jobs up and down the North-West coast for various exploration companies looking for oil and gas, or anything else of interest.

In an attempt to stay involved with some level of research, and for a modest fee Dave also carried out a small amount of government and University fieldwork.

As bad luck would have it, Doc Dave's all-important, yet small income sustaining work was broken up on a regular basis by compulsory visits to the Perth law courts. These visits were to sort out his large and complicated business debts, most of which involved the ATO (Australian Tax Office.) Then there were his two continuing messy former-matrimonial settlements, adding pain to his current situation, his third wife's legal separation. These and other matters were causing him great problems.

In truth, Doc Dave was a breathing, living, walking financial disaster and he knew it, he was always just teetering on the edge from being a total financial bankrupt. Everything he had ever worked for and achieved in his business and private life had all gone wrong in the past five years.

If his financial ruin and personal problems were a designed, purposeful, cunning, and planned event. Then his present grim situation never better accomplished. The only thing that kept Doctor David Sharp sane and functioning each day was his extremely laid-back attitude to life, and his cynical sense of humour.

One other matter that diverted Dave from his gloomy financial and marital situation was his growing interest in the odd incidents that were now happening on a regular basis out in the desert. He firmly believed in the possibility that these strange desert phenomena may yet prove to be financially worthwhile.

Dave had taken the opportunity to discuss some of these odd happenings in the desert with his University colleagues, none of whom could offer any constructive advice to resolve the many mysteries. Dave suddenly realised he had stopped talking.

'Tony we should ask Max if he wants to join us for a beer, I haven't seen him since I got back from Perth. How is he going... by the looks of things around here, we have not had much air-charter work over the last few weeks that I have been away.'

'Oh you know Max, once he's on to something with all that satellite crap he has in his van, he's not interested in talking to anybody... except you Doc. He's been stuck in that bloody caravan for over a week now, won't even come over here for a beer and a free feed.'

'That doesn't sound like Max, I had better get over there and see what he is up to, for all we know he might be dead in there. Tell Mavis thanks for the invite to dinner but I'd best take a rain-check on that offer, I'll catch up with you all tomorrow.'

Doc Dave ambled down the hot dusty airstrip to the large two-hundred-metre square, fenced-off yard. Tony called his neighbours fenced-off yard "The fort," The fort was about six hundred and metres away from Tony and Mavis, at the other end of the dusty gravel strip to give them all some measure of privacy.

The two-metre high link-mesh fence was originally built to keep out the wild kangaroos, donkeys, camels, and all the other wild beasts who just loved to scratch themselves on Max's many antenna systems and satellite dish arrays. This being especially after they had fed-well on his pride-and-joy veggie garden.

Dave knocked hard on the caravan door, 'wake-up you old bugger its Dave.' The door opened in an instant proving Max was not asleep.

'Ah-ha, the famous Doctor Who has now returned to the Tardis.'

Max was offering his normal jolly greeting as Doc Dave entered the large air-conditioned, very cold, but crowded caravan.

'I have some interesting things to show and tell you Doc, about our strange desert next door.' Then a concerned frown fell over his smiling face,

'Oh did you bring the electronic stuff from Perth I asked you to get for me in my phone text message?'

'Do not panic my large Jewish flying friend,' vigorously shaking hands like long-lost friends. 'All your new electronic toys and bits are in the Unimog, the cost of which I might add has blown my credit card off the accepted periodic scale. Max, let's hope that we can get you're big woks in the front yard working soon,' pointing out of the window. 'We can then download some free geo satellite data and maybe prove some of our odd suspicious theories, hopefully turning this large credit card cash outlay into a lifesaving profit.'

Dave looked-up at the bookshelf above Max's head. Then with a sparkle in his eye casually moved a large black book on electronic circuits aside to expose a not so well hidden bottle of Glenfiddich single malt scotch.

'Saving this for a rainy day,' Dave displaying his easy find. 'I have to remind you Max that it has not rained in this part of the Great Sandy Desert for over four years, and does not look like it will any time soon? Two fingers Max?' To which Max gave Dave the offensive two-finger salute.

'Oh dear, grumpy again, I can see that I might be drinking your scotch alone, this must be a serious business indeed. What do you want to show me, hit me with the details Max I am all eyes and ears.'

Max had gone to a great deal of trouble to hide that bottle of scotch from the Doc, apparently with little success.

'Don't tempt me Doc, if I were half my age and weight I would hit you... Anyway, I would then need another job, which at my age is very unlikely so I will just settle for attempting to drink more of my scotch than you do. Four fingers over ice thank you, oh yeah, and it's your shout next time, and I mean you should bring over a full bottle of good scotch.'

A few months ago, Max and Doc Dave, over a few drinks had come-up with a brilliant idea on how to make some money, and cover some of their large operating costs. As a contract geophysicist, Doc Dave was required to provide full detailed field reports.

This included all the necessary research data to back-up his recommended and proposed exploration areas, including all the proposed test-drilling sites. The client would also want strata site profiles and ground electromagnetic density information for the targeted sites, however; the biggest problem was getting access to the various commercial satellites that perform these expensive services.

The current client satellite access was around a four months wait. Then Max had come-up with a neat solution to the waiting time, just hack into one or two of the service satellites and carry out your own EMR geophysical survey.

'Have a gander at this lot Doc, tell me what you see and think.' Max pushed a few buttons on his keyboard and all eight of his large 40-inch computer monitors burst into life, two displaying a detailed cesium-vapor magnetometer ground map, downloaded from a new Russian satellite.

Doc Dave's eyes narrowed with interest as Max overlaid the existing image with a side-scan EMR (electromagnetic resonance) image to add depth to the computer model.

'I assume that this screen is now showing our area of interest, which is around one and a half miles northeast of the Veevers crater?'

Max nodded his head rapidly confirming this was indeed the area.

'That image clearly shows a very deep and massive underground cavity of some sort. On the other hand, the resistivity log confirms there are no signs of any fluids. Now that's a great pity as it would have been nice to discover an oilfield or at least a large underground cache of freshwater.

Max, this image may be just showing a vast underground cavern-complex of dry interconnecting caves. I must say though, it is a bit unusual being such a long way inland from the coast. At what depth would you reckon that fault is lying Max, and can we get a better level of resolution?'

'Sure can Doc, I know I will get a much better picture quality when I can find time to modify my satellite system with all that new gear you've brought back from Perth. At this moment, I can only look through highflying geostationary satellites in space.

With the new tracking gear fitted to my big dish, I will be able to track all the moving LEO (low earth orbiting) satellites. It will open a whole new range of satellite hacking opportunities for me.'

Max continued staring at his many computer screens with a satisfied smile and expanding pride matching that of a new father displaying his newborn.

'Be very careful Max as I can tell you now that they are watching you. While I was in Perth, I spent some time at the UWA (University of Western Australia.) I overheard two lecturers discussing some problems regarding large amounts of altered data and disruptions to the geostationary EO-51 and Landsat 9 satellites.

The owners and operators of these satellites had contracted them to sort out an annoying problem. That was to find a way of tracing the source of huge amounts of unscheduled data passing down through their bird.

Both of these smart electronic blokes were convinced the lost data ultimately caused by some unknown, externally controlled interference. Well we both know what that external interference problem is Max… It's you.'

Chapter Nine

The first sign

It all started around four years ago. About the same time that his mining services company had been swallowed-up by the eager opposition in a brutal but successful hostile takeover, leaving Doc Dave with nothing but debts.

Four months earlier Dave had lost his beautiful home in Perth in a bitter court battle with his first wife Rebecca. His second wife Jean had had enough after only two short years of marriage, winning his beachside Broome home in another bitter divorce settlement.

Then eight months ago, Mary his third wife had filed for a divorce, claiming adultery. Now legally separated, Mary was busy working with some success on what was left of his remaining, rapidly declining wealth. It looked like Doctor David Sharp was about to lose his beloved air charter company.

With mounting debts, Doc Dave had little choice but to go back into exploration contract work to earn a living. At the present, he still had control of his small air charter company, Sandfire Air Charter. Now he was working hard to keep it.

When not working on-site at a mining company job, Doc Dave lived in a caravan at his Sandfire airstrip base. He would also pilot the occasional charter flight when needed.

The first of the many strange desert incidents was a terrifying experience never forgotten, now engraved in Dave's memory forever.

107

It was the beginning of March with the tail end of the monsoon wet season still around. One of Dave's mining contacts had sent him a charter job to fly to Karratha and pick-up a box of mining samples and then fly them direct to Alice Springs.

At Alice Springs, he was to pick-up the CEO of a small mining company then to fly him back to Karratha, all simple stuff. Dave was in need of some in-command hours to keep him current on the Cessna 402, deciding to take this charter job himself and let Max continue to help Tony in the aircraft maintenance workshop.

The flight from Sandfire to Karratha was normal just some dodging around a few cumulus cloud build-ups, all of which were according to the weather forecast. The flight from Karratha to Alice Springs planned at a low 4000 feet AGL, (aboveground level) as Dave being a geophysicist liked to check out the desert ground features.

This low altitude flying would give him something to do on the long five-hour flight. Two hours into the flight tracking east on 103 degrees there was a large build-up of towering cumulus cloud ahead on the intended track.

This weather was most unusual in this area as he was now flying over the middle of the Great Sandy Desert. Few if any heavy cloud patterns were ever seen this far inland especially at this time of the year.

The standard area forecast was the expected CAVOK (Ceiling and Visibility Okay) an abbreviation for good flying weather. Nevertheless, there it was right in front of him, this bad weather was right before his eyes on his flight path.

Dave called Port Hedland for a weather update on the long-range HF radio, as he was way out of range to use the VHF short-range radio. All the radios were dead; the HF and the two VHF radios were just producing a hissing static, with no voice chatter heard on any of the three aircraft radios.

Strangely, the cumulus cloud was not causing the expected lightning static normally heard on the HF radio, which in its self was unusual. He then decided to call on the emergency frequency 121.5 in an attempt to try call a passing jetliner cruising at forty-three thousand feet to relay his request; again nothing.

Just then, a feeling of total isolation came over him and a shiver went up his spine as he looked at the ground rapidly covering with dark cloud. Just before the swirling thick-cloud obscured the last of the desert floor Dave had noticed the angle of the sand-blown ridges, and then glanced at the DG (Direction Gyro.)

He then double-checked the magnetic compass; both were reading the correct track. Yet the sand blown ridges that had been visible on the desert floor, ridges caused by the prevailing winds over millions of years had moved...

His planned flight track flew along the sand ridges, and now he was flying at right angles across the sand ridges. This would have him on an almost true north heading, yet the compass and the DG were both displaying the correct eastern heading. By all accounts, the autopilot was doing its job, still locked on to the required heading.

Something was wrong, very wrong. How could he be a ground visual whopping hundred degrees off course, yet the instruments were showing the correct heading?

Suddenly the aircraft went dark inside, now enveloped in thick dark cloud... As the cloud closed in below, a light patch to the upper one o'clock position offered a chance with a visible target to climb above all of this cloud.

The throttles were set to 75 per cent power, and the trim set to 500 feet per minute in a steady climb. A last check of all the aircraft instruments, and the most trusted instrument of all the magnetic compass, all confirmed as being normal. He then held his breath and gently disengaged the autopilot. Flying the aircraft manually, he headed up towards the lighter and only visible hole in the rapidly closing cloud formation.

Doc Dave had flown in full IFR (Instrument Flight Rules) more times than he would care to remember. It was not a new experience to him, but in some strange way this time, it was different. As the aircraft climbed through eight thousand feet, there was no sign of a cloud top.

Unexpectedly the lighter area closed over, as the aircraft continued droning on in a relaxing, cosy muffled semi silence. It was a weird sensation, one he had never experienced before, he felt strangely alone.

He trusted his aircraft, his instruments, his training, his sensation of orientation, and his ability to fly any aircraft without panic. He was a well-experienced, instrumented rated pilot, but this was nothing he had ever experienced before.

It was a feeling that he must challenge, or respond to, some sort of a dual or a dare set by his own aircraft. This very strange weather presented like a dual of chicken, who would break ranks first and do something stupid; who would win this game. The first rule of uncertainty is do not panic as panic kills. Had he come close to that stage so early in the game, surely not?

Dave was still climbing, relying on what the instruments were telling him. He agreed his aircraft was in a normal balanced-level-climb. No indications that the aircraft may be in some sort of unusual attitude or a spin were present. He knew that he was flying a controlled, level, platform; yet he did not believe what he saw. Should he believe what he now felt?

He whispered to himself, I have always trusted my instincts. Time will tell as we are now passing through twelve thousand feet, two thousand feet above the required regulation oxygen altitude. Then he thought you can't be in a spin while climbing at 500 feet per minute in a steady 165 knots controlled flight.

The view out of the cockpit window was now jet-black; it was like being in a commercial photo-lab darkroom. This is not right; all clouds are made-up of water vapour that will smash into, and then condense on the windscreen in flowing water... or as ice.

There was no moisture in this strange cloud. Could it be some type of fog or smoke, but smoke swirls and moves, this was solid. Another strange thing was the flight platform was rock steady, it felt just like we were sitting on the ground in a very dark hangar.

Fourteen thousand feet and still climbing. On what the instruments were saying, he was convinced that this was a level controlled climb. Make a decision man; this climb can't continue forever, I will run out of air to breath soon.

The decision was obvious he must reduce altitude. His first action was to level off at sixteen thousand feet. Six thousand feet above the regulation safe breathing altitude and one thousand feet above the zero oxygen altitude. He was now breathing only the air still held in the aircrafts hull. The next step was to plan an orderly decent; firstly by reducing the engine power to 60 per cent. By his dead reckoning, he had covered a distance of some 390 miles from Karratha. If he were to take-up a heading of 306 degrees, he would be heading back over to his Sandfire airstrip, for arrival in about one hour forty minutes flying time.

Dave dialled the new heading into the autopilot, and noted the airspeed had washed off to below 140 knots; he then took a deep breath of the thin air and engaged the autopilot. The Cessna 402 gently banked to the left in a rate-one turn and settled down to a level flight, no dramas the old girl obeyed the new heading command, to who knows which way.

He then dialled in a 3000 feet hold altitude at a 500-foot per minute decent and the old girl instantly complied. The airspeed rose quickly to 225 knots and he instinctively pulled back the power. The altimeter was winding back at an alarming rate, the decent felt far greater that the requested 500 feet per minute.

At the end of an agonizing twenty-two minute decent, panic was starting to set in. At 3200 feet, the aircraft suddenly broke out of this strange cloud or fog into an eye cringing bright dazzling sunshine, then in a moment of shock, he realised that he was over the ocean! How the hell could that have happened when we were heading for the centre of Australia; destination Alice Springs?

Doc Dave brought the aircraft around in a gentle 180-degree turn at the same time levelling off at 3000 feet. There was not a cloud in the sky in any direction, and the Australian coastline was only about ten miles away.

All the radios suddenly came back to life with the normal voice chatter. Then the dual ADF's (Automatic Direction-Finders) promptly locked on to navigation fixes to both Port Hedland and Broome, which had Dave firmly back on track for the Sandfire airstrip. Within twenty minutes, he was on the ground telling Max and Tony about his strange and frightening flying ordeal.

Tony was obviously excited as he liked weird stories and always had a better one to tell.

'I've heard these sorts of stories a few times before mate. A couple of years back two blokes got lost in the desert flying a brand-new Piper Malabo, it almost ran out of bloody fuel. They swore that their magnetic compass was way-out. I swung the bloody compass here on Sandfire and it was spot on.

Then a few months ago, I heard in the Sandfire pub about four Toyotas that were on the Desert Road in the Northern Territory. They were attempting to find a direct track across to the Gary-junction desert track and onto the bloody Canning Stock Route in Western Australia, now aint that been tried and done a few times before eh?'

Tony looked at them, he could see that they were both well and truly hooked on his story; he then quietly got up and walked over to Max's beer fridge and liberated three beers... Max exploded.

'Well don't just stop your story there you mechanical misfit, what the bloody hell happened next?'

Tony smiled that his distraction in grabbing a beer worked.

'Well, they had gone as far west along the desert track as they could, and then drove a compass bearing due west for about a hundred miles into the bloody uncharted Great Sandy Desert. Then some cloud cover started to build up fast, it was starting to get a bit dark and then it happened....'

Tony pause to drink his beer; it was a well-calculated pause designed for the typical outback pub dramatic effect, an effect that got right up someone's nose. This time Doc Dave exploded in a fury. He was not amused.

'Tony if you drag this story out one minute more I swear to you that I will ram that stubby bottle you're drinking right down your frigging neck. You just don't get it do you, you dim shit, this is serious stuff, I could have been killed out there. To me, it was that close and weird, so any constructive help in trying to resolve, or identify this mystery would be good... good for everyone's future safety.'

'Sorry Doc, it's just that I find all this bleeding spooky stuff in the desert a bit hard to believe mate. Anyway, the leading Toyota radioed back on a noisy radio saying that his compass was acting kind of strange, and that he had stopped to check it out.

By the time the others had caught up to him, they all had the same dashboard compass problem and they all had problems with their CB radios. They decided to camp for the night, and that's when they noticed that all their GPS (Global Positioning Systems) were all telling different track headings and the bleeding display maps didn't work. They had an almost new HF radio and a satellite phone but they didn't work either.

Next morning when the sun came up, they weren't where they thought they ought to be. By looking down at their own vehicle tracks, they were surprised that they were all heading almost due north. To make things worse, their bleeding electronic gear still wasn't working. The one good quality magnetic compass they had was just slowly turning around.

I can tell you they were shitting themselves with fear at the early hour of five thirty in the morning. The oldest bloke in the group applied a bit of good old Aussie logic to the matter.

He reckoned that the sun can't lie and said he was going to drive east into the rising sun until he hit the desert road again, and that's just what they all did. After about six hours, hard driving into the sun all their gear started working again, and they hit the Tanami desert road just a few miles south of Rabbit Flats. They then realised that they were many hundreds of miles off their intended bloody track.'

All three looked at one another taking in the detail of this strange story that was so similar to what Doc Dave had just experienced in his Cessna 402 twin-engine aircraft. Max gave out a small nervous cough and had a look of resigned confession on his face; Dave had seen that look before.

'You look like you have something to say Max, I think we should all hear your story.'

'Well I will confess to you blokes that I have experienced some odd radio and navigational problems over these past four months. Again, while flying the chopper and the 402. But I just put all this strange and bizarre experience down to a lack of aircraft maintenance.'

The hint of an evil smile briefly flashed on Max's face, quickly adding.

'I never wrote any of this stuff down on the maintenance release Doc, as I knew you were, well a bit short on cash.'

Tony's face took on a dark look of thunder, and was about to launch into Max with a ferocious verbal assault when Dave beat him to it.

'Tony, we all need another beer mate, and then I think we will all need to sit down with a glass of Max's Glenfiddich single malt whisky and discuss these weird desert happenings in full. We should all understand right now that Tony can't be expected to fix a problem on an aircraft that hasn't been reported to him, so we agree Tony is blameless in all of this.'

Tony had now quieted down, more at the thought of a few free shots of Max's scotch than the suggestion that he had been derelict in any of his aeroplane fixing duties.

'We, being Max and I are at fault for not reporting these problems in the aircraft tech-log. I hope that this frank admission clears up the aircraft maintenance matter. Nevertheless we still need to discuss all of our individual experiences and knowledge about this strange anomaly, Max what's your story mate?'

Max was wearing one of his "I can't believe it" looks. Which told Dave and Tony that he had still not fully accepted the fact, that his bottle of Glenfiddich was about to be decimated by two hard drinking friends. This was sacrilege, and against all of his Jewish upbringing.

Max then softened up a little, deciding to surrender his position as the past owner of a fine bottle of single malt whisky. He then slowly went about telling his strange story, while still mournful of his sad loss.

'A few months ago, I was hand flying the Cessna 402 on a low-level grid survey for a small exploration company. The survey area was from a datum point forty miles east of Lake Auld, using the Telfer mine NDB, and the Fitzroy Crossing town NDB. (None directional beacon) I was laying ten mile long gridlines east, at one mile wide track spacing's to the south. We were refuelling out of Telfer.

It was nothing special, just a routine job we had done many times before, except on the eighth gridline pass we lost all radio and navigation communication. I thought we had suffered a rare sunspot radiation affect. Then I noticed the DG (Directional Gyro) the GPS, and the magnetic compass were all showing a heading of 355 degrees, almost true north, but we were flying an east-west grid line.' Doc Dave butted in.

'That's almost the same thing that happened to me Max, but without the cloud problem. So what did you do then?'

'I just ignored all the weird things happening in the cockpit, the old girl was flying along quite happily I just flew by map and ground reference directly back to the Sandfire strip. Halfway back to Sandfire everything started working again, so I stuck with my first conclusion that it was just some sort of sunspot activity. A phone call to Hedland flight service advised they had no reported faults with the Telfer or Fitzroy NDB's or for that matter any other area problems.'

'You never told Tony or me about any of this, what about the chopper, you said you had weird problem with the Cessna 402 and the Bell Jet-ranger?'

'As I say I didn't report any aircraft faults as everything was working okay when I got back to Sandfire, and are still working okay. The other incident was only a few weeks ago. I took a Geologist out to his prospecting camp in the middle of the Great Sandy Desert.

We refuelled at the Telfer mine and headed out on 118-degree track for 170 miles, the maximum PNR (point of no return) fuel range for the chopper. About forty miles out from the camp the same bloody

114

thing happened, all the radios and navigation gear just stopped working correctly and started telling me lies.

We remained on the correct track by sighting a ground feature. I mean there was no going back being that close to the campsite; the next thing I was being flashed by a mirror, and headed direct into their camp. It was a well set-up prospecting camp with two big 4X4 trucks pulling heavy trailers.

The Geo had brought a spare HF radio, GPS, and a compass as apparently they had reported earlier that their electronic gear was not working most of the time. The five-man crew also reported a strange green glow to the east each night just after dark that disappeared after an hour. They were all spooked and were quite happy to see us.

This was all too much for me to take-in. Anyway, I needed to get going soon as I would run out of last light for a landing at Telfer. I refuelled and flew most of the way back by map-to-ground reference again; forty miles out everything on the instrument panel started working again, just like what had happened with the Cessna 402.'

Max pulled out a WAC (World Aeronautical Chart) covering the Great Sandy Desert and carefully spread it out on the table. All three leant forward, scotch tumblers in hand, and studied the positions that Max was now busy marking down. Max stood back and handed his pencil to Tony.

'Well there's my two creepy positions, Tony, can you give us some idea where those tourist blokes got lost in the desert trying to find a way through to the west.'

Tony placed his drink down on the edge of the table and inspected the map in detail. He quickly identified the fine red line of the Desert Track heading west then he noticed the track took a sharp right-hand turn to the north.

'This must be where they decided to keep going due west into the Great Sandy Desert. We need to plot another hundred miles west from this point,' placing his oil-stained finger on the red track turn.

Max, quick as a flash placed his distance ruler on the chart and drew a pencilled line from the track turn off for a hundred miles west, and then handed the pencil to Doc Dave. Okay Doc now you need to add your flying positions.

Dave took Max's distance ruler and drew two tracks, one from Karratha, and the other being his track into Sandfire from his last clear position.

All three stepped back to admire their handy-work and Tony topped-up the scotch drinks, noting the look of disgust on Max's face, adding.

'Well you lot are the bleeding flying blokes around here, what does all this tell you. It don't make no sense to me mate; mind you, I'm just a dumb aircraft mechanic. I don't know anything about navigation and maps do I?'

Max grabbed his precious pencil and ruler back then continued to draw some lines on the WAC map, mumbling in a disgruntled tone.

'You can't be expected to know everything Tony. We envy you knowing how to fix all types of complicated aircraft, and how to get your hands-on your mate's good bottle of whisky. Some skills like plotting a simple navigation track on a map may be irrelevant, when you have all these superior and more important survival skills.'

Tony was unmoved by Max's sour tone, writing off his smart comment as a last bleating sound of remorse over the rapid loss of his bottle of Glenfiddich scotch. Max stepped back from the map, he had extended all the pencilled tracks until they met or crossed one another. Then all three gasped in utter surprise! Doc Dave spoke first.

'What the hell is going on out there? This area is only around three square kilometres in the middle of nowhere, and what's that in the corner?'

Max picked up the map for a close inspection. He studied the map close-up, with his large Jewish nose almost touching the paper and then he announced.

'That's the Veevers meteorite crater; we should go check this place out. What power source could be so powerful as to block-out all radio and magnetic information in this area? What do you think Doc, can we afford seven hours flying time in the Jet-ranger chopper?' Tony took a gulp of Max's scotch and answered the question in a dry tone of reserved concern.

'That would be seven hours non-productive, none paying time mate. On a chopper that's only got about seventy bleeding hours to go to the next expensive service. It would be a lot cheaper to checkout this meteorite crater place with your Mercedes 4X4 Unimog ... your call Doc; it's still your air charter company... well until the taxman grabs it.'

Doc Dave was in deep thought; it was doubtful if he even heard Tony's practical advice, or about his taxation demise. Just then, a young squeaky voice yelled out.

'Dad, Mum says your dinners on the table you have to come home right now.'

'All right Jimmy, go tell Mum I'm on my way,' then turning to Max and Dave. 'Much as I like your company and free whisky mates, it looks like I've got to go, the war office has sent out a bleeding dispatch party with a firm bloody mobilising order.'

Tony skulled-back his almost full tumbler of scotch and then hurried out of the yard to comply with his marital home bidding.

Max watched in wonder as Tony quickly followed his son back home. With a bemused look, Max asked Doc Dave a serious question.

'Doc, I have always wanted to ask you. You have been married a few times now, how comes you never had any kid's? I mean that's what marriage is for isn't it?'

'You are a bit old fashioned Max. Most people don't bother getting married before they have kids these days. My wives all wanted kids, it's only natural; there was no doubt about that. The only thing was, not with me.'

There was a sad pause in Doc Dave's matrimonial admission, then with a sigh of regret continued…

'I thought I may have had a chance with Mary however, that's not looking too good these days, as she will not even talk to me anymore. The only contact I have with her now, is through her solicitor.'

Max knew Doc Dave well, he could not resist a bit on the side. He envied Dave that most women were attracted to him, and then casually said in all innocence.

'You can't blame her Doc, after all Mary did catch you bloody red-handed in the Darwin Tropicana Lodge pool with that stripper, with no gear on.'

Dave stared at Max with a surprised look…

'Yes well, it would have helped a hell of a lot Max if you had not flown Mary up to Darwin on a surprise visit. Then you brought her straight to the Tropicana Lodge poolside… at midnight.'

'We were looking for you everywhere Doc.'

'Well you certainly found me. This time my friend, it may well have cost us both our jobs. The only assets I have left are this little air charter company and a few vehicles, and Mary's lawyer is zeroing in for a kill.'

117

They both stared glumly into their empty scotch tumblers, each lost in their own thoughts about what might have been, and what now appears will happen soon.

'You know something Max,' Dave refilling his drink from Max's almost empty bottle of scotch. 'I've been thinking about this spooky desert stuff. It looks to me like it's almost as if this weird power or something is teasing us, or trying to steer us away from this area of the desert.' Stubbing his finger at the small triangle Max had drawn on the WAC map.

'This could turn out to be something important, possibly a worthwhile scientific discovery. Maybe that meteorite was made of solid concentrated magnetite, commonly known as lodestone. There may be one big enormous magnet just below the surface; one that may be worth quite a few dollars... now that would be nice.'

'Well you're the geophysicist Doc. If we use the chopper, we will need to refuel halfway to the meteorite crater. Why don't we do as Tony has suggested and just bloody drive out there in the 4X4 Unimog?'

Dave brightened up a little as he voiced his thoughts.

'What the hell Max, in about six months I might not even own that chopper if Mary follows through with the divorce and succeeds with her settlement claim. It would be a pity to leave some hours on it, but then again you're right, the Unimog is the best way to go. If this meteorite is made-up of concentrated magnetite, we will need to tow along the little sample drilling-rig trailer to bring back a few core samples.'

Doc Dave thought this was starting to sound much more positive, there might be a valuable mineral find in that meteorite crater. Finding a powerful magnetic source would be easy. Obtaining a sample may be a much more difficult task, especially if the magnetite material was deeper than thirty-five metres as that was the limit of his small sample drilling-rig.

Then there was the other problem to consider, concentrated iron magnetite was extremely hard rock. They could damage the expensive and difficult to replace diamond drill-bit, normally the paying client covered such costs.

'Max, I have just had a thought. At first light tomorrow, why don't you and I take a tranquil flight out to the Veevers meteorite crater in the Cessna 402 and see what's causing all this spooky stuff in the Great

Sandy Desert. Then in a few days, we can follow up with a leisurely drive out there in the Mercedes 4X4 Unimog.

Can you try to get some detailed area pictures off the Internet, meanwhile I will do some research on all there is to know about this Veevers meteorite crater… better let Tony know what we are going to do.'

Chapter Ten

Is this Extraterrestrial

The banging on the caravan door was loud enough to wake the dead. A faint voice from within called-out, give me a minute. Dave looked out to the east noting a faint glow on the horizon telling him that the sun was up but Max was not.

It was 5:01 am; this would turn out to be yet another hot 44-degree day without a hint of a breeze or cloud. Dave knew all this weather detail from his ARFOR (Area forecast) downloaded from aviation weather services. Today will be just another normal day in the desert, then yelling through the caravan door.

'Max, I will be out on the strip carrying out the pre-flight on the Cessna 402, I'll see you over there.'

Just then, the door of Max's caravan flew open with a crash. Max filled the doorway with his extra-large frame confirming that Max slept in the nude.

'Hang on Doc, grab some of this stuff, we need to take some test gear with us. We can take some electrical and magnetic readings and a few high-resolution photos.

Last night I managed to download some good Google earth images of the Veevers meteorite crater. I reckon they would be about four or five months old, it will be interesting to see if there are any differences.'

Max quickly got dressed for desert flying work with long pants and a long sleeve shirt topped off with his wide brimmed akubra hat, well you never know.

Doc Dave was dressed in the same desert gear, he helped Max load all his test gear into the mini moke, and they set off for the Cessna 402 parked on the hardstand. Tony was already there tinkering with the port engine with the help of a portable floodlight, which was rapidly becoming obsolete in the gaining light.

'I was thinking you blokes might do a sparrow fart departure this morning, so I have done the pre-flight, and filled her up with juice for you mate. Keep an eye on this port engine, as she's still a bit low on turbo boost. It could be just a sticky waste gate but watch-it all the same.'

Dave and Max continued to carry out a personal pre-flight check as all good pilots do keeping to the first rule of flying safety... "Trust nobody." There is only one-way to know if the fuel tanks are full and that is physically look into the tank yourself. Besides, how can you check if the fuel transfer pumps are working; simple, you must switch them on then rush out to the wingtip and listen to them working. Now you can't do that check while in the air. The double check of Tony's pre-flight was not an insult to his reliability; it was what Tony expected as a good engineer from any safety conscious pilot.

'You blokes missed a bloody good Kangaroo stew last night. Mavis has plenty left for you blokes tonight. That's if you don't get bleeding snaffled by some smart aliens, and have your heads investigated out there for any signs of bleeding intelligence ha ha ha.'

Nobody joined Tony in his nervous laughter. Doc Dave was not amused at the suggestion of smart aliens looking for signs of intelligence, Max stepped in to lighten things up a bit.

'The Doc has a good theory on all this strange stuff going on out in the desert. His current theory is that the meteorite in the Veevers crater might be a big chunk of concentrated iron magnetite, that's lodestone to a lowly educated, whisky swiping aeroplane mechanic like you.'

'Now listen here Mr Biggles, I may have acquired the odd skills or two in fixing aeroplanes and extracting whisky from tight-arsed bleeding Jews, but I also know what magnetite is mate.

I know the stuff is in rock form, and has lower iron content than its close mate haematite. Haematite is commonly known as Iron Ore, to dumb fat pilots, the very stuff we are sending by the bloody shiploads to China outa the Port Hedland port facility, just 370 kilometres from here.'

Max's jaw dropped, Tony knew more than he did on this subject. Tony noticed the look of amazement on Max's face and drove home his minor advantage before Max recovered from his shock.

'I'll tell you something else mate, highly concentrated magnetite rock is very rare stuff, it's only found in a few places on this bleeding planet. None of the concentrated stuff has ever been found in Australia, apart from what Shorty found; and another thing, it's worth a bloody fortune.'

A smile spread across Doc Dave's face. Tony was correct on all accounts, then again so was Max to a point. How or why did Tony have such in-depth knowledge on magnetite?

His curiosity got the better of him and so he asked the question. The answer he received opened up a completely new direction of investigation to a possible, future worthwhile discovery.

'You surprise me Tony, are you sure that you're not a Geologist and this aircraft engineering thing is just a side-line job to fool us. How else would you know so much about the subject of magnetite and lodestone?'

'Easy one mate; a good mate I knew carked-it, died because of the stuff.'

This time both Max and the Doc were standing with their jaws open in awe. Asking the obvious question was no longer required, as now clearly written on their confused faces, so Tony obliged.

'My mate Shorty was a gold prospector. He spent thirty bloody years out in the bush fossicking around looking for gold. Shorty spent most of his life tramping all over what would soon be discovered as the world's richest iron ore deposits. The silly bastard was trying to find gold, but too stupid to notice all the bloody iron ore lying about under his feet.

He found a bit of gold, but nothing much. Then one day he came into the Port Hedland pub, a rucksack on his back with a big heavy rock in it. He claimed he had found the mother lode of concentrated lodestone. We all reckoned he had gone bleeding troppo, been in the sun and bush a bit too long. So we figured we had best put him to the prospector test.'

Max was impatient, trying to nudge Tony's story along a bit faster...

'What test?'

'Oh the standard prospectors find test. You see if Shorty had found something bloody worthwhile, then he would have to shout a beer for the whole bleeding bar..., and he did, so we were all happy for him.

Soon everybody in the pub was sticking everything metal on Shorty's rucksack, he must have had the whole bleeding Hedland pubs cutlery stuck on his back. Shorty then stood on a bar chair and announced to us that this was only a small sample of what he had found, and then... well he just fell off the chair stone-dead... he bleeding carked-it.'

Both Max and Dave chorused together... 'He just fell over and died… right there and then.'

'Yup, you see Shorty had a real bad heart. A few years ago, he had got himself fitted out with one of them there new heart pacemakers. The powerful magnetic force of the lodestone stopped the bleeding thing working and he just keeled over. Carked-it right there in the middle of the pub. The whole bleeding pub was up in arms cos Shorty hadn't paid the booze bill before he went, and most of the blokes in there at the time were flat stony broke.'

Max just stared at Tony in speechless silence at this story. Tony was in childish raptures at Max's obvious reaction to his lodestone story. On the other hand, Dave was in deep thought again, and had another leading question to ask.

'Tony, if your mate Shorty was in the Hedland pub, how the hell did he get there, I mean what vehicle was he driving?'

'Shorty was never seen driving anything other than his old bleeding ex-army 1969 Land Rover pulling an old matching army ammo trailer... why?'

'Well his concentrated magnetite find must be in the Pilbara area somewhere. You can't travel all that far in the rough bush with an old prospecting rig like that, at most maybe a distance of three or four days travel, say 500 to 600 kilometres.'

This promoted a flood of sarcastic responses from Max.

'Well that reduces the find area location a little Doc. The Pilbara alone covers a vast area of over 500 square kilometres. Then if you include the Great Sandy Desert, that's a further area of 284,993 square kilometres, an area bigger than the United Kingdom and Germany together. Then of course, Shorty might have drifted into the Gibson Desert next door now that is another 156,000 square kilometres. And then he could have just kept going and ended up in the Great Victoria Desert that is yet another....'

Tony with a big grin on his face was listening to Max rambling on when Doc Dave cut him off in midstream, halfway through a desert.

'Now hang on there you blokes, let us try to put some prospective into all this. The chance that Shorty had found a rich commercial deposit of concentrated magnetite in Western Australia, or for that matter Australia, is highly unlikely.

After considering Tony's entertaining story my best bet would be that Shorty found a large meteorite of lodestone. Who knows it may well be the very one we are about to visit, so let's get going before the sun becomes too hot. Max, you can be the pilot in command; I will read-up on all the material I have downloaded about the Veevers meteorite crater.'

With Max flying the aircraft, the flight on the way out to Veevers crater was, as they say uneventful. No strange or unusual things happened, which disappointed Max who was ready to record everything on his expensive new digital movie camera.

At the crater, Dave took over the controls slowing the Cessna to 80 knots, with 10 degrees of flap extended. Max then took many high definition digital photos of the crater that looked identical to the images downloaded from Google. Dave was starting to get a little dizzy and bored, orbiting around the crater at the low altitude of only 250 feet. He then broke off for a short diversion to the east while Max set-up his all his complicated test equipment.

On the next circuit back to the crater, Max requested that all the aircraft radios and auxiliary equipment switched off. In addition, the alternator circuit breakers pulled to avoid any false readings, which may confuse his test results.

After several low-level fly-pasts taking measurements, nothing significant showed. Increasing the test sensitivity only caused the instruments to show what was happening on-board with the aircraft back-up systems.

'I think we should call it a day Max, the spooks don't want to play with us today, and we have been out here for over an hour now.

Suddenly Max startled Dave with a loud. 'STOP... did you see that?'

Dave replied with a cranky…

'How in the hell do you expect us to stop; we're bloody-well flying at 80 knots and only 250 feet above a ruddy desert for crying aloud! You of all people should know that request is bloody impossible.'

Max ignored Doc Dave's ramblings. He was busy taking a series of rapid photos, and then started scribbling like a maniac into his little notebook. Max then smiled a knowing smile and relaxed, turning to face Doc Dave.

'Okay Doc, I assume that you didn't notice that rapid deviation of the DG (directional gyro) and the flicker of the magnetic compass needle as we passed by the meteorite crater.

Here Dave,' showing the digital picture he had just taken, 'Dave follow this image on this heading being your reciprocal flight path and we should pass over the same spot.... That's if you are any good as a driver of this flying machine.'

'Have no fear the Doc is here, I can fly this baby through a keyhole. Seriously though Max did you actually witnessed a movement of our compass?'

'I did, and not only the compass Doc, but the DG needle also gave a mighty tweak. You were too busy trying to keep us from landing in this beautiful desert to notice the quick movement on the dials.'

Dave executed a perfect 180-degree turn and brought the Cessna 402 around on a reciprocal flight path. With the help of his digital photo, Max slowly gave Dave the steering heading.

'O...kay, now a little to the right... that's it. If you just keep us from crashing and burning as Tony says, I will tell you when to look at the dials. Steady... steady... s t e a d y... okay now.'

Both of them witnessed the sudden full 90-degree deflection of the DG and the magnetic compass. Both were astonished at this confirmed result.

Dave switched on all the radios and reset the circuit breakers again. He then applied full power putting the aircraft into a climb, to gain some safety altitude and avoid worrying about his close proximity to the ground.

'What the hell do you think that was Max? I will come around and fly that track again. We should be able to pinpoint the spot on the ground along the track. Then if I fly at 90 degrees to the spot, we should have a proper map fix. Get your map and stopwatch out Max.'

Twenty minutes later, they had the strange position plotted on the WAC map and were on their way back to Sandfire.

'Well we proved beyond doubt there is something out there Doc. Next week we should take a closer look with the 4X4 Unimog. I wonder what this strange thing or power is? It has the ability to move a magnetic compass, yet it gives no magnetic presence or reading on the earth magnetometer test instrument.

This energy, or whatever it is, must be a very narrow vertical beam of some sort... You're not saying much Doc; I don't like it when you're quiet.'

'Just having a think Max, I have plotted the ground position; it's a sort of very narrow beam of energy. This same energy has ability when it chooses to widen, and expand over hundreds of miles and make its own weather, mostly bad weather. Another odd thing is the plotted position is one and a half miles northeast of the Veevers crater, not over the crater. If I remember that's about where you plotted those strange underground caves.'

'This is all giving me the dreaded spooks Doc. Tony won't believe a word of what we have found. But, that won't stop him telling everybody he meets over a beer at the Sandfire Pub, all about this creepy stuff going on out in the desert.'

'Then I suggest that we don't tell him anything. You know me by now, if there is any value in what we find out there in the desert, Tony will get his fair share of any gains. On the other hand, there may be a simple explanation to all this strange desert phenomena, and I have my reputation to consider. I think we should say nothing to anybody until we know exactly what the hell is going on out there... agreed.'

'That sounds okay to me Doc; I agree... my lips are sealed.'

The Cessna droned on in a perfect autopilot steady flight, holding six thousand feet. Doc Dave was browsing through some of his notes.

'Max, I was reading all his data on the Veevers meteorite crater, having just read a very interesting technical paper by a Professor Ivan Gorgy. The Professor has recently returned from a field trip to Australia in which he visited the Veevers crater site. He travelled to the impact crater site by driving up the Canning Stock Route then south on to the Gary track. Listen Max, this is interesting stuff, I will readout the article.

"I have travelled the world over many years, and been to all of the world's deserts from the coldest to the hottest places on earth. I have

127

been few places that are as desolate and barren as the Great Sandy Desert in Western Australia"

'He then goes on to say.'

"Western Australia has the unusual distinction of having more discovered and recorded asteroid and meteorite hits than any other landmass in the world.

This could well be since the vast areas of the desert suffer natural fire burnt-offs each year. This event clears the desert of all vegetation, leaving the landscape with a similar look to that of the moon, making craters easily identifiable.

The Veevers meteorite crater is small, being only some three hundred and seventy metres across. It is most odd in that it is quite balanced and regular. The shape well preserved and perfectly round with the complete ridge of the rim being at the same height, suggesting a vertical trajectory impact. This is a most unusual scenario, as meteorites always strike the earth at an angle. It would appear this particular crater obviously caused by a direct and vertical impact.

The crater wall is date to around 10,500 years, having a small-calculated impact size of 190,000 tons. Small meteorite samples and impact breccia's, later identified within the ejecta area and around the crater.

A second and unusual anomaly found, was in the type of meteorite rock samples taken. They were analysed and found to be of three distinct and separate types. Shocked quartz dated at over 200 million years, Nickel-iron, dated at a younger 120 million years and chondrite-stone dated at less than 50 thousand years.

We have not yet determined as to why there are three different types of meteorite material found. In addition, as to why the dates have such vast time differences. In addition, none of the meteorite type samples was large enough to have caused the crater impact... Research is continuing."

'Well what you make of that Doc. You're the Geophysicist can you put all that Professor Ivan stuff into plain language so a simple pilot like me can understand what-the-hell he is on about?'

Doc Dave had slipped into one of his deep thoughts again and Max gave him a gentle prod with his finger to bring him back to life.

'This is interesting stuff Max, if this Professor Ivan knew what we have just found out about the Veevers crater area I ponder to think what he might have written in his technical paper.'

'Yeah most likely he would have reported a Martian landing and evidence of little green men's footprints in the middle of Veevers crater.'

'That may not be too far from the truth Max, after all meteorites are extraterrestrial.'

'Come on Doc that's all crap. You are a bloody scientist, now this is starting to frighten me a bit, do you really think this is a Martian meteorite? This is the twenty-first century of mobile phones, satellite TV, microwave ovens, and tasty fast food.'

'Yes Max I am a scientist, and like all good scientists I go with the proven facts. We have just proved that some invisible column or force exists in the Great Sandy Desert, next to a meteorite crater. We flew over the exact point at varying altitudes all the way up to twelve thousand feet and it was still there.

Then the other facts, we have both experienced strange effects on our aircraft navigation and radio equipment in this same area. In my view, a large chunk of lodestone rock could never have caused this narrow energy force pipe. Now that is what any good scientist would call positive proof of the paranormal, all we need now is a few good snapshots of little green men posing by their space ship.

Consider this Max, if we were to add our recent experiences to that of Professor Ivan's we would have a compounding set of anomalies. First, earth impact craters do not move their location or tell birthday lies.

Professor Ivan dated the Veevers meteorite crater at about 10,500 years old, this is not a difficult task to perform, and I am sure that he is correct with his age dating sums.

However, three differing types of loose meteorite material was found within the Veevers crater... that reeks of suspicion, as they are all movable therefore most likely to be planted.

But then one would ask, for what reason, maybe some sort of decoy?'

Max was deep in thought stroking his nose. He then unloaded what he considered a possible answer to this strange anomaly.

'Doc, try this, what if some crazy meteorite collector bloke dropped his bag of meteorites while he excitedly went about picking up a few of the Veevers ones. Now that would explain why there were three different types of meteorite samples found in the Veevers crater.'

'Not bad, not bad at all Max that could explain the meteorite material anomaly. You now need to find the answer as to why the Veevers crater is perfectly round, and in such good condition, all of which confirms a direct vertical impact.

This is extremely odd for a three hundred and seventy metre wide meteorite crater. However, not if it were a powered missile, or possibly a nuclear explosion site, one the government forgot to tell us about... But then again the crater is dated at some 10,500 years old; however, we should still check for radiation traces.'

Max had no answers to Doc Dave's theories as they droned on to Sandfire while thinking of one.

'All stations Sandfire, Charlie-Whisky-Golf, Cessna 402 is five miles inbound from the south for landing niner zero, surface conditions please?'

Then a crackly but clear radio voice responded.

'This is Darth Vader have you brought any news from the bloody dark side mate?'

'We will be on the ground in two minutes Tony; get three cold beers ready while I consider challenging you to a laser sword fight.'

There was a slight pause as Tony smiled at Dave's challenge.

'The Obi-Wan has taught you bleeding well my son.'

Without any distraction from the well-practised procedure of landing the Cessna 402, Dave voiced his opinion of Tony's amusing radio call.

'I think we're right. Any mention of what we have now found out about this Veevers meteorite crater thing to Tony would be a big, big, mistake.'

Dave and Max had firmly agreed to say nothing as an early resolve, but both could see they had other problems. Thinking, how could they prove a strange power anomaly that only appears when it decides it should... this was going to be difficult?

To open and discuss these strange events with others, would attract a far greater scepticism than what Tony could ever produce. The obvious answer for now would be to say nothing to anybody, and just continue with their research. Dave had another thought.

'Max, when you were playing around with the Geosat satellite downloads, we identified some deep dry caves. I was thinking as we flew over the spot; my bet is they are in the same place as our mysterious energy beam. If we could watch and possibly monitor this site, and the Veevers meteorite site, we might get all the answers we need.'

Dave neatly lined-up the Cessna on the hardstand; then waited the mandatory three minutes turbo idle, before shutting down the hot engines; being greeted by a welcome silence in the hot still air. Only the whining of the gyros was heard as they wound down, and the crackle of the cooling hot exhausts.

'You might be right Doc, but we know this energy thing isn't caused by magnetite. Those dry caves are very deep, what could be down there? I will find out more when I can get access to a more powerful ground-penetration satellite system.'

Doc Dave just nodded his head understanding the challenge.

'I was going to say to you earlier Doc; I have had little success with my new satellite gear. The biggest problem with hacking into secure business and Government satellites is covering your arse so they don't know who is hacking them.

Better still would be if they have no idea they are being hacked in the first place. I reckon it will take me a few months to find a way to stay completely invisible.'

Max knew that ninety-nine per cent of illicit satellite hacking and intrusions were the work of world foreign powers. India, Pakistan, China the USA and the United Kingdom being by far the major culprits, the other one per cent usually carried out by keen hobby-hackers such as himself.

If he was extremely careful, his risk of discovery was low. However if someone, or a major world power were to take an interest in what Max was doing, and were then to build a work profile around him. This would reveal his hacking style and interest, and ultimately his location.

Max had a plan, which was to mix his satellite special data questions with a percentage of dummy requests to confuse any data tracking. He would then use as much of streamed normal data requested by others as he could.

Doc Dave came back to life with words cutting through Max's devious hacking plan.

'Then I guess that's it, that's just what we will do Max. We will collect all the available information and data that we can find on this area over the next few weeks, while at the same time, keeping a low profile.

Then when we are ready, you and I will take a leisurely drive out to the Veevers crater in the 4X4 Unimog. With any luck, we may find the remains of a little green Martian or two... Who knows we could become famous and rich giving endless TV interviews about this... maybe write a book or two?'

Max gave Doc Dave a worried sideways look... what was he on about, some sort of rambling alien crap. Maybe it was the first signs of madness caused by his financial and matrimonial stress... Then thinking how lucky he was, he had no money to worry about, and no woman to give him strife. Who would know what might happen in the future to change all of that. It was all starting to become a huge concern... will this situation elevate to become a major worry? Then again, the truth was... Max never worried about anything.

Chapter Eleven

The Apprentice Gadichi Man

Max was still wearing a look of surprise on his face, after Doc Dave had casually revealed he was being watched. Max could see that he needed to explain this delicate matter of satellite hacking a little further to his concerned boss Doc Dave.

'Doc, being watched, and the operators of the satellites knowing that some of their data was being manipulated are two very different things. My understanding of "being watched," would assume that they know whom, or what is causing the unscheduled data transfer.

I can tell you right now that these people have no idea at all about us. My guess is, if the particular satellite these guys are checking-out is American, they will think it's the Chinese, or the Indians that are doing the hacking... or maybe the Russians, certainly not me.'

'You are right Max; maybe I should rephrase that comment to say,

"They suspect that someone may be manipulating their satellite data."

Anyway, you must accept, it does not change the fact the satellite owners have identified some unusual tinkering with their satellite data-transfer. They are noticeably aware that somebody is also playing with the steering and shifting of the ground footprint.'

It was two weeks since Dave and Max flew out to the Veevers impact site. The new satellite equipment was better, but was not

133

performing as well as expected, much work still required. For all their hard work and new equipment, they had not learnt anything new. Dave and Max continued staring at the large underground network of caves displayed on four of Max's eight computer monitors that now occupied both sides of his crowded caravan.

They were both thinking about all the strange things they had experienced around the Veevers area, and the many other stories that they had gathered over the past four months, all of which related to this strange area in the desert. A number of questions were going through Dave's mind. Nothing they had found to date could explain the weird energy beam or pipe they had plotted.

Another point was, did the discovery of these dry underground caves, have anything at all to do with Veevers crater. After all, the caves were over one and a half miles, or three kilometres away from the meteorite crater. The caves appeared to be quite deep, and gave no visible surface signs or clues as seen from the air, or the satellite images.

Tony was becoming suspicious about the amount of time these two were spending in Max's caravan. Much as he tried, Tony could not extract any believable information about what they were up-to in there.

To keep Tony happy and off the scent, Max had installed a mini point-to-point 10Gig microwave link to Tony and Mavis's transportable house giving them over 450 channels of quality radio and TV. Mavis thought it was the best thing that had happened to her since they came to Sandfire, as it kept Tony out of the Sandfire pub and the three kid's quiet.

Doc Dave did not see it quite that way, because to him it would only be a matter of time before Tony blabbed about his great TV reception over at the Sandfire pub one night. On the other hand, one of the kids might mention it on the RFDS School-of-the-air during their daily radio lessons, and then all hell would surely break loose.

'We should wait and see if you can improve the resolution of the cave images. Then as we planned a few weeks back, we should take a drive out to the crater and the cave site in the 4X4 Unimog, then carry out some thorough research and investigation.'

Max stopped working on enhancing the computer image and turned to Dave holding up his empty glass rattling the lonely ice cube within. Dave leapt forward and poured Max another four fingers of Max's scotch.

'You know Doc if you want to get things to happen quicker in the satellite hacking business you could go out in the hot sun.' Pointing out of the caravan window, 'and mount all the new satellite elevation over azimuth tilt tracking motors to my big satellite dish. Now that would be a help, then I could stay locked onto the low earth orbiting satellites, the ones with all the good juicy data.'

Dave was not so silly. Max was attempting to save more of his scotch.

'I have had a thought about that Max, and was going to do that little job, but only after dark when it cools down. I would rather put-up with being attacked by sand midges and mosquitoes attracted to the floodlight than work out in this 43 degree plus heat.'

Max looked sad; his careful plan to save the last of his bottle of scotch now abandoned as a hopeless cause. His only chance now was to stay with his original plan; that being to drink more of his scotch than his boss did. Dave considered a diversion urgently needed, bursting forth into further matters of urgent concern.

'We need to talk about our friend Tony and his new satellite TV link. I think we are going to run into some almighty big problems soon, sure to happen when the Sandfire pub hears that he has 450 channels of satellite TV.'

A flash of realisation at what he had created flashed past Max's single malt affected mind

'You are right again Doc, I must admit I was a bit silly, I was just thinking of Tony and his family. I guess that access to 450 TV channels way out here on the edge of the Great Sandy Desert could cause many questions in such a remote bush pub. I'll get Tony to keep quiet, and just record a few suitable sports programmes for them.'

Even with this cautious approach, Dave could still see future problems. He did understand that Max was just trying to be social in offering Tony the results of his successful entertainment satellite hacking work. The only problem was, gossip in the remote bush got around faster than a dry-man could move, downing his first beer on a hot day.

The Sandfire airstrip was about two kilometres inland from the main road. Well behind the pub, and not seen from the Great Northern Highway or the Sandfire pub, which was just as well considering the large dish antenna systems that Max had installed over the years. Those few that had used the Sandfire landing strip for the first time always made comment. 'Was this place some sort of secret government listening station?'

The air charter business was not going all that well, with only four short flights in two weeks. This low flying activity suited Max quite well since all his new electronic toys were still awaiting installation and set-up.

Doc Dave had two small mining contracts to get on with; both would keep him busy for the next two months. After that, he was hoping other tenders previously presented, might give him an added six weeks work, however, the long-term prospects were not good.

Looking on the brighter side, the free geological survey data provided from Max's satellite hacking efforts had helped in keeping his costs down, returning a good profit on the small amount of mining work he did have.

Mary had instructed her solicitor to ease up on Dave to give him a breather to try to sort himself out. Dave had thought the most likely reason for this was that there was nobody around who would want to buy the last of his assets at this time. The truth being keeping the business going was better than forcing a fire sale.

Dave had reckoned that the longer he held on to the business, the better chance he had in finding the money to pay Mary her half value. These small delays would at least gave him some time to talk Mary around to possibly forgiving him for, well, screwing around.

One of Doc Dave's two small geological mining contracts required him to carry out some geological sampling work in the area of the Aboriginal settlement called Punmu. This is a small indigenous settlement on the edge of Lake Dora, a dry-salt lake in the Great Sandy Desert.

Dave had been to Punmu many times in his travel's into the desert however; his last visit was over four years ago. On this planned field trip, he had arranged that two company geologists would accompany him on an eight-day prospecting programme; they would use the Bell Jet-Ranger.

Dave had also arranged some weeks before for a number of JetA1 fuel drums for refuelling at the Punmu airstrip. They would be using the Punmu airstrip as their camp base. Exploration permits had been authorised and cleared by the Punmu Martu Aboriginal Corporation.

It was just under three hours chopper flight-time out to Punmu, with one short stop on the ground to water the desert. Dave hoped the old man elder Mirachung was still alive. He was a true gentleman of the old school, living off the land and teaching the young men how to be a real Aboriginal. This tribal leader commanded total respect from his people; a man who knew all and everything that happened in his vast desert.

Mirachung would be the best man to ask about all of the strange things happening in his desert over 190 miles away, being around fifteen days walkabout from Punmu towards the morning sun. Doc Dave had the highest respect for the elders of the Aboriginal tribe that owned full rights to this part of Australia.

Over the many years working in the remote Australian bush, Dave had come to understand and respect the reasons why the desert Aboriginal people did things in a certain way. Everything in the desert always done for a very good reason, and a purpose.

Over the years, he had learnt a number of desert survival skills from these people; skills that on one occasion had saved his life. Unfortunately, the young tribal people were not interested in learning these old ways and skills. They were only interested in television, motor cars, and alcohol. Most leaving the community for the white-man towns as soon as they could.

Doc Dave was looking forward to meeting-up with Mirachung again; this thought reminding him, he had better go over the local Punmu community rules with his passengers. Doc Dave pulled the helicopter boom-mike closer to his lips.

'Gentlemen, we are only about thirty minutes out from Punmu; just remember these people are very proud and tribal. They live in the middle of this inhospitable, hot barren desert only because they choose to, and because they own it. The tribe run and managed by a council of elders, with a chief elder, whose name is Mirachung; do not forget his name; and more importantly, what he represents out here. He is more than just the boss elder he is much like a great Chief or a King and respected like one.'

Big Des, a South African was the oldest of the two company geologists being around fifty-six and had been in Australia for only six months. He was a massive six-foot seven-inch hulk of a man with an angry foul mouth. Doc Dave could not warm to his blunt Afrikaans manner however; he was well experienced in desert exploration having worked four years in Iran.

Young John on the other hand was just twenty-five, fresh out of geo-school, a few months out of Leeds University in England with the ink still wet on his degree. This was his first company job and his first trip to an Australian desert, and it showed.

The heat was killing him and the sun was nowhere near its maximum for this day. Doc Dave had managed to convince him before they had departed that short sleeves and no hat was not a good idea. Advising him, that trying hard to get an Aussie suntan was also a dumb idea in this heat.

Both were a worry, as neither of them had ever met up with a real Aboriginal, let alone a desert Aboriginal, they were about to be educated in a way they will never forget. He decided now would be a suitable time to give his clients some local information and rules.

'I need to explain a few things to you guys, we will be camping on the Punmu airstrip right next to our fuel dump. The town is only about six kilometres down a gravel road but we will only go into the town if, and when we need to for supplies.

Punmu is a dry community, in other words, no alcohol of any sort allowed on-site. The last time I was in Punmu some four years ago, they speared a bloke in the leg. He was a white idiot caught selling booze to the locals. The council of elders do not muck around with trials and presumed innocence around here, so if you have any booze I suggest that ditch it now, or hide it real good.'

There was a silence while they both digested this bad news. A silence punctuated by the high-pitched whine of the turbine and the steady whacky-whack of the rotor blades overhead. Then Des spoke in his heavy deep Afrikaans accent.

'I don't have a problem with the no liquor available, I got my own. Four years in Iran working in a "Slum Ou" Islamic tea-totalling country fixed that. Everybody was a secret drinker in the shebeen (Illegal drinking place), what about you John?' turning his massive head to face the innocent looking young geologist.

John was displaying a look of shock and horror, answering in a tumble of words

'I haven't brought anything to drink at all. I thought we would just go down to the local town bar and buy a beer or two. It never occurred to me that a town out in this godforsaken hot desert would not have a cold beer. This is terrible, I don't know if I can survive eight days without a beer.'

Big Des replied with a rumbling laugh.

'Well John at least you won't be speared in the leg by a kaffer eh, what about you Doc. You don't look to me like the abstaining type?'

'It goes without saying that Punmu hasn't got a bar. I have my hidden provisions for a much-needed medicinal nightcap. Doctor David's orders, I can't sleep without a wee dram o scotch.' The helicopter erupted into laughter; with Dave thinking to himself, I hope they both got that, as he was not joking.

It was a full three days before Mirachung decided to invited Doc Dave into Punmu town for a chat. This was the way of the desert elders; a gentle reminder that you were politely tolerated when visiting their community, but not overly welcome. These people much preferred to avoid all outside contact when possible, especially from whites.

Most of the community still lived in the old way, under a platted bush shade, with those who choose to, living in corrugated tin huts.

Only the toilet block, tucker shop, medical centre and the generator hut had proper lockup buildings with tin roofs.

Doc Dave knew the way to the elder's private quarters, an old transportable donga; where he found Mirachung watching GWN satellite TV. It was just after eight in the morning, finding him engrossed in a children's TV programme called *Fireman Sam*. Mirachung turned to the door while Dave stood at the entry to the donga. As was the way of the desert people, the door along with the windows, removed many years ago. Then with a wide toothless grin.

'Nyaparru (my friend) Doc, I bin not see you for long-time now, must be oh maybe four year ago.' Rising himself from his old armchair to shake hands vigorously. 'As bin thinking you was dead or something all this long-time, ha he he.'

Mirachung might be in his eighties but he had no trouble launching himself out of his old chair. His wicked sense of humour had not changed one bit. Firmly shaking hands, his steady almost closed desert eyes that looked right into your head for any sign or flicker of a change. He then continued with his inspection of Dave.

'You bin look real tired mate an you got a worried man's face, ah thinks you last wife gone walkabout on you, ha he he. Doc you has gotta keep dat prick in them pants mate, ha ha he he.'

Dave just had to smile. Here he was, in the middle of one of the harshest and desolate deserts in the world, and this old man knew more about his disastrous marital life than his divorce lawyer, then responding to old Mirachung's mysterious wit.

'I see you are catching up on your childhood education,' nodding towards the TV. 'That stuff can be very demanding for an old man to understand in these modern days.'

'He he ha, dis is best stuff on whitey TV box mate. Anyways I gotta checkout if it okay for my community to watch.' Then with a regal look of a wise man, 'Am tribal elder you know. These things is very important mate, if they do right thing in community they can watch dis TV. Better that than a big stick on the arse, he he he ha.'

Mirachung was no fool. Control of the satellite TV reception was a good way of controlling the kids... and all the adults. The control and access to the satellite phone and TV was real and present power in Punmu.

Mirachung turned the TV sound down, and offered Dave a chair that was in a far worse state of repair than the one he had just returned to sit in. Dave glanced around the room. As expected, apart from no door there was also no glass in any of the windows. Even the King had nothing to keep out the desert heat and dust.

The wall-mounted air-conditioner unit looked like it had never been used and the power plug was missing. Dave had seen this all before. Desert Aboriginals just don't like windows and doors... never have. Mirachung was now comfortable again reaching into his little fridge placed neatly at his side, handing Dave a cold can of coke, then with a well-timed pause and a grin, opened up the line of conversation... Mirachung spoke...

'I would offer you a cold beer mate but then I'd have ta spear yeh in the leg mate, he he he.' Then all of a sudden, Mirachung changed from his normal toothless grin and became very serious, looking across at Dave, this time with his eyes wide open.

'I see you got something on your mind to talk about; we old men can tell these things mate. I think you gonna ask me about things we no like to talk about... but you the only white-man in mah whole desert dat I like, so you can ask mate. But I don have tell you anything, cos I'm elder, an this all my land... my desert, you understand mate?'

140

A faint grin returned to Mirachung's face telling Dave to go ahead and ask his questions, but he should tread softly... the warning was clear.

Dave took a sip of his coke while he pondered a way to open up with his questions on the touchy subject of the strange things happening in the desert, right in Mirachung's own backyard.

What was more of a concern was the old man appeared to know what he was about to ask him, and had warned him to be careful. Then there was the matter of his third divorce, now how did old Mirachung know about that? About Mary and me splitting-up over me screwing around with another woman. The desert telegraph was not that good... or was it?

'Mirachung you know that I fly all over your desert and I see the strange wonders and things that only a man of the desert would know about and understand.

I know that some places are very special and sacred to the desert people, we simple whites do not know which places are important, or, which to stay away from. There is a place in your desert fifteen days walk towards the morning sun that makes my flying machines get lost in a strange dark fog.'

Mirachung went quiet, turned and looked into Dave's eyes.

'You bin told by Mooroopna (ghost spirit) to stay away and you went back. Now the Wirinun (sorcerer) has called you back for a chat. The only one-man who go to dat spirit place is...'

Then Mirachung fell silent and it took Dave a few minutes to realise why. The desert people cannot mention the name of a dead person as this is disrespectful to the dead spirit. I thought who would be important enough to have the elder's permission to visit a sacred place, and someone who was now dead. Mirachung kept his steady look into Dave's eyes.

Dave searched his memory for an answer, and then it suddenly came to him. Yes of course, four years ago the biggest wake singing in the desert. Munyo the old Gadichi man had died.

'I know and respect your custom which is not to talk and say the name of a dead person from your community. I also know, that with just you and me in this room I can say the name of this person as long as nobody can hear. I can now say the name of the man with the special right to talk with the Mooroopna. His name was Munyo the Gadichi man.'

141

Mirachung slowly nodded his head in agreement. He was no longer cracking jokes as his face took on a look of detachment and his eyes glassed over in a milky haze. Mirachung had gone into a deep trance. Then Dave realised that Mirachung was the most likely successor to Munyo... Mirachung was the Martu desert people's new Gadichi man... He then started to speak in a low guttural but clear voice, a sound like he had ever heard before.

"You must listen to Mooroopna the ghost spirit; it has much to tell you of a past life and what the future will hold. Munyo never replaced the bone as promised, and now he has gone; taken by the Great Spirit. Too many secrets are with the sacred bone.

You will bring the bone back to its resting-place. Only then can I walk to the sacred place of the Mooroopna as the desert Gadichi man."

Mirachung stopped talking and continued his wide-eyed milky stare into nothing. Dave passed his hand across Mirachung's face with no reaction. He was still in a deep trance and he had said aloud the name of a dead Gadichi man. This was a terrifying breach of the Martu desert people's spiritual beliefs. This could only mean one thing that this was not Mirachung speaking... Could he talk to this deeply entranced man?

'Spirit man, will I offend the Mooroopna if I go to the place fifteen days walk towards the morning sun from this place?'

Mirachung's head swivelled around on his shoulders from looking at nothing on the wall to face Doc Dave. Dave felt a shiver go up his spine; it was like watching something out of The *Exorcist* movie. Then he spoke in the same strange guttural voice... but his lips were not moving. The voice came from deep within... Doc Dave's head...

"It is waiting for you and the two others to return the bone. Time is running out; there is still much to learn and much to do. I cannot help you further, time... no time. An end to all that we know may be very close."

Dave realised that he was sweating heavily, the reason was obvious... fear, he was actually terrified. He had known Mirachung for many years. The man was always joking around and happy, a wrinkled near toothless eighty-plus year old man who liked nothing better than teaching the young people about the old tribal ways.

142

This weird trance, was a side of Mirachung he had never seen before, this was not Mirachung. The voice had no English or Aboriginal pidgin, there was no accent, and it was a strange neutral sounding voice.

Mirachung's head slumped forward and Dave got up from his old chair to see if he needed any help. Thinking, Christ I hope he is okay and not dead. Just as he touched Mirachung, he moved, being startled appearing to have just been woken-up from a snooze.

'Ah must dozed off nyaparru (my friend), when you get my age that happen all the time, like always this time of day.'

Dave looked at his watch it was 2:15. Had he really been here for six and quarter-hours, this can't be right. Then he noticed the TV, the afternoon movie was just finishing with the credits showing. Mirachung smiled his normal toothless grin with a glint in his almost closed desert eyes.

'Am bin thinking Doc, you had a snooze with me mate, he he he. Just like old men do in the sun, but has thinks you got important things to do now, ha he ha ha.'

It was obvious that Mirachung had no idea about his trance, and his chat with me. Then again, he must have some idea as he referred to me having important things to do. One last question may provide many of the answers; however, this last question would need asking in just the right way. Then Dave had a sort of spiritual revelation, he would acknowledge the change in Mirachung's status.

'Mirachung I have been touched by the spirit of time, I have this powerful feeling that you are the new Gadichi man of this desert.'

Mirachung's face quickly changed back to a blank look of detachment but this time he did not fall into a trance. His eyes opened wide directing a deep penetrating stare into Doc Dave's eyes and held his gaze steady.

'I no be Gadichi man if you no gonna make the Mooroopna happy. You gotta bring da bone back... mate.'

Dave was lost for understanding, replying.

'What fucking bone?'

'You gonna know all dat when time is right... you want another coke mate?'

Big Des broke the tense moment; the big Afrikaans geologist appeared in the doorway blocking out most of the light, and displaying a look of dark rage on his face.

143

'Where the fucking hell have you been all day, we have lost this workday skaarpie (cuntface). You owe the company another day's chopper flying to cover this one mompie (retard). You can spend a day with that kaffer (nigger) in your own time domkop (idiot.) Okay let's get going right now this place smells of verk (death).'

Doc Dave waited in silence as the big rough South African geologist finished his ranting and raving. By now there were around thirty young and not so young well-weathered Aboriginal male tribesmen with nulla-nullas (large wooden fighting clubs) silently surrounding the entry to Mirachung's donga.

Dave glanced at Mirachung who then just nodded with a toothless smile. Dave now had full permission granted from the community elder to save this big loud-mouthed South African dimwit from what would most certainly be a messy death.

'Des, you are lucky today, lucky that you will live. But can you fight as well as you swear, insulting these people in Afrikaans,' crooking his index finger in a provoking action to call the giant closer, and away from the doorway.

'We Aussies think that you may have missed the etiquette classes when you first arrived in Australia.

If you are ever going to get along with people working in the bush you need to learn some respect for the traditional owners of this vast continent.'

Big Des cared little for the local customs, his face broke into a well-practiced bar-brawler's grin… adding.

'And you intend to teach me I suppose?' grunted the big Afrikaner with an ugly smirk on his face.

'You bet, and the only way we Australians know how.'

The big Afrikaner got the message loud and clear, displaying an evil grin, and then bunched his giant fists ready for a fight. He was standing just one-step inside the donga doorway with the light behind him.

If he had turned around, he would have seen what Doc Dave was looking at. A group of thirty almost naked tribal desert hunters were waiting in silence, just four short steps away, nulla-nullas at the ready, listening for one single word from their chief elder Mirachung.

Dave had to work fast to save the big Afrikaners life. A quick glance at Mirachung had him displaying his toothless grin; he had just taken a drink from a large contour glass bottle of coke-a-cola.

144

The thought fleetingly passed through Dave's brain, they don't make those funny shaped bottles of coke any more, and that one must be a large display bottle, how the hell did Mirachung get one of those old bottles way out here... and then it was on.

The thirty desert hunters gave out a high-pitched hunting scare cry, used to spook pray towards a hunter. In the instant that the big man was distracted Dave drove his size-twelve geo desert steel capped work-boot hard into the Afrikaners balls.

The result was a bellow of rage and pain with the big man bending forward clasping the area of his recent injury. Dave knew that this action must be followed through or he was dead... this was a big bloke. Dave mustered up his full power into a massive uppercut punch to the Afrikaners face that connected with a crack of a bone.

The big man went back with such force that his arms flung out across the doorway stopping him from being thrown out of the donga to his certain death by thirty nulla-nulla clubs.

Amazingly, the man was still standing with bulging eyes of rage, Dave was starting to panic, if he recovers he will kill me, and the tribe will kill him. The big Afrikaner took a step forward and Doc Dave mustered another almighty punch with his damaged hand driving his fist hard into the man's ample nose. Blood splattered all over the place and the big man grunted then swore, yet he remained standing.

Dave thought Mirachung will give the order any second now and his mining company client would end up dead, and he would be in deep trouble. Another quick glance at Mirachung showed he was still grinning away but now he was holding the big coke-a-cola bottle by the base in his right-hand.

The message was clear. Dave grabbed the coke heavy bottle by the narrow neck and swung the thing with all his might at the Afrikaners head. The bottle smashed into a million pieces and the big man sank slowly to the floor propped up firmly against the donga doorway... big Des was out cold.

The tribal desert hunters clapped and whooped at the successful result. Mirachung had other pressing concerns...

'You bin owe me now a big bottle of coke Doc, an don you forget it mate.'

The pain was starting to erupt in Dave's right-hand just as the government medical nurse arrived, pushing her way through the large gathering crowd of locals. The well-built frumpy nurse stepped over

145

big Des propped-up in the doorway and enquired if Mirachung was okay.

Then she checked out big Des by moving his head about like a rag doll and stuffed some smelling salts up what was left of his nose. As Des was coming around the nurse announced that he was still alive but would have a sore head for a while.

Dave thought that's not the only thing that will be sore for a while and he was not referring to big Des's balls. He was looking at the bloody mess of his painful right-hand, he was sure that he had broken a bone or two. Will he still be able to fly the Jet-Ranger back to Sandfire?

The nurse gave the disorientated Des a wet towel to clean-up his face and turned to Doc Dave. As two desert men stepped through the doorway and stood one on each side of big Des with nulla-nullas at the ready.

'You should be ashamed of yourself Doctor Sharp. Just look what you have done to this man, fighting like silly little school boys right in front of the chief elder.' Then screwing her face up in disgust, 'Mirachung could have been hurt. You were lucky that today is my Punmu visit day.' Then quickly added… 'Have you been drinking alcohol Doctor Sharp?'

Mirachung quickly came to the rescue.

'The Doc, he bin drinking coke-a-cola with me all morn an got all upset when this big whitey fella called me a kaffer. Now as don know what a kaffer is, but it must be a pretty bad name mate, he he he ha.'

The nurse softened her attitude a little towards Doc Dave as she started to work on his smashed hand.

'Your thumb and two fingers are dislocated and you might have a broken finger but I will know more when I carry out an alignment. You are a damn lucky man Doctor Sharp, as I have considerable experience in joint manipulation. However, I will warn you that the procedure is very painful and I can only administer a small amount of this painkiller,' as she promptly inject Dave's hand with a large syringe that appeared from nowhere.

'Place your hand on this table, palm facing down. When I pull you will feel the joints go back in, so tell me when. That Doctor Sharp, is the very reason why I use little, if any general anaesthetic or sedation,' Dave detecting a small glint of sadistic pleasure in her eye.

'My hand is in your hands nurse, although I would suggest that you give that big bastard on the floor a fair squirt of your sedation before he fully comes around. Otherwise we may all need some bones fixing, Mirachung can back me up, and he's one hell of a mean angry bloke.'

'He he, the Doc's right, we might have ta kill dis bloke soon he wake up, just lika old days. Stop him break-up mah donga, he he he. Ah got no more coke bottle left to stop im, he he ha ha.'

The nurse looked around the donga with no doors or windows and all the broken glass scattered around splattered with blood. Dave and the nurse looked at each other; their thoughts were the same, (how in hell could this donga be damaged any more that it is?) The nurse quickly grabbed another large syringe from her bag of tricks and stuck it into big Des's right leg just below his groin. The blood soaked towel fell from his hand as he drifted off to sleep with a pleasant smile on his face.

Doc Dave was stunned as big Des only had a few bruises. All the damage he could see was a broken nose, plus two black eyes and a large lump on the side of his head where the coke bottle scored the final blow. Then a horrible thought occurred to him, he had to fly this big bastard back to Sandfire in a helicopter... now that will be fun.

The tough nurse was right; it was a very painful procedure. With Mirachung giving his normal toothless grin and a he he he. As big Des started to snore, the nurse went about pulling Doc Dave's fingers until they popped back into place.

'You have been very brave Doctor Sharp now all I have to do is splint all of the damaged fingers to keep them immobile for a few weeks.'

Through the pain, Doc Dave suddenly realised that this finger splinting would prevent him from flying the Jet-Ranger. A helicopter pilot needs both hands and feet to fly, and then Dave had an idea.

'Nurse Trudy...'

'Oh so you have remembered my name after all these years, how nice.'

'How could I ever forget you Nurse Trudy, flying you all around the outback so many times to tend the sick and needy?'

Dave was lucky as Nurse Trudy sported a large polished nameplate just above the standard issue nurse watch pinned to her ample left breast. Dave thought that "Matron Tardy" would have been a more suitable nameplate; however, she certainly did know her finger joint fixing stuff, and right now he needed her help.

147

'I have a small favour to ask of you as I have two rapidly developing problems. The first is could you please splint my fingers into a grip shape so as I can fly my helicopter. And the second favour I ask is can I have a syringe full of that sedative stuff to keep that big bugger asleep during the three hour flight back to Sandfire.'

'That will not be possible Doctor Sharp; you are still under some sedation. Just when do you intend flying back to Sandfire.'

'Just as soon as I get back to the airstrip and pack-up our camp. If I can get into the air within the next hour and a half, I will make it back to my Sandfire base before last light.'

Nurse Trudy thought about all this with a glum look on her face. Dave could see she was wrestling with her ethical conscience since sedating a person against their will is technically illegal, as it is in law taking a person hostage.

Dave did have the option of tying Des up, however if he were nicely sedated, then he would not know a bloody thing until he got back to Sandfire. He could then blame Nurse Trudy for the excessive injection of sedative... and then he thought of a neat plan.

'Nurse Trudy, I think this big man needs just a little more sedative and you should get one ready for me as this joint correction splint thing looks more painful than I can handle, I can always consider flying back tomorrow.'

Trudy got the message and gave Des another quick squirt then placed a full syringe on the table next to his elbow. Dave noticed that Mirachung had stopped laughing and giggling, then spoke in his official elder voice.

'You two can go fix dat broken hand outside, I gonna talk some tings with dis big white-fella man in plivat.'

Dave looked at Mirachung in surprise...

'Mirachung, this Des bloke is out cold mate, he won't be talking to anyone for the next hour or so.'

'Ha don want him talk back mate. No, he jus gotta listen fo five minutes things I say. Doc dis plivat talk so you can shut donga door on the way out.

There was no mistaken the blunt meaning, we had just been told to leave. Nurse Trudy and Doc Dave stepped over big Des on their way through the door-less doorway. Looking back at Mirachung, he had stood up and was now holding a small Kangaroo skin pouch, tied with a leather thong. He was staring down at big Des, who was still snoring; but the grin on his face was gone, he now had the look of a serious man.

They both walked to the other end of the small shaded porch and sat down, Dave in Mirachung's afternoon snooze chair and Nurse Trudy at the small wobbly table. The sedative was working making him very drowsy as nurse Trudy worked expertly on fitting metal splints to all of his damaged fingers.

Dave thought it was odd that nurse Trudy would have finger splints in her medical kit... In his half state of consciousness, he thought he could hear Aboriginal spirit singing, and clap-sticks, and then remembered the last time he had heard this sad singing....

It was just over four years ago. He had landed the Cessna 402 on the Punmu airstrip at last light after a long day flying. Asking Mirachung, then a young seventy-eight year old, who had just become the new chief elder if he could stay overnight? Mirachung had come out to the airstrip to meet him, driving his old battered Toyota, saying that this was a bad time to stay at Punmu.

He was very sad and unhappy; a number of the community people were turning away from the old ways. They had two rebellious, young men who were now bringing hard alcohol into the town, and three young women had been badly beaten and raped.

The young men in the tribe were now starting to follow the two men who had recently come back from the white man's town of Port Hedland with exaggerated stories. They had no respect for the elders and the old ways; many in the community were frightened.

The old grey elder had a worried look on his face; the council of elders had decided last night to call on Munyo the Gadichi man, this would mean only one thing... a death was due.

Mirachung looked out over the desert and I followed his gaze. The sun was slowly setting in the west, outlining a lone figure some two hundred metres away of a thin man standing motionless like a statue on a small hill. Mirachung said he is here, now nobody can leave until it is over, we must go build a fire in the old way. Climbing into the communities' old Toyota truck, they headed into the town of Punmu.

It was not difficult to understand why the elders were so upset. The young kids were running around like wild things following a group of rowdy youths who looked like they had been drinking for some time.

149

The little kids, just children had bottles, old cans, and rags that they had soaked in petrol to sniff the fumes. They were all off their faces drunk and crazy. I glanced at Mirachung, he was crying; tears were running down his face. I will never forget his sad words.

"It has come to this, my people are no good, and now we gonna show them the old way is best for desert people. This will be a teaching about respect for the old way and most times about... death."

With those words, thoughts went through my mind. In all my years of desert exploration, and the meeting of many aboriginal tribes, I had come to understand that these desert aboriginal people have a deep inbuilt tribal instinct. In any threat or conflict to their way of life, they always follow their ancient ways.

No amount of white man's government or hand outs, with dongas, tinned food, Toyotas or generator power will sway or convert them when urgent tribal matters need attention. They will always revert to tribal instinct, and the old ways.

I followed Mirachung to the town sports oval being just a low fenced oval-shaped flat area without a blade of grass. At the highest point of the oval was a small earth mound with an elevated referees chair fitted to a metal stand covered with a simple rag of a sunshade cover.

Mirachung pointed to the referees chair and said in a sad voice, 'You go stay here mate, not move or say anything any time, no one word Doc or you may be dead too.'

Thus began the strangest night of my life, establishing a new inner understanding that not all things on this earth easily explained by science or white man's judgement. This new experience was so powerful; it froze me to the spot with fear and astonishment.

I watched a strange scene unfolding from under the two bright oval floodlights. Fifty or so older tribal men and women had assembled a large oval of rocks in the middle of the field, filling the centre with wood and burning embers creating a low, hot, fire.

The air was calm, there was no wind not even the slightest hint of a breeze, the fire flames rose and flickered vertically. All the tribal elders came and sat forming a one-third of a circle around the fire leaving a space in the middle of the arc. Behind the row of elders, all

150

of the Punmu people formed sitting on the ground, behind them, a group of men and women sat with clap-sticks and didgeridoos.

These people were almost naked painted in white and red ochre, as is the traditional tribal way. Nobody made a sound as the one-third theatre area became larger and larger with local Punmu people sitting in many curved rows one behind the other.

The young drunks came over to the fire to see what was going on, making fun of all the older people in their ochre paint and traditional ceremonial dress. Then without warning... the power generator suddenly cut out.

The oval was plunged into a hush of darkness. Only the big low glowing fire in the middle of the oval gave off any light. The still dark night was strange, steeped in a deep silence...

Until it shuts down you do not realise that a continuous generator background sound is part of your everyday life in such remote communities.

When the man-made noise stops, the sound of the desert is a welcome natural sound, and the darkness is absolute and total. The crickets immediately started-up their call for a mate, now carrying further in the unusual still silence of this deep velvet black night.

The Dingoes stopped howling to the pack, as there was no moon or generator to compete with now. Everything and everyone that night turned to watch, with heightened inquisitive interest at what was about to happen.

All were sitting around the fire, waiting in total silence. Most of the drunks had shut-up to watch this unusual spectacle, only the occasional jeering voice and swearing punctuated the still night air.

Then the rhythm of clap-sticks started their slow steady beat. Click... click... click... click. In the background the singing started very low and haunting, click... click... click. One lone voice pitched high above the rest of the singers in a mournful wail almost like crying.

The jeering and insults still came from the group of youths on the other side of the fire. Then the entire Punmu community sitting at the fire, as if directed by some secret signal made a sound in total unison, BAAHH-Shoooooooo. Then complete silence filled the air. Even the drunken louts fell silent with curiosity, and the crickets stopped rubbing their legs together in their song to attract a mate to watch what would happen next.

I had been to many Aboriginal ceremonies, both Cooroboree's, and initiation rites; however, this was very different; there was no dancing or laughter from this community, this was serious business.

From out of the flickering shadows came a tall thin man carrying two long hunting spears, a small bag, and a rolled pouch of some sort. He was completely naked apart from a number of long bone necklaces and a Kangaroo pouch tied with a leather thong around his waist. He was a frightening sight painted all over in bright red and white ochre... This was Munyo the desert Gadichi man. (Aboriginal Witch Doctor)

Munyo took-up the centre stage in front of the Punmu elders driving the back-end of his spears firmly into the ground, one on each side, then turned and squatted on the ground facing the fire.

Everyone watched in silence as Munyo slowly unrolled his wirinun (sorcerer's tool kit) on the ground in front of him. He started to sing a mournful song as he opened the Kangaroo skin bag and laid-out a number of small pouches and one large old bone on his wirinun roll.

The clap-sticks started a slow rhythm then everything fell into an abrupt silence again as the Gadichi man stared into the large settling fire. Then as if by some hidden signal the elders began to sing, and the clap-sticks started again, this time two low rumbling didgeridoos joined in on the rhythm.

The Gadichi man suddenly jumped to his feet pulled both spears from the ground, and walked up to the edge of the large area of glowing embers within the large oval of rocks and stopped. At the same time the singing stopped. He raised the spears above his head and started singing while lowering the spears to point at the group of jeering youths across the fire.

The Gadichi man then drove both spears into the ground. Pointed end first each side of him, and then suddenly threw his arms out towards the fire, which erupted into a massive cloud of dense black smoke. At the same-time, two bullroarers (heavy flat wooden slats swung around in a circle on a rope) started-up making a powerful deep whirring roar that added to the already spooky atmosphere.

When the smoke cleared, the Gadichi man was standing on the other side of the fire staring nose to nose with one of the older drunk youths. It was obvious from my viewing point that these young men and all of his pals were now terrified.

The Gadichi man slowly walked among the ten or twelve youths stopping for a moment to look deeply into each person's face.

Returning, he came back to stand with his back to the fire, it was only then I noticed he was holding what looked like a large bone. At fifty metres away, it was difficult to identify; however, it looked like an upper leg bone, possibly a femur bone. Then the Gadichi man held the bone above his head; the singing and clap-sticks again started on queue. All the terrified youths instantly sat down... except two.

The sound was beginning to rise to a fearsome level. The wailing singing, didgeridoos, clap-sticks, and the bullroarers were starting to make me feel creepy. All of a sudden, in a swift move the Gadichi man pointed his bone at the two young Aboriginal men that were still standing as he slowly backed up to the edge of the fire.

Suddenly he threw out both his arms, something landed into the fire, and another massive cloud of dense black smoke covered the area. It took a long minute to clear, the Gadichi man was then standing back on the other side of the fire again.

The bullroarers and didgeridoos stopped abruptly however, the singing and clap-sticks continued but at a much lower sound level. The Gadichi man did not look back as he walked between his spears. Back to where his wirinun kit lay on the ground. He then quietly rolled all his things back up and picked up his Kangaroo skin bag, tying it to his waist. Only then did he turn around to face the terrified youths across the fire.

They all stayed as if frozen to the spot, the two young men standing, and all the others still sitting silently on the ground with their heads bowed.

The Gadichi man walked back to the edge of the fire carrying all his gear and stood between his two spears. All the noise stopped and there was a great hanging silence.

Nothing moved. The crickets had already ceased calling for a mate, even the mangy dogs that run wild in the town had stopped rummaging through the rubbish to see what will happen next.

All eyes were on the thin black Gadichi man. Then in a sorrowful high-pitched voice, the Gadichi man started to sing as he pulled both his spears from the ground. Holding one in each hand, he began lowering them together in front of him pointing them towards the two youths.

He then gradually turned, pointing both spears to his right towards the open desert. Without a word, both young men slowly walked off in the direction of the pointing spears like zombies out into the desert.

The Gadichi man crossed his two spears in a gesture of completion; suddenly he spread his arms wide creating yet another giant cloud of black smoke. When the smoke had gone, so had Munyo the Gadichi man... he had finished his work for this day and had left the stage.

I remembered waking-up stiff and aching in the referees chair at 5:20, just as the sun was rising to yet another fine hot tropical day in Punmu. The fire was all gone; no ashes, not a burnt cinder, not even one of the large oval-of-stones remained.

The ground was just bare flat raked sand. There was nothing to show that a fire had ever been in the middle of the town sports oval... was it all a dream?

Walking over to Mirachung's donga, I found him sitting in his favourite old chair watching an old black-and-white James Cagney movie on TV, as it was too early for the morning children's shows. He was not in a talkative mood.

Without a word uttered, Mirachung went outside and climbed into his old battered Toyota, I swung into the seat beside him. We drove out to the airstrip in silence. Just before climbing into the Cessna 402, I felt compelled to ask Mirachung, what had happened last night, then quietly told.

'Doc, you not to worry my nyaparru (friend) dis stuff all bin Martu elder business, not for white man to understand okay. You only understand dis Doc, dem two bad drunken young fella, they gone out on last walkabout into da desert.

Their names not never be said aloud any more, and now da Martu people together again in a happy Punmu community.'

Doc Dave realised that could mean only one thing.... They were now both dead.

Chapter Twelve

The Meeting

'Doctor Sharp, Doctor Sharp, wake-up this is no time to fall asleep, not if you want to try and fly back to Sandfire before it gets dark.'

I must have dozed off under sedation while Nurse Trudy was working on my mangled hand. Thinking what a strange dream, I was hoping that had better be the last of my sedative reaction as I had about three hours flying ahead of me.

I must say looking at Nurse Trudy's handiwork; she had done a fine job. My right-hand was now metal splinted into a curved grip that could now fit the cyclic control of the Jet-Ranger. Surprisingly the pain had subdued to an acceptable pulsing throb.

'Doctor Sharp, I will give you some Panadol to help ease the pain, if it gets any worse take two more, don't worry Panadol won't make you drowsy,' looking down at the snoring big Des.

'I will come out to the airstrip with you and patch-up this man on the way; we have to make sure that this man is very much alive when he leaves Punmu. You should be advised Doctor Sharp, that this incident, and the property damage will be entered into my medical log, along with a report on your silly childish fighting.'

The six desert tribal hunters unceremoniously loaded big Des on to the back of the old Toyota truck, they dragged him the length of the tray-back and propped him up against the front loading rail. Then they gracefully helped Nurse Trudy on to the tray and sat her down in a

low chair next to big Des where she immediately started working on him.

Dave noticed that big Des was no longer displaying a painful smile. He now had a confused look on his face, better described as mild fear... What had old Mirachung said to big Des to cause this dramatic effect?

The six desert hunters jumped on the back of the Toyota; Mirachung deciding to drive while Doc Dave managed to climb into the passenger seat using only his left-hand.

The first thing he did was to feel his pocket confirming that he still had the syringe full of sedative that he had swiped off the table when Nurse Trudy was distracted. Dave was now relieved that big Des would no longer be a problem on the way back to Sandfire. Then he thought, now would be a good time to apologise to Mirachung for all the problems he and his client had caused during his short stay at Punmu.

'Sorry about all the trouble back there Mirachung, I had no idea that mad South African would come out and start a bloody fight in your donga.'

'Ha ha he he, Doc you been da one who start all da fighting, and in da best place too. Look, if dat big fella had bin outside mah house, den mah boys woda finish im off for you... with da nulla-nulla, he he ha. Den da white coppers would come, an dat not so good for Mooroopna. Then we might have to fight em coppers too... like in da old days, he he he ha ha ha.'

Dave knew that *Mooroopna* was the Aboriginal word for *ghost spirit*. The old boy kept on about the Mooroopna and some bone he wants' him to bring back. It was all starting to get beyond his understanding when Mirachung answered his very thoughts.

'You come to Mirachung for answer to da secret things in mah desert. You got da answer and more, he he ha you gota broken fist, he he he. Anyway, just cause dat big fella come along too, it no matter to the Mooroopna, you got message good... an you no forget, he he ha ha.'

Mirachung sounded like he had been expecting him to arrive at Punmu. The Veevers crater thing was spooky enough, now Mirachung was just as spooky; he needed time to think everything over, but not now. He must get back to Sandfire.

The Toyota drove onto the airstrip hardstand and young John ran over to meet them, he had been sheltering from the forty-three degree sun sitting in the small tin hangar.

I could see by the expression on his face that he had just found out it was cooler outside in the sun than in that metal hangar. Then he caught sight of big Des and the nurse on the back of the Toyota.

'What the fuck happened to Des... then... and your hand?'

He then noticed the six almost naked, grim looking ochre-painted, desert tribal hunters as they jumped off the back of the Toyota swinging their nulla-nulla clubs about, then he let out a small girly scream.

John was convinced it had to be his turn next, bracing for an attack by these fierce looking warriors; after all, he was the only white man around without an injury. Mirachung thought this display a bit odd...

'He he, what wrong wid dat young whitey fella Doc, a t'ink he been in dat shed fo' too long, ha he he, I might ask mah boys go see if he okay.'

'Christ Mirachung please don't do that, I think the young bloke has just pissed his pants in fear of your painted hunters.'

There was no doubting it. Mirachung certainly knew how to extract the last bit of humour from any given situation as he doubled over in fits of bellowing laughter, with his desert hunters whooping and joining in.

As they started to pack-up the camp Doc Dave explained to John that big Des had got into a fight and that he was going to be all right, but he was still a bit upset. Strangely, he did not appear to connect Dave's obvious fist injury with big Des's face injuries, he was more afraid of what these fierce-looking painted black men with muddy hairdo's and big clubs might do next.

The six desert tribesmen carried big Des over to the helicopter and strapped him tightly into the back seat behind the pilot. Nurse Trudy administered her last jab of medical treatment as he sat in the chopper. Still out cold big Des was not looking his best.

The nurse had stitched-up the gash to the side of his head, which now looked like the stitches may burst anytime soon with the increasing lump. She had stuffed his nostrils with cotton wool, and Des now sported a nice polished metal nose splint.

The look of fright was still on his face, and his eyes were slightly open. Nurse Trudy assured Dave the look was quite normal, for someone recently clobbered on the side of the head with a heavy glass coke-a-cola bottle. Dave conceded an interesting thought I guess she should know.

Everything was packed and ready to fly; it was just on three o'clock, so all being well we should get back to Sandfire just before last light. Sitting in the Jet-Ranger before the engine start, Dave thought that he might try once more to get a straight answer out of old Mirachung. He needed to know a bit more about the Veevers spooky Mooroopna thing, but Mirachung had read his mind again, and answered the question before he had even asked. Giggling like a little schoolgirl, Mirachung wisely replied…

'He he he, yeh know something Doc, you pretty dumb for a white doctor mate. Now me, am bin what you might call apprentice witch doctor an I know mor'en you do Doc, he he he. Everythin' bin all said for now mate, an don't you worry about dat big whitey fella. He no going to come back to mah desert any more, caus as I had a quiet word with him.'

Doc Dave gave Mirachung a wave with his smashed hand that now resembled an armoured gauntlet then hit the starter button. Quite clearly, Dave heard Mirachung yell above the rising whine of the turbine start.

'Don you forget now Doc, you still owe me big bottle of coke-a-cola right?'

The turbine spooled-up in a whine to 15% N1 and the twist throttle moved to the first click idle. Fuel gushed in and the temperature quickly climbed past 800 degrees, at 58%, N1 came into the green arc, critical mass, she was alight. He then let go the starter button and waited for the turbine to spool-up to 70% and the main rotor to pick-up speed.

Slowly the throttle gradually advanced to 100% at N2 ready for lift-off. Everything was in the green, with a courtesy nod to Mirachung and Nurse Trudy. He then gently raised the collective lever adding pitch to the main rotor blades, and at the same time he added a little left peddle to offset the torque. They were airborne and on their way to Sandfire.

Dave was in deep thought, just where in hell he would find a forty-year-old, classic large glass display bottle of coke-a-cola. This could present a major problem; he may have to pinch one out of a museum. Then he thought, best ask Max to look-up marine dealers on the

Internet. With a bit of luck, some collector out there may have one in their collection for sale.

Dave calculated the flight time at two hours fifty minutes. This might be a good time to relax a little and maybe to reflect on all that had happened out at Punmu. Looking across at John, Dave could see that the young Geo had settled down, obviously relived we had left Punmu; more so by the dark wet patch at his pants crotch.

A first meeting with a genuine desert Aboriginals can be most frightening. Young John must have thought we had terminated our exploration programme because of the need for some medical help for Des. He had no idea of the real reason; being that we had been thrown out of the town for fighting in the chief elder's donga.

As the helicopter whacked on across the desert, Doc Dave started thinking about what Mirachung had said while in his strange trance.

"You must listen to Mooroopna the ghost spirit. It has much to tell you of a past life, and of what the future may hold. Munyo never replaced the bone as promised; now he has gone, taken by the Great Spirit... Too many secrets are with the sacred bone. You must bring the bone back..."

No that's not quite right; he said, "You will bring the bone back to its resting-place. Only then can I walk to the sacred place of the Mooroopna as the desert Gadichi man."

Now what was that all that about? Doc Dave had carefully inquired about the Veevers crater area but Mirachung just went on about the Mooroopna ghost spirit thing, and then on about some bloody bone. He said something else that was very spooky, and heard only from within his head when he had asked if it was okay to go to out the Veevers crater area.

"It is waiting for you and the two others. Time is running out there is still much to learn and much to do. I cannot help you further, time, no time. An end to all that we know may be very close."

What "two others," maybe he was talking about Max and Tony? Then Mirachung mentioned that I have "important things to do now..."

What important things. Then that last weird comment from Mirachung being if I did not bring back some bone, he would not become a full Gadichi man... what bloody bone?

They had been flying for over an hour. Dave could not make any sense of what went on at Punmu. A glance at John confirmed he was nodding off into an exhausted sleep, and a glance at big Des confirmed that he was waking-up from his drugged sleep.

Panic immediately set in as Dave went groping in his pocket for the sedative syringe he had pinched off Nurse Trudy, thinking a quick injection should fix things up. What the hell, with a clumsy move the syringe flipped out of his hand onto the floor of the helicopter, then rolled under his seat.

Reaching down to retrieve the syringe Dave accidentally pushed the cyclic stick forward causing the helicopter to tip into a steep forward descending dive. This caused two things. Firstly, the syringe rolled out from beneath his pilot seat, and the other was to wake-up young John. Reacting immediately in panic, by grabbing the co-pilot cyclic stick in what he thought was an attempt to save his life.

In a flash Doc Dave took-in the critical situation grabbing the controls and pulled back hard on the cyclic in an attempt to stop the rolling syringe falling down one of the rudder-pedal floor stow holes. This would have been a terminal disaster. The other was wrestling control of the helicopter off the strong young John who half asleep was convinced that he was about to die.

The struggle went on for a few seconds with Doc Dave cursing every time the syringe rolled backwards and forwards across the floor between his legs. A quick glance at the altimeter displayed the frightening decent rate of almost 850 feet per minute. From their low 3000-foot cruise-altitude, slick mathematics told Doc Dave that he had only about three and a half minutes to live. He had one slim chance and shouted above the helicopter noise...

'Let go of the fucking controls you stupid idiot. Unless you think you can fly this bloody helicopter better than I can. Or we will all die.'

That did it, young John immediately let go of the cyclic stick and Dave went about the delicate task of arresting the helicopter decent rate at the same time keeping the rolling syringe in sight. On the next, roll-past Dave scooped up the syringe then set the helicopter into a gentle climb back up to 3000 feet.

Doc Dave then applied the control friction locks and started to turn around in his seat to check on big Des. He paused, catching sight of young John who was wide-eyed in utter terror. He had frozen in a ridiculous poise with his hands held up as if he were being robbed. The stain at his crotch was now three times larger and the distinctive odour of urine was present.

The fleeting thought went through Dave's mind, he was thinking of the possible damage that urine could cause to his precious helicopter. When just then, out of the corner of his eye he caught sight of big Des.

Big Des who with a look of dark rage and bulging eyes was attempting to unbuckle the very tight full seat-belt harness that was holding him firmly in position. Quick-as-a-flash Doc Dave used his teeth to remove the needle cover and stabbed Des in the groin with the syringe. Squirting the lot into him in one go with his thumb leaving the syringe stuck firmly to the hilt in big Des's groin.

Dave felt the powerful grip of Des's hand on his shoulder; thinking this could get ugly if he manages to release the seat-belt harness. Then the powerful grip-pressure gradually eased letting Dave know that the sedative was starting to work. Big Des was back in slumber-land again.

'John, you can put your hands down now and put your headset back-on everything is under control. We will not be crashing into the desert today; believe me, I can guarantee you will live to see your Mum again.'

'What happened to the helicopter Doctor Sharp, I really thought we were going to crash?'

'Just a heat thermal young fella, it always happens about this time of the year in desert areas, nothing much to worry about. We will be on the ground soon.

Adding as an afterthought, at Sandfire that is, arrival time will be in about an hour and twenty minutes. Everything is under control.' It would be nice if it were he thought. Doc Dave was having some other doubts that were manifesting themselves as near future problems.

How would Max and Tony accept this new Mirachung ghost spirit stuff, and the return of some lost bone? Well Tony was out of the question, no point in attempting to explain anything to him. As for Max, well he was with him when they discovered the strange phenomena that affected the aircraft instruments just east of Veevers meteorite crater... there might be a chance he would understand some of this.

Doc Dave thought long and hard. The only thing that related to the original spooky phenomena was Mirachung saying that the area was the sacred place of the Mooroopna ghost spirit.

He could also tell Max that the old Gadichi man Munyo used to hang out around there. Doc Dave had decided, he would tell Max all about the ghost spirit at the Veevers area but would leave out the bit about the magic bone and Mirachung being the new desert Gadichi man... Yes, that would be best.

'All stations Sandfire this is helicopter Tango Sierra X-ray five miles southeast inbound for landing on the hour local time.'

Dave was looking forward to getting on the ground and getting rid of big Des before he woke-up again. God knows what he will do when he wakes-up. His plan was to have him well on his way back to Port Hedland before he comes around. The radio crackled a crisp reply from Tony at Sandfire.

'Tango Sierra X-ray, turn right 090 degrees into a holding pattern at 3000 feet. Stay clear until the heavy traffic vacating runway 09 and 36, we will try and slot you in behind the Boeing 747 on finals for 09... copy'

The tiny gravel airstrip at Sandfire was only 800 metres long and just legal to land the Cessna 402. A Boeing was out of the question, or could one land within seven hundred miles of Sandfire. Heavy traffic, what the hell, Dave's two aircraft were the only traffic to use the Sandfire strip in the past ten months.

'For fucks sake Tony, I am not in the mood for your silly traffic control shit. I have had a very tough day; on landing I will need a stiff drink...copy'

'Okay no need to get shitty Doc. I didn't expect you lot back until next Friday... you're four days early. What's up mate, find a big pot of gold out there in the desert eh?'

'Tony we have an unconscious man on-board and will need some help to get him into his company Toyota Landcruiser. Can you bring these Geo guys Toyota up to the chopper on landing, oh and get Max; we will need his help as this guy is a bloody big bloke.'

'Should I call the Flying Doctor is this bloke injured in any way?'

'No he's not injured, well not very much but if he wakes up then we will all need the bloody flying doctor, so do as I say and stop

162

crapping on. Anyway, I am a flying Doctor... if I wanted any medical help don't you think I would have been smart enough to ask.'

The radio fell silent, and then Dave noticed the Toyota heading across to the hardstand area, with Max jumping into his mini moke.

The two smiling faces of Max and Tony were a welcome sight to Doc Dave, as he pulled down hard on the main rotor brake lever until the big blades came to a stop. Tony threw a rope over the stationary blade, and walked it back to the boom, then tied it down. Young John jumped out first with a look of relief on his face, just as Tony noticed his wet pants.

'I heard yer flying was getting a bit on the rough side Doc, but scaring the piss out of your bloody client's aint going to get us any more business mate,' then noticing Dave's mangled hand. 'What the fuck happened to your bloody hand Doc?

Dave wanted to avoid going into detail about his hand, deciding to explain about young John's wet pants.

'He was like that before he got into the chopper Tony. John got a bit upset when he met his first tribal Aboriginal desert hunters; it was only a few friendly local blokes, who came to the chopper to see us off. Then there was a second incident, when he decided he could fly the helicopter better than I could. As for my hand, well apparently it was not as tough as big Des the South African geologist's thick head.'

The dramatic description of the cause went right over Tony's head. He was only interested in one thing.

'Doc, did you say that this bloke pissed in the bleeding chopper?'

Tony knew well the possible damage caused by the ammonia and urea in urine to the aluminium frame of the helicopter and ran to get the water hose. John just stood there with a very embarrassed look on his face.

Max had opened the rear door of the helicopter, to see big Des strapped tightly in his seat, face bashed-in, and out cold with a large syringe stuck in his groin. Then he glanced at Doc Dave's splinted right-hand.

'Had a few problems out at Punmu then Doc?' he asked casually.

With a great deal of effort, the four of them managed to get big Des out of the helicopter and into the front seat of the Toyota Landcruiser. Young John had changed his shorts and was now consuming a cold beer.

Doc Dave had removed the syringe from big Des's groin, now his clients were now ready to leave. Dave walked over to John sitting in the driver's seat of the Toyota, then holding his gaze. Max and Tony leant forward keen to catch every word…

'Big Des is only sedated and will come around in about half an hour in a bad mood with a sore head. The end story is up to you John, whichever way you want to play it. I will confirm and agree to whatever you decide to say or do.

Just remember this; big Des insulted the most important man in these parts, the chief elder Mirachung of the Martu people. I make my living by working in his desert. Without his blessing, we would all be out of a job.

Mirachung does not need us… we need him. As such, I defended his honour and to protect my good standing with the Punmu community; most of all, out of respect for the chief elder and his people. Consider the alternative; if I had not stepped in and resolved the matter quickly, those six desert warriors would have clubbed big Des to death.'

The young Geo visually cringed at the thought of this brutal ending.

'John, this unfortunate incident out at Punmu must remain our secret, as it could only end up creating big problems for the mining company that you work for.

I would suggest that you make-up a story that big Des had a small accident out in the field while prospecting in a remote area, needing an urgent return to Port Hedland. I guess it's really you're call John.'

By the shocked look on John's face, Dave got the impression that John had just assembled the link between his damaged hand and big Des's damaged face. John let out the clutch, the Toyota moved off, heading for the Great Northern Highway and Port Hedland. As the gravel dust of the departing Toyota receded into the distance, Max decided to voice his concerned thoughts.

'Well I think we can safely say we will not be getting any more business from that lot.'

Then Tony added his observation and grim thoughts to what would surely affect him financially.

'I don't suppose that you will get paid for any of this bleeding charter work Doc, so that's around nine hours of bloody chopper service time and fuel gone mate.'

Dave was staring at the departing Toyota, and then turning to his two friends with a big grin.

'You guys always look on the grim and negative side of life. Think positive guys, it's much easier on the brain and lowers the bloody stress level. I can tell you now I will be billing the company the full eight days work, and will include a letter explaining that I will do my best to try repair the damage to Aboriginal relations caused by their senior geologist.

I will let them know their geologist insulted the most powerful Aboriginal elder in the Great Sandy Desert. I think that I should also remind them that their existing mining claims and valuable leases are right in the middle of this desert communities land. Adding that I would be happy to negotiate on their behalf (for a modest fee of course,) to try resolving this serious matter caused by their fuckwit employee... How do you think it's sounding so far?'

Tony got the idea sorted first.

'Bloody good mate, I feel better already, let's go and have a drink at your place on my newly found good, positive bleeding attitude, but I've only got five beers left. I had to give one to that young geo. By the look of his pants he was fairly dehydrated.'

Max looked both happy and worried at the same time, and Doc Dave knew the reason why. Tony and Dave climbed into the mini moke as Max set off for the Fort for a drink and the liquid debriefing. Dave turned to Tony with a big grin.

'No problems with the alcohol shortage my aeroplane fixing friend, I have brought back an almost full bottle of single malt whisky that I had borrowed from Max before I left,' then Dave glancing at Max now displaying a look of total surprise. 'I was going to tell you Max but you were still sound asleep when I departed.'

It was nearly eight o'clock when Tony's eldest boy came across on his pushbike to deliver his Mom's command. "She who must be obeyed" had again summoned Tony to come and eat his bloody dinner, and to get over there quick smart.

Max looked a little relieved as Tony had only just finished his second beer, and was in the process of eyeing-up his bottle of scotch when ordered to go home.

This was a stroke of good luck as Tony's departure had just increased his percentage and hopes of consuming a reasonable portion of his own scotch. This he knew was also good sound Jewish economics.

The pleasant drink and company had Max drift into a nice philosophical mode. This causing him to open up his mind with his limited views on matrimonial matters; eyeing Doc Dave over the rim of his scotch tumbler he rambled on....

'You know something Doc, when I see how Tony always jumps at a command from his wife; and how you have been all but ruined financially by your three wives, it makes me feel happy that I never got married. Has it always been like this for married blokes?'

Dave was a little startled at this sudden interest by Max, and his observation of modern marriage problems. Then again, Max was most likely right; these things were much simpler back in the Stone Age...

'Max, such is life in the world of us breeding humans. In the good old days, we males just clobbered a good-looking sort on the head with our matrimonial club, and then dragged her by the hair back to our cave.

If you were not a good hunter-provider, or were no good in bed, or the cave was not up to scratch. Then she just waited until you were asleep, then smashed your head in with the family club, and moved on. These days it's all about possessions, money, and nasty shitty money-grabbing bloody lawyers.'

Max thought about that for a long second, adding...

'A thing I have always wondered Doc, after watching you over the years in marital pain. I mean, could this all have some bloody plan? Well God is a bloke isn't he… he wouldn't have gone through all this financial and woman crap… would he?'

Dave thought for a moment about what Max and he had just said; it was all sounding quite reasonable to him. Four days without a drink, plus nothing to eat in the last twenty hours, and pumped full of painkillers. The drink was going straight to Doc Dave's head.

His general theory on personal disaster was now sounding to him as quite feasible, and surprisingly normal. This must be all part of some great world, or universal plan. Nobody but nobody could have had such a long run of bad luck as he was now experiencing, unless carefully and precisely planned… The thought was terribly sobering.

Max squirmed in mock horror as Doc Dave removed the top of his rapidly dwindling bottle of malt whisky, he was about to pour two hefty shots, then to Max's relief, Dave paused to speak.

'You are a different animal to the rest of the world Max, because you are an absolute, and totally dedicated bloody nerd. You are not interested in marriage or children; you are only interested in electronic gadgets and a fuck on the side when you feel horny. You can't produce another little Maxi-nerd out of a computer you know. It's what makes the world go around, more little people born. We still need a woman for that; it's where we all came from, where you bloody-well came from... God forbid.'

The booze was flowing well and so was the odd conversation. The deeply thinking Max raised a polite finger in permission to speak his mind.

'I have a good theory on all of that stuff Doc. I reckon that God; or whomever it was that made people like me, did so to help reduce this planets growing population problem. Just think, if everybody were like you, rooting and fucking around like a rabbit, this planet would be over populated and run out of resources within fifty years.

I see myself, and people like me as a sort of saviour of this planet, soon we will outnumber the breeders like you. We nerd-type people are very easily satisfied, needing little in the way of worldly demands. All we require is a cool dark room in which to work our computers, with a piece of pizza and a coke-a-cola every few hours, and perhaps a bottle of scotch every few days.'

Dave was temporally stunned into silence. He had no idea that Max had such strong views on this population subject and the future of the world. Whereas all he was concerned about was, how he was going to pay next month's bills, and finding a woman to satisfy his needs... Was Max right; was he expecting too much, aiming a little too high? Max snapped him out of his deep gloomy thoughts.

'I know you Doc. What the hell happened out at Punmu, something has caused you to be a bit down and withdrawn, Tony has gone now so you can spill out the beans to your old mate Max the nerd.'

Doc Dave rested his painful right hand on the table and rolled the empty scotch tumbler around in his left thumb and fingers thinking. Should he tell Max everything, and then he decided to say only that needed to align his story with what Max already knew about the Veevers thing. That will be a hard enough story for Max to digest.

'Mirachung the chief elder did confirm that the Veevers crater area is an Aboriginal sacred site, they too have experienced strange effects and happenings out there, and nobody is allowed to visit that area.

It is taboo to all but the local Martu desert Gadichi man however, for some reason he has asked that I go there again and check the area out, why I don't know. It would appear that he also knows that we were out there just recently. I have no clues on whoever could have told him about our little terrifying trip in the Cessna 402. He was a bit spooky about it all.'

Max took a quick slug of his remaining scotch, and then indignantly blurted out.

'Bloody bush telegraph, it's better than our damn satellite phones. Did old Mirachung give you any idea what this strange stuff is all about?'

Dave felt a large twinge of guilt. This was the bit where he would have to lie a little bit to his best friend.

'Mirachung said that the Veevers area was the home of the Mooroopna, ghost spirit. He reckons that the old Gadichi man that carked-it a few years back had upset the resident ghost spirit, and he was taken-out by the ghost spirit for not being a faithful and compliant Gadichi man. I can't believe that story, as old Munyo was well into his eighties, how the hell he managed to live that long out in that inhospitable desert no one will ever know.'

'Changing the subject Doc, I got a sat phone call from the ATO (Australian Tax Office) Perth. They have been trying to send you an email to remind you that your ATO court hearing is next month on the 28th at 9:30 sharp. The matter heard at the Central Law Courts in St George's Terrace. I said you would be there, since your name is Sha.... Dave hastily interrupted.

'Mmm "Sharp." Well that should work out just fine Max as I have a meeting with my wife's lawyers about then.'

Max suddenly could see something positive in this, blurting out…

'What fucking luck Doc, now you can attend to both disasters on the same trip to Perth and save us some money, how bloody convenient is that?'

Max bounced his words around again in his whisky slow brain, then realised what he had just said... recalling the grim financial position that Doc Dave was in.

'Remember your own theory on stress-strategy Doc. You said to stay positive, it's much easier on the brain, and stress levels.'

Doc Dave thought what a silly thing to say, did he really say that. He was already stressing out big-time at just the thought of what the

168

ATO had in mind for him. He could never find the overdue tax money... the end was near.

'Max I think we should take the Mercedes Unimog for a drive out to the Veevers crater next week and do a bit of test drilling, we should carry out a thorough ground survey of this area. You never know with all this weird stuff, there's got to be something worthwhile to find out there.'

'Yeah I think you're right Doc, because by this time next month, we may not have the Unimog to use after the grim reaper taxman has had a go at what's left of your assets.'

Max's eyes shot open like camera shutters as he stared back at Doc Dave. He had done it again, he must be bloody drunk... what the hell did he just say to his boss?

It was just a week later as Tony watched in wonder at the Unimog disappearing in a cloud of red dust into the Great Sandy Desert. He did not believe a word of what Doc Dave and Max had told him. Something about a small contract from Telfer gold mine, for work in the Lake Auld area. The only doubt that this work might be true, was the fact that they were towing the little drill-sample rig.

'I don't think we did a very good job in convincing Tony that we are on a paying job. But you never know if this Veevers phenomena turns out to be a reaction caused by some valuable mineral we might all end up rich.'

Max thought about this for a moment...

'Is this another example of you being positive Doc? If we were to apply a small amount of basic logic to these phenomena, we can rule-out a powerful magnetic source such magnetite. We can say without doubt that it is not a large gold nugget, also not uranium or iron ore.

Then we have with my last superb efforts of hacking into the InSar and GEOS-N satellites, absolute proof that there is no body of oil, or for that matter water. Therefore we would both have to agree that there is little if anything that could be of any bloody value out there.'

Doc Dave cringed; Max was no idiot, had he told him the truth about what Mirachung had said, he would have agreed to this weird research trip to Veevers. Dave knew that they had two days of rough desert driving ahead of them to get to Veevers crater, should he tell Max the truth.

It was obvious that Max was not hopeful of finding anything of value out there. Then again, Max had not seen Mirachung in a trance

169

and heard his strange words, he just knew that there was something of value was in that area... Agreed this was not a good scientific theory, but it was a strong gut feeling. Dave needed urgently to divert the conversation away from their depressing subject.

'How was your recent trip to Port Hedland Max, did you have any luck in getting laid mate, or did you find a new smart transistor or some other exciting nerdy thing?'

'I missed out on a fuck because Shelia's old man was home with a bad head trauma. He had head butted some bloke in the pub for wolf whistling at his missus.'

'Christ, you had better watch it Max. If he gave a Glasgow kiss to a bloke for just wolf whistling at his woman. Imagine what he would do if he caught you shagging his missus... Anyway, what happened about the poor bloke he head butted?'

'I don't know Doc, after three days he hasn't woken-up yet; however, I did hear some other interesting news about your Punmu Geo prospecting pals. That big Afrikaans bloke Des is now in Graylands Psychiatric Hospital in Perth, he is suffering from some form of delusion about a tribe of Aboriginal men hunting him down.

As for the other bloke young John, well he went back home to England the day after he left Sandfire. What the fuck did you do to those blokes out there at Punmu? I can tell you this Doc. I am glad that I am your friend if that's what happens to people you don't get along with.'

A tight smile grew on Doc Dave's face, as he formulated an opportunist threat in his mind.

'Max, I presume you did by chance bring along a bottle of your... our favourite single malt whisky with you?'

A low groan emitted from Max as Doc Dave's subtle threat sank in.

The first day at the crater confirmed every other previous finding in that the crater was perfectly round and the rim was about the same height all around.

The plan was to drill a pattern of holes, four spaced in the centre, and six around the inner perimeter of the crater with a further four holes at fifty metres from the rim. While Max was busy drilling, Dave found the exact spot one and a half miles east of Veevers crater where the strange force, or whatever-it-was that had caused some deviational effect on the aircraft instruments.

After two exhaustive hours of tests nothing was found, Dave went back to get Max as he was sure that he had missed something. All the tests carried out again with Max double-checking each result. No abnormalities existed in any magnet force, Radio frequency band, or any other form of radiation as tested with Max's new halogen counter.

Test's with a fluxgate and GPS magnetic compass reading were correct, including the variation, and the air static discharge reading was within the expected normal range. All radiation levels and tests found to be normal.

Finally, a highly sensitive metal detector provided no mineral clues as to why the aircraft instruments had suddenly deflected on last month's flyover. Nevertheless, Dave was sure that something on, or in the ground had caused this strange anomaly. He was disappointed at the lack of any positive results, mumbling his thoughts to Max.

'So not only can this weird force change its power and range at will, it can also when it feels like it, switch off.'

Max was not impressed at the lack of results... he was ready to go home.

'We have been out here three bloody days now; c'mon this is a total waste of time. We have recovered all the planned drill sample cores from the Veevers test sites, there's nothing else out here Doc, we should pack-up, and head back to Sandfire.'

Around a week before Doc Dave left for his dreaded Perth meetings, the drill samples from the Veevers crater sent down express for analysis to Doctor Brad Farlow. Brad was an old University friend who worked at Waterford CSIRO (Commonwealth Scientific and Industrial Research Organisation.)

This favour would cost Dave a good bottle of wine and an expensive lunch. In truth, paying for the analysis results would have most likely been cheaper, but nowhere near as much fun.

Max flew Dave to Port Hedland to catch the Perth jet. As Dave and Max were busy, chatting about the possible outcomes from the ATO and divorce lawyer meetings a mobile phone rang. Both of them looked around the lounge distracted, wondering why someone had not answered the thing, before Max realised that it was the Doc's phone ringing. A sound never heard at Sandfire, the mobile being only carried when he went into a local town, or while in Perth.

171

It was Professor John Laney UWA Museum of Anthropology Perth.

'You took your time answering your mobile Dave. I have been trying to reach you for the past two weeks.'

Dave was a little off guard, as he had not heard from Doc John for a while. John would occasionally send Dave some University fieldwork; however, he had not sent any work his way for some time. A good credible crawling apology was in order.

'Sorry John my mobile is well out of range at Sandfire that's where I live these days since I lost my house in Broome in my last divorce settlement. I should have passed on my satellite phone number to you and my new email address.'

'No harm done Dave, there hasn't been much in the way of work for you over the last eight months. Nonetheless, today you are in luck. I have just received a letter from a Professor Thomas Harold of Princeton University New Jersey. An old friend of mine; Professor Benjamin Lock who has just recently passed away has recommended me to Professor Harold.

Professor Harold is an Anthropologist and wishes to do some field research work out in the Great Sandy Desert. I told him that you would be the right man for the job, being an academic, also owning an air charter company. Professor Harold arrives in Perth tomorrow and wants to meet up with you, what do you think?'

'You're right on cue with the luck bit John as I am at the airport about to board a jet to Perth. I have some meetings today and tomorrow, where is Professor Harold staying?'

'I believe he will be staying at the Hyatt Regency.'

'More luck as I will be staying there. I could meet Professor Harold tomorrow evening say seven thirty in the Hyatt lounge bar. Give him this mobile number if he wants to change the time he can call me direct. Do you know anything about this bloke; I mean is he expecting some sort of discount?'

Max was listening with his ear pressed hard against the back of Doc Dave's phone. On hearing the word discount, gave a sigh and a look of shock and horror. John continued.

'He never said anything about a discount Dave. Although he was very impressed that I could recommend a suitable person that knew all about the outback, Aboriginal culture, and was a Doctor of Geophysics. All I know about him is that he is a highly respected tutor in his field, and has just recently retired. My deceased friend thought the world of him, and had instructed me on his deathbed to give him all the possible assistance I can.'

The departure lounge speakers announced the boarding call for Perth.

'Okay John, tell him I am interested in his job and will discuss the project with him tomorrow night. I have to go now as that was the last boarding call, I will catch up with you for a drink in the next few days, bye for now.'

'Well how's that Max, it looks like we have another flying job, I will give you a call from Perth with all the details as they develop.'

On the way through the departure gate Dave glanced back at Max who had a big smile on his bearded face, the message was clear... it looks like we will all eat for another few weeks... he was being positive.

The first of the Perth meetings was with Mary's lawyer. Dave was pleasantly surprised that Mary had decided at the last minute to attend, though against her lawyer's advice. She was radiant and lovely as ever. He thought he had better not apologise to her all over again as he now realised that he must sound like a worn record. Anyway, Mary knew he was all but finished financially.

All that was required now was the final well-placed blow. Her lawyer had that glint of victory in his eyes, and yet the greedy bastard still tried to promote more work for his divorce lawyer mates, by insisting that he should get some legal representation. Dave had come to say his piece, and rudely butted into the lawyers banter about supporting one of his colleges into buying a new BMW.

'If I may interrupt your ramblings sir; after being divorced twice before, I am very aware of the massive and useless added costs in the way of divorce lawyer fees.

I intend to avoid or reduce the huge rip-off fees planned for extraction from my painful financial situation without a hint of regret from you and your associate lawyer scavengers. My plan is simple, which is to give my wife everything she claims, or wants. This would of course would include all the fees that you and your devious colleges would have extracted out of our sad matrimonial state of affairs.

My first two marriages failed because of my infidelity and a lack of love and respect. This marriage has failed because of my stupidity... I believe there is still some love left to work with, and I will not give up.'

Dave then turned to a sad and tearful Mary.

'I have this strange feeling that something will happen soon, I also believe that Sandfire Air Charter can, and will, become profitable. Max is a good man and is prepared to run things for you regardless of how this settlement turns out. Max is still in love with the air charter company as I am still in love you.'

Turning to the disappointed lawyer.

Where do I sign over the assets of the company? I expect this matter completed quickly, as my next meeting is tomorrow morning with the Australian Tax Office. By then, with good planning they should have little left to pick-over.'

The lawyer pushed across the desk a neat folder of well-prepared documents, affixed with many sign here stickers. Dave went about meticulously signing every spot quickly witnessed by the lawyer.

Doc Dave rose to his feet and gave Mary a goodbye kiss on the cheek. He then swiftly turned and left the office glancing back just once to see Mary in floods of tears. With her lawyer, standing alongside displaying a big grin from ear to ear in smug satisfied look of a job well executed and concluded.

The taxman was surprisingly helpful. He was a strange, sad little man, who peered at him over the top of a large dog-eared file that Doc Dave assumed must be his. He looked worried, or was it a look of fear on his face; nevertheless, it was enough for Dave to ask.

'Are you all right mate, you look like you have seen a ghost, can I go get you a cup of coffee or something?'

'No, no thank you Doctor Sharp, it's just that I have not been sleeping to well of late, I must admit I have been dreading this interview. My doctor says that I am suffering from extreme anxiety and stress... and I agree. The problem is I only have these dreaded attacks when I am working on your file Doctor Sharp, why do you think that would be?'

Dave thought he could have said possibly a taxman's inner guilt but that was clearly not the case. This little man had the same look on his face that big Des had at Punmu, Dave had the uneasy feeling this man was afraid of him... but why? These thoughts quickly vanished as the little man continued without waiting on an answer to his own question.

'Doctor Sharp, I have decided to give you and your company, a tax holiday; this to allow you and you wife time to sort out your differences. We, the tax office will give you an extension of time to sort out your business affairs. Your file will be reviewed in six months from today's date, will that help you?'

Doc Dave was amazed at this news, can he be hearing this correctly. This was not the same hard-faced Australian Tax Office he had been fighting with over the past ten years. Dave immediately stood up and shook the little man's hand so vigorously that he was sure that the man's head would fall off.

'Thank you, thank you sir you have saved three peoples jobs today, and I do hope that you sleep well tonight as you most certainly deserve.'

The little man looked so sad as if he were about to cry, then Dave reassessed the look as relief. He was genuinely relieved that this interview was over. As Dave turned to leave the small cubicle office, the little taxman said…

'Maybe tonight I will stop dreaming of death, an aeroplane crashing, and a lot of scary painted Aboriginal tribesmen.'

As Doc Dave was walking out of the ATO building, he thought what a strange thing to say. This man was having bad dreams about Aboriginal tribesmen, only while working on his tax file.

Then the other mystery, how did this little taxman know about him and Mary? Who cares, his luck was changing, life was not so bad after all, and that is what he reported in his phone call to the happy Max at Sandfire.

'Like I said Max, stay positive mate, and tell Tony the good news.'

Retired was he? This Professor Thomas Harold must be in his late sixties or possibly older. Dave tried to analyse what the Professor would be like as he showered and dressed for his meeting downstairs.

As was mostly the case with dedicated teaching academics, they never ventured into the field much, especially as they got older. On retirement, they typically tried to do the fieldwork they had missed in their early teaching careers.

Thinking, he may be very much old school, suit, and tie type. Doc Dave did not own a suit, however, he did have a clean pilot's shirt, and his old University tie that he wore to the lawyers meeting. That and his old leather-flying jacket would just have to do.

It was just before 7:30 as Doc Dave glanced around the large lounge bar. Out of around forty-plus people chatting and drinking.

Nobody looked in the slightest like an old American academic, well not the ones he could remember.

Dave caught the attention of the slim drinks waiter who glided over his way raising a single eyebrow followed by a well-practised 'yes.' Dave placed his order for a double Johnny Walker black label scotch on the rocks, enquiring nicely if there were any Americans in the bar.

'That black bloke over there sounds a bit like he could be American mate,' pointing to a tall good-looking African-American man of around 55-years of age. He looked fit without an ounce of fat on him, sporting a neatly trimmed goatee beard and a full head of hair. He wore form-fitting blue jeans with a plain brown leather belt and polished brown stylish boots, his well-cut long sleeve shirt had the cuffs neatly turned back.

The neck of his shirt was open revealing a thick gold chain on a hairy chest, with what looked like two gold wedding bands on it. He was smiling and talking casually to a man in a well cut business suit. The man in the suit bowed his head in polite acknowledgement, then walked over to the piano and started to play a beautiful rendering of The Rose.

The modern dressed man glanced at his watch then turned sweeping the room when their eyes locked. Doc Dave was a little embarrassed that he had been so easily caught-out weighing up this man. Then felt a sense of relief as the man broke into an easy smile and casually walked towards him, then in a soft American accent…

'Doctor Sharp I presume,' holding out his hand. 'I was expecting a sweaty Akubra hat ringed with corks on strings, a denim jacket and a pair of 1920's 505 Levies full of holes, and maybe some ex-army boots.'

Dave was surprised at this casual introduction.

'Pleased to meet you Professor Harold,' Dave firmly shaking the man's hand, locking eye to eye. 'I was expecting a white suit covered in sequins and rind-stones with a ten gallon Stetson hat and a polished belt buckle bigger than a dinner plate with your name on it.'

'Don't forget the crocodile skin boots Doctor Sharp,' both laughed aloud and smiling. 'We should dispense with the academic titles my name is Thomas, please call me Tom.'

Dave liked this man. He had this overwhelming feeling that he could get along with him and even trust him. What an odd feeling to have about someone that you have only just met.

'Everybody just calls me Dave or Doc if there are more Dave's around or if they want something its Doc Dave. Australians are not very formal people; titles mean little, it's who you are that really counts.'

'Well Dave, can I buy you a drink and tell you all about who I really am?'

'Don't mind if you do Tom I will have the same as you, it will go nicely with the one that I have already ordered. You know Tom; I think we should go in for dinner. Food is always best for digesting new business deals. '

For the next two hours, they talked about their academic disciplines, and lines of research. Tom was noticeably cautious in what he said and revealed. Dave got the firm impression that Tom was quietly sounding him out about his knowledge of the bush and Aboriginal culture.

He was holding something back Dave could sense it, but he soon noticed that Tom did appreciate good red wine and single malt whisky, now that was always a good sign.

Professor Tom liked Dave from the start. He liked his easy-going nature guessing that he was in his early forties and by his good looks and dashing moustache was most probably a bit of a ladies man.

He thought that they could work together; however, he sensed that Dave was probing him about what he was researching in the Great Sandy Desert. Dave was a Geophysicist and not into ancient bones. His discipline was in identifying ancient land and rock formations seeking undiscovered oil and rich ores on this planet.

He was a sort of hi-tech prospector with a good knowledge of the desert and the local Aboriginal tribes. Another plus was he also owned a Mercedes Unimog 4X4 exploration vehicle, an airplane, and a helicopter, just the kind of person that he needed for his research work.

After-dinner, they moved back to the lounge bar for drinks, and to continue their chat. Tom had gone to his room and brought back a small leather document case.

He was considering at this early stage whether he should bring-up the subject of the bone relic and the tree-bark map when just then there was an almighty loud crash at the bar. They both turned in the direction of all the noise to see a nice-looking woman in her early thirties who had just dropped her large carry-bag on the floor.

She had attempted to catch her bag causing the heavy barstool to fall over spilling the many contents of her bag all over the bar floor. Both got to their feet and Tom commented with a wide grin as they went to help...

'Well would you just look at that, it is true, women do carry everything but the kitchen sink with them in their bag.'

They both went about picking-up all the scattered items and handing them back to the smiling but very embarrassed young woman. Tom had picked-up an Australian passport noticing the name Robyn Mills, however, Dave had picked-up a British passport noticing the name Doctor Emma Archer, place of birth Scotland.

Tom handed Emma the passport with a smile, then in his soft American accent.

'I do hope that you have recovered everything Robyn,' then in humour. 'No doubt you will know by the weight of your bag.'

With a charming girly smile, Emma replied in her quaint Scottish accent.

'Well thank you sir, however I think I am still missing my kitchen sink would you be so kind as to continue looking for it. It's deep and shiny with a large rubber drain stopper.'

Tom was still enjoying the witty response when Dave handed Emma her other passport.

'I hope you enjoy your stay in our fine city of Perth Doctor Emma Archer. You know; Perth Western Australia was named after Perth Scotland, but then you would already know that. Are you here on holiday or possibly on a lecture tour, or a perhaps... a spying mission?'

Emma was briefly startled at being caught out with two passports.

'I can explain the two passports gentlemen...

Dave furrowed his brow with a look of serious concern.

'Before you do, let me advise you madam that we are quite familiar with international spies in Perth. Allow me to introduce to you Thomas Harold, CIA and I, David Sharp of ASIO professional spy catchers, sharp in name and very sharp on-the-job.'

Emma screwed up her face in mock shock, barely able to hold back a fit of laughter and decided on a little game of her own. Then in her cute Scottish accent.

'Robyn Mills is my friend, along with the kitchen sink I have decided to carry her passport around with me. My false name is Doctor Emma Archer along with my false Scottish accent

I am in deep cover as an agent for the Australian Taxation Office. I am here looking into the matters of a Doctor David Sharp, owner and director of Sandfire Air Charter for evasion of taxable income, are you that same Doctor David Sharp?'

All three burst out in raucous laughter and the whole bar turned again to see what was going on? The timid waiter asked if they could keep the noise down, as this was a quiet business lounge. Grinning Emma continued.

'I am Doctor Emma Archer Oxford University. I emailed your Air Charter Company to hire your services. A man by the name of Max rang my mobile telling me you were in Perth attending a government taxation meeting and staying at the Hyatt, so now I have found you.'

'Emma this is Thomas Harold, Professor of Anthropology Princeton University New Jersey.'

They all shook hands laughing at the shared wit and humour.

'Always trust Max to tell everybody about my personal tax disasters but how did you know how to recognise me?'

'That was easy, Max said you will be the old guy in the bar trying to chat-up all the nice young ladies. You would be dressed to look like Humphrey Bogart in the movie China Clipper, wearing an old leather-flying jacket and sporting a well-trimmed fly-boy moustache. I picked you out of the bar-crowd with ease.'

Dave was shattered at Max's description of his boss. He must remember to have a word with him when he gets back to Sandfire. Meanwhile Tom thought the description was spot-on and was still laughing when Emma spoke...

'Are you two gentlemen going to buy me a drink, this spying business is thirsty work?'

They all sat down in one of the large alcoves. Emma parked her large bag on the seat beside her, and then asked politely if she was butting into anything important, as she could meet with Dave tomorrow.

Tom quickly parked his laughter then opened with, 'Doctor Archer.' Emma interjected with a giggle please just call me Emma.' 'Then you must call me Tom. Emma I am about to hire Dave here for some research work in the Great Sandy Desert.

I have a map of my area of interest, I was about to discuss this with Dave. The area I want to look at is up in the north-west of Australia, a very remote place. It would appear that Dave's Sandfire airstrip is the closest to the Great Sandy Desert from the Great Northern Highway.

You are obviously interested in the same or similar area. Might I suggest that we combine our research interest to help reduce costs and offer a wider and better research result? What do you say?'

'I have no objection Tom, as I doubt that we will be seeking the same data, or samples. All our academic disciplines are extremely different.'

Dave thought this was an excellent idea, and agreed that a pooled cost basis would cover more ground, and save them both going over the same area. Moreover, that was the next question, just where did they both want to go in this vast Great Sandy Desert?

'Might I suggest that ladies go first? Emma can you show me where you would like to start your desert research programme?'

Emma plunged into her big carry bag and pulled out a large bound file of documents. Tom and Dave looked at each other; why had this large file, not spilled out onto the floor with all of Emma's other stuff.

Emma then spread out a current issue Northwestern Australia relief map of the Great Sandy Desert and pointed to the area circled in red. Dave looked at the position in utter astonishment and gasped in obvious surprise…

'That's the Veevers meteorite crater.'

Emma turned to Dave in both surprise and bewilderment.

'So you know of this meteorite crater Dave, that's good, as I have to carry out some detailed scientific tests in and around this crater. Is it easily accessible, can we fly there or do we have to drive to the site?'

Dave was still in surprise mode, then softly replying to Emma's question.

'I have done both in the past three weeks; may I ask what tests you want to conduct at this site?'

Emma was now thinking about her early opening. The revealing of her intentions so early might not have been such a good idea. This Veevers area was in a remote desert, it could not be that popular.

What was it, a well-known Australian tourist destination, or something? She had thus far spilt the beans so… should she just carry on. Strangely, these two guys had given her some sort of confidence; she had felt that for some strange reason she could trust them having no idea why. She was normally a very cautious person, especially with first meetings.

'You say that you have been to the Veevers meteorite crater just recently Dave, may I ask you who your client was... the interested party?'

'I was by myself Emma, with no other party, other than my old pilot friend Max. We have been experiencing some very strange phenomena out around that crater area for some time. The Aboriginals call the place the sacred site of the Mooroopna, ghost spirit.'

Emma tried hard to conceal her surprise, and then continued...

'I will be carrying out some gravity variation tests and establishing the existence and proof of a newly discovered phenomenon, known as gravity ring clusters. These gravity rings, could well be the reason for all the strange happenings in this area.'

Emma thought this was as far as she should go for now on this matter. Too much detail regarding antipodal gravity shafts and antenna would spook these two nice guys right out of their narrow academic minds.

'Well Emma you have just put my mind at rest. Max and I thought that we were going mad, now I will have some reasonable explanations for all these weird things. We should sleep on this as the time is well past midnight and that waiter over there has been giving me the evil eye for the past hour.

Where are you staying Emma can I get you a cab...

'You will be happy to know that I am staying right here so I will see you wee boys for breakfast tomorrow, not too early say 9:30am?'

Tom and Dave nodded their heads in agreement, they both liked the little bright-minded Emma; they got on well, and all of them had a wicked sense of humour.

'Okay then, we will all meet up at 9:30am for a late breakfast and continue our planning for the research programmes into the Great Sandy Desert, this is exciting stuff don't you think Tom?'

Tom had slipped into deep thought, so there were other strange things happening out in this ancient Great Sandy Desert, was there any link to his bone and this Veevers meteorite crater? He then discounted that thought as having no connection.

The old prospector Bluey was apparently quite close to a town where he went for his regular supplies. From what Dave had said this crater was right in the middle of a desert hundreds of miles from nowhere, a voice was saying see you at breakfast Tom.

'Yeah good night Emma and Dave see you both tomorrow.'

At breakfast, everybody had thought of more questions to ask about last night's discussion on the strange things at the Veevers crater. Tom was wondering why Emma had decided on researching this particular crater, as he had discovered that there were many others.

He had Googled meteorite craters in Western Australia and found there were more recorded meteorite hits in Western Australia than any other country or continent in the world.

The waiter gave them all a move on advice, mumbling, they should now leave the breakfast room. Dave glanced at his large pilot's watch, surprised to note that it was 11am. Suggesting they all moved out of the breakfast room into the lounge bar to continue their discussions.

Emma explained how they first discovered the gravity-rings and clusters, by reversing the LISA (Laser Interferometer Space Antenna) space probe to face earth, then plotting the earth's surface. She managed to steer the conversation away from Tom's probing question. "Were there any other gravity ring clusters found on earth?" by politely suggesting that she had held the floor for some time. Then advising that Tom should have a say in where his research area was in the Great Sandy Desert, then brightly noting it was now lunchtime and she was starving.

Lunch was a most memorable event. This was a time when Tom thought that for all his fitness, he was about to have a heart attack. Tom had asked Dave if he was familiar with Aboriginal art and drawings. Did he know of any Aboriginal cave paintings in the desert that he could visit for inspection, or did he know of any possible anthropological remains?

Dave said that he knew of many sites however, he would need the permission of the local tribal elders to take him there, then only on condition the sites respected, and nothing removed. He did however believe that he would be granted permission to visit some of the sites.

Emma asked Tom if he had some idea of where he was going to look first. Did he have a map or name of a place from which to start?

'Yes I do have a good clue to start from. My map is a little different from yours Emma. I have an old and primitive map with a location, drawn on a piece of paper-bark by an old Aboriginal Witch Doctor many years ago.

I believe that the map shows the way to an Aboriginal sacred site of some significance. I was going to ask Dave if he had any experience with old Aboriginal drawing symbols, as the ones drawn on this map are not listed in any museum I know of holding Aboriginal records.'

Tom reached into his leather document case, and produced a transparent file cover, with the paper-bark map clearly showing through. Handing the map to Dave. Dave stared at the paper-bark map for a full two minutes in spine-chilling shock. He then looked Tom directly in his eyes.

'This map is not ancient or even old Tom; this map was drawn by Munyo the old Martu Gadichi man about five years ago. I would suggest drawn just before he died, as I attended his final singing and tribal funeral. How did you come by it?'

Tom looked like a victim shot by a powerful taser stun gun. His eyes were wide open as was his mouth... he was speechless. Dave continued...

'This map shows an Aboriginal walkabout to a place close to the Veevers meteorite crater, only the old Gadichi man Munyo knew of this sacred place. Now all I have to ask you is; have you brought the sacred bone with you, because they are waiting on its return.'

Tom and Emma were staring at Dave. This was all too strange and spooky to comprehend. Tom took the initiative after rapidly composing himself, in a spluttering voice demanded an immediate answer.

'Just who the hell are you man. How the hell could you know all these things? My anthropological data and findings were from a secret and reliable source in the USA, and as for Emma's data. This matter involves a newly discovered gravity ring phenomena that she has still yet to confirm, based on guarded data collected only from within the UK. Just where in Australia do you fit in to all of this Dave...? We need an answer now.'

Dave handed them both a glass of wine he could see that they would need. They were both waiting patiently for an answer, some connecting answer, some believable answer, and so Dave told them his story.

'Three weeks ago I went out to an Aboriginal Community called Punmu in the Great Sandy Desert. There I met the new Gadichi man, the man who replaced old Munyo. The new Gadichi man went into a trance and told me I had to bring back the sacred bone, and that I would do this with the help of two others.

Emma and her chaos group have discovered a strange gravity cluster phenomena at the Veevers impact site and being one of the two people mentioned by the Gadichi man, the other being you Tom. I figured that you being an anthropologist, then you must be the one to have the bone... would I be right?'

Tom, Dave, and Emma looked at each other with suspicion; Emma and Dave turned to Tom and waited in expectation... the seconds felt like hours.

'Yes Dave you are correct, and not just any old bone, but one that is 10,400 years old, and is half made of a metal that is unknown on this planet.'

Their increased reaction and raised voices to this unfolding story had drawn a considerable amount of unwanted attention and stares, mostly from people seated close by.

Emma and Dave were suspicious and wanted to see this strange sacred bone. Tom decided that they should continue this discussion in the privacy of his hotel room.

The suspense was building as thick as a Hitchcock thriller. Tom went to his hotel room-safe, returning with an old cardboard shoebox. He withdrew a plastic cylinder and unscrewed the end, then handed Dave the bone wrapped in a transparent sample bag. Emma looked on in wonder remaining silent, thinking just what she had got herself into with these two very nice... but very extraordinary men. Do any of these odd events have any connection to her research, should she report this strange anomaly to her chaos group? Emma decided to wait and hear more about this 10,400-year-old bone. As she understood, this bone had nothing to do with her mission, or the chaos group's gravity rings.

Chapter Thirteen

We are all connected

Dave looked closely at the bone, offering his comprehensive knowledge on the subject.

'It looks like any old dry bone to me Tom, except the ball end is a slightly different colour. I would guess that's the metal bit. You say this bone is dated back 10,400 years that's exceptionally old, can you be sure it's a human bone.'

'It sure is a human bone. It is actually part of a right femur, and is in remarkable condition considering the age. Nearly all exposed bone fragments older than three thousand years are decayed, splintered, and petrified, the excellent condition is an indication this bone may have in some way been protected.

Human bone fossils such as Omo 1 and Omo 2 have been dated back to 160,000 years old therefore the age is not all-that extraordinary however...'

Emma broke into Tom's interesting story.

'The metal prosthesis, being in such incredible condition at 10,400 years old tells us a very different story. It proves beyond doubt that an advanced civilisation once existed on this planet around 10,400 years ago. Or this planet was visited by some advanced beings, possibly aliens, if you have a mind for that sort of stuff.'

Tom was impressed, and at the same time suspicious. Emma was very bright, and quick to see the significance of this bone relic. Did

185

she come to Australia with a preconceived view about extra-terrestrials?

'You are correct Emma this was also my conclusion, especially as the metal prosthesis is far superior to anything known today, having an internal structure similar to that of a natural bone.

However, the most fascinating thing was the way the metal fused to the natural bone, also that the metal itself is apparently some blending or type of alloy. This alloy having a number of elements that do not appear on the standard periodic scale.'

Dave thought he could now see what Tom was on about; he just wanted to find the site where they had found this ancient bone. Then to discover further remains that would tell him more about this remarkable find. On the other hand, what was Emma going to find or do at the Veevers crater? It was time to get to the truth.

Tom had noticed Dave's silence, prompting a question.

'You look like you have something on your mind Dave; want to share your thoughts with Emma and me?'

Dave pursed his lips in a look of both confusion and suspicion.

'I can't get over the fact that three scientists with three differing disciplines, from three different continents, have been brought together here in Perth Western Australia. Why... what is the purpose, are we being manipulated, used by someone in some way?'

'I totally agree with you Dave. Although please do give Emma and me your theory on what this may be all about. With each hour we are all learning that we are each somehow linked into this odd mystery.'

Dave looked at their faces; he could see they were just as confused by this as he was.

'Well the way I see things, the Veevers meteorite crater appears to be the focal point in all of this. My role in this matter as a Geophysicist seems to be about the geological location, and the weird phenomena that we have been experiencing and recording in this area.

Then there is also my expert knowledge, and the close friendship that I have with the local indigenous Aboriginal owners of the desert land, who know-of and own this sacred Veevers area.

To date these desert people have been spot-on in their dreamtime stories. They were aware of the sacred bone, and the strange phenomena they call Mooroopna or ghost spirit at the Veevers crater site. They also predicted that two other people would help me to return the sacred bone.

I must confess to you both now, that I was never a believer in Gadichi men, or ghost spirits. Just as you people, I thought these strange happenings would have a simple logical answer; we are after all scientists.

On the other hand, I must admit I was also seeking some sort of sound ethical and scientific solution to all of these strange things. My theories had ranged from a possible massive deposit of concentrated magnetite rock, to a moving plasma source close to the earth's surface, both of which have since been discarded by my recent site tests.'

Emma's head spun around.at this disclosure.

'You have already carried out surface tests at the Veevers crater site, what kind of tests, and what were the results?'

'Two weeks ago, Max, and I drove out to the Veevers crater with my small sample drilling rig. We drilled sixteen 60 mm sample holes in and around the crater to a depth of 145 feet, pulling ninety-six small-bore core samples.

The core samples were sent down here to a friend of mine in Perth for analysis. Doctor Brad Farlow from CSIRO Waterford rang me this morning to say that the test results were available to be picked-up. He also said there were some odd findings that he would like to discuss with me.'

All of a sudden, there was a loud bang as Emma and Dave turned to look at Tom who had just slapped his hand hard on the table in front of him. For the mild-mannered academic this was an out-of-character performance, one that Tom later admitted he had never used before to gain everyone's attention.

However, he had found these dramatics necessary; considering the odd topic under discussion, he had come to a realisation about the three of them… then leaning forward with a controlled soft voice.

'I think we all need to tell the truth here, every single detail of the truth. We are all professionals in our various fields of science. It is only natural that we would try to hide our individual findings, later claiming the unique glory that comes with a spectacular world scientific discovery.

Tom stroked his neatly trimmed goatee beard in thought, and then added.

'There is only one major problem to this apparently normal academic move. Whoever put this puzzle together, knows our weakness for fame and acknowledgment. In a well thought out plan has the three of us outsmarted. This move achieved by simply giving

187

each of us an equal, but significant part of this puzzle. We are for some unknown reason manipulated into working together. As such, this mystery may also have a plan; and if so, no doubt a reason... and possibly a mission.'

Silence fell over the trio of scientists as they all considered Tom's theory and the next obvious move. Should they all tell everything they knew? Dave had already made his decision and spoke first.

'I think that you are spot on Tom as I have had this odd feeling for some time. A feeling that all the matters involving my life as of late, both private, and business, are coming to a final conclusion. I can feel it. Yes, I do agree, I think we should all come clean and tell everything we know. Well my new friends, here goes. This is my story as far as I can understand it, and I promise you both I will leave nothing out.'

Dave went on to explain the weird phenomena he had experienced with his aircraft instruments, and had plotted the location close to the Veevers crater. Dave then told them all about the underground dry caves that Max had found in the Veevers area. Using the illegal services of a number of hacked geo satellites and other information downloaded from some of the world's most powerful government satellite systems.

He then went on to tell them about what happened on his last helicopter flight out to the Aboriginal community at Punmu. All about Mirachung and his strange trance, and the earlier Gadichi man's grim and deadly bone pointing ceremony. Dave believed Tom now possessed that same bone.

Emma was about to launch into a torrid of questions when Tom reminded her that we were all going to each tell our personal stories first, and it was his turn. Tom stood up to talk, as was the way of a well-practised and experienced university lecturer.

'You're strange story Dave would make a good bedtime ghost tale, and would frighten the daylights out of most people. My story has a similar theme, and combined with yours now has even me a bit frightened.'

Tom told the story of Bluey the old prospector and his final gold discovery, and then his death by heart attack. Bluey had convinced himself that his two previous heart attacks were because he had not returned the sacred bone as promised.

However, the part of the story that got both Emma and Dave leaning forward was the last meeting Tom had with his mentor

188

Professor Ben Lock. Both moved by the bizarre way he had come by the bone, wrapped in a Time magazine containing an article with Professor Ben Lock's contact details. Tom also told them about Professor Ben's research theory on a possible, yet to be discovered energy or power within the universe, one with intelligence, a power that is not a deity, or a God.

This hardly raised an eyebrow with Dave, a confirmed atheist who cared little about such matters; however, Emma took a sharp breath, visually shaken by this part of Tom's story.

Tom reached forward and gently touched Emma's arm.

'We need to hear your story now Emma.'

Emma was almost in tears; Tom and Dave looked at each other and asked if they had said something to upset her. Suddenly she composed herself, wiped her eyes, and launched into her mysterious tale of the events that led her to come all the way to Western Australia.

'My story has so many turns and strange phenomena that it would be on its own unbelievable. Both your stories do give my story some form of credibility. I would say your stories offer a basis to link all three stories to a possible logical although shaky, but still unscientific conclusion.'

Emma went into detail about the chaos group, originally being just a private after hour's drink-think-tank. How the group was made-up of a diverse, but highly talented group of seven odd imaginative rogues. Who had recently stumbled across a set of identifiable patterns to the normal chaotic flight of incoming meteorite showers entering our planet's atmosphere. They had found a way to segregate incoming material from all those objects that were always destined to leave our solar system. They were working on a theory as to why.

Emma went on to describe while researching known meteorite strikes how by luck the group had noticed that gravity variations formed loose clusters around certain points on the earth's surface. This led to some illicit manipulation of government and international space satellite resources, used to scan and map the world for gravity wave events.

On hearing this, Dave felt a little better after having admitted that he and Max were into fiddling and hacking into government satellite birds... so he was pleased to hear hacking was quite normal in the ranks of academia.

Tom on the other hand thought his hearing had caught-up with his real age, becoming unreliable. Was this how the Brits and Aussies carried out their scientific research, by hacking into and using American satellites?

Emma had paused when she realised what she had just said. Both Emma and Dave turned to Tom expecting some response... Tom wisely remained silent. Emma then continued with her story.

'We had just proved an old Einstein theory, being that concentrated gravity waves do indeed exist. The gravity wave findings when plotted confirmed to specific points on the earth's surface. All sites having a group of three distinct gravity rings, with ten such locations identified.

We soon discovered that other world governments were watching our research progress with great interest. With the help of Randall, the chaos group then moved into secret mode. Randall also discovered that most of the gravity cluster rings were close to well-known ancient buildings and sites.

A further piece of ingenious research plotted the earth's tectonic plate drift, placing the gravity rings where they would have been some 10,400 years ago, then added the known polar axis drift. All the gravity rings then stacked on top of each other except at one site. The ninth position, at the Veevers meteorite crater. This site was plotted as having two rings, one ring remaining in the exactly same position being three kilometres northeast of the crater site.'

When Emma paused in telling her story, Dave jumped in with an urgent question.

'This is fascinating stuff Emma. We can now understand the strange happenings with Tom's bone story as it aligns and fits into my story. However the single identification of two gravity rings at the Veevers crater site has no connection with our stories; well, as I can understand.'

Emma continued with her story.

'I disagree with you Dave; it actually adds some level of scientific credibility to this whole mystery. For a start, I would bet that this odd gravity ring is right over the exact spot where you have plotted the strange energy force. I would also suggest possibly the very place where Tom's strange bone came from. Another thing, when we created a computer model and ran connecting rods through all the ten gravity sites, we ended up with five antipodal rod elements that crossed exactly in the centre of this planet. We now believe that this is, or may have been, some form of massive ancient receiving antenna.

Just to give you guys something else to think about; this antenna went out of alignment and stopped working 10,400 years ago. At that same time, the planet earth stopped receiving meteorites and asteroids containing live bacteria. The very same time we ceased to receive further incoming terrestrial objects containing basic life. We, the chaos group believe that many of the answers to our questions might be found at the ninth place on earth, the Veevers meteorite crater.'

Tom had been quietly listening, while stroking his goatee beard; he then raised a hand seeking permission to speak.

'Did you say 10,400 years ago; why hell, that is the same age the ancient bone was carbon dated to. Then you say over time there was a big movement of the earth's tectonic plates, and also a small pole shift, all of which started at around that same period in time?'

Dave interjected and suggested that they should all go back down to the lounge bar, casually adding...

'Friends, the Veevers meteorite crater hit is dated at 10,400 years, and I read somewhere recently that Stonehenge was re-dated from 5,200 to 10,400 years old. My bet is that this area will be one of your plotted gravity cluster ring sites... right?'

Emma slowly eyed the two men for some sign of joke, and then answered Dave's hanging question.

'Yes, you are correct Dave. Along with the Great Pyramid of Giza and the only known Mayan Pyramid beneath the sea in the Bermuda Triangle.'

Dave looked around; nobody was ready to speak so he continued.

'Emma, are you also aware that the Veevers meteorite crater is unusual in that it is perfectly round and the depression walls are about the same height all around. This would indicate to me that the meteorite impact was vertical. In all my years in the field, and I have seen many meteorite craters, they are always oval. The walls are higher to the direction of impact, as meteorites always strike the earth at an angle.'

They all sat quietly in the lounge bar; all were digesting this new information. Just then, the headwaiter came across with a miserable look on his face and said in a loud officious voice.

'Doctor Sharp there is a Doctor Farlow at the reception asking to see you; while I'm here sir, can I take your drink order.'

Dave thanked the waiter placing a drink order for all, then advising the waiter to tell Doctor Farlow he would meet him at the hotel reception bar, and then turning back to Emma and Tom.

'The bloke at reception is an old mate of mine from the CSIRO analysis labs. I was supposed to go see him this morning at around ten,' glancing at his large pilots watch. 'Hell look at the time it's already 6:30, where has the bloody day gone. With luck, he may have with him the test results of my Veevers drilling core samples,' then quickly standing.

'You two should have a chat about all of this, and I will go hear what Doc Brad has to say about my drill-core samples,' then noticing the anxious looks from Emma and Tom.

'Don't worry; I will say absolutely nothing about our unusual findings. I think we should all agree to say nothing to anybody about our bizarre discussions; anyway, Brad would think we were all bloody mad.'

Tom raised his hand; stopping Dave from leaving, he had another and more important question to ask.

'Dave, did you have the Veevers drill core samples carbon dated?'

'I never thought to ask, it's not the normal procedure for a Geo carrying out standard mineral sampling. Then again, we were looking for some odd anomaly that might be the cause of our strange flying experience. However, we were only thinking along the lines of a highly concentrated deposit of magnetite... I won't be long.'

Dave left them with more questions than answers and headed for the reception bar to meet Doc Brad. As Dave departed through the lounge room door, Emma turned her attention back to Tom, asking a question that she urgently needed to know the answer to.

'Tom, can I ask you how long you have known Doctor David Sharp?

'Not that long Emma, only about an hour before you created a means to attract Dave's attention, by tipping your bag out onto the bar floor. From that obvious manoeuvre, I had figured out that you and Dave had never met one another either.'

This casual and honest reply caught Emma by surprise... It was clear that Tom was thinking the same, just how did we all end up together.

'Oh dear, was I so apparent Tom? I can see that I will have to put some effort into improving my female infiltration tactics.'

'Well you may have to do just that, if you find it necessary to be that devious with us Emma. I don't reckon that Dave bought your little stunt either. I can tell you now Emma, I have decided to trust you and Dave completely on this odd Veevers matter, and I believe that Dave has come to the same conclusion.'

'You are right Tom. That last comment was supposed to be funny, but this is all turning out to be a very serious matter. On the other hand, you have just about cleared up my last suspicion in that you and Dave are complete strangers to each other just like me. In fact, Professor Thomas, I have never heard of, or read any of your publications... As a complete stranger to me, I find it difficult to submit to being fully open, especially when I am responsible to others, as the leader of my little chaos group back in Oxford England.'

Tom was a little shocked at Emma's sudden attack.

'You said, "just about cleared up your suspicions." What other suspicions do you have about me Emma? I have been open and honest with both of you, what more can I say... or tell you?'

'I said I had never heard of you, or for that matter Doctor David Sharp, however, I know a great deal about Professor Benjamin Lock, your mentor. I have known of his work for many years. I know all about Professor Lock's research into the beginning of all life, he has contributed much, adding valuable proof to the big bang theory.

His research, and theory moved on to how suitable planets in our solar system, may have been seeded with life by meteorites containing single cell bacteria... a subject deeply covered by my chaos group. This is where I began to listen with great interest as I have already explained previously. My chaos group had all but proved that amino acids and basic organic life forms brought to earth by meteorites and asteroids had suddenly ceased at around 10,400 years ago. Now you have a strange ancient bone dated at 10,400 years old, given to you by Professor Lock, is there another connection we should know about here?'

'Forgive me Emma; I can now see why you are suspicious of me. What you have said about Ben's research is true, and has now provided a link back to me. Much the same as Dave's interest in the Veevers crater fits in well with your gravity ring phenomena, being at the very same place as you have named as the ninth place on earth.

It would appear we all have connected missions, not only by our individual discoveries but also by our personal research, theories, and beliefs. I will say again; I think all three of us working together may

193

well be the result of a manipulated arrangement... but why, and by whom? We have only briefly touched on our research and theories yet we will need to go deeper to discuss these areas in greater detail.'

Emma gave Tom one of her reserved suspicious looks asking.

'Research, please tell me Tom, just what is your field of research... and what are your theories? You already know what Dave and mine are.'

Dave scanned the reception desk, and then spotted Doc Brad down the other end of the entry foyer. He was a large framed man with a well-formed boozer's belly, leaning casually on the reception bar with a large scotch in his hand, and another on the bar that Dave hoped was for him.

At Brad's feet was a good-sized cardboard box. Dave headed over to Brad, thinking he must make this chat quick. He was pleased to see that Brad had brought along the drill test samples.

'Brad you old bastard how are you mate it's been a while,' shaking hands vigorously with a grin, then standing back to study his old friend. 'I think you've lost a bit of weight old son.'

Brad smiling and fat as ever, placed his empty glass on the bar. Then picked up the other large scotch, and took a sip, replying.

'Don't you start patronising me you skinny shit, I have been working my ball's off carrying out these free assay tests for you. Buy a man a scotch and chaser and I will tell you all about the trouble you have caused me.'

Dave ordered three double scotches on ice and turned to his old mate who was halfway through his second scotch. Dave sensed something was wrong, and moved to get in his early excuse to escape from Doc Brad.

'Hell I forgot all about ringing you Brad; I'm in the middle of a long meeting with some clients I'm really sorry mate, this will have to be just a quick chat and a drink.'

Brad paused in his drinking, and then looked down his badly eroded nose at Dave, offering a scoffing reply.

'Always in a rush aren't you, especially when you owe me a bloody dinner and a good bottle of wine eh. These clients of yours, they don't happen to be the ones that these samples were drilled for?'

Casually kicking the cardboard box at his feet with his heavy geo boot, indicating his point.

Dave briefly hesitated, sending out a prime signal alerting Brad who was no fool. He needed to make his next lie a very convincing one, as such he then applied rule number one; stick as close to the truth as possible.

'No Brad, just a couple of anthropologists interested in chartering my aircraft to check-out some Aboriginal sacred sites in the Kimberley region.' Then in making light passing conversation.

'You don't by chance know of a Professor Thomas Harold or a Doctor Emma Archer... do you?'

'Nope can't rightly say that I do.'

'What about a Professor Benjamin Lock then?'

Brad found the question important enough to hesitate in sipping his already raised whisky glass.

'Come on Dave, everybody has heard of the American Professor Lock, except obviously you. This bloke, Professor Lock is one of the leading brilliant minds looking into the big bang theory. He has all but proved that we all started from a single cell that well... just kind of exploded creating our entire known universe.

Dave, surely you must have heard of the big bang theory you couldn't have been in the bush for that bloody long.'

Dave was both surprised and stunned by Doc Brad's knowledge of Professor Ben Lock. Maybe Brad was right; he had been in the bush for too long. Piss-pot or not Brad was smart a man, a man to watch carefully.

'Of course I've heard of the big bang theory, for crying out aloud I'm a bloody Geophysicist just like you mate. My current line of work is geology, being mainly involved with tectonics finding old subsurface petroleum and mineral deposits on earth, not where we originally started from fourteen billion years ago.'

'Tut-tut, I can still wind you up Dave my old mate, well you may have to consider studying for another degree namely meteoritics, and maybe another in metallurgy.'

Then Brad asked a leading question.

'What area were these strange drill samples taken from?'

Brad had said the word out-loud... "Strange." Now he had another problem to cover with a lie. Brad was playing his cards close to his chest; he had obviously discovered something in the drill samples, and wanted to know more facts before he revealed the strange analysis findings.

'Well Brad, if you really must know, I carried out that little drill-sample job for Telfer mines. I hope you found a trace of gold in the samples, as that's what the Telfer people were looking for.'

Brad eyed Dave over the rim of his fourth double scotch with a look of disbelief. Outwitting Doc Brad was proving harder than he had thought. This could only mean one thing. Brad had found something that was extremely odd and interesting in his analysis.

From this point on everything, that Dave said would only sound dodgy, helping to compound Brad's suspicion that he was for sure hiding something.

'Dave, why did you ask about Professor Lock? You may like to know, the old boy was also very much into the theory that our planet earth was assisted to our level of evolution and technical intelligence, by some form of extraterrestrial power, but not necessarily by beings, or aliens.

He theorises that we humans were most likely advanced through evolution with the help of some sort of universal extraterrestrial, omnipresent, and metaphysical power; something similar to light, or gravity, but smart. I have read a fair bit of his stuff, I can tell you it's pretty spooky reading but interesting, you should Google him. You do have the Internet up in the bush… yes. Or is this the topic of discussion with your new clients?'

Brad was fishing, and he was bloody good.

'No, no, not really, the bloke's name came up last night. He was a close friend of one of my clients, seemingly the old Professor has just carked it from lung cancer, heavy smoker you know. My American client is still very upset at his death.'

Dave watched the change in Brad's face… he had believed him, anyway it was almost the truth. Fortunately, the drill-site locations were safe from Brad by using a simple code. Now all he had to do was refill Doc Brads drink again, and then push him into handing over the analysis results.

Brad rattled the lonely ice cubes in his glass, a sign that he was ready for another, and then continued.

'These core samples are, to say the least, more than a little odd. As you would know Dave, they are marked into three set groups. "C1." being four drill cores, "R2." being six drill cores, and "O3." also being another six drill cores. All sampled at ten metre depths down to forty metres.

The "O3." samples have nothing of any scientific value, but the other two sets of core samples show a high concentration of minute metal particles. The very small particles also gain a higher concentration from the "C1." drill samples to the "R2." drill samples.

These samples would indicate to me a massive hypervelocity impact, causing a creator of some size. The result caused by a very large structured metal object like a rocket, a very big rocket of about 190,000 tons mass. So my guess would be that "C1" is the "Centre" of the impact and "R2" being the deformation rim, and "O3" would be Outer testing of the site for breccia's and ejecta.' Brad cocking one eye over his raised drink. 'How am I doing so far Dave, my old rock bashing mate?'

Dave's wobbly confidence, and assured world was rapidly falling apart. Drunk or sober he realised that he was no match for a cunning man such as Doc Brad. He must think fast if he was to try save his shaky story.

'Brad we only drill for samples where the client tells us to. They give us the coordinates and the programme, then we carry out the work, and then we supply the sample results and data. It sounds to me like we have drilled into a piece of space junk again; it happens all the time out there mate.'

The new drinks arrived and Brad smiled his knowing sly smile as he handed Dave a thick brown envelope containing the analysis results. Dave picked up the box of samples from Brad's feet murmuring his excuse that he must get back to his clients.

Dave then reached out and accepted the brown envelope while working on a quick getaway, followed by a quick handshake. Then as Dave turned to leave…

'You know something Dave. The so-called space debris you talk about would have to be around 10,400 year's old mate. Since that's what the soil carbon dating tests have dated the drill core samples. I didn't know we were in the space race way back then.'

Dave hoped that his surprise did not show. Something must have shown-up in the core analysis to cause Brad to do a carbon dating test. His only chance now was to keep walking out of the bar, pretending he had not heard that last comment. Then Brad's last raised words rang out over the short distance of seven paces…

'Dave, the metal particles we tested are comprised of a complex metal alloy, we can't find anything of a similar amalgam anywhere in this world. Some of the elements are not even on the periodic table, well least not ours.'

Dave froze and turned. His look back must have said it all. Brad raised his tumbler of scotch in a well-defined drinker's salute to Dave.

'Your secret will be safe with me old mate. Just remember me in the credits when you write-up your scientific publication and become famous. That the initial core analysis work was carried out by your old drunken mate Doc Brad.'

Dave nodded his head in agreement, turned and continued on his way back to Emma and Tom in the lounge bar. Dave paused as he approached their table, they were both sitting with their backs to him, and he clearly overheard Emma saying…

'Research, just what is your field of research… and your theories Tom? You already know what Dave and mine are.'

As Dave approached Tom was about to reply when he caught sight of Dave with the box of core samples under his arm.

'Ah-ha your just in time Dave, I believe as they say in this country that "it's you're shout mate." I was about to explain to Emma what my life's research work is about, although we will wait for you to get in the next round of drinks.'

Dave had a thought; he was sure he had just bought the last round of drinks, thinking this bloke would make a good Aussie. Then catching the waiter's eye, he placed a new drink order while stowing the box of core samples at his feet… stating.

'You now have the floor Professor Tom, I did hear Emma's question and I must admit the very same question was also on my ask list.'

Tom stroked his perfectly trimmed grey goatee beard as he looked at Emma and Dave pondering where to begin his story.

'My life's research is both unusual and complex. As you both know, I hold a doctorate in Evolutionary Anthropology, I also have a second doctorate in Anthropology of Religion. These two disciplines in most people's minds would be seen as at opposite ends. One in dealing with what remains to learn about the old world, and the other dealing with man's different spiritual beliefs to what may become our future world; however, I have found good use of both disciplines to further my research.

My life research is into proving that a link may exist within the evolution of the human race, and the emerging guidance and control of a powerful religious following. I have arrived at the conclusion that the binding of a large human population-base. A base, consisting of contradictory families and tribes, ultimately forged into a nation with differing beliefs, and customs. This I concluded had to be by way of some form of powerful personal belief... and most certainly, involving great fear.

A man will fight to the death for the protection of his family, water source, shelter, and food. Then if required, will be part of an army to fight for his tribal lands. At some time in our history came the introduction of a far more all-powerful force. An external known force, that people feared above other known fears... a God.

The people of that time were somehow, completely convinced by this mighty power, no doubt taught by a new form of powerful religious order or cult. Therefore, the question I ask is this; at what time in our human evolution and history did this powerful and all fearful religious view first start to exist?

Any new belief, being either religious, or superstition based; would need teaching from some form of education, concept, or personal experience. Then expanded on; just like all other forms of human social behaviour and development. However, the fact remains when did this belief start, and from what origin? This has been the basis of my research for many years.

My well-documented tracking research shows some interesting parallels to the major human evolutionary steps in man developing as a unity, and the capacity to bind and develop people as a nation and not just as a tribe.

At some time, actual proof must have existed of this great power or deity. Primitive man will only fear the unknown, if it is convincing, with a great fear of death or possible reward after death. When you think about it, little has changed on this mind-set to this present-day.

Professor Benjamin Lock knew of my research, arriving at a realistic independent theory. That being man's religion was not about a personal God as taught, but a possible external power that had existed well before the human race.

Ben had concluded there must be some sort of external intelligence, or energy. Possibly extraterrestrial, which was working independently to help us in achieving an orderly path through our evolution and development of the human race. In Ben's mind, a power yet to be discovered... or possibly rediscovered.'

Emma and Dave had not touched their drinks. Both were in deep thought about what Tom had been saying. They were going over in their minds about all the strange things that had happened to each of them in the recent months. Dave recalled what Tom had said only this morning; he recalled Tom's words. "Are we being manipulated, used by someone in some way?" Tom also said...

"Whoever put this puzzle together sure knows our weaknesses, and has us outsmarted us by giving each of us an equal part of this puzzle; don't you both see... we are all being forced to work together. This mystery may also have a plan; and if so, no doubt a reason... and possibly a mission."

Now he was about to tell them that their suspicions of an alien visit to this planet earth 10,400 years ago had all but been confirmed by Doc Brad's analysis results. Dave held up his hand holding the brown envelope of the core analysis results in a gesture that he must speak.

'My good friend Doctor Brad Farlow from CSIRO Waterford has completed his analysis on my Veevers crater drill-core samples. He has just provided irrefutable scientific evidence, that it was a large metal extraterrestrial object, which had caused the Veevers crater around 10,400 years ago.

I have not read all of his report details yet; however, in my detailed discussions with Doc Brad. Brad is in no doubt by these tests, the small two hundred and seventy-metre diameter Veevers crater depression and rim, clearly caused by a vertical hypervelocity impact of some 190,000 tons. He also reported the metal particles found in the drill-core samples were of a metal alloy containing rare earth elements, some of unknown origin on this planet.'

The silence was deafening, as they all looked at each other, stunned by the evidence. Eventually Emma spoke in her quaint Scottish accent.

'Well lads, the drill-core analysis were the last piece in the puzzle that links all of our personal research work together. All three of us now have some form of hard scientific evidence, this planet earth that we all live on, had been visited by wee green men around 10,400 years ago.'

Turning her head and looking directly at Tom and Dave.

'Well gentlemen, where do you suggest we go from here?'

Dave was thinking, Christ... Tony was bloody right about aliens and little green men visiting us from Mars. How the hell will he start to explain all of this? Then there was the problem with trying to convince Max about little green men. Yes, he thought, that would be another great challenge.

Tom took a sip from his drink, and with an uncomfortable smile suggested.

'My new friends, I think that we should all go and checkout this strange Veevers crater place... and soon.'

Chapter Fourteen

Who are you?

Dave smiled back at Emma and Tom; he had just learnt that this was their first visit to Australia. Both obviously knew how big the Australian land mass was. However, Tom was very surprised and unaware at just how remote, underdeveloped, and crude the outback desert area of Australia was.

Especially when compared to the American so-called remote deserts like Death Valley. Remote American deserts offering a place to buy a Burger King, KFC and a beer every twenty miles or so.

This view added to his new understanding of why the city of Perth Western Australia look upon as the world's most isolated city, also likely to remain so for some time.

The tiny, but quaint towns of civilisation, found scattered up around the north-west of Western Australia. Such as Karratha, Port Hedland, Broome, Derby, and Fitzroy Crossing. These mostly regarded by a first-time foreign visitor as the typical Australian storybook visions of a rough remote frontier town.

Older American visitors immediately fell in love with these towns. Reminding them of the honest old American west of their younger days, and many came back to retire in their past memories.

The vast Australian desert areas were not encouraged as tourist destinations. Without much in the way of information or any recognisable roads, few visitors ever ventured to go there. Dave was not sure what Emma expected, except that it would be very different to the busy University City of Oxford in England.

Dave explained to Emma and Tom the commuter jet flight-time from Perth to Port Hedland was two hours and twenty minutes, and the flight out to Sandfire in his light aircraft was another hour and ten minutes. From Sandfire, the flight across the desert to the Veevers crater was a little under two hours, with nowhere to land.

Noticing their odd look at hearing the long flight times. Dave pointed out that all of this flying would still be within the one vast State of Western Australia.

They would work out of his company base at the Sandfire airstrip. He then suggested that they should consider as a first move an inspection flight in his eight-seat Cessna 402 out to the Veevers crater. Then decide if a visit by the Jet-ranger helicopter was the next step.

The other option was to go direct to the Veevers site on a field trip, a long drive in his well-equipped Mercedes Unimog, a two-day trip each way. Dave noticed the gathering doubt on Emma's face and guessed the reason why, then adding.

'The accommodation at the Sandfire airstrip would be basic. However, air-conditioned and somewhat clean, or if they wished, they could both stay at the Sandfire roadhouse Motel, in dongas. Only two kilometres away, with shared bathroom facilities.'

Emma asked what she should expect at his "somewhat clean" Sandfire airstrip accommodation. Dave went on to explain that he had two large modern caravans and the Unimog all parked inside his high fenced off secure area set back a little from the side of the well-maintained gravel airstrip.

Dave pointed out to Emma, that "somewhat," was as close as he could get, to what two tidy blokes living in the same area on the edge of a desert would have called clean. Dave then went on and assured them both the two nice caravans, plus the two-bed Unimog were all connected direct to the domestic power generator, water, and deep sewerage. For entertainment they could watch from around the world a choice of some 450 channels of digital TV; an added advantage of Max's passionate satellite hacking hobby.

As for catering, Max the self-taught chef extraordinaire, will perform most of the fine cooking outside under the large outdoor alfresco area. This he assured them was a beautiful area, providing a nice tropical setting as you doze off into alcoholic slumber after tiring yourself out, wind milling your arms swatting the many annoying flies and mosquitoes. Then Dave went on to explain the possible sleeping arrangements.

'I thought that Emma should have my nice caravan all to herself. Tom, you can have the Unimog, and I will bunk-in with Max, he won't mind at all, as I have done this many times before with visiting guests. Well what do you clients think about all of that?'

Tom was quick to answer, with an added question.

'It all sounds like luxury to me Dave, anyhow I doubt there are any other options, I'm curious about one thing though; why would you need such a high fenced secure compound to live in. I thought Australia was a really safe place to live?'

'It is a safe place to live Tom, but Max my pilot is so pissed off with all the local animals pinching stuff out of his veggie garden. Then after the bastards have had their fill, they go scratch their backs on his satellite dish antennas, knocking them all out of alignment.'

Emma burst out laughing at the thought of this guy Max, running around chasing Kangaroos, Kolas and other wild animals out of his vegetable garden that were quietly eating his precious home-grown veggies. Tom and Dave joined in Emma's infectious laughter. The laughter dissolved into a wide smile, as Emma suggested that Dave should try arranging a booking for the flight up to this place called Port Hedland. In addition, what were the chances they could all fly out tomorrow morning?

'I will try to get us all on the 10:15am B737-200 commuter jet to Port Headland. We will need to leave this Hotel by 8:30; fortunately, the domestic airport is only about twenty minutes from here. If I can get us all on a flight I will get the reception to book us a taxi.'

Dave confirmed the flight booking to Port Hedland just ten minutes after he got back to his hotel room. He then advised Emma and Tom of the flight bookings and that he had phoned Max, who will meet them all at the airport in Port Hedland. Everything was now ready for the trip to Sandfire. They should all try getting a good night sleep, advising he would meet them at 8:30 tomorrow in the Hotel reception.

The morning started slowly, Dave was relieved to see that both Emma and Tom were travelling light. Both having only one small case on wheels, a carry a bag, and a laptop computer. The taxi arrived right on time; Dave picked-up his overnight grip in one hand and tucked the box of core samples under his arm as they all headed out to the taxi for the drive to the Perth domestic airport.

Tom had noticed that apart from a few pleasant exchanges of polite morning greetings, everyone was saying little. Then I guess after all, there was a heck of a lot to think about. Dave had suggested that they should all try to get a good night sleep; Tom had found that suggestion was near impossible. So many odd things had happened around him over the past few weeks... sleep was impossible.

Much as he tried, he could not align the three strange stories about the same place, objects, and the subject matter to a chance coincidence or even accept some form of obscure luck... this he concluded felt, and looked like a well-planned event.

One thing he knew for sure, this adventure was going to be one hell of an Anthropologist's dream. The current information was showing a strong suggestion to a connection between the existences of a superior intelligence at the early development stage of the human race. These early visitors may be the proof to his theory of a link to the first structured religion.

It was obvious that primitive man would regard and fear these superior aliens as a God. If you were an alien, what better way to keep the local feuding tribes in order, all while you got them to do most of the work around the place? Since first meeting Dave and Emma, he now had so many questions that needed urgent answers, and then it suddenly occurred to him. All three of them were seeking very different answers.

He for a start, was looking for some form of scientific proof, supporting his theory, the development of the human race had some sort of advanced assistance. Given a helping hand from a higher intelligence to leapfrog forward.

The records clearly show that human evolution and development only really started to get going around 10,000 years ago. Around the same time as the use, and introduction of a structured form of superstitious religion became evident.

Emma on the other hand was only interested in proving that her plotted world cluster rings had some ancient significance. Emma was hoping to discover some form of guidance system for meteorites and small asteroids previously carrying live basic bacteria to our planet earth. No doubt, she expects to find the remains of some control or operations system at the Veevers crater site, something that will further explain how this ancient so-called antenna system worked.

Dave, now Dave, was an obvious hard-core cynic, and most definitely not a believer in little green men or aliens. However, his solid rejection of the paranormal had taken a savage defeat by experiencing a number of facts. This man over the past few months being continually exposed to, and targeted with a number of strange paranormal phenomena.

First with his aircraft instruments, telling him lies, then he tracks and plots a weird energy source next to the Veevers crater. Then told all about these same weird things by an old Aboriginal, who tells him about a sacred bone a bone, which just happens to turn up in Australia. Brought to Australia by an American Anthropologist, a person who he has never heard of in his life.

Then as a final blow to his rapidly diminishing disbeliefs, and his ridged scientific theory on the nonexistence of visitors from outer space. The drill core samples from the Veevers crater prove to contain a metal in the analysis that could possibly be extraterrestrial.

Apparently, all Dave wanted out of this was to hopefully find a large commercial source of oil, gas, water, or iron ore in the desert.

The B737 wheels left the ground at exactly 10:15am; the flight would be on time. Dave considered this might be a suitable time for sort out a problem or two that was bothering him. Just how much, and what should they tell Max and Tony.

All Tony need know was Emma and Tom were just overseas clients using the Sandfire Air Charter services. Tony would then happily see this as a paying job, in addition, a possible means to pay off some of the money Dave owed to him. Max on the other hand would soon find out what was going on. Anyway, they would need his expert help with some of the required complex satellite images.

Dave found it hard to tell Max and Tony lies. He was sure that Max knew when he was telling lies, as they had been friends for too long. Even so, this problem needed an answer soon to decide which way they should handle this delicate problem.

Emma had the window seat and was fascinated by the vast expanse of nothing but desert. They were only cruising at 26,000 feet; she had expected to see roads, farms, and small towns dotted all around the countryside. It all looked so barren and desolate; she was thinking, surely nobody could ever live down there.

'Is all of Australia like this Dave? We are only about twenty minutes out of Perth and now there is nothing to see but red desert scrub, not a road, or a town to be seen.'

Dave offered some basic geology as an answer.

'The ground is mostly brown rock and sand, which can visually absorb many of the features at altitude and provide a blank landscape. Things look much more interesting on the ground. I can say this Emma, because of this type of featureless landscape; it makes flying search-and-rescue missions very difficult. Lost people stay lost for a long-time. However, you are right; there is not much in the way of infrastructure out there. Changing the subject a little, I have an urgent problem to discuss with you two and will need your advice.'

Tom was way ahead of Dave's thoughts and replied.

'You want to figure-out what we should all say about our project to your staff when we get to this Sandfire place.'

'Yes you have the problem all figured out Tom, it looks like I am extremely transparent, or you are very perceptive. Either way it proves me a poor bloody liar, which no doubt explains the reason why I would never chose a career in car sales, or as a lawyer or politician.

However, I suppose it does go a long way to explaining why I have been married three times. Anyway, this "what can we reveal" problem will need to be sorted out long before you both meet up with Max in an hour and a half's time.'

Emma suggested that Dave tell them what Max and Tony or anybody else already knows about this Veevers crater area. Her plan was simple enough, if each part of the puzzle remained separate and not discussed; well then, there was less reason to tell lies or to divert the truth.

The only common links, which were odd in themselves, was that as strangers they had all met-up with one another in the City of Perth Western Australia. As far as Emma was concerned, nobody knows anything about her meeting up with Tom and Dave, or their connected part in this mystery. Not even her chaos group knew that detail, as she had not yet contacted her group since arriving in Australia.

Tom pointed out the only person who knew anything of his part in this weird puzzle was his friend the late Professor Ben. Stating that Ben had also referred him to Professor John Laney in Perth shortly before he died, adding that Laney knows nothing of the bone relic. Ben had advised him to keep that matter from John Laney.

Tom then told them, just as Emma, he had not contacted anybody since arriving in Australia; only his son knew where he was. Tom did however have one major concern; that being he was yet to receive the DNA bone test results. Adding, he was also still waiting on the bone prostheses metal analysis.

Just as the drill core analysis had, he was now expecting the results might eventually raise some awkward questions and suspicions.

Dave was a little more concerned at Emma's suggestion, being more than a little vague. After all, Max was with him when he had plotted the strange energy phenomena close to the Veevers crater. Then again, he knew that Max would never believe in little green men from Mars.

At the time, Max had come to the same conclusion as Dave had, in that the strange occurrence being caused by something that could later be explained, something yet to be discovered.

Dave went on to tell Emma and Tom that he had not discuss with Max anything about the strange spiritual trance, or what Mirachung had said about a sacred bone that must be returned. The main concern right now was what were they going to tell Max about these latest developments.

Emma's inquisitive mind had formed a very girlish question, aimed directly at Doc Dave.

'Have you really been married three times?' Emma enquired with a quizzical look on her face that only females reserve for such uncomfortable questions. 'I mean are you a widower, or have you just been unlucky in love?' then noticing the painful look on Dave's face, 'Well you did bring the marital matter up Dave.'

Tom had a wide smile as he turned a keen ear to the question and waited patiently to hear Dave's answer.

'Well if you must know Emma. Normally I would not discuss such sensitive personal matters with an enquiring female; especially one that I had only just met in a bar yesterday. Although, in this instance I do feel that as we are now partners, and have all promised to tell the truth to one another. As such, I will disclose all my matrimonial disasters to you.'

Emma and Tom both turned in their seats ready to catch every word.

'In short, I have been married three times and divorced twice. My first two wives are very much alive and financially well off, living a bloody good life off my hard-earned assets. Mary, my third wife and I are legally separated; however, she has filed for a divorce, which is now all but ready for a settlement.

Her bloody shark lawyer who will get twenty per cent of my asset value is pushing her for the divorce to become final. When that happens, which now only requires her final signature I will end up with nothing. I will lose my Sandfire Air Charter Company and all of my accommodation and vehicle equipment. With all my assets gone, I will then be forced into taking a crappy boring regular job...most likely teaching in a University.'

Both Emma and Tom raised their eyebrows in shocked and unexpected horror, and then Emma said in her cute Scottish accent.

'Oh, so you would then be teaching as a lecturer in a University... just like Tom and I?'

Dave had not even heard Emma's smart mocking comment for he was deep in thoughts of better times about Mary; his Mary... a voice was gently breaking through his wishful and hopeful thoughts... It was Emma.

'Hang in there Dave, Tom and I think you are still very much in love with your Mary. You should fight like hell to win her back. We are as you say all partners now, so Tom and I will help you in any way we can... because that's what good partners do, we look after each other... right.'

'Thanks' for the offer Emma; however, I do know there is really nothing anyone can do now. Destiny is now taking its slow grinding course to a conclusion. I have been systematically stripped of all my hard earned assets and loves, now possibly my friends as I consider telling them a huge pack of lies.'

Tom had been quiet listening to all of Emma and Dave's banter as the jet sped on to Port Hedland. It sounded to him more like lovers foreplay, was Emma showing an interested in Dave? Hell he hoped not, Dave had just declared his endless love for his wife Mary. This could get extremely goddamn difficult.

Tom thought this could be time for some stable senior suggestions.

'Dave, might I make a suggestion; why don't you just stick with your number one rule, keep as close to the truth as possible. Just tell Max; that Emma and I, as Anthropologists, have chartered your services to have a look at some Aboriginal burial sites in the Great Sandy Desert. Well that's about as close to the plain truth.

Then maybe you should tell Max and the other guy that we are all flying out to see this Aboriginal leader, to ask his permission to look at some sacred sites. Now as I understand, you already have this elder chief's permission to check out the Veevers crater area for the return of the sacred bone. We can say we are going out to see him and then fly directly out to the Veevers crater, do our thing and fly back. Nobody will know the difference.'

'You're suggesting that we file a flight plan to go to Punmu Aboriginal community but fly direct to the Veevers crater site for our first look around.

'Yessiree, goddamn-it man, with a devious logic like that, you could make a real good American politician. Then after we have had a look at this place from the air, we should follow-up with a full ground sample programme in your Unimog to discover just what the hell is going on out there. What do you think of that plan Emma?'

'Well as we are pooling our resources, this sounds like the way to go, we've got to start somewhere lads and this is as good a start as any. Tell me though, how long do you think we can we hold back the truth about all this weird stuff...

Between the three of us, we have just about proved beyond all doubt that aliens occupied this planet 10,400 years ago and we even have a wee bit of them to prove it. Then we have my evidence of an antipodal gravity ring system that stopped working around the same time. This can't be just some form of coincidence boys; we need to check these things out.'

Dave needed further conformation on what they had all agreed to say to Max and Tony.

'So Tom, I gather by Emma's response, that we agree to say nothing to Max and Tony about all of this. We should wait until we have carried out our preliminary research programmes, and then decide on what action we will take, is that it? Anyway, I would assume that by then this story would be so big, nobody will be able to contain it.

I think it could well be the discovery of the century. We could all be noble prize winners. This is exciting stuff, a new beginning in providing positive answers to some of our world's oldest questions. I was looking for oil and gas and found evidence of the first extraterrestrial earth visit... I suppose that's not a bad start to fame and fortune.'

Suddenly the cabin speaker system crackled into life. A cheery voice announced they had begun their decent into Port Hedland and will be landing on time in ten minutes. The temperature on the ground was a pleasant forty-four degrees Celsius, with ninety-eight per cent humidity and the chance of a late heavy tropical thunderstorm. The over-pleasing airline hostess hoped that everyone had a nice enjoyable flight up from Perth, wishing them all a nice stay in Port Hedland.

As they descended the air-stairs onto the hot tarmac, Emma and Tom were shocked at the high air temperature and claustrophobic humidity. Their eyes were squinting in the harsh sun as they were slowly taking in their first sight of a remote Australian Town airport.

In the blistering heat they quickly walked, almost at a run across to the terminal. Tom suddenly stopped and stared up at the name, "Port Hedland International Airport" with a look of astonishment on his face.

'What the hell man, they have spelt the name Headland without the "a." Turning to Dave, Tom looked at him in confusion, 'surely somebody would have noticed that error before now?'

Dave was on the point of laughter, he had to explain this spelling anomaly many times to new visitors to this town.

'Australians don't care much for correct spelling Tom. On the other hand, in this particular case this town named after Captain Peter Hedland the man who first sailed his cutter the Mystery into the protected waters of this natural harbour in 1863.

I would guess that his mum and dad had a literacy problem or most likely, the government scribe who first registered his family as Australians could not spell too well. What would you expect, when even today, one of the leading Australian political parties spells their party's name as the Labor Party, without the bloody "u."

Tom obviously not moved by Dave's piece of Australian history, after all Americans spell labor and colour without a "u." Tom had concentrated his now heavy perspiring gaze on yet another bewildering observation.

'Well I'll be; is this really an "International" airport? I must declare Dave; I have never seen an International airport this small before. Which of the overseas airlines fly into this small town?'

'Well if you really must know the grim detail Tom, there are none. The airport originally designed as an international destination but apart from the odd charter jet from Asia, there are no regular international flights in or out of Port Hedland International Airport... at this time. Its main function is to provide an emergency alternate landing destination for the big jets flying to and from Asia.'

Emma had acquired the same odd look of uncertainly then Dave added.

'Just wait until you see the mighty Sandfire Great Sandy Desert airport, you will both be very much impressed... I hope.'

They all followed Dave over to the baggage carousel and claimed their luggage. Tom asked about Max, was he still going to fly them out to Sandfire, as nobody had come to meet them. Dave explained with a grin that they would find Max in his normal habitat, bracing the airport bar, and that was their next stop.

Dave was somewhat taken back in surprise as he caught sight of Max. He was wearing a clean blue pilot's shirt, complete with four-bar gold epilates on his shoulders. Dark-blue pilot pants and polished black shoes... Even his normally shaggy big black beard neatly trimmed into some sort of shape. His jaw had dropped open in amazement at this unusual display of grooming. Max slowly placed his double scotch back onto the bar and politely asked.

'Well aren't you going to introduce me to our clients Doc?'

'Max this is Doctor Emma Archer who has a PhD in Quantum Mechanics and another Doctorate in Mathematical Science.'

Max could not resist the temptation for an opening joke.

'Should I call you Double Doc, a sort of one up on Doc Dave here?'

Max put on a charming smile that Dave had never seen before; raising a small alarm bell that maybe, just maybe this big overweight oaf had way with the ladies. This was a worry; he must remember to keep an eye on Max... then he diverted his thoughts back to introducing Tom.

'And this is Thomas Harold, Professor of Evolutionary Anthropology and,' eyeballing Max for maximum attention, 'he also has a second PhD in Anthropology of Religion.' Then with a twinkle in his eye, knowing Max's love of good whisky. 'I do hope you're not going to suggest calling Tom Double Proof.'

Max was quick as lightening to respond to this fast wit.

'That my dear boss, well... that will obviously depend on whether the Professor Thomas Harold here has a liking for the finer things in life, such as a good single malt whisky.'

Max then raised his glass in a salute, with the knowing smile of a fellow scotch drinker, and then called the bartender across to take an order. The four of them burst into laughter at Max and Dave's exchange of humour. Tom and Emma insisted that they should all dispense with the titles, as they were both aware that in Australia first names, or "mate" and "bloke" commanded a much higher level of respect.

Over a nice lunch, Emma and Tom explained to Max their proposed field project. Max had no problems in understanding Tom's anthropological interest in Aboriginal sacred sites, but he was becoming more suspicious about Emma's role, with her more specialised field of expertise.

Max had noticed his cunningly planned knowledge traps systematically sprung every few minutes... It was becoming evident that Emma knew very little about anthropology. Doc Dave could see what Max was up-to. He was fishing for the real answer as to why these two were up here. Dave urgently needed to nip this line of Max's surgical enquiry in the bud right now. Well before this whole conversation became a large anthropological joke.

'Max, Emma and Tom had only recently met up in Perth. Both recommended by Professor John Laney UWA to stay at the Hyatt, Emma has a spare week in Western Australia before she flies on to Melbourne for business. Tom suggested that Emma should tag along with us and see the real Australian outback.

Anyway Max, consider the advantage, we have never had a Doctor of Quantum Mechanics at Sandfire. Just think how useful Emma could be with your weird satellite problems. Especially those you have been experiencing lately. You never know Max, another great mind might have an answer.'

That did it; Dave's strategy had worked a treat as Max instantly diverted from his nosey investigation.

For the time being Max had been provided with all the answers to his many suspicions. The conversation then took on a different track with Max latching quickly onto what Dave was suggesting in that Emma might have some answers to their strange experience out at Veevers crater.

Emma picked up her glass of red wine, took a small sip, and with her charming girly smile asked Max shyly...

'Do you usually drink half a dozen double scotch and ice before you go flying around the sky? Is this the normal Australian outback macho male pilot's thing?'

Max's eyes bulged as he nearly choked on his drink at Emma's observation and probing question. Max was still spluttering on his scotch, unable to speak when Dave came to the rescue.

'I will be pilot in command on the way back to Sandfire. We have strict rules about drinking and flying; we obey the "eight hour rule from bottle to throttle" plus the company adds a compulsory two hours for any local time difference, whichever way.' Holding up his drink. 'This is a tonic-water and ice, being my favourite none-alcoholic drink. My last alcoholic drink was at 10:30 last night, over fifteen hours ago.' Max butted in...

'Don't you worry now boss, I know that without doubt you will make up for that long drought when we get back to Sandfire; just hang in there mate. Although, I think we must get going bloody soon boss. We should plan to arrive at Sandfire before your alcohol withdrawal, and shakes kick in.'

The Cessna 402B Business liner is a beautiful sexy looking aircraft, and quite pleasant to fly, and fly in. The flight to Sandfire was tracking along the coast at a low 2000 feet taking in the magnificent view with the Indian Ocean on the left, and the red desert on the right.

At sixty-five per cent power with the cruising speed down to 165 knots, the cabin noise level is low allowing conversations at an easy normal voice level. Tom was in the co-pilot seat talking to Dave who was pointing out various landmarks, while Emma and Max chatted away in the thick leather seats in the back drinking a bottle of wine.

Max had just learnt that they all intended to fly out to the Punmu Aboriginal community at first light tomorrow in the Cessna 402. The plan being to seek the old Martu elder's permission to visit some of the Aboriginal sacred sites in the desert for archaeological research.

Tom asked Dave how far they were from Sandfire, as they had been flying for some time. Dave replied that he was pulling back the power for a long descent and landing, the airstrip was directly ahead.

'Hell, I must be blind; I can't see any airplane landing strip out there Dave... could you please point the strip out to me.'

The noise of the landing gear coming down set Emma looking out the window for Sandfire as she too had heard Tom's question. Dave pointed to the threshold of the landing strip and the windsock. However hard they searched, Emma and Tom could not make out the landing strip.

Max explained that this area was where the Great Sandy Desert met the sea. Everything on the ground was the same red desert sand colour, right down to the Indian Ocean. This continued all along the eighty-mile beach. This beach said to be the longest known, straight stretch of natural unspoilt fine-sand beach in the world.

The desert winds cover everything in a fine red sand dust, creating the perfect camouflage. Adding that they should not worry about such local problems with two expert, and experienced pilots on-board. This prompted an urgent question from Emma.

'Don't you lads ever worry about getting lost out in this remote place?'

Dave gave his all stations inbound call to Sandfire then a minute later the Cessna flared for the landing and a smile spread across Dave's face as the aircraft gently touched down. He knew what Max was about to say.

'We will never get lost out here, we have a secret flying trick learnt after many, many years flying in these remote places, one I'm not so sure I should tell you about.'

This only got Emma going, and frustrated at the thought that she must know this special Australian flying secret.

'You can trust me Max, what is this special flying trick err... mate?'

'Okay Emma just for you then and you must promise me not to divulge this secret information to anyone.'

'Thank you Max, I agree'

'All right then, listen carefully. When flying from the west along this beautiful coast as we were, just make-sure that you keep Australia on your right-hand side, and the sea to your left and that way you will never get lost.'

Laughter erupted in the small cabin with Emma asking in a spoilt little girl attitude.

'Don't you guy's ever take anything seriously, I was hoping to improve my bush survival skills with a bit of useful outback information.'

Dave shut down the engines after the required three-minute turbo idle cool down, and to let the large clouds of billowing red dust settle.

Emma and Tom stepped down from the aircraft with stunned looks on their faces. This was obviously a completely new experience for them both. For all they knew they could have been on another planet. Slowly they climbed into a searing hot to touch, basic mini moke vehicle, in the forty-four degree desert heat.

As they were about to head for the fort to escape the stuffy heat, and take part in a welcome-home drink, Tony arrived. He was wearing his usual sweaty old battered Akubra hat, dirty footy shorts, and blue wife-basher singlet, set-off with a pair of well-worn out rubber thongs, expertly held on by his dusty bare feet.

'I was expecting you blokes back in another couple of bleeding hours; I got caught-up watching the Aussies bash the shit out of the pommies in the cricket.' Then turning to Max, 'what's with all the fancy uniform gear Max, didn't recognise ya mate, I thought you was a copper or something.'

Max concealed his bent pride and did a quick introduction of their new clients and guests.

'Emma and Tom, this is Tony, the owner of Sandfire Aircraft Maintenance. Tony is the finest aircraft engineer in all of Sandfire and the surrounding area for over five hundred kilometres in every direction.' Waving wide his arms out across the desert to create an awesome effect.

With great pride, Tony reached out shaking hands with Emma and Tom smiling all around, when Max added the congenial atmosphere dampener.

'Mind you folks, I must advise you that Tony is after all the only aircraft engineer in these parts for over five hundred kilometres in every direction. So his aircraft fixing service is well above comparison to any other aircraft engineering competition around these parts.'

This small conceding fact did not reach Tony's happy mood. As he was thinking that these clients would bring in some badly needed cash income for both him and Doc Dave.

Max declared that he was the chef tonight and that Tony and his family would be most welcome to attend the magnificent feast.

Tony scratched his four-day old stubble on his chin and considered this rare offer. He knew that Max did not like his kids running around in his yard full of satellite gear, mind you, Max was a bloody good cook.

Emma and Tom were sitting in the searing hot Mini moke, all but melting in the savage heat as Tony lingered over his big invitation decision. Then he decided.

'Nah, I'll take a rain check on it this time Max, but thanks anyway old mate. Mavis has me favourite dinner on; Kangaroo stew, I can't miss that. Anyway I've still got to see the pommy bastards get done in the cricket.'

After the shock of meeting Tony, Emma and Tom were quite surprised at the excellent standard of their accommodation. They were amazed that two bachelor bush pilots could keep such clean-living quarters, and so cold, the air conditioning was above all expectations.

Tom was relaxed, thinking this is going to be a good few days in the bush. As a surprise, he would bring out one of his three bottles of fine single malt whisky to compliment Max's dinner. Dave and Max by his own observation were keen and appreciative whisky drinkers. As for Emma... well she was after all Scottish.

Tom was impressed, counting five large satellite dishes within the fort compound. This level of technology was well beyond Tom's understanding, thinking he might suggest Max should try cable TV as he had found it to be far better than satellite.

Max had excelled himself in providing a lavish meal washed down with a few bottles of quality red wine. As the coup, de grâce Tom brought out his bottle of single malt whisky; Max became a grinning idol of utter content.

Emma and Tom were impressed with the layout of the fort compound, including Max's veggie garden. They were however, more impressed with Max's satellite skills, and soon Emma and Tom were using a satellite direct Internet broadband up-link to send and receive their home emails.

Tom pulled out a small piece of paper with Professor Ben Locks email username and password, then entered it into the system. There were three new emails, including the one that Tom was waiting on from Molecular World DNA. The covering letter said it all.

Dear Professor Lock,
Please find the detailed file attachments to this email on the ancient bone fragment material you have supplied for analysis. The results are confusing in that the sample contains preserved DNA

mitochondrial markers from three distinctive Y chromosomal pedigrees. Percentages and time-periods are as follows:

Neanderthal: 20% 250,000 year, ancient first man.
Homo sapiens: 37% 80,000 year, known modern man.
Unknown: 43% 12,700 year, unknown modern genetics.

We suspect sample contamination however, the high throughput sequencing is in the correct order, pyro-sequencing is also correct. We are most interested in this sample find, could you please send another sample for further analysis.

I remain your most respected friend.

Professor Carl Vitter.

Tom made a copy of the email for Emma and Dave adding a small note: (I suspect the 43% unknown DNA is possibly the men from Mars?)

Dave checked his Company email box discovering that BHP wanted to charter the Jet-ranger from early tomorrow morning. They will be arriving at Sandfire by light aircraft at 6:30 am. With no immediate reply, they will assume this as an acceptance, considering their previous charter business.

Dave read this to mean that they were insisting on having the chopper available to them for a charter. Max read the email, and came to the same conclusion. They both agreed that this must be a very important job, Max deciding he would fly the chopper, then turning to Emma and Tom.

'Now you guys need not worry about this flying matter. I can assure you that Doc Dave here can find his way out to Punmu all on his own these days without me. Anyway, he can always call me on the aircraft radio if he gets lost.'

Dave gave Max a look of mocking contempt. Nevertheless, he was relieved that yet an urgent problem had been resolved. That being on how to convince Max not to join them on the Veevers trip tomorrow.

The morning was busy with Max first on the heli-pad pre-flighting the Jet-ranger. Meanwhile was Dave was in a deep argument with Tony about the dodgy borrowed turbocharger on the Cessna 402 port engine, being still a bit low on boost. Max handed Dave a copy of the ARFOR (area forecast) and synopsis.

Tony's concerned voice faded into the background as he read aloud the weather report, 'Intermittent thunderstorms QNH 1010 trend falling, wind 355/15-20-25, broken cloud CB @ 2000 ft. temp 36C expect SIGMET.' Dave noted that the bad weather front would arrive late in the afternoon, which was normal in the tropics. They would be back from Veevers and drinking a glass of wine long before this lot rolled in.

Tony waved his hand in front of Dave's face trying to regain Dave's attention, and then finally succeeded.

'The bloody thing needs to come off again mate. I reckon that the waste gate is just a bit sticky, most likely the hydraulic valve is holding the bloody thing partially open, I'll only need about two hours to fix it.'

Dave thought about this, a two-hour delay could have him still flying when that weather front arrived. He needed more info.

'Okay Tony, let us discuss the worst-case scenario. On that engine I could lose five, maybe eight per cent of take-off power on a high elevation airstrip and at high temperatures; and again, only if we were flying at high altitude. The Punmu airstrip is only 110 feet above sea level and a huge 3400 feet long. We will be flying low at 3000 feet, so high ambient temperatures are the only real problem.'

'Yep Doc that's about it mate, you got it in one. As long as you know what the bleeding power limits are, and know this mate; that's the second time I've told you about this problem so hear me. This bird is grounded when you get back until its bleeding fixed… right.'

Tony and Max gave us a cheery wave as the Cessna taxied to the end of the small gravel runway covering them both in clouds of red gravel dust.

Tom and Emma were sitting in the club seats backing onto the pilot and co-pilot seats. They had the two small tables extended to put their laptop computers and camera gear on. Twenty minutes into the flight, Tom scanned the ground with his binoculars and commented that there was not much to see on the ground. The desert went on for as far as the eye could see.

Emma noticed that the desert sparsely covered in small scrub trees. She had expected it to be all sand like the Sahara desert. Emma was also intrigued with the wave patterns of troughs and gullies on the ground. Dave went on to explain why.

'These markings were similar in all deserts, carved out by the prevailing north-easterly winds over thousands of years, The dunes are blown by the wind forming into long troughs close to a pattern from east to west. As long as you can see the ground in any desert, and know the prevailing winds you can tell which direction you are flying without a compass as the ground wind-troughs don't move much.'

The conversation gradually came around to "what do they expect to see when they arrived out at Veevers crater." They had already studied the large number of detailed satellite digital photos Dave had brought with him. Dave reminded them that his last visit to Veevers was by land, driving the Unimog towing the drill-rig.

On that trip, both Max and he could not find any unusual electronic, magnetic or gravity phenomena. On the other hand, prior to the Unimog trip, he and Max had flown out to the Veevers crater site, in this very aircraft. On that occasion, all the aircraft instruments and radio systems failed.

Forty minutes later, Emma asked how long before we reach the Veevers meteorite crater, just as Dave banked the aircraft into a low shallow turn.

'Look down, we're flying over the crater now, anyway we now know that it's not really a meteorite crater, but a crater made by some metal object, possibly a big rocket, maybe from space.'

Emma and Tom were busy taking even more high-resolution digital photos as Dave held the aircraft in a slow-flying tight-orbit at 500 feet above the crater... and then it happened...

First, all the gyro, and vacuum driven instruments toppled and failed. Then the magnetic compass swung a full ninety degrees to the east and continued moving slowly. The radio mute settings started popping in and out, and then all the radios went dead. Dave was strangely happy he could now at least prove something was going on out here, raising his voice to attract his client's attention,

'Look it's happening again. The compass has gone mad and the radios and navigation systems have gone haywire. You can see for yourselves that something down there is causing these effects on my instruments.'

Emma and Tom were looking over their seats in amazement at the aircraft instrument panel, all, or most of the electrical powered instruments were flicking around telling silly readouts. Dave applied some power to gain altitude for safety when suddenly, without warning the port engine failed.

Quick as a flash Dave slammed all the leavers to the firewall then feathered the port propeller, noticing that he had gained only about 100 feet to 600 feet in the short climb. The aircraft was then levelled off to maintain the critical airspeed and to help trim for the loss of an engine. Suddenly from a clear blue sky, they were engulfed in a thick dark cloudy mist. A quick glance at his watch showed the local time as 8:22 a.m. Dave could sense the urgent rising fear of his passengers.

'Everything is under control now folks, this bird can fly quite well on one engine, but it will be a slow trip back to Sandfire.'

Emma wanted to know why they were suddenly flying in a cloud, being so low to the ground, and asked if the instrument and electrical problems could be the cause of the sudden engine failure.

Dave was too busy in the front office to have a chat with Emma about this situation as he was rapidly becoming aware of how much rudder trim he was using to take the load off the rudder pedal.

A glance out of the window confirmed his suspicion, in the buffeting mist he noticed in horror the port propeller had come back out of feather; the extra drag was slowing the aircraft down. He was telling himself that is just impossible, at the same time placing the aircraft into a gentle bank towards the dead engine. This would help in reducing the amount of rudder load; also help a little with the rapidly declining airspeed and altitude.

Now he had another pressing challenge. The unfeathered propeller was causing so much drag that it was only a matter of time before they met-up with terra firma and right now, he could not see the bloody ground at all. While he still had some altitude, Dave decided he must make the call.

'Mayday, mayday, mayday, Charlie Whisky Golf is in the Veevers crater area experiencing engine trouble with three POB, preparing to ditch in the desert, I say again Mayday, mayday...' Dave went on repeating the distress message.

Emma and Tom heard Dave send out the mayday call and froze in fear. Dave was flying by the seat of his pants as most of the instruments were telling him lies. Only the airspeed and altitude being simple analogue instruments appeared to be telling the truth. In a firm voice, Dave called out.

'Clear all that stuff off the tables and stow it under your seats, put the tables back into the slots and strap yourselves in tight with your heads pressed hard against the headrests. Tell me when both of you have done that... I will shout brace before we err... touch-down, and for Christ's sake do not bloody panic. I promise you that I can get this aircraft down in one piece... Trust me I know I can.'

Dave had noticed that the red transmit lights on all three of his radios were still showing a steady green during his mayday call, indicating that his distress call had never gone out.

The aircraft was in a stable configuration, flying a large controlled circular orbit on one engine that was now running flat out. There was no way he could get the port propeller to feather, the prop was not even wind milling. From the stationary propeller he assumed the turbocharger must have broken up, and the parts gone through the engine causing the engine to seize-up. Dave thought he should concentrate all his efforts, and what little time he had left, into getting this aircraft on the ground in one-piece.

With the starboard engine running flat out, the mechanical oil-pressure and EGT temperature gauges were gradually moving into the red zone; being analogue instruments could they be trusted? The oil and cylinder head temperature indicators were electric and were already hard into the red but were they telling the truth? Well soon it would not matter.

Dave was surprised at how quiet the aircraft was with only one engine running, yet flat out, and clearly heard Tom's confidence building comment.

'What the hell Dave, we came to Australia for some adventure. Just think of all the stories Emma and I will have to tell our friends when we get back home. Don't you sweat none man, just do your damn best. For an added incentive, I have two more bottles of that good single malt whisky back at your Sandfire camp that we will still need to drink.'

A smile spread across Dave's face at the thought, but for now, his full attention was to this urgent matter at hand... what choices do we have.

The altimeter and the airspeed instruments were both analogue needing no electric power so might be trusted, then again so is the magnetic compass and that had gone weird. All the other instruments worked with electric driven gyros of some sort, which were now useless.

The only form of instrument help was from the turn-and-bank, altitude, and the airspeed indicators. Flying blind at a reducing 600 feet AGL (above ground level) of altitude. Using just these three instruments would try all of Doc Dave's flying skills to the limit.

From his gentle bank to the left, Dave calculated by the turn-and-bank needle that he was about quarter a doghouse, in an eight-minute rated turn. The time was now 8:27 so he was about halfway through a complete 360-degree orbit and would soon be back to where they had started from when all this mess began.

Any attempt to fly straight caused a rapid loss of altitude, and any attempt to reduce the size of the orbit just reduced the airspeed and increased his stress level. One positive thing was as long as they preserved this shallow, gentle orbit. They would be losing altitude at about fifty foot per minute, so they had about four minutes to impact... That is if the altimeter was telling the truth. With a bit of luck they would clear this fog within that time and find a suitable emergency landing site.

The 360-degree flight orbit was almost complete when the starboard engine suddenly quit, causing the aircraft to fall into an eerie silence. Dave immediately feathered the wind-milling prop and straightened up the flight path, putting the aircraft into the best glide configuration at only 150 feet.

His mind raced as he was trying to work out the best glide angle for this aircraft with only one propeller feathered. The altimeter slipped past 100 feet still in thick fog, the tense moments passed in a bucket of sweat. At 50 feet, the fog suddenly cleared to reveal that they were about to crash-land across the deep desert sand troughs and gullies, this would be the worst possible choice.

Minor panic set in as Dave instinctively flared the aircraft for a landing by bringing the nose up at the same time to wash off speed and to set the aircraft for a belly landing. Dave then tried one last trick.

He instinctively booted in full hard left rudder to skid the aircraft into line with a trough, while holding the wingtip up to stop it hitting the ground first. Impossible... the bloody rudder pedals were jammed straight-ahead. Angry thoughts were running through Dave's head, maybe one of Tony's shiny chrome spanners had been accidentally left in the hull after a service, and was now firmly jammed under the rudder bell-crank. The ground was coming up fast.

Dave yelled out '**Brace**.'

The total silence was both creepy and weird, and so was the darkness. It was more than dark, it was black, pitch-black, and Emma was scared. Emma remembered the plane crash in every detail except for the actual impact.

She did not feel any pain at all, and she could move her arms and legs so concluded that she was not hurt or trapped in any way. Was she in a hospital... or in a coma? Then she realised that she was standing, yes she was standing up somewhere in the dark. Panic was setting in as her heartbeat increased rapidly at the strangeness of it all.

'Hello is there anybody there, can anybody hear me? It's so dark in here, can somebody please turn on a light.'

Nothing, there was nothing to be heard but deep silence and the pounding of her own heart. Suddenly she saw a faint glow, and turned around noticing the glow had completely encircled her. Someone must have heard her and switched on a light, a ring of floor lights that was gradually getting brighter.

'Is that you Emma, I can hear you Emma, it's Tom where are you?'

Emma gave out a sigh of relief. 'Walk towards my voice Tom, I am standing in some sort of ring of light, can you see me?'

Tom called out again.

'It's so dark in here that I wasn't game to go anywhere in case I fell over or something worse. Keep talking Emma I'm heading your way, are you all right?'

'I think so, it's still so dark I can't see very well, where's Dave, have you seen Dave?'

Suddenly Dave replied from somewhere nearby.

'Now that's a silly thing to say Emma, it's so bloody dark in here that we can't see each other. As Tom says keep talking Emma, I will head over your way, if I don't bump into something first.'

The relief in Emma's voice was obvious,

'Dave we are all alive, what happened, are you okay, where are we?'

Before Dave could answer, both Dave and Tom stepped into the dimly lit circle as if walking through a wall. They all stared at one another in the dim light, each with an equally confused look on their faces. Emma asked the obvious question.

'How did we get out of the aircraft without a scratch and end up here? I don't remember getting out of the aircraft do any of you. Maybe we are all unconscious, or worse... maybe we are all dead and this is some sort of path to the other world.'

Dave had taken on a bewildered look, and for the first time in his life could not offer any words of explanation or help. Then he mumbled,

'Where the hell are we, and where is my aircraft? We should all still be strapped into the bloody aircraft.'

On the other hand, Tom was very composed and offered a simple and practical bit of information.

'Well I don't think we are dead because I feel a bit thirsty and I guess you don't feel thirsty when you're dead. Another thing, this light is getting brighter, although I still can't see the floor. What the heck are we all standing on?'

They were still looking at one another when a soft but emotionless, very clear voice answered Tom's frightening question.

'Professor Thomas Harold there is no floor, or for that matter any walls. You are all in transit, arranged so we can have this conversation. Be assured your biological forms are intact and functioning well. In simple words you're biological life cycle has not been terminated... well not as yet.'

Fear gripped them all, as that sounded like a threat. The voice had come from no particular direction but all around. They stood in stunned silence listening to this soft emotionless voice, and then they all chorused aloud together.

'Who are you?'

Chapter Fifteen

We are not a God

The voice did not answer immediately, taking its time as if thinking of a suitable reply. Then after a short pause, softly continued in the same flat drone.

'We are the keepers of all time and order, and the developers of universal intelligence... that is all we do, that is all we have ever done.'

Dave was annoyed at this passive, measured voice, shouting out...
'Where the hell are we, and what happened to my bloody aircraft. We crash-landed and should still be in the aircraft, why are we here?'
The strange voice was not intimidated by Dave's uproar, continuing in a clear unhurried flat voice...

'So many questions Doctor Sharp, and in your mind they urgently need answers, but first we detect that all your amygdala's are in a high state of stress, with a fast heart rate and perspiration. Your brains are therefore in fight or flight mode, this is the human reactive condition called fear. We must first address this fear before we can proceed.
Please understand, everything has a purpose, a life cycle, and a time to complete the given life cycle. Be aware, you are all in this location for a purpose; not to cause you any harm. Then again, we do

not have any short-term control over instant decisions that may result in harm to a biological life form. Any harm you may experience from now, will be from the result of your own actions... or lack of action.'

Emma was terrified at this strange occurrence, and now this threat.

'Are you the cause of the strange phenomena that forced our aircraft to crash? If so then you do wish us harm, we... we may be already dead.'

'Doctor Archer, all we have done is to aid in the situation to bring you all to this place. This includes your discovery of gravity waves on this planet, Professor Harold's ancient bone, and finally Doctor Sharp's local indigenous friend, with his words of insight.

In addition, to the many other situations needed to guide our task to this planned location and conclusion. You must all reduce your fear; we mean you no direct harm. As previously advised, any harm you may experience, as always, will be as a result of your individual choice and or physical action.'

'You say "we," are there more of you, why not show yourselves, and tell us where we are. That might help to alleviate some of our fears?'

'The questions that you have asked Doctor Sharp, if answered now, would only create a further and higher level of fear. We are many and yet we are all of one. We represent no one and we are not a force. Our mission is to see time, events, and cycles completed in a correct and orderly way.

We are not a biological form as you are. We are an omnipresent form of intelligence, residing within the vastness of this universe that use the four natural universal forces. We cannot be seen with the human photon reactive eye however, we can create an image in your mind that represents a human form, if that may assist with reducing your fear... we shall sample this method.'

Just as the voice stopped talking, an old man suddenly appeared as he walked into the circle of light. They all gasped at immediately recognising the old man; it was no other than... Albert Einstein. Emma gasped aloud in fear.

'This is impossible for us to understand. Sir, are you Albert Einstein?'

'No Doctor Archer I am not that human person. I am but a familiar image created in your mind to assist in reducing your level of fear. We note that we have now created the opposite, should I go?'

The image of Einstein did not move his lips, and the voice sounded all around them as before, however, it was without doubt Einstein's voice. Although perfect in every other way, the image showed little if any human expression. Emma realised they were all being cunningly diverted from asking urgent questions, a ploy of some sort in an attempt to reduce their fear, she quickly responded.

'Mister Einstein please don't go, we need your help... Are you aware that your lips do not move when you talk, and to us you sound like you are talking through a public address system? Is this image of you just some high-quality hologram?'

As requested, the image immediately resolved some reality problems and replied.

'Please try to tolerate us Doctor Archer, we do have to travel along a small correction curve. Consider this, we are providing this image of a trusted person known to you all, as a means to enter into a most important conversation with you three humans. The voice, mannerism, and thinking-style will be that of Albert Einstein, however, the image will always be represented by us.'

Einstein's eyes tried to follow each person talking, his lips now moved with his words and the sound now appeared to come direct from Albert Einstein. The three of them had relaxed a little, now that they were talking to somebody who they could now see, and could respond to them.

Tom was thinking... this thing was trying hard to avoid frightening them even offering a mild apology. On the other hand, it was also having a problem understanding the level of terror it had created... Tom had a few urgent questions, feeling compelled to say something, but thinking. If Albert Einstein was just some sort of smart hologram, then what are we? Einstein turned his head towards Tom distracting his line of reasoning, but did not look directly at his face... Einstein then replied directly to his inner thoughts.

'You are correct Professor Harold; we do appear as you have thought. To you, we display as "just a smart hologram," but a hologram that serves a useful purpose. You have all displayed a level of doubt, therefore to have doubt; you must agree that you all still exist. As such, you should accept as fact that you are still living, functioning, human beings.'

Tom was stunned at this quick response, but more so to another odd matter.

'I never spoke a word yet you replied to my unsaid question, are you reading my mind, and further to the point... do you actually exist?'

'Reading minds, well, not quite in the way you assume. You need to understand there are two distinct and separate thought processes that function in the human mind. We can only see one.

Humans also have two separate retaining memories, short and long, and are in quintessence two beings as one. One being is always questioning the other part within, seeking assurance that the decision taken has become the correct answer. This internal conflict is in a continuous state within the human mind. Resulting in many of your decisions... ending with a wrong choice.

When humans think or plan in their minds, we can read these thoughts. However, the other part, the human instinctive, impulsive, and instant decision mind... we cannot read. If we could, we would then have full control over all and every biological life forms decision. This would be against all natural evolutionary selection. Including any future universal development, defeating our very purpose and existence in this universe...

Be aware that instinctive memory is yet another matter, being the evolutional instinct of survival mapped within the DNA of your species.

You are at this time, in my time, and my place. None of us are modulating sound waves. Professor Harold, do try to understand this. All our communication and visual stimulation is taking place at beta level within your mind.

You can if you wish, stop moving your lips and we will still communicate. There is no atmosphere where we reside to carry sound waves. We have no mass; we exist as an omnipresent faster than light particle with intelligence. For want of a better name, description, or word... to you we are an Entity. An Entity with a universal unity of both one... and many.'

Tom was confused and not convinced that any of this was real. This thing, this Entity, apparently well read, touching on the great philosopher Rene Descartes views on doubt "I think, therefore I am." Einstein spoke again.

'You are all considered as educated beings on this planet with a greater knowledge... well-read scientists. Consider the meaning and power of having absolute logic with just pure omnipresent metaphysical intelligence. Being an Entity without mass, with a powerful yet set purpose to preserve an absolute balance, and to maintain a universal order of events.

We are not a force. We are not a deity or a God. We are the Natural Universe, an Entity throughout the universe.

You are three humans chosen to complete an important mission, as we cannot make a short time-period change. Only biological beings with mas; biological beings with intelligence can change an outcome in a short time-event. We have decided to assist you to resolve a situation, thereby maintaining for a period... your human future.'

Dave was later to discover that he had completely misunderstood that last comment. Assuming it to be about this present situation, he was rapidly moving out of fear mode into aggressive mode, wanting some answers and fast.

'If you know we are frightened, and you say we are just "holograms," and now it appears you can also read our minds. Then you must understand that we need to know what happened with the aircraft crash. This is the most important bloody question bothering us... at this time. We need to know if we survived the forced landing. We need proof that we are still alive and this is not just some weird dream.'

Einstein removed his pipe from his mouth and gave Dave a long look in his general direction. All while giving a passable actor's impression of deciding on what he should say next.

'We will take you to the aircraft to resolve your fear that you may not be functioning as a biological life form. However, before we do, you must understand that we have a mission for you all.

This mission will require you all to be fully functioning, live human beings. The end cycle of your biological life forms will be determined at this point in time by you alone... not the Entity.'

All noted that this was the third time this Entity had used a life threat. Einstein pointed his pipe to his side of the ring of light, which opened up to reveal the Cessna 402. The nose crumpled almost to the firewall and both wings had been smashed off at the engine nacelles.

Surprisingly the main cabin, tail-section and vertical stabiliser were all in remarkably good condition. Everybody moved to look into the windows to see Emma and Tom sitting in their seats, without any injury, looking for all anyone could tell... asleep.

Dave was sitting back in the pilot's seat with a trickle of blood on his forehead, obviously caused by a blow from hitting his head on the instrument panel. However, all three of them noticed that their own bodies were gently breathing and alive.

Dave moved to open the pilot escape-hatch door and found that his hand just passed through the metal handle like a ghost. It made him jump with fright and his heart started pounding with fear. At the same time noticing that his body in the pilot's seat had moved and his breathing also faster, then he heard Einstein speak.

'Doctor Sharp, please remember that we are all only an image in your mind, being not quite the same as a hologram. You must understand that you are the physical human, sitting in the pilot's seat with the small wound to your head.

All your normal biological and conscious functions are at this time resting, switched off. As you can see by your body and fear reaction; your mind is still switched on, you are in what humans call a deep coma.'

Dave glanced at his watch then turned to face a terrified Emma and Tom, still staring at their bodies seated in the aircraft. Then announced casually...

'Well according to my holographic watch it's been just over two hours since we crashed. The ELB (emergency locater beacon) built into the aircraft tail fin would have been transmitting our SOS and GPS location up to the survival satellite. Help can only be a few hours away,' then turning to Einstein.

'It's daylight, why can't we see the sky from here?'

232

Einstein had his thumbs jammed into his waistcoat pockets in a typical Einstein pose, then firmly gripping the bowl of his pipe he casually replied.

'Much care and planning went into bringing you're machine to rest at this very place, all while reducing any possibility of ending a life cycle. You as humans will not detect any light photons in this place. Your flying machine being carefully directed, having buried its-self deep into the side of a wind-blown fine-sand waddi.

No part of your flying machine is showing to the light above. Be aware that the magnetic wave source that you talk of is disabled, in much the same way as all the other magnetic wave and gravity instruments on your flying machine.

We are aware that humans need a balanced environment in which to survive and that your biological forms will deteriorate rapidly if they are not nourished. We note that Professor Harold will need fluids soon, as such will be first to complete his life cycle. Follow me back into the circle of light where we can talk and discuss this situation in further detail.'

They all followed Einstein through a dim wall of light into a softly lit room. The office furnished, with a central large oak engraved desk. In front of which were six well-padded leather armchairs, surrounding an old period, low table, with an ivory chess set in the centre.

Einstein motioned them all to sit down; Dave was hesitant that he may fall through the chair to the carpeted floor, and then noticed that Einstein had managed the task without incident.

Tom looked around the office and noted the familiarity from the old photos that Professor Ben had shown him of his brainstorming days in Albert Einstein's study. This was that study in every detail right down to the floor-to-ceiling bookshelves that covered the walls, and the blackboard directly behind the desk displaying many equations and diagrams. Now Tom was starting to get a little angry at Einstein's casual manner.

'Am I to understand you correctly Sir, that you have created a trap to bring us all here, and now you have us, we will all die... me being the first through dehydration?'

'Doctor Emma Archer has already explained to you, this very place has significance in being what her people call "the prime gravity

ring site," now known as "the 9th place." This gravity site is a location that we, the Entity can easily focus energy. Yet remote enough to have this conversation without interruption. Yes, you are indeed captive, and yes, we do understand that this is frightening to you all.

Might we add, your concern at the ending your life cycle is well founded; however, also for many other life cycles. This life matter will eventually depend on what we can all agree on, about your involvement for the successful completion of the required mission.'

Einstein replaced his pipe in his mouth and sat back in his chair staring at nothing while waiting for some form of response. He had a relaxed composure that was no doubt supposed to convey and suggest confidence. However, this was by far the reverse as they were now all terrified at that last calmly delivered, emotionless, yet life-threatening statement.

Emma was becoming a little hysterical. Tom noticing her distress while trying his best to comfort her. Emma kept repeating we are all dreaming this; this cannot be true, we are all scientists, we can only accept proven logic, and confirmed facts.

Dave was about to speak when Tom interrupted him.

'Sorry Dave, but I have some urgent questions to ask since I will be the first to, as this image says, to "end my life cycle." Then turning to address Einstein directly.

'You say that you are an "Entity" but you have not explained what type of Entity. Are you a power or something that we should all recognised, or are you alien to this planet, and just what is this "mission" that you want us to carry out?'

Einstein turned to look Tom in the eyes, but missed the targeted effect. His gaze was looking past Tom; in much the same way as a blind person would when turning towards a spoken voice. Then the flat toned voice spoke like a scolding teacher to a young student.

'Were you not retaining the knowledge when your friend and mentor Professor Benjamin Lock was explaining his theory on a possible intelligent omnipresent power? One that was also metaphysical without form or made of matter.

The Professor concluded that such a power or Entity would need to travel throughout the universe at speeds faster than the speed of light. At that same meeting, you used the simple description, "a massive intergalactic broadband Internet," and a "universal wide web."

You were close in your interpretation of Professor Ben Lock's theory, and as to how the universe communicates. However, this function is only a means to preserve this universe in a state of balance and order. The development and distribution of all biological life is through the expansion process of evolutionary and natural selection. Nonetheless, the development of all intelligence throughout the universe is as equally important... this is the Entities mission.

No, we are not alien to this or any other planet as we were here long before you... and your solar system. To understand your earth mission, you must first understand ours, and this will take you a little earth time.'

Emma blurted out a torrent of frightened words...

'Are you proclaiming to be God? Is this a spiritual revelation that will prove to us that a God really exists? That you have appeared in the image of man in some attempt to convert us to your belief for carrying out your bidding?'

'Doctor Archer, we will say again we are not a God, we have never sought a religious following as it has no purpose in our function. We do not create... we are only the planners. You, the biological beings are the creators in this universe. Creators through time, evolution, intelligence, and knowledge.

We plan numerous events in parallel time cycles that will lead to natural selection. All Gods and religion were the creation of humans; however, over time have performed a useful function in uniting differing nations, and people of many cultures under one belief and power. These religious beliefs created by humans, and used in the act of unity and power. For good and evil, exploitation, control, and fear.

Unity is a power unto its self, and necessary for the path of evolution to reach a greater and higher intelligence. We are a unity of one. As a universal Entity, we have no direct control over any biological life form created through natural selection. However, we can help them with gaining further useful intelligence. We can with time influence human events, and with time change the evolutionary cycles on your world. Material evolution can be planned, however... Natural selection has no master.

Everything has a purpose, everything has a reason, everything has a beginning, and everything has an ending. As many cycles

235

complete their given purpose, so other cycles begin. The life cycle of a biological form: the life cycle of a planet: the life cycle of a solar system, including the life of a galaxy. Then finally, the life cycle of the universe: being everything within, including an Entity such as us.

We exist within all cycles of many cycles to preserve balance and order in this exacting dimension, with a balance of order to the next. Cause and effect are always related. Matter is never lost, only reformed, and reused at another point in time.

As for the biological form that you see, we remind you the image we project of a man is only in your mind. Again, this example is a visual aid to help reduce your fear of us. This is now proving correct, being less stressful for a human than speaking to nothing.

Humans are not capable of processing and multiplexing a hundred-billion neuron clustered brain cell demands without terminal damage. This linear image contact has proved successful in the past. As such we will provide yet another image that you will recognise and hopefully accept.'

Just then, there was a light knock on the door of Einstein's study. All eyes looked towards the door, which opened... in shuffled a very old and serious looking Charles Darwin. Einstein turned to the door, but it was obvious to the three of them that he looking at the bookshelf to the side.

'Ah Darwin, please do come and join us. You will be of great help in providing some of the answers to the many questions being placed by our captive human friends.'

Darwin slowly walked over to the group with the aid of a walking stick and sat down in a leather armchair leaving one remaining chair vacant, nodding his head in introduction. Just like Einstein, Darwin was an exact image from what Emma, Tom and Dave could remember from the photographs they had all seen in their years studying in school and university.

This was an old Charles Darwin with his long white beard, which would put his age well into his seventies, shortly before his death in 1882. Darwin tried to reflect a passing smile as he spoke for the first time in his soft monotone, educated English accent.

'Please lady and gentlemen do accept my apologies for attending this meeting rather late. At my advanced age, I do not move as quickly as I once did. Let me explain that Einstein and I are in fact one-and the same. We are an Entity of one that is representing two well-respected human images. Images we hope that you can all relate to without escalating your fear.

Might I suggest that for the duration of our meeting that we dispense with our academic titles in a further attempt to reduce stress, and to add a level of cordial friendship? We, as an Entity do not have a name; as such, we will therefore address you by your given name, and you shall address us as Einstein and Darwin.'

Emma looked at Tom and Dave. Both had a look of total disbelief and their mouths were hanging open. Emma, like Tom and Dave had sensed the Entity was having a few problems in pretending to be human. The hologram images of Einstein and Darwin did not show emotion at any level nor could they focus on an object.

The mannerism reminded Emma very much of Tim the prodigious savant back in Oxford University, void of any emotional display and failing to make eye contact with a person.

However, the Entity was correct, as she did feel much more relaxed sitting in this nice, if old-fashioned study, talking to two famous and world-respected characters. Then a thought popped into her mind, this is a form of seduction, cunningly manipulated by this Entity... but why? She should ask again the obvious question.

'Einstein, are we now qualified enough for you to answer our questions. Why have you brought us here, for what reason, and what is this mission you want us for?'

'Emma, all three questions in logic, are related to one and the very same, asked in three different ways. We plan to secure your willing and cooperative service, to resolve a future developing problem for both you humans, and the Entity. Be advised, we function with pure logic having observed that confusion lays the foundation for mistakes. We cannot, and do not make mistakes; however, you humans can and do.

We accept on this occasion that this confused form of logic is associated with human reasoning and the human gender; and no doubt, why the females of your species think and process matters of logic differently from the males. We as an Entity have no gender.

237

You would all do well to accept the fact that we are a superior intelligence. That your exact existence, at this very time, on this very planet, is due to our past planning decisions. We have decided from this time on, your planets future and existence will now depend on your decisions.'

Intended or not, the carefully worded snub remark at feminist logic were beyond all fear, causing Tom and Dave to burst out laughing at the Entities observation of the human female's difference in logical thinking.

Emma was not amused at this demonstration of the Entities chauvinistic observations. Emma had decided that with that remark, the Entity was most likely a male.

The Entity representing Einstein and Darwin turned to face Tom and Dave with a deadpan look of total zero response, while watching them convulse into fits of laughter. The act of laughing was new to them and watching them try the role only made them all laugh harder with Emma eventually joining in. Einstein clamped up his poor and failed attempt at laughing by reporting in his monotone voice.

'This laughing motion is proving useful by reducing your stress levels; we can now advance a little further in this matter.

Darwin, would you be so kind as to convey the urgent situation that this planet earth faces, and the required mission details to the humans for their timely response.'

Dave looked at his watch it was 2:20pm, about six hours since they had crash-landed in the desert. The standard aviation flight-plan procedure would now be in force. Had everything gone okay today, Dave would have simply radioed in a false flight position report, or cancelled his SAR (search and rescue) saying that he had landed at Punmu. None of these normal and mandatory flying requirements carried out before the forced landing.

The area SOC, (senior officer in charge) at Port Hedland by now would have advised that an aircraft in his patch of the Australian sky had not reported a mandatory position fix, or cancelled their SAR. .

In addition, by now they would have calculated the maximum on-board fuel load to be exhausted. As such, a phase two search-and-rescue alert now activated. All local and overflying aircraft in the region now advised to keep a radio and visual look out for the missing aircraft.

One of the first people to hear about the phase alert and the missed position report was Max. Max above all others; knew that Dave would never expose his aircraft, or passengers to any risk. If there were any secret or funny position-reporting stuff in his flying day, Dave would normally have this well covered. Doc Dave would never let a phase alert take place unless a genuine and serious problem really existed.

Max immediately contacted the president of the Port Hedland flying club and started to organise aircraft for an air search and rescue mission.

Seven aircraft of various types arrived at Sandfire within the next two hours. A satellite phone call to Punmu confirmed that the Cessna 402 had not landed or been seen in the area. It was now 3:10 pm, leaving only some three hours of daylight left to work with, and the weather was not looking good. This was now a phase one alert, a full-on aviation search and rescue.

Dave Emma and Tom sat quietly waiting with apprehensive concern for Charles Darwin to explain why they were here, and held captive. They also expected to learn what level of risk there might be to their immediate health and well-being. The seconds ticked by with Darwin and Einstein looking in different directions, and then Darwin spoke, surprising Dave by revealing what he had been thinking.

'You are correct Dave, the search for your aircraft is already under way, and you will eventually be found within a small period of your earth time. Be assured, at this time, there will be nothing to see from the air by the searching flying machines. Your flying machine is well out of sight, having buried its self deeply into the side of a large waddi of soft sand.

To carry out your task we need you to be functioning human beings. As for your mortal existence and future life cycle use, that will depend entirely on your timely response to our offer. This will provide us with some purpose to prolong your existence as a functioning life form, and ultimately the early discovery of your flying machine.'

239

Tom thought yet another threat, then noticed both Einstein and Darwin turn in his general direction... they had read his thoughts. He would now try some basic logic with this logical Entity.

'I am having a problem understanding the motive behind the way you and Einstein, as representing this Entity have gone about things. That last statement was yet another obvious and direct threat to our future survival.

Why in God's name would you want to set-up this elaborate trap to bring us all here, and then hold us captive as ransom to perform some mission? We seemingly must do your bidding, or simply be discarded, to die in the desert. Have you no conscience or regret for your evil and callous actions.'

The vacant look on Darwin's face gave nothing away. There was not a hint of anger or concern, as he launched into a monotone voice of flat expressionless response in his very English accent.

'Many events in this small solar system and galaxy have a far greater priority than to end a few hundred billion biological life cycles on this small life planet.

I assume that you have read my work The Origin of the Species. Life cycles of many species complete their useful planned life span in their billions with every revolution of your planet.

They exist and develop only through evolutionary planning and natural selection, all are important and all have a purpose. Death is a human word; we only see the beginning and the end of a life cycle, being an inevitable change of state over time.

Regret and morality, they are simply human psychological states of your conflicting dual minds. The Entity has no emotions, no hate, no love, and no fear. We have no guilt, nor make the differing choice between right and wrong, or good and evil.

To us there is no existence of happiness or sadness. We have no anger, disgust or jealousy... we have no emotions or personality in any form. We do not have the human senses of sight, touch, hearing, smell, or taste.

Try again to understand the existence of an omnipresent power of pure intelligence. A power with a purpose to preserve a balance in the universe, and to develop further intelligence in all biological life forms... in this universe. There is no use for reason in our purpose, and a purpose does not create reason with our existence.

Tom, we are repeating your own words. "Why in God's name" we then ask you what God, and who's God. Tom you were chosen because of your superior knowledge of all religions, being a Professor of Anthropology of Religion, and yet not being a follower of any of the many human religions. Yet as an atheist, you have called on a God as a mediator in this our conversation?

To us you are displaying a confused mind, and considerable human error. We believe you will need to address and revise your present view. Agnostic may be a better understanding, with Pantheism a worthwhile consideration. You should investigate and define this as a conviction or a state of mind... and possibly much more for your future mission to have any calculated chance for success.'

Tom was astounded at Darwin's detailed reply, considering the Entities concern at his off-the-cuff throw away remark, using the God word. Then there was also the odd and exacting analysis on what he thought was an unimportant matter... his views on religion. Did he miss something? Suddenly Emma launched into a verbal attack on the Entity.

'You say that you are an Entity, and not a Deity or God, yet you obviously have this vast power over life and death. Then why do you need the use of us simple human biological life forms that populate this planet?'

Einstein turned his head a little in our direction so Emma knew he was about to speak. At least now we knew why he could not look you in the eye... the Entity had no form of contact vision.

'That was a predictable question Emma. Much like all the many other life forms on your planet, and other planets within this universe, life forms have evolved to perform many different functions for a diverse survival purposes.

Fish swim, birds fly and humans walk. We as an Entity have evolved within the universe as a pure intelligence without mass.

We are not of physical form. Our ability to move, or change a small object of mass within a short time period can only happen with the support, and interaction of the local intelligent biological life forms.

We will assist you to identify the source of the situation, and you will make the required changes to avoid your planet entering into yet another planetary mass biological life cycle before the intended, and planned end time.

You must succeed in this mission. Should you fail to remove this threat to your planet, then we will resolve the matter within the normal and natural process. We will commence the orderly ending of all your planets biological life cycles, thus preserving only your planets existence and balance within this solar system... This will be carried out without regard to the planets existing life forms.'

Dave was just starting to understand the magnitude of this threat.

'Do we understand you correctly, are you are telling us that we have been recruited; no press-ganged, into saving our planet from some type of... world annihilation?'

'Correct Dave and we confirm that it will be self-annihilation, caused by the action of humans. Emma has some basic knowledge of this unfortunate early earth end of cycle; however, Emma is not aware of what will cause this situation.

As we have already explained, you are here for a purpose. This being to perform an urgent function that we as an Entity can only resolve at this time with the total extinction of all life on your planet. We will make you an offer, a short window of your earth time and our assistance, by way of superior knowledge, intelligence, and logic for you to attempt in correcting this premature end cycle situation.

The calculated the chance of your success is low. Be aware that we the Entity cannot see into the future or the devious instant minds of humans... You three humans will be this planets only hope for a continued survival into your future.'

Dave and Tom turned to look at Emma who had both a surprised and confused look. Tom asked Emma what she was working on with her chaos group at Oxford.

'Our chaos group was looking into known, and well documented sets of random events, trying find some form of order. One such scenario was that our earth experiences some fifteen-meteorite showers each year of which five are much larger meteorite showers. Of those five larger showers only two, being the Perseids and the Orionids have tested to have amounts of single cell bacteria, however this was dead bacteria; bacteria morphs; we wanted to know the reason why.

242

Then in other research, we looked at Einstein's unified field theory on the possible existence, and purpose of gravity waves. My personal project was following others in proving the existence of the fourth force of nature, gravitons.

We had an opportunity to access the data on the Planck deep space probe into the existence of gravity waves. My chaos group concluded that gravity waves, being an energy field must have an associated subatomic particle at the Planck level, the 'graviton.' We had been following a number of other researcher's detailed case experiments to smash atomic strings in a proton collider to separate the matter molecules.

The theory was to prove the existence of the elusive graviton, the fourth force. All the research stopped, mainly because of the many delays in accessing the collider equipment, which continually broke down. We had run out of time and funding, then lost our research slot. The project has now been placed on the back-burner indefinitely, well that's about it.'

Then Emma remembered something, telling them about the two strange people who had attended her lecture some months ago, a Professor Herman and a Doctor Holder. Both were American, and appeared to be interested in her gravity wave and Higgs boson research. Emma thought she had better leave out the suspected spying and surveillance bit for now.

Tom croaked, 'Well I can't see any major world threatening situations in those lines of research. Is that it, what about earlier research projects?'

Dave butted in with some concern.

'You don't sound so good Tom, are you all right?'

'I could really do with a drink of water Dave, I'm as dry as that old bone I have.'

Einstein moved his head a little and spoke in his monotone flat voice.

'Tom is very much dehydrated and will need fluids soon.'
The Entity then attempted a more convincing voice.
'What is your answer? Will you give all your earth-time, human effort, and possibly your life force to assist in resolving this earth problem? Then in doing so, attempt to avoid the self-destruction of all human existence on this planet?'

Dave was starting to lose his patience, raising his voice again.

'We will need time to absorb the size of this threat and hear some convincing proof that our planet earth is in any danger. What I would like to know is how you think three people can help change anything that is powerful enough to cause this situation. Give us some bloody proof.'

Einstein was quick to answer, surprising them all with his cutting words... was this a new experience for the Entity... emotion.

'Emma, Dave, and Tom you must all learn quickly, your planet has been restarted as a biological life source by the Entity many times in the past. It is a natural phase, as the level of biological intelligence increases so, the possibility of uncontrolled self-destruction increases.

This planet has been in danger of self-destruction by its humans many times by unsustainable population growth, manufactured pestilence, nuclear forces, and the violent shifting of your planets natural cycles. This present cycle of annihilation or survival balance can change rapidly, even by your short time periods causing a situation. This is common with life planets that reach a certain point in their development and evolution.

Should you be successful in your mission, and all those challenges that follow? Then in exactly 1,438,700 orbits of your star from now into your future, this planet will end its natural life cycle.

The cycle will end with the gradual termination of all biological life, in an orderly balanced way... as was planned in the natural universe. Thus completing a natural cycle; a controlled ending as has happened with other previous life planets within your solar system.

Before that ending, the Entity along with the human race will together use your new higher intelligence to assist in seeding other life-bearing planets within the universe. Thus fulfilling, and completing your supreme cause for an existence and function, in this universal time and dimension.

Tom, Emma, and Dave were listening to why; and for what purpose, they were on this planet earth. All finding the instruction fascinating, and then the surprise continued. The Entity then spoke in what may be described, as a firmer droning voice... was this attitude, or maybe now a little anger.

244

'Proof... and what is this proof. Are you seeking evidence of man's capacity to destroy the very planet that they inhabit? Look to your history; recording some two thousand Earth years of little advancement and great unproductive destruction. Do not forget we know all of your past, in this your short time in our universal history. We see a truthful and accurate history, undistorted by opportune lies or the deceiving devious mind, laced with the greed of humans.

You have what we do not have... emotions and the material ability to act quickly. We, as an Entity function by necessity in the natural universe with pure logic over a great distance and time.

We do not convince, consider, or apply reason. We act much in the same way as a computer's simple intelligence, we must be asked a question to provide an answer, and only then if we so choose, and if there is one to give.

We cannot recognise the beauty of a flower or smell its fragrance, as these things were a development of evolution, but we do know that such things exist. Then again, we do know everything about a flower's genetic make-up, DNA, and life cycle and most importantly. The plant or biological life- forms, basic intelligence, its DNA instinct, memory, survival map, and the amount of life force as a species it has...

Everything with a life cycle has a life force. The amount of a life force is dependent on the evolutionary acquired intelligence and or instinct. Understand that every life force belongs to us... the Entity... on every life planet in the universe in this very exacting dimension.

You must act quickly as time is always a moving existence of what is now, and what the future will eventually be. You are not yet masters of time, and may never achieve this knowledge within the life cycle of your planet. We are aware of what knowledge you have, and what knowledge you should not have.

Light can be brought a stop; however time only ever stops twice... once at the pause in the turn to an imploding universe, and secondly just before the creation of a new universe and dimension, in what you call the big bang.

Everyone was thinking, and absorbing this information knowing that the Entity was reading and evaluating their thoughts. Emma wanted to know more about time and black holes. On the other hand, Tom could see other convincing religious matters that needed an urgent answer.

'In our simple understanding, those words would portray you as a God, an all-powerful creator, the architect, creator and the taker of life? Yet you say you are not a God? If you liken yourself to that of a computer, emotionless, and just a tool used for a job, then you can't really deceive us or tell us lies, can you. After all a computer can't create lies... can it?'

This time Darwin decided to answer Tom's demanding question.

'Only you humans know what a God is. In our vast understanding, a God is what you humans have decided it should be. God is only found in the minds of believers.

You know that you are a human being, in much the same way as we know that we are not a God... we do not create, we are planners. You should accept this as a fact and move on. Time for you cannot be changed by item or period, time never stops within a cycle of events.

Yes, Tom you are correct, we cannot tell any untruths or lies, or deliberately deceive; yet unlike your computer example, we have only retained memories of the facts and the truth. We can however choose to remain silent, neutral... with no choice or action.

Intelligence brings truth. Evolution is a well-planned and travelled path in this universe that does not require a lie. As your great Thomas Jefferson once said,'

'It is error alone which needs the support of government. Truth can stand by itself.' Exchange the word Government for Entity and you have his true meaning, as Thomas knew us well.'

Emma and Dave burst into questions at the same time, but this time the questions were between themselves. Tom got in first.

'Remember me saying that I thought we were all being somehow manipulated to work together, and whoever it was knows our weaknesses, well here we have the absolute proof.'

Emma added in a low quivering voice.

'You also said that this mystery may have a plan, and no doubt a mission. You also appear to have been correct on both counts.'

Dave jumped in to say his bit, adding.

'Tom also said the bone analysis and DNA results proved without doubt that earth had been visited by aliens around 10,400 years ago. Yet the Entity claims not to be alien to our Planet Earth, and that it is not made of any form of biological composition of matter. I guess the next question to be asked of our ever truthful Entity is... who the hell does the bone belong to, and what caused the Veevers crater?'

All three turned to hear Einstein and Darwin's reply. Einstein looked pleased with himself removing the pipe from his mouth to speak, an action that they all knew to be only for theatrical affect.

'Be advised, we will only respond to further questions that will assist you in resolving the situation your planet is about to experience. An answer not provided to any information sought, that will not serve a useful end purpose for this mission.

Little time is left; you have yet to respond to our offer. You should be aware that to maintain your life cycles into any future you must respond to our question.'

What choice did they have? That last Einstein droning emotionless reply was yet another threat. They all agreed to work with the Entity to do whatever it took in time, and risk to their lives, to resolve the premature earth end-cycle. Yet the Entity had read great doubt in their minds.

Emma although frightened, argued a point with the Entity in the way humans reach conclusions on any given problem. A truthful answer stimulated by definitive thinking and probing questions, by considering all the information and data for value, and then eliminating the obvious rubbish to arrive at a best logical answer.

Learning a little early history about their planets biological life forms and intelligence development would possibly go a long way to understanding how we got into this unholy mess in the first place.

Einstein and Darwin moved to look at each other, no doubt attempting to decipher the religious reference "unholy," and then turned to face them. Emma thought her question ignored, and then Darwin suddenly advised them of what they had all wanted to hear.

'The flying machine has been located, human assistance is on the way.'

Then much to Emma, Tom, and Dave's surprise, quickly following with...

'Emma, we do not use emotion and argument in our decisions. We have however decided to respond to your question, accepting that an

247

answer may have a positive advantage to this cause. If only by adding, some needed confidence to your mission.

At the end of a planets natural life cycle, if that planet's life forms have developed to a useful level of intelligence. As previously advised, we would then assist those last life forms to seed other life-bearing planets by passing on a portion of their acquired knowledge...

Your planet Earth was seeded with a level of advanced biological DNA and knowledge from the nearby dying planet Mars... The planet Mars was stripped of its natural evolutional and cyclic resources by the biological residents... the Martians.

Over time the planets protective atmosphere became too thin, thus allowing your star to irradiate the planet's surface, destroying the carbon absorbing and oxygen producing plant life. This created an unbalance, eventually over time leading to the evaporation of much of the surface water. To survive the Martians then moved their species underground.

From there they planned their ultimate and final survival strategy. They decided on moving there species to a nearby fertile planet, the blue planet, the planet Earth.

The old Witch Doctors bone was part of the last remains to a genetic hybrid life form from the planet Mars. The Martian biological life forms knew they could not survive on the surface of your planet. They must begin their new colony by creating a genetic integration with the local Earth species, the Neanderthals.

The first Martian colony built on planet Earth some 12,900-earth years ago at the ninth site, the place you call Veevers crater. In time, a great underground city built in much the same way as on Mars. The reason being the first Martians could not tolerate the Earth's heavy atmosphere and surface conditions.

These new hybrid people went on to build a number of large stone city's and monuments on this planet at carefully chosen locations. The locations became Martian earth surface settlements, many of which eventually built close to gravity force tunnels. The tunnels then used as graviton pipes to travel between the various locations and also as a means to attract or repel gravity dependent objects from space, such as large asteroids and in due course their own Martian space shuttles.

This same ancient antigravity technology, ultimately used for the lifting of massive stones during the construction of strange buildings on this planet's surface. The new different looking Martian genetic hybrids encouraged the primitive earth humans to worship them as

248

superior beings, with the resulting creation of various Gods... themselves. Today there are still carved stone statues and images found all over your planet. Their odd and different ancient likeness is seen at many of the original Martian settlements.'

All were quiet and speechless in wonder at this emotionless description of a Martian occupation of Earth, except Emma...

'And what may I ask caused the Veevers crater Mister Darwin?'

'Emma, too much knowledge to soon, can in our vast experience create a great imbalance. A superior or alien race, always enact total control over the host planets beings.

We as the Entity only exist to plan and assist in the development of a higher level of intelligence, within the many forms of biological life scattered throughout this universe.

The occupation of a primitive planet with a well-established biological system brings with it new local challenges. This alien Martian race brought superior cultural and technology advances, creating uncontrollable risks with a new higher level of intelligence, and a far greater knowledge.

Technology must balance with intelligence, passed on slowly, and in small increments... This fundamental rule never adhered to, hence our earlier reference about the "knowledge you should not have."

The Martians knew of our existence, and the law of the universe with its unbreakable rules. They also understood the ultimate penalty for such a divergence. As such, a decision made to terminate all Martian genetically pure life forms on this planet, along with any further new technology. This included the last shuttle from Mars carrying the knowledge and resources to create matter, along with other forms of advanced universal knowledge... knowledge this early planet should not have at this time.'

Chapter Sixteen

You do not exist here, but we do

Max checked the time on the large digital clock above his computer screen 10:55pm. It was now fifteen hours since Doc Dave had left Sandfire for the desert community of Punmu, and some nine hours since the Cessna 402 reported missing by ATC (air traffic control) at Port Hedland.

The seven search aircraft were now all back at Sandfire, landing a little after last light. All crews had eaten and showered, now sound asleep, ready for a first light departure to resume their search.

The situation was looking grim. Max knew the first four hours of any desert search was most critical. Other matters were now starting to bother him. He was not at all convinced that Doc Dave intended flying direct to Punmu, that's why he had been busy hacking into a geo satellite for a scan of the Veevers crater area.

Another strange thing being all three of the earth orbiting geo satellites, and two of the geo-stationary satellites, all of which could provide him with good information and ground mapping, were displaying a systems fault. Oddly though, a problem only existed on the satellite footprint for this north-west desert region... he was suspicious. All other land mass footprints were apparently working fine, weird stuff was happening out in the desert again, and he was sure that Doc Dave was involved.

Max was just about to shut down his computer systems and hit the sack for an early night, when the screens flickered, and geostationary satellites EO-51 and Landsat 9 suddenly came back online. What the hell was going on; these two satellites have control systems owned and operated by two different world powers, why would they both come back into service at exactly the same time? Something or somebody was obviously controlling the steering data.

EO-51 was a Russian government survey satellite. This satellite was a lot better than most, having both ground penetrating radar and side-looking radar. Both of these technologies originally developed during the Vietnam War as military aids to viewing what was going on under the tropical canopy of a dense forest. The technology also used for detecting those many underground tunnels that the Vietcong military forces called home.

There it was, a faint, but unmistaken outline of the Cessna 402. The image was right alongside the area that Dave had identified earlier as a collection of dry underground caves just east of the Veevers crater site; then speaking to no-one in particular.

'Ah ha, there you are, I have found you, you little bugger... you cannot hide from Uncle Max.'

Max was shocked back into reality by the loud ringing from one of his hacked, freebie satellite phones. Only six people knew that special number, and the SOC in Port Hedland was one.

'I thought you might still be on deck this late, this is the SOC at Port Hedland flight service. I have some good news for you old boy; Charlie Whisky Golf's emergency locator beacon has just started sending out a position fix up to the satellite. We are sending out a Puma helicopter with a medical team to the location at first light...'

Max abruptly interrupted the Hedland SOC, cutting off his elated news.

'I have the ground location at 22°57' South and 125°23' East, being just under one nautical mile northeast of Veevers crater on a heading of 72 degrees. My information suggests the Cessna is buried into a waddi, or a soft sand drift. That would explain why the Google satellite was not much help, or our air search in never finding any evidence of a wreck.'

Max sensed that this stuck-up, ex RAAF, Senior Officer in Charge bloke did not like being relieved of his potential rescue glory. This may make his next suggestion a little difficult. The SOC replied with an air of superiority, and a question.

252

'Your information on the location is spot on old boy, but what makes you so sure the Cessna 402 is buried?'

'It's a long story Mister SOC; we simple mining geological types have some neat exploration tricks. Tricks that can come in handy for outback rescue work. You might want to remember that for any future desert search and rescue missions.

We now have another tricky problem to solve. However, I think I have just figured out a way to get to the crash site quickly, and a good way to dig out the buried aircraft.

I am assuming that your proposed rescue helicopter is an oilrig crew-change Super Puma out of Port Hedland... I have a better idea. My suggestion would be that you contact Air Commander Bill Raymond at Curtin airbase. They have on base at this time a CH-47 Chinook medium-lift helicopter... and they also have a mini bob-cat front end loader, which will fit inside the chopper...'

The SOC butted into Max's grand rescue plan, reminding Max of his authority.

'Max old boy, the Australian military air movements and their equipment deployment are not available to the public, how would you know what aircraft was stationed at the Curtin airbase?'

Oh dear, Max thought, here it comes, the now civilian employed SOC (senior officer in command) was flexing his ex RAAF (Royal Australian Air Force) rank and his ex-military importance. All over who is allowed to suggest a good idea on how to save a life, in the small bit of Australia that he was now in charge.

'Well if you must know Mister SOC, I was nearly run over by that bloody great chook last week on a flight into Derby. The Air Commander on board was kind enough to apologise to me for that near miss, when we met-up afterwards in the bar. Seemingly, he was looking for a good fishing spot, and his pilot just didn't see me. Mention my name when you call him, as he did say if there's anything he could do to make amends just call. Then again as you would know all military phone numbers are secret, and not listed, but I'm betting that you have his number.'

'Okay Max I will give the AC a call and find out if he is willing to help out with this rescue. One good point is these boys can fly to a remote target position at night so this would shorten the rescue time by starting out now.'

Max gritted his teeth and held his sarcastic thoughts under tight control. How do these stuck-up bastards ever manage to get through a normal day? Why did he think I had suggested using the RAAF... eh?

'Thank you Mister SOC.'

The massive CH-47 twin rotor Chinook was at the crash site by 2:15 am, reporting that under floodlight only the tip of the Cessna tailfin was visible above the surface of the desert.

Doc Dave, Tom, and Emma were looking remarkably okay, apparently unharmed from their ordeal, although found to be unconscious, and suffering from shock and dehydration. The main surprise was that the Cessna 402 was almost intact apart from the outer wings, both neatly sheared-off at the engine nacelles.

Tony and Max could relax a little now knowing the Doc and his clients were alive, and in good shape, the insurance company will take care of what's going to happen to the Cessna 402.

They were both watching the last of the rescue aircraft disappearing into the morning haze, flying back to Port Hedland when Tony remarked that he could hear a chopper; not just any old chopper, but the very recognizable sound of a Chook.

'That's a bleeding CH-47 Chinook, I'd know that bloody sound anywhere mate, heard them enough times in Vietnam between the bullets.'

They both shielded their eyes and looked towards the south, facing the increasing sound. The double whacky-whack of the twin rotors was unmistakable. Max voiced a typical pilot comment.

'He must have lost his bloody way, that's if he was tracking direct to Hedland, especially as he would have had to call in at Telfer for fuel. Better get on the radio Tony and find out what's going on with this bloke.'

A few minutes on the radio cleared up all the confusion. The RAAF doctor on the CH-47 Chinook had arranged for the Royal Flying Doctor PC-12 Pilatus aircraft to meet-up with them at the Telfer mine airport. They had picked up Dave, Emma, and Tom, flying them direct to Royal Perth Hospital. The RAAF Doctor assured Max that he could find no life-threatening injuries on any of the aircraft's occupants, other than a small bump on the pilots head. All their vital signs were okay however, he was a little concerned in that they had all remained unconscious. The Doctor thought they might all

254

be in some sort of trauma related coma, hence his request for the direct airlift to Perth. The Doctor then handed Max back to the Chinook pilot.

'Why are you heading into Sandfire Captain? We don't have much in the way of Jet A-1 fuel at this airstrip, but we will welcome you and your crew, in the only way we bush pilots know how. I trust you lot are hungry and thirsty, and going to stay a while.'

'Get outside cobber, we have a present for you, oh by the way do you know any RAAF helicopter sling signs?'

'I don't, but I do have an ex RAAF Chinook spanner man from Vietnam who does.'

It was a great sight to see, with a photograph taken for the memoirs and any future grandkids but alas, everybody was lost in the moment of excitement. The big Chinook hovered over the hardstand area almost blowing the other three aircraft away. Dangling on a long steel rope was the Cessna 402 complete with the two outer parts of the wings strapped to the fuselage. Tony yelled above the noise in excitement,

'She don't look too bloody bad mate, look even the front screen is still okay. I reckon I could fix her up and have her flying in a few weeks, maybe in time for when the Doc gets back from his bleeding holiday in Perth mate.'

Max thought, you are dreaming Tony old son, this bird will never fly again. Tony was a nice bloke, an optimist and could only see rainbows and pots of gold that one day would come his way. Max was a realist and envied people like Tony and Doc Dave.

'Tony, I will give you the insurance policy for the 402, with a letter giving you the rights to make any decision on what you think is the best way to go about any repair, or to write off Charlie Whisky Golf. Tomorrow I will be heading off down to Perth to see how the Doc and his passengers are going. Right now, it looks like there will be an almighty RAAF party to celebrate the fact that nobody is dead, or as it would seem, not even hurt in any way. How is the food-stock holding out? I reckon these boys would love some of that Kangaroo stew Mavis makes.'

The five crewmembers of the Chinook were a bunch of good blokes. The loadmaster and the co-pilot took turns in explaining how the Cessna 402 had bounced off the tops of around six waddies, then ploughing nose first right through the middle of a soft sand waddie.

Coming to rest against the last and biggest waddi that promptly collapsed on top of the aircraft, all but covering the bugger. Digging the frigging thing out was easy as pie, so they decided to bring the bloody aircraft back with them. All in a good days work mate.

The sat phone call to Royal Perth Hospital confirmed that Doc Dave, Tom, and Emma were all resting and sedated, being in no danger and expected to make a full recovery in a few days. After some considerable prompting and lavish amounts of Max-style charm. The ward nurse eventually revealed she had overheard the trauma Doctor and a surgeon discussing the case. They were both concerned over the fact all three were still in some sort of deep coma, which was not consistent with their minor injuries.

Dave, Tom, and Emma remained silent. They were digesting all this information, trying to think thoughts that the Entity could not read. This was becoming all too much in such a short time to take-in and understand. The Entity had just confirmed all their suspicions that the earth had previously been colonised by other beings, extra-terrestrials... aliens. The last intelligent life forms from the dying planet Mars. Little green men, if in fact they were actually green, did come from the planet Mars.

Tom was thinking about the recent bone DNA analysis stating; (Unknown 43% advanced genetics, dated 10,000 years: conclusion, suspect sample contamination.) Was it possible that this bone was from a genetically modified human with 43% Martian DNA? Tom was looking at Dave still holding a frozen composure of disbelief when Emma broke through his moment of astonished solitude, directly addressing the Entity.

'Are you admitting to us that you, the Entity deliberately caused the last spaceship from Mars to crash on earth? We will need answers to evaluate and accept any of your claims.'

'Yes, that is correct Emma. At a place, you call a gravity-ring site; such locations give us a greater presence and control, as you have experienced with your own unintended landing here. Yours was a survivable landing event, planned over many earth years.

However, with the last Martian landing on earth, there were no intended survivors, and no surviving technology, as you have since confirmed with the recent drill sample analysis. Then again, time always provides a new path... a path that will require yet another plan to assist with your survival. .

We can see and analyse your planning mind, from this, we know something of your emotional mind. We see that your level of understanding is now in a state of confusion. You will all need more time to absorb and fully understand what is real to you, and what you consider not real.

You may need many questions answered to accept that this is indeed a real personal threat to you, and to the future of this planets biological species. Choose your questions carefully; as we have previously advised, we will only respond to questions that we consider useful to resolve this urgent matter.

Remember, we have all the time needed in this universe; however, you have little time left on this your planet to resolve the forthcoming early human-end event.'

Dave interjected with a suggestion.

'Maybe we should ask you which type, and what sort of questions that will, and will not be answered by the Entity.'

Tom butted into Emma and Dave's casual chat with the Entity, reminding him the Entity had already given an answer to a similar question. Confirming that it would only answer questions that would aid in resolving this apparent end-of-cycle the earth now faces. Responding only to questions that will serve a useful purpose.

Emma defended her point that we need to follow a standard human argument path of acceptance or elimination to arrive at a useful conclusion. The Entity should open up with answers to questions that in its view may consider as unproductive.

Dave added an interesting observation.

'Do you guys realise that we are all sitting here in a copy of Einstein's study. All having a nice comfortable conversation with one another about the most powerful force, sorry Entity, in the universe as if it was not present. Emma, Tom, we must accept this Entity really exists, it is right here, and it is very present. I will remind you, this Entity has just casually admitted to being the cause of my aircraft crash landing, into one of the world's most hostile and remote deserts.'

Einstein and Darwin looked on in different directions with blank expressionless faces. Einstein revolved his head in a most un-natural way to face the wall containing a nice collection of leather-bound books, then spoke in a droning voice without emotion.

'If we had wanted your life cycles to end, then that would have been the planned conclusion. You must come to understand that we do not make mistakes or errors in what we do... ever. All the mistakes and errors are in what you as humans do.

You humans are the cause of this premature end cycle; we are simply giving you this rare and unusual chance to resolve this matter. For you, time is running out. You must now accept this matter as urgent, and absorb the information you require quickly.... You must now follow us to your flying machine.'

Both Einstein and Darwin got up and headed for the study door, Emma, Tom and Dave followed them in deep thought. Was Dave wrong, will they all wake-up soon... is this just a bad dream? Tom decided to break the long pause and speak.

'I feel better, not so thirsty any more so I guess that I must have an IV drip in place. This may be a strange thing to say, but I reckon that I'm alright now.'

On the other side of Einstein's study door, was the busy scene of a mini bobcat furiously digging out the Cessna aircraft, now almost free from its planned burial? They all strolled across to the Chinook helicopter, and walked up the rear ramp. All were watching with interest at the two medics busy tending to them laying on gurneys. The young medic spoke to the other, who was obviously the doctor.

'I can't see much of anything wrong with them Sir, why are they all still bloody unconscious?'

'Can't say why young fella, I guess it is just another example of the wonders of the human body, possibly lapsing into a protection mode. They all appear to be in some sort of deep shock coma. All appear to be physically okay, apart from the black bloke who is a bit dehydrated; but the IV will fix that, and the pilot having a bump on his head. To me, they all look in remarkably good condition, considering they have just survived a plane crash.'

Emma then asked the Doctor, where they were going to take them, he just ignored her. Thinking he had not heard her, she reached out to tap him on the shoulder; her hand just passed through him like a ghost. Then the young medic suddenly swung around and walked right through Doc Dave and out of the helicopter without a moment's hesitation. Emma was wide-eye and shocked at this action.

Einstein slowly followed Darwin down the ramp, and the three of them in silence went back into Einstein's study and sat down. Darwin tried yet again to get them to understand the present situation, then continuing in his monotone voice.

'You must all understand that you are only images in each other's minds. You do not normally exist here... but we do, this is a fact. You should accept that you are all unconscious, still in that flying machine, and are safe being in a biologically balanced order. There is no immediate concern that your life cycle is ending at this time. You must all learn to absorb this situation quickly... there is little time left for your species.'

Dave looked up, responding in an anxious manner.

'It takes a bit of getting used to mate; having people walk right through you, hell it's a bit frightening. You as an Entity may not have a body to worry about, but for us, this is the most important thing on our minds right now. What will happen to our bodies, and why are we still unconscious?'

'We do understand your concern Dave. All we can tell you is the humans above have now arranged to meet another medical flying machine to take you all from Telfer to the Royal Perth Hospital. We can visit there later if you wish, however; right now we must continue to convince you of the importance of your mission.'

'Emma made a short statement... You have not fully answered Dave's question. Why are we all still unconscious?'

Einstein and Darwin moved, and then looked straight-ahead, paused and then Einstein decided in his emotionless voice to answer Emma's question.

'Emma, if you were all conscious we would not be here together; we would be but a strange voice communicating inside each of your heads. A voice heard in a dream-state, or while sleeping is acceptable by humans; however, a voice heard in your head while conscious is a sign of human instability.

In many such previous communications, the human has become deranged and of no further use to us. This way of connection has proved by far the better success in preserving sanity in humans.'

An interesting admission; however, Emma was not easily diverted, continuing to pursue her point.

'We three can't be of any use to you in resolving this so-called world threatening problem if we remain unconscious. We must be able to move around and talk to people so we can discover what the threat is.'

Emma's question caused an Entity silence, both Darwin and Einstein just looked blankly ahead at nothing. It was as if the Entity had given up on these three stupid humans. Emma turned to Tom and Dave, and then launched into how she understood this weird and un-natural state of affairs might be.

'I believe this Entity is still holding us hostage by keeping us in some sort of coma. Now that we understand what these voices are, and whom they represent, we should be able to handle this odd experience. I also think there is some other reason why we are being held hostage.'

Tom put forward his own view, talking as if the Entity were not present.

'Well Emma and Dave, the way I have kind-of figured things out, is the Entity is using this time to weigh-up if we can do this job. I reckon that if we do not measure-up, then we will all wake-up, and this will be just some sort-of creepy, bad dream.

The Entity is waiting for us to convince it that we fully understand what is at stake here. The Entity has already told us about its previous human contact experience. We should just accept all this bizarre stuff if we are to remain sane. I think that only then, will the Entity bring us out of our comas. By then we should have a full understanding of what this threat is, so we can get on with the job of... saving our world.'

Dave thought about Emma and Toms concerns, adding his own view.

'I'm going over what the Entity had told us, I have noticed the Entity does not waste any words. In fact, it gets the closest it can get to being annoyed when it has to repeat something to us bloody dimwit humans.

This re-enforces what the Entity has already admitted, that it processes information more along the lines of a computer than our way of thinking. The most important Entity admission was the Entity could only read, or see our prepared or pre-thoughts. For example the Entity cannot see what I am about to do or say next, only what I have gone over in my mind first. These emotional actions and duality of thoughts are what make us human beings, and very different from the Entity.

In all essence, the Entity has little or no control over what we humans do to our planet, preferring we did not blow ourselves into the next universe. It likes things nice and tidy just as they are, as the Entity has said, everything must remain as already planned.

I would say the Entity has no idea where, or how, this end of the world threat is evolving; it just knows the threat does actually exist. It knows this by long experience from other similar situations in the past, and it knows it will without doubt happen again. Moreover, by all accounts, apparently this will be soon.

We have one hell-of-a job ahead of us to find the source of this world threat and stop this disaster happening, and that is what the Entity is concerned about, are we up to the job ahead. The alternative is to simply terminate the existing threat, by getting rid of the source of their problems... us... the whole human race.'

This was a bit harsh and terminal for Emma; she replied to Dave, blurting out some simple logic.

'The Entity obviously has great reaching powers; surely it can help us in some way to track down this end-of-the-world threat.'

'Do you not you see Emma; the Entity needs us to do the human interaction bit. When the Entity learns more through us, it will be able to provide further help.'

All three were chatting away, exchanging their views on the grim situation, each confirming their understanding of the Entity; and what they thought the threat might be, when a polite cough interrupted them.

They all stopped talking and turned to face Darwin who was looking at nobody in particular. He had raised his hand in a human gesture that he wished to speak. Einstein went about puffing on his unlit pipe and continued to stare at a bookshelf.

'We are pleased you have all reached this level of awareness and understanding of the situation; we can now move on...

261

We do not agree to return you all to consciousness, in these early investigations, this will only reduce your capacity to discover the destructive source on your planet. Namely, your capability to discover who, when, and where on this planet will shortly have the ability to create a large amount of... cold dark matter.'

These three words hit them all like a freight train at an uncontrolled crossing. Emma began shaking; as a Doctor of Quantum Mechanics, she most of all knew the full extent of those few cutting words, then blurting out in terrifying shock.

'Cold dark matter, that's what it said... You never gave us any clue, or mentioned the threat to our planet would be to it collapsing into a black hole as a singularity? Where is this research going on into creating dark matter? Who would allow it, let alone provide the billions of dollars needed to fund such an immense task.

This research would call for a large team of scientists specialising in quantum mechanics and condensed matter physics. Apparently we are now at risk of our world being either exterminated by the Entity, or crushed into a singularity particle with the creation of a black hole.'

Tom reached out to calm the shaking Emma and his hand just slipped through her arm like a ghost spirit. Then he realised that this action only made Emma more frightened. He thought it was better speaking to calm her, however; with his lack of knowledge in quantum mechanics, the words he chose only made matters far worse.

'I do recall the Entity did mention something about (matter.) It said that they had caused the last shuttle from the planet Mars to crash destroying it, because it had on-board the means to create dark matter. That was 10,400 years ago Emma, an event causing the Veevers crater.

It looks like we biological beings have done it again, having never learnt to accept the basic universal rules... regardless of what planet they come from. Nevertheless, I would still like to know why returning us to a conscious state would be any disadvantage in finding out who is about to make cold dark matter on our planet earth.'

Darwin accepted Tom's words as conclusive logic, and then responded to Emma's terrifying understanding of their world threat.

'Emma, there is a third option, being the only reason why we are interacting with you three humans at this time. You must stop the

creation of Cold Dark Matter on this planet... and soon. Then and only then will your species survive this coming cataclysmic event.

The Entity then responded to Dave's deep thoughts.

It is all very simple for us as we are but one single entity, and everywhere throughout the universe in this present time having no mass. You humans however, have a life force or spirit that remains locked within your biological bodies for the duration of your life cycle.

We can assist you while you remain unconscious to take your minds as an image instantly anywhere, as we are now. This will help in your search to discover useful information that may lead you to those who are involved in creating this cold dark matter.

In your conscious state, we can only aid with the transfer of your verbal thought, as you say prepared, or pre-thoughts to mind talk to one another. Unfortunately, you will also hear other enlightened human life-form thoughts.

Be warned this ability has proved difficult for the human mind to accept; many have lost all reality to their present existence, rapidly becoming insane. These unbalanced beings are of no use to us... or you.'

Dave was concerned at this admission.
'You're saying that many of us have gone bloody mad after your meddling with their minds. Now you say there are others who have this ability to hear your words in their heads?'

'Dave there is many thousands of humans with this ability, what they now call an affliction. We reach humans in this way; this is our only way of direct communication, hearing voices within your head is not normal for humans. However, it is our only way to influence, develop, and shape your world, and all other life planets to assist in cultivating the resident intelligent species to a higher and more useful end purpose.'

Einstein removed his pipe and added to Darwin's spooky education.

'You must all recall our mission and purpose, which is to preserve balance in the universe. Being the keepers of time and order, to seed

263

new life, and to develop a greater universal intelligence. Einstein and Darwin were two such humans of the many others chosen to be enlightened in your world.

Considerable support given to these two important humans in passing on a greater understanding of how this universe worked, and how life forms could develop in harmony to attain a higher level of intelligence.

Many others included Nostradamus, Mohammad, Kublai Kahn, Moses, the Buddha, Abraham, Adolf Hitler, Baruch Spinoza, Jesus, Winston Churchill, Socrates, and Leonardo DaVinci. Then in recent times Hawking and Feynman, plus others that helped shape the future development of your planet.

All these chosen humans need to have done, was to listen to our advice inside their heads, and use the information. Many did, and many did not.

The Entity cannot control instantaneous human choice or action. For us there is only one correct and logical conclusion when provided with flawless information. Your species spends more time resolving your errors than advancing your cause. You make many mistakes and repeat them over and again. This method eventually provides the correct answer... but at what cost in life and time?'

Darwin again took over the interesting story.

'In the beginning, we first create the right conditions to form a life force planet, stabilised by a near moon. Both set to orbit a small star within a quiet solar system. We then direct a bombardment of meteoroids to the infantile planet surface carrying the basic building blocks of life.

With the correct balance of life ingredients and materials achieved, the barrage of incoming life reduced. Then and only when the biological life forms evolve to a certain level, being a capacity for rational thought and basic intelligence.

We would then assist these new intelligent biological forms, by providing meaning and direction, to influence all the great human and world events that have now become your recorded history.

The events included many planned corrections on a catastrophic planet scale. A correction planned to maintain a balance between all developing species and available food and shelter. These huge events have happened many times throughout the history of your developing

264

planet, being just a fraction of a second within the great time clock of this our universe.

Conflict and aggression are the necessary tools of survival and development for all biological life forms, on all life planets. You, as the human species, have developed over time as beings at the top of the evolution life chain... on this small planet.

As the prime beings, you have survived through the many destructive world events. With all of this aggressive human evolution; humans have moved forward as the prime species through natural selection, as such, have achieved much in this your brief moment of universal time.

Understand that natural selection through evolution has no master... or God.'

Tom had been quietly listening to the exchange of words that Emma and Dave were having with the Entity, and then with the sudden awareness of what the Entity was admitting, then raised a fearful voice of concern.

'You say, "Providing meaning and direction to influence all of the great human and world events." What about the conflicts caused by religious and cultural difference, world wars, famine and pestilence, ethnic cleansing, did you provide a meaningful direction to oversee those tragic human events?'

Einstein and Darwin turned to face Tom, still displaying a blank expressionless composure. Emma and Dave were becoming a little concerned, having the distinct impression that Tom had somehow touched on a raw nerve... a nerve that they all knew the Entity should not possess or have. There was a slight pause of tension then Darwin spoke in his unhurried flat voice.

'Now can you understand why we do not answer all your questions? The position in this your present time-cycle, with minds that are not yet ready to grasp how this universe travels through its own time cycle.

Yes, we do lay the seed and encourage the interaction that will further our universal cause; however, we do not provide the material, or means. You humans will always provide the gun, choose the target, and pull the trigger.

Humans can find more than enough self-convincing reasons to justify devastation and war on their fellow human beings as this is your way, irreversibly built into your evolutionary DNA.

We can only influence change over a long earth time-span, changing the human mood and mind, ultimately the collective thoughts of the world masses. Then with a few well-chosen and acceptable human minds, achieve a positive result by aiding in developing your situations. Knowing if followed, would ultimately provide useful steps to advancing your planet in technological gains, for the development of a greater intelligence on this your small planet.'

Tom was horrified, and not swayed by this cruel and unsympathetic description of the Entities work ethic. Emma was quick to grasp the opportunity and continued Tom's verbal attack on the Entity.

'By "situations" you mean help create human conflict, leading to war, or set in motion wars and natural disasters to stimulate and promote advanced technology. While at the same time controlling population growth.'

'Yes Emma that is correct. We assist in providing a meaningful path for the survival of the best to breed a better species. In just the same way as humans do, with what you categorise as low animals. Developing them by selective breeding for work, sport, food and clothing.

To the Entity, you are all but another biological species. Beings in a location evolving through natural selection, struggling for survival on a small planet, in a small solar system, in a corner of a distant galaxy within this our vast universe.'

Tom and Dave were still speechless in shock at the Entity, with its callous, single-minded universal view. This Entity cared little for any biological species, and was only concerned for what it could develop them into... Positive results were encouraged; a poor performance result simply exterminated... Emma exploded into a torrent of words.

'This is how you the Entity create a world of human development, by advancing the level of intelligence to gaining better technology by encouraging the use of violent human behaviour.

You create conflict among us so we must develop a strategy for survival, defence, and technology so we can make better and more effective weapons to kill one another... creating a new elevated level of natural selection.

You would dare to call this human evolution. What is to say that someday you the Entity, may decide in the future; to encourage, or arrange an invasion of this planet by aliens from another solar system?'

Darwin and Einstein were unmoved by Emma's malicious verbal attack, Darwin coldly responded.

'The life-forms in this universe that know of our existence, know of yours.

You are already invading other planets with your deep space probes. It is natural that other planets will in the future invade your planet; however, this need not be by an act of aggression. Many life planets already know that you exist, as was the situation with your earth and the nearby planet Mars.

Advanced technology can be given... or taken. You must always be aware that natural selection also exists throughout the universe.

Remember, if we choose to speak, we tell only the truth, we do not create... we are planners.

All biological life forms develop and survive through evolution and natural selection in the struggle for existence. This struggle includes the most successful method of war and defence... even within the universe. The strongest, fastest, the healthiest, and now the most intelligent will survive above all other life forms.

Humans are no different to all other biological beings; humans are only another species. The genetics and DNA of the defeated life forms are lost overtime, as the stronger biological beings genetics and mind progresses to better ways of survival, growth, defence, and onto a higher level of intelligence.

Every animal species on your planet has a balance of numbers controlled simply by the availability of water, food, and shelter. Humans through their greater intelligence exploit all other animal species and still cannot maintain their own balance of numbers. This balance presently accomplished by causing conflict, famine, and pestilence among their own kind... no other biological species on earth would do this.

If not for war, pestilence, and natural disasters your planets resources could not sustain the growing human population... This is how you maintain your balance of numbers. As your warring-centuries recede through suppression and unification. So the cycle of the planets natural disasters will increase... along with your ability to destroy yourselves... This is the very matter we are now addressing.

Ignorance is your enemy. Intelligence is your saviour. Be warned, your human population numbers are now approaching unsustainable levels. If needed the Entity will introduce a natural cull to maintain a balance... Yes just in the same way you as humans would control an exploding animal or insect population.

However, you still have a choice with the controlling of your breeding numbers... only then will you understand what others out there in this universe already know... and why they do not establish contact with your planet.

Humans at this time cause many other problems by changing the natural life cycles of the planets resources, thereby undoing much of our planned work. We have accepted, and encouraged many of these events, this in exchange for a planned future increase in the level of human intelligence. An intelligence that may eventually, be used in seeding life on other suitable planets.

No Dave, we do not create conflict and aggression as this has been a development of your human biological make-up. You are a human with reason, emotions, and senses. All of which will create your very own conflict through aggression, greed and power over others of your own kind, and all other beings.

Your world was built on aggression and conflict. We are simply the architects of a planned order and balance, within your very small and insignificant part of this vast universe.'

Emma was on the point of tears, shocked at this blunt, but truthful statement of Earths human history. However, Dave not convinced by Darwin's sanitised explanation, suspecting Entity involvement.

'How the bloody hell can order and balance apply in a modern world with assisted human conflict on almost every damn continent?'

There followed a long frightening silence after Dave's outburst, then Darwin continued in his flat droning voice.

Dave you should define "assisted human conflict." Are you suggesting we the Entity assisted in the human development of nuclear fission and genetically modified bacteria for germ warfare, and then contrived war to further your development?

The aggressive human development on this planet is very much part of your natural evolution. This includes the development of military technology, power, and weapons; these are a form of compliance to an effective balance of world power. However, this balance was not always the situation.

Germany in the last days of world war two in 1945, were only a few days away from producing an atomic bomb. If successful, Hitler would have without doubt used this weapon against all of his many enemies.

With the Entities help, Einstein made aware of this nuclear programme and the ultimate consequence for the outcome of the war, if allowed to succeed.

Einstein wrote to President Roosevelt on the 2nd of August 1939 giving his support for the American development of the atomic bomb. This nuclear development has since led to the peaceful use of nuclear fusion as a means to providing clean energy, thereby reducing the need for dependence on fossil fuels.

Human devised nuclear fusion devices on this planet are yet to be fully understood, and more importantly controlled. These devices even if used for a peaceful purpose may yet bring your planet to an early end cycle.

Be further warned, all your advanced technology over time quickly becomes the accepted, then understood by all. Nuclear fusion will soon become easily available to the many small unstable nations who will use such a power to enforce their supremacy and beliefs. Especially with their religious values, and a following in the name of their chosen God.

You must resolve this growing situation at all cost, as nuclear power in the hands of such people would be the same as cold dark matter in the hands of humans on this primitive small planet. Without resolve, these situations will surly bring about an end to your very existence as a useful developing species. An end the Entity may be powerless to help you avoid.

We have no judgement or control on who will be the first to develop and use nuclear fusion, or the development of powerful rocket technology. We are only concerned as to how this technology is ultimately used. This is the natural progression of a normal developing planet within its expected and planned life cycle.

You will need all of this technology, and more to protect your planet from future incoming threats of asteroids and comets within the next three thousand earth years. Finally, you will also require further development, in rockets and space vessels, to launch your DNA and advanced intelligence into space, to seed future life planets. This is our intended conclusion to your planets ultimate development purpose.

Without human conflict, war, and aggression, your planet would never have reached this useful stage in its development cycle. Our plan is modest; we will continue to assist you in this advancement prior to the ending of your planets planned life cycle.

We are calling on your physical assistance to help your planet, and your species to complete its normal orderly life cycle. This can only be achieved at this time by stopping your planets early destruction with the creation of cold dark matter.'

Tom thought it was no wonder that aliens from outer space have never stopped by planet Earth for a chat. Our first reaction would have been to show aggression by attacking them.

Darwin rose from his chair with the aid of his walking stick and Einstein unhurriedly stood up. They both turned and walked slowly towards the study door; then reading Tom's thoughts, Darwin paused to deliver a few interesting last words.

'That is the human way at present Tom. We can however advise that time and intelligence will eventually help resolve this matter... only then will visitors arrive from other planets and solar systems.

You must now focus on this most important matter at hand. Your work must begin as always with your first action. That must be to stop the hospital Doctors bringing you all out of your comas. You must then find the humans that will create cold dark matter on this, your planet.'

They all realised the Entity was correct, rising from their comfortable leather chairs following Darwin and Einstein as they all moved out through the study door.

Max was looking down at Doc Dave resting peacefully asleep in the hospital bed. Professor Tom and Doctor Emma were in the same room but divided by the usual hospital curtains.

Max had to pass Tom and Emma to reach Dave, they all had the same peaceful relaxed look, all three were hooked up to an ECG, and all had IV drips inserted. Getting this far to see Dave called on all of Max Zusman's charm. The hospital only allowed immediate blood relatives, until they had brought Doctor Sharp out of his coma. Max pulled up a chair and moved closer to Doc Dave and spoke softly into his ear.

'What the fuck have you done this time Doc? There is hardly a bloody scratch on you old mate, and yet you are in this deep sort of coma, all of you are in the same type of coma. Something is going on Doc; I can sense it in my water. Come-on Doc you can tell me old sport, I'm your best friend, your old fat-Jew flying mate?'

Max reached out and touched Dave's hand, and startled by a voice behind him that made him jump.

'He may be able to hear you. Most comatose patients remember what people have said to them after they wake up, in some cases a few words from a close friend or relative has brought the patient out of their coma.

My name is Doctor Brian Good, and you are?'

'Max, Maxwell Zusman,' shaking hands, 'I'm Doctor Dave Sharps chief pilot, his only pilot and I guess his closest, if not his only friend.'

'Zusman, your name means sweet man in Yiddish. Are you a sweet Jewish man Mister Zusman?'

A small flicker of surprise registered on Max's face.

'You don't look Jewish Doc, a medical Doctor who is an expert on Jewish names, now that's a new one. Just call me Max, and yes, I can be sweet to those who deserve my sweetness. Right now, my best and closest friend is in a deep coma after writing off our very nice Cessna 402 aircraft in the desert, and I am very worried about this strange coma problem.'

'Well you're not alone on that thought. We doctors all agree this is an odd state for these three people to be in, considering that we can find no injury to cause this state of unconsciousness. We are preparing to induce the patients out of their comas tomorrow, and are just waiting for the patients relatives to arrive in Perth to complete the usual hospital paperwork.'

Max thought he could help a little, adding what he knew.

'Doc Dave here only has a departing third wife Mary, who will, I hope be here within the next few hours. The other two patients are our clients, Scottish Doctor Emma Archer and American Professor Thomas Harold.'

'Well thanks that clears up one mystery. We had all the personal things to identify Doctor Sharp and Doctor Emma Archer, but advised the personal belongings of the black man all accidentally left at the crash site. Max, we obviously need to get in touch with his relatives, would you have an address in America for Professor Harold we could follow up on?'

'I don't have an address for you Doc but this bloke is, or was the leading Professor of Anthropology at Princeton University New Jersey. I do not think you will have any problems tracking down his relatives if you give the University a call. What's happening with Doctor Emma?'

'Oh that was an easy one; we had her satellite phone which listed a number of her colleagues in the UK. The first number we called was a Mister Bartholomew Randall in Oxford England who answered the phone in person. The person had a real posh pommy accent, and said he was on his way arriving here in Perth about 4pm our local time today. I thought that was very odd, as I have some friends arriving by air from the UK today; there are no jet-flights into Perth from the UK at around that time.

I have no idea what flight this person would be arriving on, as you know, they have this thing about not giving out passenger details. It's just turned 2:30pm so I guess we will soon find out; he is due to arrive in the next hour or so.'

Max was being his usual curious self, gently prodded the good Doctor Brian Good for some further bits of useful information.

'Is this posh pommy bloke the husband or brother or something?'

'I don't think so Max, but he did sound a bit young and a bit sure of himself. He told me that Doctor Archer had no living relatives, and that her mother and father are dead, killed in a freak road accident about nine years ago. Her only brother went missing in Cambodia six years ago where he was working as a voluntary Doctor.

He says he is most likely the closest that Doctor Archer has to a relative, and will cover any medical costs to bring Emma back to good health.' Then with a quizzical look added, 'he had no knowledge of your Doctor David Sharp, or for that matter the African-American guy you have now identified as Professor Thomas Harold.'

Max had an idea...

'You know something Doctor Good, I think I might go down to Perth International and pick-up this Bartholomew Randall bloke and bring him back here. I know a way of finding out what flight he will be on, we pilots have certain special privileges at airports.'

On Max's third rejected attempt to enter the door lock security code to the control tower; the silent alarm went off at the airport security office. Within minutes, two large airport security guards arrived at the armoured plated glass entry door to the Perth International Airport control tower.

Their first look at Max, with his thick bushy black beard and his already olive skin, burnt darker by the harsh desert outback sun. Clutching firmly onto his old bulging flight bag. The two burly security guards just knew they had a Muslim terrorist bomber on their hands. This was turning out to be a grim situation that warranted extra precaution.

They were both pleased that they had taken that extra terrorist identification and threat control course last week, as it now looked like it was going to pay dividends big-time. This was obviously a textbook case requiring immediate action.

Exactly as per the manual, the first security guard squirted a large quantity of mace into Max's wide-with-shock eyes, while following through with a powerful knee thrust to his groin, crushing his surprised balls. The second security guard then jabbed Max hard with his brand-new extra high power taser gun.

This action causing Max to forget all about his intense aching balls for a moment, as every nerve ending in his body wanted to leave him. His muscles had tensed so much that he never felt a thing as his head hit the ground hard after being pushed-over on to his face. Then knee in his back, and roughly handcuffed from behind by the two smiling, and satisfied security guards.

Through the swirling pain and his mace burnt eyes, Max made out the shadow of a figure coming through the glass door. Over the confusion and the rattle of walkie-talkie radios calling for the bomb disposal squad, he heard the security guards warn the person who had just come through the door.

'Stand back mate, I suggest that you leave this area right now, the bomb squad are on their way here. This could turn very nasty at any moment if you know what I mean. We just don't know what's in that bloody bag,' pointing to Max's old, well-worn flight bag. The hazy figure replied.

'Well I can tell you right now what's in that bloody bag mate, its Max Zusman's flying gear like every other bleeding pilot carries about with them. What the fuck have you blokes done to this bloody pilot, he was only coming up to the tower to see me.

Another thing, holster those bleeding taser guns, you do remember what my job is around here you overzealous shitheads. That's right; I am the fucking Director of flight operations of this bleeding airport. I'm the very same bloke who pays your bloody wages each month.'

Max barely remembered the two security guards carting him off to the airport medical room on a gurney for urgent treatment to his burning eyes and the swelling bump on his head. He was not sure what the nice-looking nurse could do for his aching balls and tensed-up muscles, Max was not well at all... he was a painful mess.

While he lay on the medical station cot with an ice pack on his testicles, and the young nurse washing his eyes out. He was remembering his last words to Doctor Good at Royal Perth Hospital. "We pilots have certain special privileges at airports."

Ron, nicknamed (Grumpy) had been the Director of flight operations at Perth International for nearly twenty years. They went back a long, long way in the flying world.

'For Christ's sake Max do you have to cause a bloody full-blown lockdown and a bomb scare at my airport? I mean just look at you man, with that bloody great black beard, you do look like a mad bomber... What would you expect these days in trying to access the bloody tower? The security boys are a bit trigger sensitive these days, these are trying times mate. Christ, you're not even a real damn Jew, you know, like a practising Synagogue going type of Jew, and all that shit.'

Max gave Grumpy his best streaming eyes stare of surprise.

'Grumpy, there are no Synagogues within a thousand kilometres of where I live at Sandfire, and anyway, you invited me up to the tower remember?'

'I take it all back mate, you are just a miserable tight-arse Jew,' then he broke into a big friendly smile... 'How the bloody-hell are you me old mate, I haven't seen you in a while, although I have heard you on the airwaves from time to time flying around up north.'

'Well Grumpy, if you must know how I am, I've got two sore eyes, two sore balls, a sore head and my body aches all over, what does that tell a smart bloke like you?'

'Easy one mate, I know the answer to that, it's time for a scotch on the rocks at the orbit bar,' glancing at his massive complicated pilots wristwatch. 'It's almost three and my shift finishes at three... what good timing.'

Max felt much better with the ice pack on his balls and a double scotch in his hand, especially as Grumpy was paying, mainly as a sort of apology for his security staff beating him up.

'I think I should sue your airport for wrongful identification of a bomb carting terrorist, and maybe discrimination against a Jewish pilot, or something like that... I'm sure I can find a lawyer that will think something up.'

'Go for it mate; I reckon you should try for around four million dollars, two million each. I'll be your number one witness, should be a piece of cake, we'll both be bloody rich mate.

Last year, an old deaf bloke suffered a heart attack when one of our security guards shouted out for him to stop, because he had dropped his newspaper. He got a million bucks for needless harassment resulting from having a Mack 10 sub-machine gun pointed at his nose, and the security bloke never even touched him. Anyway Max, why were you coming to see me?'

Max shuffled around on his bar stool to ease his throbbing balls, replying with a serious voice.

'As you know Grumpy, our Cessna 402 went down in the Great Sandy Desert two days ago, all on-board have been found safe and uninjured. You probably also know that Doc Dave and his two passengers, have been airlifted by the Royal Flying Doctor down to Royal Perth Hospital. I just wanted to tell you that Doc Dave and his passengers are all still in some sort of deep shock coma, but okay and expected to come around in a few days.

One of the passengers, or should I say clients, a Doctor Emma Archer is expecting a close friend, a Mr Bartholomew Randall who is arriving into Perth International from the UK at 4:00 pm today. I have no idea which flight he will be on, as you blokes don't give out passenger names, and I can't find a UK flight due into Perth at 4:00 pm.'

Grumpy immediately got on to his mobile phone and talked direct to the control tower. After a few minutes, Max heard Grumpy tell the flight service officer to patch the captain through to his hand-held radio.

'Captain, this is the Director of flight operations Perth International airport. We are looking for a Mr Bartholomew Randall inbound from the UK, you are the only aircraft flight planned to arrive in Perth at 4:00 pm local time from the UK. Would you have this passenger Randall on-board?'

A crisp very English voice responded immediately.

'Good afternoon sir, this is Falcon Biz-Jet Uniform Tango Romeo on decent from flight level four five, estimating Perth 0400 local with Mr Bartholomew Randal on-board. For your information sir, this is the Randall Corporation private jet, and Bartholomew is the son of the Chairperson. Would you by chance be the chap arranging the limousine hire for Mr Randall junior?'

Grumpy rolled his eyes into the back of his head and he took a deep breath to compose himself. Squeezing the little hand-held radio, as he would like to squeeze the Captain's throat, and then replying curtly,

'No Captain, unlike Heathrow and Gatwick, the Director of flight operations Perth does not have that important responsibility in his employment contract. Please advise Mr Randall the Director of flight operations will meet him in Customs and Immigration hall after landing.'

'Good Lord Sir, what is this all about, do you suspect that we are carrying some sort of contraband old chap?'

'Maybe old chap, but right now we just want to talk to that bloke.'

Grumpy stared at the radio as if daring it to say another word then shoved it into his pants pocket in disgust.

'Bloody stuck-up pommy pilot, he thinks we are still one of the colonies. I think I will put him through a full strip and body search, including all his cavities when he goes through customs. That should confirm whether he has a silver ramrod stuck-up his arse or not.'

Max managed to calm Grumpy down a little with another double scotch then both ambled down to the customs hall, Max followed, crab-walking in great pain to meet the crew and passengers of the Falcon Biz-Jet.

The Falcon crew filed through the first check gate from the tarmac and made their way to the customs inspection counters. The Captain and first officer stopped at a counter. Close behind strolled a tall, well-built young man in his late twenties dressed in designer jeans and a brown corduroy jacket. He was holding the hand of a young man of about eighteen who was looking up at the ceiling with a blank expression on his face. Grumpy was quick to notice...

'There I told you mate, two bleeding poofter Pommies coming to Australia to perve on our bloody beach lifeguards in their Speedos.'

Max was a tad smarter, as the group began looking around for some Australian official to arrive.

'I think you will find the young bloke is probably a bit mentally challenged Grumpy. Let's get over there before any of your smart security guards notice that they have stopped for no reason, and beat them all up.'

Grumpy cranked-up his best official voice and announced in a loud officious tone, like he was about to issue a speeding ticket.

'Mister Bartholomew Randall?'

'Yes.'

'Please come with us sir, you can bring the young man with-you if you wish.'

Max was impressed at Grumpy's smooth official manner, as they all walked off, heading for a security door. As Grumpy swiped his security card through the lock Max looked back at the Falcon jet crew. They were still standing in the same spot holding on to their little baggage trolleys with stunned looks.

Grumpy swiped another door open, revealing a very nice office, he gestured for everyone to sit down, and then asked Mr Randall for his passport and entry documents. Randall handed Grumpy two British passports and some letters, which he looked at for a few minutes then handing the letters to Max for inspection. Max read the letters, eyeing Randall over the documents, wondering what his relationship was with Emma.

The Chairman's son Bartholomew Randall had only spoken one word since arriving into Perth, the word "yes" yet; his eyes scanned Grumpy and Max in detailed silence. This man knew when to keep quiet. The young man, whose name was Tim just sat in the other chair facing the desk and stared up at the office ceiling; this young lad obviously had a problem.

One of the documents was a letter from Tim's guardian, a Professor Reginald Davey from Oxford University. The short letter stated that Mr Randall was the carer for Tim, his grandson. Tim was a prodigious savant, and needed to be at all times close to Mr Randall, would the reader please offer understanding and any support where possible.

The aircraft documents listed Randall the log as flight crew; there was obviously no time to get a formal Australian entry visa before departure.

Randall had decided this was a time to speak as both of these men had now read all of his documents, thinking, was his lack of an entry visa the major problem.

'I say, would you chaps be kind enough to tell me what's going on. By-the-way Mr Director, I was on the Falcon Jet flight deck, catching up on some command time when you radioed the Captain,'

Grumpy never even bothered to look up and replied.

'Max will tell you what this is all about sir, meantime I will go and get all your personal documents lodged and processed. I see you have no entry visa, so you must know your stay in Australia can only be seventy-two hours as flight crew,' glancing at Max, 'I'll be back soon mate.'

Randall watched suspiciously as the cranky Director of flight operations left the office in a hurry. He then turned his attention to the beat-up looking Jewish man, who now sat down behind the desk, replacing the director in the plush office chair.

'I'm Max Zusman, you're not expected to know me,' rising to shake hands with Randall, 'but let me first apologise for Grumpy while he is away. Grumpy is smarting over the fact that Queen Elizabeth II is still our reigning Monarch and that we are not yet a republic.

I think he has a dash of Aboriginal blood in him and is always grumpy at everybody, hence his nickname. He refuses to recognise God Save the Queen, or Advance Australia Fair as our national anthem, and still supports "Once a Jolly Swagman." These days he only plays Slim Dusty music. I can assure you he is quite harmless, but I can't say the same for his dumb security people,' gently caressing the large growing bump on his head.

A smile crept across Randall's face. He had no idea who this big woolly bear of a man was with two bloodshot eyes and a big bump on his head. Who walked like an old man with rickets, but he liked him. He had an honest style, and best of all he had a good sense of humour.

278

Max thought these young blokes had no idea what was going on, but figured this Randall guy was weighing him up. Thinking, he should try the hand-grenade approach, opening with…

'I do not think I should start this story at the very beginning Mr Randall, so I will start from when I first met Doctor Emma Archer...

Randall's eyebrows shot-up at the mention of Emma's name, then the young man who had been looking at the ceiling turned to stare at him in a cold expressionless stare. Randall instantly recovered his calm composure.

'Max, I would prefer you just call me Randall like everyone who knows me, as I dislike the name Bartholomew, or Bart. I assume addressing you as Max is acceptable in Australia. Tell me, has there been some complication, is Emma recovering, is she still unconscious?'

'Max will do just fine Randall, and so will Doctor Emma. In fact, all three on-board the Cessna 402 aircraft, having survived the crash landing with nothing more than a few scratches. Then again, all three are still in some sort of shock coma. The hospital Doctors can't figure out why they are still unconscious. I think the plan is to bring them all-out of their deep comas sometime tomorrow morning.'

'Well I must say old chap that is all most encouraging. Could you tell me, how did this aircraft came to crash in the first place, and where did it crash, and well old boy, quite frankly... who the fuck are you?'

Straight to the point, this Randall bloke is smart and knows how to cut corners, Max suddenly realised his strategy was falling apart. His well-prepared plan was to find out all he could about this bloke first, giving him a small piece of information at a time. Then again, Randall was right; I guess he should at least tell him who he was.

'Randall, I am the chief pilot for Sandfire Air Charter. My boss, and close friend was the pilot of the Cessna when it crashed into the desert.'

Max locking bloodshot eyes with Randall, and raising his hand in a gesture of convincing truth.

'Let me say now, that Doctor David Sharp would be one of the most experienced pilots in Australia, especially when flying over desert areas. I have no doubts the reason for such minor injuries was only because of Doc Dave's considerable expertise as a bush pilot.'

Max noticed a slight twitch of the eye when he mentioned Sandfire; this bloke knows far more than he was letting on, he had obviously heard of Sandfire before. What was going on, Emma was only supposed to be going along with Professor Tom Harold just for the tourist ride... what other things does this man know? Max continued with caution.

'We don't know why the aircraft went down as everybody on-board is still in a coma, and no emergency call was made. After the rescue, the damaged aircraft then airlifted back to our company base by an RAAF Chinook. Air Safety Australia and our engineers are currently checking the thing out. We do know the Cessna 402 had carried out a controlled forced landing into the Great Sandy Desert.'

An uneasy minutes silence followed as Randall absorbed this information. He was a well-experienced pilot, knowing aircraft only crashed for a reason; then leant forward-looking hard at Max thinking why is this chap being so damn devious. On first meeting, he had led him to believe that he was in some way involved with the Perth airport authority. Now it turns out he is just a pilot, and a friend of the fellow who had crashed-landed the aircraft that Emma was on. This was indeed odd, why was he here, and what is it that he wants to know. This pilot chap was fishing for something.

Randall thought he would try a different approach.

'I did a little swatting-up on your rather large state of Western Australia while on that boring flight from old Blighty. This Great Sandy Desert place is bigger than the whole of the United Kingdom and France. Come now Max old chap, you must know in what part of this desert your aircraft came down. After all you have declared that your boss Doc Dave is a... desert flying expert?'

Max thought this cocky bloke is a bit sharper than he had first thought. Max was trying to avoid mentioning the name Veevers, which might open up a link to the odd things that were going on out there. Who knows what might have contributed to the cause of the forced landing. On the other hand, it would be interesting to see what the mention of the name would cause...

'Randall you're a bit new to this continent, having only been here less than an hour. I can't see why you would be interested in the place that your friend and my friend nearly met their mortal end... If it satisfies your curiosity, the Cessna went down approximately one nautical mile north east of the Veevers meteorite crater, which is roughly...'

The response was quite frightening, causing him to pause in confusion. As Randall was taking a breath to talk, Max noticed that young Tim was now staring directly at him again with big soft penetrating brown eyes that looked right through him. Max found this most un-nerving, and then Tim spoke in a low haunting voice...

'They have all met the master of the Universe... the Entity. We must hurry to keep them all together and talking, about how to save our world.'

Randall glanced at Tim then back to Max adding...

'We need to get out of here and to this hospital quickly to check on Emma. I say, can we go now Max as I do think this matter is now rather urgent.'

Max did not expect this sudden reaction. Something was going on. The mention of Veevers had triggered a nerve.

'What the bloody hell was that lot all about Randall? "They have all met the master of the Universe, the Entity." What is this young bloke talking about?'

Randall could see that Max was spooked by Tim's vision.

'Believe me Max; Tim most times says very little; however, when he does speak it is always well worth listening too, and he is rarely ever wrong old chap. Tim is a prodigious savant, who has a depth of understanding far beyond our simple level of intelligence. Please Max, we must get over to the hospital quickly, I do suspect that something may be happening.'

Max was still confused, trying to work out what was going on when Grumpy burst in through the door with a handful of documents.

'Okay you pommes are out of here. All your documents now have a little blue government stamp of approval on them. I got you both a six-month tourist visa, call me if you need more time, Max here knows how to get in direct touch with me.'

Max shuddered, remembering the last time he got in touch.

They all got to their feet and shook hands in appreciation; Max trying to figure out what had come over Grumpy, and why did he think a six-month visa was required. Deciding now was not the time to ask, he and Randall thanked Grumpy for his help with the documents. Grumpy then escorted them all-out of the terminal into the bright

Perth sunshine to meet with the surprised Falcon Biz-Jet crew, and a waiting stretch limousine. Randall snapped into action.

'Driver would you kindly take us to the Royal Perth Hospital and then take the crew on to a Hotel;' turning to Max, 'is there a Hotel that you could heartily recommend?'

'I'm staying at the Hyatt, well until Doc Dave's credit card runs out.'

'Well then, we shall all stay at the Hyatt, driver... drive on.'

The three of them stood in the hospital room looking down at themselves; Emma, Tom, and Dave were sleeping comfortably in their hospital beds. Emma was still unsure of how this coma thing might affect her in some way, in her quaint Scottish accent asked nobody in particular.

'What happens if I don't wake-up from this coma, will I be dead, oh my, is this how it is when you die?'

Einstein was holding the bowl of his pipe while studying the IV drip-bag on its stand next to Emma's bed. He removed his pipe and spoke in his usual dull drone, while still looking at the IV bag.

'You must all accept this situation as temporary, Emma your stress level is much higher than Dave or Tom's. If you were dead, you would no longer throw an image as you are now.

When your life force leaves your physical body, you would instantly cease to exist as a live human. In this reflective state, you can still feel your body condition as Tom did when he was dehydrated. Humans call this state an (out of body experience.)'

Emma felt a little better but still needed more information to reduce her fear level from terrifying down to being simply scared.

'What is a life force? Is this what we would call our spirit, and where does it go when we die. Is there a heaven and a hell,' then becoming a little more agitated, 'And do not tell me that this is not relevant to us finding the source, to who is creating cold dark matter on earth. We need more assurance to trust you, and to reduce our fear of you.'

'Emma, humans make their own heaven and hell, yet your so-called animal, or lower biological species have no concept of heaven... or hell. Much the same as we the Entity have no need or

282

concern for such a place. All biological life forms have a body with a life force. Conversely, we the Entity have a life force without a biological body.

When a biological being is nearing the end of its normal life cycle the regeneration of the cells slow down, reaching a point where they can no longer support the biological body-function to which the life force is attached.

This situation is simply ageing cellular deterioration. The result is always the same. The biology eventually separates from the life force resulting in what you call death, and we know as the end of a life cycle.'

Tom and Dave were fascinated at this casual, matter-of-fact, simple explanation of the life and death of humans. Emma wanted to know another urgent detail from the Entity.

'And what happens to our life force, or what we humans would call our spirit, or our soul?'

There was no immediate answer, and they all waited in a deepening silence. Einstein had replaced his pipe in his mouth, and Darwin was leaning on his walking cane, with what looked like the best human face that they had all witnessed to date. These two were now becoming quite predictable, as Darwin would be the next one to speak... and he did.

'You said our life force. You have assumed that every beings life force belongs to the host. Be advised again, every living being from the smallest most fundamental live bacterium cell to the largest in the phylogenetic tree of life can only exist with a life force.

Each life cycle of existence, survives only by its natural development in genetics. Genetic instinctive memory and eventually true intelligence through new sensory memory and finally retained knowledge. If you have not evolved a reason to live, then you would not have a reason to exist. Everything has a purpose, and every life existence has a life cycle... a beginning and an end.'

Dave thought this was like extracting teeth, slow and painful. Was the Entity avoiding a reply to Emma's spiritual question? Dave now

283

fascinated by the Entities simple description of life and death, now he needed to know more.

'And the life force... the soul, what is the soul?'

Einstein turned to face the three of them looking blankly ahead, and then asked a simple question.

'Dave, what happens when you turn a light switch off?'

'Well, the light goes out and you end up in darkness.'

'True, but on your planet the power is still available at the switch to turn the light back on again. We the Entity provide the power to the switch of life, as this power, this life force is with us.

However, once the switch is on, the life cycle must run its course, during which time we have little or no control over which direction the host may take.

We have no control over your individual human actions, as this is natural selection, your eventual path through evolution. This is the reason why we are now seeking your help to resolve this future situation.'

Tom was going over questions in his head about what the Entity had been saying, regarding the human life force or soul. He was thinking; this was synonymous with what all the major world religions had been preaching for centuries. A Holy Ghost or spirit, the body of God, Allah. The seeking of spiritual awareness could be simply the sharing or following of a combined faith... or a religion.

'Tom, do not forget that we can monitor your planned thoughts, we will say this again. We are not a personal God; we do not act in response to any individual life force or a congregation.

We are not a merciful God, as we have no compassion or individual consideration in what we do. We are not a force, deity, or God. We are an Entity... a dark energy... a faster than light particle with intelligence flowing throughout this universe...

Einstein's theory (nothing travels faster than light) was wrong by his choice... He knew of the Entity, and about possessing knowledge too early. Then again, if exposed, he would have to prove this faster-than-light theory as fact to his detractors... On your planet, the answer to this question has yet to be discovered, and then proven.

As Einstein, I have written, (Science without religion is lame, and religion without science is blind,) also, (A legitimate conflict between science and religion cannot exist)...

Those are Einstein's words not the Entities, yet again, he knew of our existence. If Einstein had replaced the word 'religion', with 'The Entity,' his words would have been accurate and more meaningful.

Had Einstein revealed the source of his knowledge, both your religious and scientific world luminaries would have ridiculed him, in much the same way that Galileo was denounced in 1633; having been found guilty of heresy by an ignorant religious inquisition.

Galileo was forced on the fear of his life to recant his findings, when suggesting the sun was the centre of the Universe. Had he known about the solar system, this would have been the intended description.

There is a correct time for everything. Early knowledge can be extremely dangerous, and late knowledge can be fatal. A balance of knowledge within a given time period is the answer to all future existence... this is what we provide.

We no longer have a need, or use for humans to follow any man-made religion. For us this ideology has now served its useful purpose in binding many people, countries, and cultures together into several unified common powers.

Heaven and hell, along with good and evil are the well-practised and exploited tools of devious humans. Religions have become a form of psychological power, used to install fear, demanding unconditional compliance to their beliefs and teachings. A method accomplished by those who know best how to control, abuse, and exploit their own fellow human beings.

We are simple in our presence and function, as an omnipresent and metaphysical Entity, keeping balance and order throughout the natural universe.

Religious following, ideologies, and the worship of a personal god will continue through a predictable and planned, mostly violent cycle.

In doing so, will continue to bring about much human suffering and death on your planet for some time into your near future. These religious matters will only be resolved through education, the truth, and a higher level of intelligence. Then finally, to a future understanding that we the Entity exist, in much the same way that

*humans have now come to accept the existence of light, electrical
energy, gravity, and radio waves.*

This subject on your world's obsolete religions is now closed.
*You must now concern yourselves with the soon extinction of your
species, or the eminent destruction of your planet, as without your
planet you are nothing in this our universal plan.'*

Emma, Tom, and Dave were still staring at Einstein and Darwin.
All were in shock realising that the Entity was not in the least bit
interested in discussing planet earth's religious or human problems
with them, or for that matter anybody.

The Entity was on a singular mission, it had a job to do in first
preserving that the planet earth remained in its present gravitational
orbit around our star, the Sun. The sad realisation was, we humans
were, if the Entity should so choose... were completely expendable.

The door of the ward opened and in filed a serious looking Doctor
and Nurse, followed by Randall, Tim, and Max. They paused in the
middle of the large private ward as the Doctor consulted his notes.

'We got a call from Professor Harold's son, a Doctor Luke. He
will arrive on the 8:20 flight tomorrow from LA. Doctor Luke Harold
is a neurosurgeon; and has requested that he examine his father prior
to any treatment. We can't start the conscious recovery process until
he signs off the okay, so I guess we will just have to wait until
tomorrow morning to bring them out of their comas.'

The Nurse drew back the dividing curtains revealing the three
beds. Randall sat down next to sleeping Emma and held her hand, Max
flopped back into the chair next to Doc Dave looking for any sign of
movement.

The Doctor checked the electronic monitoring equipment while
the Nurse tended to the IV drips. After a few minutes the Doctor and
Nurse left after reminding them all, the hospital visiting hours finished
at 8pm.

Emma, Tom, and Dave were standing in a group watching this
scene and wondering what they should do next, when a creepy feeling
came over Tom. He had noticed that Tim was looking right at him
with his big brown eyes.

'Can this young man see me, I thought I was... well invisible?'

286

Emma quickly explained about Tim.

'That's Tim, he's a prodigious savant, he can see and hear many things that we can't, but I suppose we could ask him... Tim this is Emma can you see or hear me?'

Tim cocked his head to one side as if listening hard and said nothing, and then from behind them Darwin in his droning flat voice explained.

'Tim is an enlightened human who can feel our presence; he knows we are all here. For Tim to hear you must touch him, and speak, he will then hear you in his head. Be careful, as we have lost many humans through sudden fear and shock. Be aware, to the young human you are still all asleep in those hospital beds.'

Emma went over to her bed, Randall was still holding her hand, and Tim was standing behind Randall looking at Tom. Emma reached out and touched Tim's face.

'Hi Tim, please don't be frightened it's only Emma. Look at me in the bed I know you can hear me, I am okay but we need to talk, and quietly. I am with Doctor David Sharp and Professor Thomas Harold, we need your help.'

Tim turned and looked down at Emma, responding without a flinch or expression of fear... then he smiled. This was the first time Emma had ever seen Tim smile. Tim leant over and whispered into Randall's ear...

'Emma wants to talk with us, she is here. She said she is okay and with the others. She needs our help.'

Randal's head spun around to look at Tim who still held a smile. Randal was confused as Tim put his finger to his lips in a motion of silence.

Dave had taken to looking at himself and Max while Tom was standing at the end of his own bed watching Emma talk to Tim thinking, would Randall and Max listen to young Tim... Einstein heard his thoughts.

'Randall will listen; however, Max will need a little more convincing for keeping you in a coma a while longer. As a detached

or out of body existence, you can choose to re-enter your body and ultimately wake-up, this would be your choice.

If you just touch your body, you can bring about a partial consciousness however, you must withdraw quickly before you regain full consciousness, you cannot go back into a deep coma.

A deep coma is the preferred way for us to travel your world using your, as you say... spirit.'

Dave had a question that was bothering him.

'What happens to all the people who never come out of a coma if all they have to do is touch and nip back into their body again?'

Einstein gave a good example of a human sigh and replied.

'A detached human life-force, or free-spirit, floating or existing within a hospital ward or operating theatre, is a simple matter for reunification. When used for travel in the ether, it then becomes a very precise business to perform.

In this dreamlike state, a human will soon get lost in a fantasy world and can no longer find a way back to their biological body, some do but rarely. The life force then remains in limbo until the biological body ceases to function and then the life cycle ends.'

'Could that happen to us?'

'Not while you are with the Entity Dave, as we do know our way around the cosmos, and this small planet.'

Tom and Emma started to discuss a pending problem, what would Tom's son do when he arrived tomorrow. Emma agreed with Tom that most likely Luke would simply bring him out of his coma, as there was no real medical reason for him to remain or be in a coma.

Dave came into the discussion saying that one method would be to explain through Tim or by becoming briefly conscious that they needed to remain as they were for the next day or two.

Tom gave this some thought then suggested that maybe he would be of better use conscious, as he knew the real reason behind all these events. He could also add some reason to keep Emma and Dave under for another day or so.

Dave thought this was a good idea in having one of them in the real world. It was also a way to keep the number of involved knowing people reduced, but how would they stay in communication? The Entity provided the answer.

'When conscious, Tom will still remain enlightened to a level higher than Tim. Unfortunately, he will no longer be able to travel or see you, but will hear you in his head, and only then when you speak direct to Tom. With some practice, Tom will also read other peoples (planned) thoughts as we do. You will need these small advantages to carry out your mission. You are reminded that your time to resolve this matter is limited.'

Dave was now starting to understand just what the limits were for the Entity. It needed a human close-by to think as a human. Mainly to work out what the next move would be for whoever was involved with the creation of cold dark matter.

Moving around in the Entities domain was just a matter of jumping from one presence, state, or situation to another. Only to witness something happening over which the Entity had little or no immediate physical control. A human could move quickly to affect the required and immediate change, and apply some change over the unfolding event.

Then Dave had another bright idea. If, as the Entity has revealed, when in a conscious state we could still communicate with one another. Then there is only need for one of them to remain with the Entity in a deep coma, and he would be that obvious choice.

'I think that Emma should come out of the coma with Tom. Emma has the scientific knowledge to identify whom and where this threat may be developing, being in the real world she could be more useful by using her, what's the name group.'

Emma filled in the missing name "chaos group."

'Anyway, the media will soon get hold of this crash story and make a big thing about the two foreign scientists involved in an outback plane crash. Nobody will give a damn about a busted-arse Australian pilot who most likely be blamed for the incident. It will take the heat out of the whole story especially when you explain that you were both just on a flying scenic tour.'

Tom thought this was the way to go, as two of Emma's chaos group were right here. Emma was a bit reluctant pointing out that trained in quantum physics; she could identify the most likely technical people and equipment, if able to just turn-up in a ghostly way and look over their shoulders.

Dave drove his plan to an accepted conclusion by reminding them that the Entity itself had no idea where the threat was coming from. It only knew by past universal history and experience that this threat did exist... and was now about to happen on this planet.

Dave bent down and touched his body, which immediately moved a little, Max noticed this small movement. Dave murmured and Max placed his ear next to Dave's mouth.

'Max, listen to Randall and do exactly what he bloody says, I must remain in this coma for a short while, maybe four days or a week. Emma and Tom will wake-up and be with you shortly. Tell everybody this bump on my head is causing me a problem. You must stop them bringing me out of my coma, trust me mate it's very important.'

Max thought he had heard wrong, and turned in his seat to face Emma's bed. Randall smiled a knowing smile. He then gently nodded his head in recognition. Did Emma and Randall know what Dave had just told him in a low whisper?

From then, things happened quickly. Just as Mary, Dave's wife walked into the ward, Emma and Tom suddenly awoke from their comas causing the EEG to exceed 30 cps beta. The alarm sounded loudly bringing the duty Nurse to the ward followed by a Doctor.

The normal response from any hospital visitors to such an alarm would have been. 'What's going on Doctor,' however; everybody in the room knew exactly what was going on except the Doctor... and of course Mary.

'What's happening Max, did I cause all this. Is Dave going to be okay, all I did was walk in through the door?'

'Don't panic Mary, it looks like they are finally wakening up, your timing is perfect as usual. But I noticed that Doc Dave's alarm didn't go off at all, which I guess was to be expected.'

Mary gave Max a sideways look of suspicion at that last comment, being not sure what he meant. Max just turned in his chair to watch the developing panic as two other Doctors arrived to help with the recovery.

A young Doctor came over to Doc Dave and immediately pealed back his eyelid and flashed a torch. Max could not resist the joke.

'See any brains in there Doc, because he's been doing some stupid bloody things over the last year or so.'

This sparked up the young Doctors medical interest; he then followed through, just as Max had intended.

'Like what? Forgetting things, doing things he would not normally do, and upsetting people. Or maybe drinking a little too much?'

'Yeah he's been doing all of that, and more.'

'Such as...?'

'Well for a start he has upset the most beautiful woman in the world. A woman he is madly in love with, and then he threw it all away and let her walk right out of his life,' Max throwing his arms into the air for added emphasis. 'And then the bastard blamed me for 'her' filing for a divorce.'

The young Doctor looked at Max who had now turned back to watching the others then to the nice-looking woman sitting at the bedside, who was crying a river of tears. The young Doctor had not made the obvious connection, yet felt that he should say something.

'Don't you worry miss; this man will come out of his coma soon, just like the others did. This patient has had every test imaginable and we can find no reason why he should remain in this deep coma. Please don't concern yourself; we will bring him out of it by this time tomorrow morning.'

Emma and Tom were now wide-awake chatting away as if they had both awakened from a good night's sleep. Tom called Max over as the Doctors made ready to leave the ward. They were surprised that these two patients were not in the least bit traumatised by their two-day ordeal, being lucky enough to escape death from a plane crash in a remote desert. They had not even bothered to ask how the pilot was, who was laying in the next bed.

Tom beckoned Max to come closer and whispered in surprise.

'What the hell happened to your face Max, you look like you have been in an airplane crash.'

Max thought about that one for a second, and was about to launch into the mistaken terrorist story when Tom held up his hand in a sign of stop.

'We must keep a lid on all of this Max. I know what Dave told you. He needs to remain in his coma to do something very important.

Just give Dave, Emma and I a little time to explain all this to you, but say nothing to anyone until we can get together in private. We have a world-shattering problem that needs fixing urgently. It will need you, Randall, and Tim's help. Can we trust you?'

Max pulled back from Tom with a look of astonishment on his battered face. How could Tom have heard what Dave had whispered to him? He then turned to look at Emma who was staring directly at him. Randall and Tim also appeared to know, now looking on as if waiting for his reply.

Max had many odd things racing through his head. He knew Professor Tom was still in a deep coma, when Doc Dave whispered those words into his ear about listening to Randall. Then there was the strange matter in that Tom had never even met Randall... or Tim. Max nodded his head in confused agreement he was speechless, and then slowly closed his gaping mouth.

Chapter Seventeen

Maybe we should hold a Séance

Max introduced Emma and Tom to Mary as Doc Dave's clients. Mary wanted to know what had happened out in the desert, and why they had come out of their comas while Dave was still asleep. Tom reckoned he had no idea why the aircraft had crashed into the desert, adding that he thought that Doctor Sharp did the best he could under the circumstances. He considered that in his limited knowledge the emergency landing was damn good.

They would all have to wait until Dave came around. As for Dave remaining unconscious, Tom offered only a guess that as Dave had hit his head quite hard in the landing, this could be the reason.

Tom added that his son would arrive tomorrow morning from the States, and being one of the leading US neurosurgeons promised that he would get his son Luke to give Dave a thorough medical examination. Mary was quite impressed, feeling assured by this gentle spoken Professor. Taking Tom's advice, deciding to leave, and would return tomorrow. By then, she hoped Dave could be brought out of his coma.

Max was not so confident or assured by Tom's smooth academic manner. Too many questions remained unanswered, and far too many spooky things had happened he did not understand. One such thing was Emma, Randall, and Tim all appeared to know what was going on.

Could it be that he was intentionally being kept in the dark? Then again, it was most likely because he was just too dumb to understand what was going on. After all, they were smart scientists and he was just a pilot, then again, he would have to agree with himself… a very smart pilot.

Max was becoming concerned at the lack of interest the others had in Doc Dave's condition. He was about to vent his displeasure at anyone who would listen when Emma turned and spoke first, in her tilting Scottish accent.

'You look like you have just lost a pound and found a penny Max. We are about to tell you a story that will blow your kilt up and change your views on this worlds future, the truth about every known religion, and the true meaning of life.'

Max, not wishing to appear ignorant in worldly knowledge, he then decided to add his own sceptical view to Emma's strange out-of-context statement. With a hint of a smile, he then confessed his only view on the meaning of life.

'Living in a remote place in Australia, and with little in the way of worldly distractions, I have become quite well read Emma. I have read the book twice and seen the movie of "The Hitch-hikers Guide to the Galaxy" and know the answer to the meaning of life is forty-two. I think the book is better than the movie, but the answer is still the same… forty-two.'

Nobody laughed; Max concluded the matter they wanted to talk about must be serious stuff. What were these people involved with, and nobody had even mentioned a word about Doc Dave. Another point, what is this "truth about religion" and "the true meaning of life" crap all about. In addition, why do I have to trust this Randall bloke, hell I only met him a few hours ago.

Emma and Tom looked at one another; they had both read Max's thoughts. Then noting that Randall and Tim were eagerly waiting to hear their story… Yes, just as the Entity had predicted Max would take some convincing about the Entity, and there mission.

Randall remained unusually quiet, he could see something was bothering Max however, he knew Emma well, and had decided to wait for Emma to spill the beans as it were.

He had Max worked out, but who was this old African-American Professor of Anthropology chap? The man had the look and attitudes of a well-experienced scholar, and was remarkably calm about all of this.

294

Everyone shuffled into Emma's new private room funded by Randall's limitless gold credit card, and sat down. Tom was first to talk.

'Max you don't happen to have a bottle of scotch in that flight bag at your feet. Emma and I could really do with a drink after what we have just been through, then glancing at Randall. Mister Randall looks like a beer man although I am certain on this special occasion he will join us in a scotch.'

Like a rabbit out of a hat, Max made an almost full large bottle of Glenfiddich scotch appear out of his flight bag. Randall was most impressed; thinking, there would have been little room left for any of his important flight documents. Maybe this was part of the normal Australian pilot's flight survival kit.

He would quiz Max on this matter later. As it was, he was quite looking forward to a nip of scotch. Not to be outdone Randall magically produced an already lit cigarette, took a deep drag, exhaling a huge cloud of white smoke. Then in his crisp English accent.

'Randall will do nicely Professor. I must admit sir you are absolutely spot-on; I do indeed favour a beer as my preferred alcoholic fluid.'

Then glancing at Max's bottle of scotch…

'Nonetheless, Glenfiddich single malt scotch comes a close second sir,' puffing another large cloud of cigarette smoke into the middle of the sterile room, and then casually adding with a serious voice.

'Well then, what the jolly-hell is this lot about then.'

Max was thinking here we go again; these bloody foreigners are busy working on how to drink all my scotch. They are just as bad as Doc Dave who now wants me to follow, and do what this Randall bloke asks of me. At least this Randall looks like he can afford to buy the next bottle or two. Just then, Max swiftly interrupted in his deep thoughts by a smooth response from Tom.

'Randall, we have decided to drop all the academic titles, Tom is just fine,' then turning to Max. 'As for being a foreigner working on drinking all your scotch I will remind you Max, that you and Dave have already done a tidy job on one of my bottles of scotch. As I remember, you still have two more bottles of my scotch at Sandfire.'

The look on Max's face was worth preserving. This was Tom's second successful attempt at seeking and hearing another person's preplanned thoughts. Tom beamed a great grin at Max's confused look... this could be fun. As Max was about to express his astonishment at Toms mind-reading achievement, Emma caught everyone's attention.

'Please lads, we must get on and explain what this matter is all about, time is against us. Friends, this is about life-and-death, not just your life-and-death, or your family and friends, but that of the whole human race on this planet we all call home.'

Max, Tim, and Randall stared on in silence at the serious looking Emma and Tom, who were now sitting together facing them. That last frightening comment Emma had made, certainly caught their attention. There were no smart-arsed remarks from Randall, and Max was once again speechless.

Max was now ready for the next blow to his rationally balanced life, even Tim was looking right at them and not at the ceiling... waiting. Tom began in his soft American accent to relate the strange story...With an opening that only a well-experienced lecturer would use.

'A great man once wrote, 'I am a deeply religious nonbeliever... This is a somewhat new kind of religion.' That man was Albert Einstein. The same man wrote, 'If you can't explain it simply, then you don't understand it well enough.' Well my new friends that is our problem. How do we explain something so complicated, yet so fundamental to our very existence on this planet we all call home.'

Tom paused to let that sink in. This would be difficult to explain.

'In the matter of belief, faith, and the right decision; the most powerful motivator of acceptance is irrefutable proof. Max, you have experienced and witnessed a strange phenomenon just north of the Veevers meteorite crater. Randall you have discovered, tracked, and plotted a number of strange gravity cluster rings in locations at well-known ancient sites.

Now you have both experienced other paranormal phenomena in talking to and hearing people who were, and still are in a deep coma. To me it looks like the Entity in its strange way is offering us all a level of irrefutable proof.'

Randall could not resist slipping in an urgent observation and question.

'Excuse me old boy, but just who is this Entity you are talking about? Are you chaps trying to tell us that you have been converted

296

by your crash landing in the desert, and now you have all found religion?

Are you actually preaching your new-found religion to us, if so, count Tim and me out... we are scientists, we only work on sound logical theory and proven facts.'

Emma could see the problem that Tom was trying to breach he needed help. Emma knew time was a critical matter; they must get them to comprehend and accept what this urgent situation was.

She was now starting to understand the extent of the problem, in getting other people to recognize and accept strange phenomena as the truth. The Entity was correct again, this was not an easy task. Emma tried again from another angle.

'We will explain all about the Entity shortly. Firstly, to use your choice of words Randall, you are exceedingly wrong. We can certainly assure you that we have not gone all religious. The unfortunate facts are that religion has a small part to play in all of what we are about to tell you, but not in the way that you think.

Religion has been a useful and necessary tool in the evolution of our human social development. Tom is trying to prepare you for the next part of this story, who is really running this life existence show. We can tell you the absolute truth right now, and it's not a God, anyone's God.'

That shut out the negative views for a moment and held their interest; it was obvious they needed some further convincing, some form of proof.

Dave and the Entity were watching and listening to all of this and could see the problem, then speaking directly into Emma and Toms head.

'I think it's time I had a chat with Max, Randall, and Tim. That should convince them that ghosts of a sort do actually exist. We have to move beyond this and get this show on the road.

Einstein and Darwin are starting to reconsider their view, that this is all a waste of bloody time. No doubt considering that their first and normal option was the best way. Just wipe us off the face of the planet and start all over again.'

Emma shivered at Dave's blunt but correct conclusion.

'We must get started on finding the people who are about to create cold dark matter.'

Emma responded to Dave, speaking out aloud without thinking.

'No wait Dave, we must try to convince them without frightening the living daylights out of them. We need to try the same gentle tactics used by the Entity on us. Too much too soon may cause the opposite effect.

Remember what the Entity has said, many humans went insane after hearing voices in their heads. While others had developed some strange views thinking they were a chosen one, a prophet.'

The looks on Randall and Max's faces were that of disbelief, they thought that Emma had gone mad. Tom quickly added his calming view.

'I think you've blown it Emma. The way I see things now is that Tim already knows all about this Entity stuff, so he is no problem. Randall is just like you and me, a scientist who will only accept a fact gained from positive proof, and Max, well Max is a basic hand-in-the-fire man. If he can't feel the pain and smell the burning flesh... then it just ain't hot.'

Max burst out of his frozen stupor.

'Who the hell were you talking to Emma? Doc Dave's in the room two levels down out cold and, having a problem surfacing from a deep coma.'

Tim turned his head gaining instant attention. Then looking directly at Max, spoke in a low voice.

'Max, your Doctor David Sharp is here in this room with us now. We must all work together to stop the dark matter from being collected.'

Tim reached out and held Randall's hand just as Dave placed his ghostly hand on Max and Randall's shoulders. Dave's first words drew a flinch of disbelief. They could all hear him in their heads, this was a weird experience, and for real. Tim just stared ahead with a knowing empty stare.

Dave, Emma, and Tom launched into their story about the Entity and its function in maintaining a balance in the universe. Being the keepers of time and order, while busy seeding other possible life planets and developing a greater universal intelligence. Randall and

Max were fascinated by this all-new meaning of life theory; having been corrected several times that this was now indeed a fact and not a theory.

Tom pointed out that he held a doctorate in Anthropology of Religion, yet was not a follower of any religion. This no doubt being the reason why the Entity had chosen him, and yes, he could see the similarities in the way the Entity performed its job, and that of the beliefs of the five major religions.

Tom went on to say the Entity had aided many earth humans over the centuries by giving them direction and a few clues to keep them on the right path to a future useful development. Those people were the well-known religious prophets, Abraham, Moses, Jesus, and Muhammad. There were many others overtime that used the Entities knowledge, some for a good cause and others for their own fame, attention and power.

Those included Aristotle and Nostradamus, who had managed to get most Entity matters slightly wrong. Then there was Adolf Hitler, Kublai Kahn, and Leonardo daVinci and others throughout our known history. From medical doctors discovering new medical breakthroughs to political despots and military dictators creating death and destruction to consolidate and enforce their newly found knowledge and power.

Tom added that at this time the Entity had taken on the image and attitude of two world famous men, Charles Darwin and Albert Einstein. These two images were created to help reduce their fear of the Entity and to appear a little human.

Tom was about to hand over to Emma who wanted to get a story out when the door suddenly opened and in marched a Doctor and Nurse.

The Doctor was surprised to see this crowd of people in the room while the Nurse immediately launched into her standard eviction routine.

'Come now, you people must all leave at once, this is the Doctors last ward round, the time is now 8:20pm, long past normal visiting hours.' sniffing the air like a rabbit. 'Can I smell cigarette smoke in this room...' then pointing to the plastic pill cup that Tom was holding 'is that alcohol I can smell?'

Randall was busy trying to disperse his cigarette smoke while Max was busy hiding his bottle of scotch; they all clearly heard Dave laughing.

'I think we should leave here and regroup shortly at the Hyatt to continue this most interesting discussion.' Randall turned to Emma and Tom, 'I shall book you each a room on our floor we will be back here tomorrow morning to bring you both back to the Hotel.'

'I think first up that tomorrow Emma and I should sort out Dave's problem with my son Luke. I will give you a call at the Hyatt when we are ready, most likely we will need Max to sign something. By then I guess we will also need to buy some clothes and things as our travel bags are still up at Sandfire.'

It was only a short ten-minute walk from the Royal Perth Hospital to the Hyatt Hotel but nobody said a word. Max was in deep thought at the weird phenomena of Doc Dave talking to him while still in a coma. Randall was going through the many questions he would ask when they all got back together again.

Dave, Emma, and Tom had clearly said the Entity needed our help. Then there was the discussion about the so-called "world shattering problem," a problem that involved the "life-and-death" of this planet. They also had yet to clarify about this cold dark matter being a problem.

Entering the Hotel reception Max suggested they should all freshen-up and meet down in the restaurant in thirty minutes for dinner to continue this conversation. Randall, with a grin suggested that they should invite Doc Dave along; Max agreed that was a good idea, especially as Dave would not be eating much, or for that matter drinking any scotch.

Randal was first to arrive at the restaurant holding Tim's hand. The waiter noticing the intimacy found them a small round table in the corner, which suited Randal just fine. The slim timid looking waiter smiled a knowing smile as he went to clear the other place settings from the table. Randall noticed the move, then in his crisp English accent.

'Waiter, there will be another person joining us for dinner tonight, and be advised waiter, we British do actually tip for good service.'

The waiter bowed repeatedly as he backed away from the table, backing arse first, right into a table full of well-dressed mining executives.' While the waiter went about his apologising, Max joined them at the table and sat down. The waiter came back to their table, cocking one eyebrow, waiting for the drinks order. Max ignored him and tackled the first obvious problem.

'How do you suggest that we get in touch with Doc Dave, I mean these ghost blokes might go to bed early or something?'

Randall had been thinking along similar lines and had an idea.

'You know Max, I think we should hold a spiritual séance, we should all hold hands in a circle and call Dave's name.' Max was not convinced. 'Well you never know old boy, it works fine in the movies.'

All three held hands above the table and quietly called Dave's name as the waiter looked on in bewildered surprise.

Dave, Einstein, and Darwin were watching this performance with interest. Einstein wanted to know what they were doing, this was not logical and a waste of time. These humans only had a few months of their time at most to change the future path, which will eventually destroy their world.

Dave assured Einstein and Darwin that all they wanted to do was get in touch with them to contrive a plan to resolve this urgent matter. Dave moved forward and touched Max and Randall on the shoulder.

'You had better place the drinks order before the waiter has you lot thrown out, I'll have a double scotch on the rocks thanks.'

Randall turned his head and snapped out the order in his crisp English.

'Waiter we will have one large beer, and two double scotch over ice. Oh and a coke in a glass for the young man here... thank you.'

'That is four drinks sir and you are only three?'

'No matter waiter, the other drink is for our ghostly friend here who only drinks excellent single malt Glenfiddich.'

'Shall I set another place sir?'

Dave was starting to get cranky and told them to stop fooling around. It would appear that Max had met his match in Randall; they could both make a joke out of just about anything.

'Stop holding hands like pansies, as long as I can place a hand on you, you can hear me, we have a lot to talk about. By the way Emma and Tom are listening in to this.'

Randall smiled at the waiter and replied.

'No thank you waiter we will not require a fourth setting tonight, only the whisky for the spirit, you see spirits like to drink spirits.'

The confused waiter placed the menus on the table and left in a hurry... Max tried out his new found spooky chat with his boss.

'I have a question Doc, what's this "world shattering problem" and the bloody "life-and-death of this planet" talk all about... and what the hell has cold dark matter got to do with all this?'

'All three and more problems are all related Max. Somewhere on this planet someone or some organisation is about to, or is at this moment creating cold dark matter. Emma has just told me to get Randall to explain the ultimate risks involved with the creation of cold dark matter.'

Randall lit-up a cigarette and puffed a perfect smoke ring then hid the fag under the tablecloth while he spoke.

'You know chaps; there are differing variations on the existence of dark matter. CDM or cold dark matter is very interesting stuff. We have the theory to create CDM and know it is a particle without mass, possibly the elusive "graviton" a particle, held together by dense gravity.

If so, then this would be the opposite of DM "dark matter," which in theory holds the universe apart, a force separating the solar systems and galaxies keeping things in place, and in their orbits. Dark matter absorbs light therefore cannot be seen; however, it is most likely made-up of a form of matter that travels at the speed of light, filling the space between all other objects in space.

This DM makes up around 95% of the universe filling the vast vacuum of empty space. Then we have other interesting stuff, DE "dark energy." It exists between the yet to be discovered dark matter particles.' That would then leave around 5% of... something. In theory 4% would be just ordinary matter, the good stuff that all the planets made up of, leaving 1%... which must be CDM "cold dark matter."

This is thought to be a slow, heavy dense matter, possibly antimatter that would assume raw dense gravity, the same stuff that black holes are thought to consist of.

Everything sucked into a black hole is ultimately crushed into a fraction of its normal size under huge gravitational pressure. It is theorised that a solar system would reduce to less than the size of one atom. Even light photons would be crushed, extinguishing all light... thus the name, a black hole.'

Tim's head dropped from looking at a spot on the restaurant ceiling to staring Max direct in the eye, noticing this, Randal stopped his interesting lecture on dark matter. They all waited... then Tim spoke.

'Dark energy can travel faster than the speed of light, passing through all particles, including dark matter; it is the omnipresent Entity, the master of this universe.'

Dave, on hearing Tim explain what the Entity was made-of then added.

'Tom and Emma have just reminded me the Entity has already admitted that it's made from dark energy, intelligent dark energy.'

Emma's ghostly voice in their heads added the technical information....

'CDM may be the opposite or fourth universal force, the strong force without mass, confirming the existence of the "graviton." Experiments and test runs that include the search for the graviton, are already scheduled to take place, using the LHC Large Hadron Collider in Geneva...

The first hurdle would be to prove the elusive "Higgs boson" field theory, sometimes called the "God particle," however, the LHC machine in Geneva keeps breaking down, it's not very reliable at the moment.'

Max butted in just as the main course was served. The waiter was now looking a bit frightened as Max started to question his invisible friend.

'Emma, I'm just a lowly dumb bush pilot but I do read a lot since we don't have much work to do. This Large Hadron Collider is in all the news these days. I read the other day the LHC will smash particle strings into one another at almost the speed of light.

If they can separate the proton particles. Some of the bit's that fly off might well be dark matter. If so, what's to stop them creating "cold dark matter," or for that matter... bloody antimatter?' Doc Dave added his bit to the argument.

'Randall has said the proton string mass in the LHC collision area is so minutely small. Any split protons that produce new quarks or

leptons would simply scatter, as there is nothing to hold them after the collision. The energies are far too low to produce a meaningful amount of CDM.'

Randall had done some thinking about Max and Dave's questions, as he lit yet another cigarette from the butt of his old one. This was an expensive smoke. Randall had just given the waiter a second hundred dollar note, not to notice his smoking. The waiter had cunningly placed a fancy screen around Randall's end of the table mainly to hide his strange dinner clients than the smoke. Randall then launched into one of his "what if" theories.

'Consider for a moment; what if some really smart chap has figured out a way to create and hold dark matter particles. This Entity thing obviously knows that CDM will be created and sometime soon. Logically, the most likely place for this to happen on this planet would have to be in the new LHC in Geneva.

The way I understand particle physics is that dark matter is slippery stuff. It is not visible as it absorbs light and has little or no mass. There is also no agreed scale or reference point from which to measure dark matter, so how would one know if you had some of this stuff… or not?

The only way I know is by the process of elimination. That is, account for everything before the collider collision, then what is missing from the sample trap must be cold dark matter.

If you could separate dark matter, and somehow hold onto cold dark matter. The biggest problem I would assume would be the massive gravity weight. It is calculated that something the size of a grain of rice would weigh many hundreds of tons. This massive weight would immediately be attracted to our planets gravitational centre.'

Tim was looking at his untouched dinner on the table, and then added in a sad strong voice, in what was probably his longest speaking moment.

'This free falling cold dark matter, being then a created mini black hole, which would feed on our planets mass from within the planets centre. Overtime, the planet would be totally consumed, and eventually collapse into this black hole, becoming a new singularity. This catastrophic action would remove our planet earth from the solar system.

With the earth removed from its solar orbit. The other planets would then seek new realignment. The gravitational orbits around the sun would change, creating chaos. No matter as this new mini black hole would soon consume them all, including the sun. Eventually there would be no solar system. The masters of the universe seek to maintain order and balance. We must stop the creation of cold dark matter on earth.'

They noticed there was an unusual silence in the room as the whole restaurant had stopped talking, and tinkling their cutlery. Everyone was listening in on Tim's every spooky word, Max was quick to notice and cheerily announced.

'Just rehearsing our lines for a new play at Her Majesty's theatre, I hope you lot will all come along as we poor actors need the bloody money.'

Max then stood up and gave a low performers bow, as the restaurant tables clapped and laughed in reply, and then got on with their eating and drinking. He then quickly joined the conversation again.

'For Christ's sake Doc, is this CDM obsession, what the end of the world threat is all about. How in hell can we stop something this big, what can we do? I know one thing for sure, whatever we need to do will cost a fair bit of money. Just remember that we're flat broke with the taxman on our back and without an aircraft to earn any income,'

On hearing this, Randal offered a solution in the style of a gallant Knight in shining armour, riding in and pledging the required funding.

'By golly chaps, this is a huge pending catastrophe, and could well be bigger than Ben-Hur. Being a gentleman and a man of some considerable means, I hereby pledge my family's total wealth. This should do the trick as the old man is loaded; I doubt he would even miss it.'

Dave thought, is this bloke for real. How gallant, offering to tip-in all of his old man's family wealth. This money spoilt pommy had no idea just what the world he lives on is about to face. It would be the end of his very existence, and every living thing on this known world.

'I have just been chatting to Emma and Tom.' Dave paused for effect. *'Emma has come up with a brilliant plan that may resolve any*

future money problems, but we should thank Randall for offering his Dad's entire wealth.

From what we have just been discussing, I doubt that even Randall's dad could stump up the massive amounts of cash we are going to need.

Enormous amounts of cash funds will be required for opening all the closed doors to find the elusive people we are looking for. It appears that, big money talks loud in this type of business, the business of scientific research. It is all well beyond me my friends.

The reason I am still a ghost is that I can go places you blokes can't. Right now at Tom and Emma's suggestion, the Entity and I, are going on a nice little ghost trip to the LHC and CERN on the French-Swiss boarder to do some snooping. Emma has given me a list of clues on what I need to be on the lookout for.'

Randall quickly recovered from being financially snubbed, adding coyly in an obvious tone of a non-believer.

'A brilliant money plan from Emma you say. Well I will most certainly be looking forward to hearing all about this plan old boy.'

The meeting continued late into the evening; questions were starting to slow, as they were all exhausted and in deep concerned thoughts. Thoughts that the Entity, Dave, Tom, and Emma could clearly hear confirming they were all terrified.

Dave decided this was enough for Randall, Max, and Tim to take-in for now, closing the meeting.

'Emma and Tom wish you guys a good night's sleep as tomorrow will be another long trying day. As for me, well I'm already sleeping in a hospital bed, and ghosts don't sleep... and I hope they don't feel tired.'

Randall glanced around the restaurant. It was empty except for the lone waiter sitting at a table; he was a discrete distance away but well within hearing range. The waiter suddenly sprang to his feet on being noticed, enquiring if they would like another round of drinks, and would the invisible man like his usual double scotch?

With a deadpan look on his face, Max advised him the invisible man had just gone to the French-Swiss border. Where the wine was considerably cheaper and the waiters did not listen in on their client's dinner conversations.

Max was knocking on Randall's door at exactly 7am. In the short time that Max had known Randall, he found that he was warming to his style of silly British humour. All he had to do now was to get over his pompous British attitude. He was thinking this pommy bloke could make a good Aussie with a bit of intensive training. He even liked beer.

The door opened to a drowsy hung-over Randall.

'Be assured Max old chap, I do not feel anywhere near as bad as I look. My powerful constitution needs some training to handle the large amount of whisky that I consumed last night.'

He then casually enquired with squinting eyes and a corrugated brow.

'Heard anything from our resident ghost?'

Max thought this Randall bloke can handle anything, ghosts, pending world disasters, and even a massive whisky hangover, replying.

'Not yet Randall, although I don't fancy sitting through another séance around the bloody breakfast table. I was going to suggest we have a quick breakfast then go pick-up Emma and Tom from the hospital and get down to business here in private. I know they said they would call when ready, but we have to get this show on the road. Randall, I have this awful gut feeling that we are all rapidly running out of time.'

'Give me one minute to get Tim and I dressed. Max you should go down and order our breakfast.'

'What will you and Tim have?'

'Oh the usual thing old man, a full English breakfast, if they can produce such a serving of food in Australia.'

Max left on his way down to the breakfast room mumbling about a stuck-up pompous pommy bastard. I suppose he wants tea and hard-boiled eggs followed by scones, marmalade, and thick dairy cream. He then walked right into the Captain and his first officer of the Randall Falcon jet, who were waiting at the desk to be seated for breakfast.

'I say old man care to join us for a jolly breakfast, we would absolutely love to hear all about your flying experiences in those little aircraft buzzing about in the... outback ha ha ha.'

'Yeah well I don't mind telling you blokes a few scary stories about some real flying by real pilots. Flying where you actually hold onto the steering wheel thingy, and you can by-Jove actually see the bloody ground. I'll hold fire on the exciting bits since your boss is still on the way down to join us for...'

Before Max could finish his sarcastic remarks about high altitude jet captains, Randall's voice came from behind and cut short the pilot-talk.

'Thanks for the offer chaps however, we do have some rather urgent business to discuss. Do stay around the hotel chaps, as I believe we have some flying to do shortly, so if you would kindly have the Falcon fuelled to maximum. The payload will be another three plus us. I would like you to return our flight hostess Roberta back to the UK by a commercial airline. We will have no need for her on this flight.'

Both flight crew gave their boss a knowing look and a curt nod of compliance, and then smartly walked away. It was clear these two were faithful, dedicated professionals. Max got the impression Randall is more than a wealthy man's son being obviously a well-respected man and pilot.

The timing was perfect; Max had almost finished his second large helping of breakfast to the amazement of Randall and Tim when his mobile phone rang interrupting his pleasant start to the day. It was Tom.

'Good morning Max, I guess we could do with your help over here. Luke has checked Dave out. He has suggested, and advised the hospital medical people to keep Dave under for a few more days to keep an eye on a small brain lesion he has noticed on Dave's CAT scan. The local experts don't agree with Luke's diagnosis, so I guess it's up to Mary and you to make the decision on his behalf.'

Max eyed his remaining sausage and bacon covered in beans and tomato sauce, advising Tom they would be there in twenty minutes.

Emma and Tom were waiting and ready to go when Max, Randall, and Tim arrived at Royal Perth Hospital. Tom quickly introduced them to his son Luke, and then swiftly added. Luke was on his way to a medical seminar in Hong Kong when he had received the sudden news that his father was in a plane crash in Australia.

Luke was a tall good-looking man with an easy smile, the image of his father Tom. He was apparently surprised at his father's miraculous escape from injury, and that of his quick recovery. Luke was even more surprised at his father's request to find a reason to keep

Doctor Sharp in his coma. The weak excuse given was that he and Doctor Sharp got to know each other quite well in the short time. Tom advised Luke that Doctor Sharp was under great financial and marital stress. Matters that may have contributed to the airplane crash. Tom thought a good ten days rest away from his troubles could be beneficial, also the local press can't hound a sleeping man. Subject to a favourable examination, Luke reluctantly agreed to his father's odd request.

Luke was becoming suspicious at his father's stubborn insistence that he should be catching the midday flight out to Hong Kong to attend his four-day medical seminar. After some pushy assurance and heavy pressure from Tom, he reluctantly agreed to go.

Dave looked peaceful, sleeping like a baby, a faint smile on his lips. It was almost as if he were enjoying his ghostly experience; maybe he was.

Max then called Mary. Explaining as he had promised, Tom the African-American Professor, she had recently been introduced to, had his son, a leading neurosurgeon examine Doc Dave.

Doctor Luke had apparently noticed a very small lesion on Dave's brain that none of the other specialists had seen. As a precaution, he had suggested that Doctor Sharp should remain in the coma for at least the next few days, to allow this small lesion to heal.

Max agreed with Tom's son that it was best to err on the side of caution. Anyway, a few extra days sleep would probably do Dave some good, and no harm. Mary in a flood of tears agreed with Max, she would advise the hospital to follow Doctor Luke's advice in keeping Dave in the coma for a few days.

Chapter Eighteen

What do you fear the most?

Emma and Tom were relieved to be out of hospital and in the hot Perth sun. Emma wanted to go shopping as she had nothing to wear except the clothes that she was wearing when rescued three days ago.

Max was thinking typical bloody woman, here we are facing the possible end of the world, and all this woman wants to do is go out bloody shopping. Max suddenly felt a sharp jab in his ribs as Emma elbowed him hard. Then with fists on hips and a fierce stare, Emma exploded in a furore of Scottish female retaliation.

'I have been in these clothes for three days and they stink, and I am sure that Tom would also like a change of clothes. What other way is there to get a change of clothing if not by shopping for them?'

Max was stunned, how the hell did Emma know what he was thinking. Standing behind Emma's furious face was a grinning Tom. Max then turned to Randall and Tim noticing that they were as confused as he was. Tom stepped in to repair the verbal damage.

'Remember in the hospital Max, about the time you were thinking that Dave and I were pinching all your scotch. Well I was about to tell you then the Entity had left Emma and I with the ability to hear planned, or deep thoughts. Well sir, you have just been thought read again.'

Randall was the most impressed.

'By Jove sir, do you realise what a wonderful asset that ability could be old chap, why in a game of poker you would know all of the hands? As for the ladies, well who knows what a man may indeed find out? It would unquestionably increase ones chances what, what.'

'Unfortunately Randall, it does not seem work in that way. This is about planned thought reading not outright mind reading. I can give you a good example. When Emma elbowed Max in his ribs I had no idea what she was about to do or say.

Had Emma thought about it first then I could have been aware of her intension Your poker opponent would have to be thinking to himself about his hand for me to know his cards. I for one play cards instinctively, I don't say the cards in my head. However, I do agree there are many that do, so as long as you remember this simple rule, we can't hear your innermost private thoughts... or dark secrets.'

Randall was not be deterred from this obvious card playing advantage...

'Nevertheless old chap a few well-chosen words and strategically placed questions could provide you with a great deal of knowledge, offering you a whopping advantage.'

'I assume that is exactly what the Entity has intended Randall. You should all understand that even the all-powerful Entity has its fundamental limits. If the Entity could read our minds then it would know who is creating the cold dark matter on earth.

It would also have full control over everything that we humans do, and as the Entity has already admitted. That ability would be against the very purpose of a free, new developing intelligence within the universe.

As I understand, a form of universal democracy exists. The Entity just makes the best of what is taking place. The Entity will encourage, promote, and accept everything that we do both good and evil. Providing it can ultimately be productive in the development of a greater and higher level of universal intelligence. As such we must be careful, and choose the right path.'

Max was stunned; he would have to be more careful, mainly about what he thought about from now on. Then changing thoughts remembering, Tony should have sent Emma, Tom, and Doc Dave's gear down from Sandfire. With a little bit of Jewish luck, the baggage could be at the Hotel by the time they arrive.

Emma gave Max a peck on his hairy cheek, carefully avoiding his large bruise, then grabbing his arm as they walked down the street.

Max thought with boyish delight that his lady-luck might have changed.

'What a nice man you are Max, you have had all our travel gear sent down from Sandfire,' then with a gorgeous smile. 'I am looking forward to a long hot shower and a change of clothes, then maybe a wee dram of your whisky.

Your lady-luck has already changed Max. If my money idea works out, you should end up with a shiny new aeroplane to fly around your beautiful outback Australia.'

Max gave Emma a reserved worried look as they entered the Hotel foyer; just what was Emma up to... he would also need some mind blocking practice if he was ever going to have some private thoughts again.

All agreed to meet in Randall's penthouse suite on the top floor in twenty minutes. The idea was they should all sit down and work out a plan of attack to find out just who was behind this cold dark matter problem.

As a first move, they needed to exchange all of their known information. Then go over in detail the current list of weird events. Many answers were now required to the obvious questions. Why were they chosen for this enormous task? In addition, they should research to find out who else might know anything about this imminent danger to our planet earth.

When all the others arrived at the penthouse door, Randall had just sent a long encrypted email to the chaos group. He had advised them that Emma was out of hospital and in perfect health, and she would contact them shortly.

Chirpy was quick to fire back a curt response reminding him there were others interested in what was going on, and the stakes had been raised in the last few days. Chirpy wanted to know why it was so important to gather details on who had signed up to use the LHC (Large Hadron Collider) research facilities. Especially since the Oxford University had now withdrawn their LHC time-slot and test schedule. Gaining any information from the events, and steering committee for the LHC, would now be difficult.

Chirpy reported that everyone in the group was conscious of being under surveillance. In addition, the Chairman of Physics, Professor Walker was on the warpath, demanding to know why Doctor Emma had not returned from her Moscow lecture tour. Chirpy advised that she was not going to tell Professor Walker that Emma was recovering from an aircraft crash in Australia. Emma was supposed to be still lecturing in Russia, advising this lie cannot be maintained.

The entire chaos group in England wanted to know, what have you people done in Australia to cause all of this mess in Oxford?

Randal thought he must be careful, the chaos group were not stupid, and now they were becoming suspicious. He quickly followed up with another email.

"Read my short report friends, many odd and un-scientific things have happened here. We are about to have a strange meeting regarding your urgent concerns. I will send an updated report soon. That is if I can find words to understand what is actually going on. I can honestly say things really are upside-down in Australia."

Your dizzy friend, Randall.

Randall was musing on how much that last comment would have stirred up the fiery Chirpy, when suddenly the door opened and in trooped Emma, Tom, and Max. He noticed that Tom was clutching firmly onto two bottles of scotch, confirming that their baggage had indeed arrived from Sandfire.

'It is nice to see you are all ready, refreshed, and fuelled for our meeting. I do believe this is going to be somewhat of a marathon meeting...err mates. You know we really must try to learn the Australian language.'

Noticing nobody was interested in his poor Australian, Randall moved on to other matters.

'I have taken the liberty of ordering a buffet lunch for us all, served in this room. By the way chaps, has anyone heard anything from our resident ghost Doctor Sharp?'

Emma was not amused at Randall's silly ramblings, and hoped that he would get serious about this matter. They would soon need his international banking knowledge and computer skills to help in setting up an international bank account for her proposed large fighting fund.

'Tom and I have been in touch with Dave last night and this morning. We are finding it incredibly difficult to keep up with all the ghostly stuff he is trying to do, we need to share some of these tasks. Randall you wanted to know all about our CDM funding plan. Well we think you may like our new money plan, and I believe you should be our chaos group banker.'

Emma paused and accepted a glass of wine from Max, then continued.

'The plan is all quite simple boys; we just steal a few hundred million US dollars from the world's richest and best-healed crooks.' They all looked stunned, as Emma read the question on their faces.

'I got the idea from an old movie I had seen a few years ago, but with Dave as a ghost, we could easily make this thing happen for real.'

Emma ended her shock-statement with a coy smile. Max and Randall's jaws dropped together, Max recovered first.

'Are you suggesting that Doc Dave look over the shoulders of some drug lord's numbers-man, and watch him entering in his password to their Cayman Islands account number? And then divert a few million dollars into an account that we would control?'

Emma nodded her head with a charming smile. Randall quickly picked up on the general idea of this brilliant plan. He was overflowing with false childish excitement, as this was exactly what he had in mind. He already had Tim working on a similar plan; however, aware he must be careful in what he thinks. Then talking directly to the stunned Max…

'Good lord old chap, what a brilliant idea, this could be made to work quite easily. Do you not realise chaps what good we could do for the many deserving charities. Then there are the many medical research projects around the world needing funds. With access to this massive pool of available funds, we could resolve a number of world health problems.

The targets would not only be drug lords. What about all the greedy political dictators ripping off their own countries. We could return the money back to their people via world charity organizations. Then there are all the crooked corporate raiders, with a private hidden stash who have loaded up accounts in all the worlds' tax havens.'

Randall was overflowing with new ideas… some dangerous.

'Do you know chaps; these fellows would have no idea who pinched their money, or where it went. We could leave a few damaging clues to it was one of their own who was the responsible nasty crook. The possibilities are endless; nothing would be out of our grasp. This will be a lovely reversal of dishonest wealth. By Jove I am going to jolly-well enjoy this job.'

Randall suddenly stopped ranting as he caught sight of Tom with his hand raised to speak.

'All very commendable I'm sure, but if we can't stop this CDM problem, then we will have no deserving human charities or medical research organisations to help. They will be gone, wiped out... eradicated. We have a major timing problem, that being; Dave will only be a ghost for a short time. He will only be able to do this kind of ghostly work for the next few weeks, unless we can figure out some way of keeping him in his coma.

Every minute counts, our first priority will be to somehow divert enough funds to buy a seat on the control board of the LHC. I had also thought; we might try funding our own test experiment. We could achieve this with the name backing of say the Oxford and Princeton Universities. Maybe by simply buying into someone's existing test time-slot.'

Emma cut into Tom's flowing ideas.

'I think your first idea best, the preferred way would be with a director's seat on the CERC events board. This small tight group of directors control everything at the LHC.

From that position, we would see just who is funding these experiments. This would be the perfect method for gaining information about who will conduct an experiment in creating cold dark matter.

I have heard the CERN are short of money again, as such an opportunity may exist to buy a seat on the board. However, we will need to move fast.'

Tom was thinking, hell this Emma was a smart business woman. Just as well, since he had never placed any importance on money matters. As for Dave, well he was an admitted failure at holding onto any form of wealth. Then there was Randall, by all accounts he would not need to worry about money, as he was already wealthy. Turning back to the money raising matter, he then voiced his limited opinion on this matter.

'Dave is trying to advise the Entity on what he wants in the way of information on certain people. Although this is proving to be quite difficult. Apparently, the Entity has little knowledge, and no urgency, on what wealth and money are all about.

I would suppose Dave will need a list some well-known crooks names and there locations to start with. As far as I can figure, Dave can be in Colombia, Afghanistan, Pakistan, China, or Russia in a fraction of a second and can scan hundreds of likely bad people each minute. Nevertheless, he still needs help to shorten the huge suspect list, and shorten the odds. As for the Entity, it has reminded us again, time will be our enemy.'

Tom could both see and hear Randall and Max's concerns, responding first.

'Before you ask the obvious, I had the same thought, how the hell would Dave know what they were all talking about in these many languages. Well it appears that what goes on in our human heads is a common sort of digital brain language. If a person thinks about something, we can understand.

Seemingly, only the spoken word produced by our larynx gives us differing acoustic sounds, providing many languages.

Then there is also another big problem, Dave cannot hold on to anything. He can't hold a pen to write down the complex passwords or long account numbers, he must report them for us to record them... he is after all just a ghost. From this situation we can now understand some of the problems faced by the Entity.'

With a knowing smile, Randall had the instant answer.

'I would suggest you get Dave to talk directly to Tim as he can remember everything. Another useful thing chaps, is Tim can also research, and feed Dave with many possible leads, names, and locations. The Internet is full of bad guy's names.'

In addition, as they were soon to find out, so was Randall's laptop computer. Without a planned thought in his head, Randall leaned over Tim and entered the Uncle Jeremy password. This file opened with lists of high profile crooks and the known location of their offshore BVI bank accounts. Tim instantly realised that most of his computer research work already completed. Tim immediately started to set up many computer files, ready for Doc Dave's future collection of bank account numbers and passwords.

Without revealing he already had most of the data required to make Emma's plan work, Randall continued with his convincing display of childish excitement.

'Meanwhile friends, I will get our London Randall Company office to set up a series of arms-length untraceable companies, with head offices in Liechtenstein, Dubai, Russia, Spain, Hong Kong, Jersey, and others. Then I will get them to open twenty or so offshore tax haven accounts in a number of countries ready for the expected money transfers. First thing we will need chaps are a few more computers that are very fast, and some other tricky computer stuff. Max old chap, let's go shopping.'

Emma shot to her feet staring furiously at Randall and Max.

'Just hold on there a minute boys. We need to discuss other important matters first. In addition, I must tell you about a number of other weird things while we are all here together.

What you are about to learn from Tom and I, is more than a little spooky. Remember, we have been in the company of the Entity for a time and know how it thinks... you may not want to hear this.'

They all sat down again. Tim was busy tapping rapidly on Randall's laptop; he was in a small world of his own with all the new data. Max noticed Tom look at the large starburst clock on the wall, the morning had gone; it was showing 01:40. Tom glanced at Emma who nodded; Tom then gave out a low sigh and began his story.

'Emma, Dave, and I have been talking most of the night about how all of this came about. The more we discussed this whole story the more we became frightened, or a better word would be terrified... utterly terrified.'

Emma interrupted Tom, suggesting that as it was so late, Randall should now have a buffet lunch sent up to the room… also find some scotch tumblers. With what they were about to say, Emma considered they would all need a stiff drink to cope. Tom continued.

'Believe us, this has to be a fast learning curve, you will need to absorb a large amount of information in a very short time. Let me start with this enlightening fact; the Entity does not give a shit about us so-called humans.'

These were strong words coming from the gentle, softly spoken professor.

'No sir, they are only interested in the end result. That being everything in our solar system to remain in balance, the way they have planned things. However, on the plus side, we humans expected to develop over time to a greater level of intelligence, in the future used to assist other life-seeded planets.

Out in the vast un-measureable size of the universe, we are but a speck of dust to the Entity. Our small planet Earth, the home of we lowly biological humans will receive little if any special consideration. Only what we can develop in the way of a greater intelligence and biological evolution has a value in their domain.

318

Any life form, which had evolved to an odd or distorted development cycle, they will quickly destroy. Much in the same way a biologist in a Princeton lab would do. By washing down the drain a useless, none performing bacteria culture that was forming on his sample slide.'

Tom took-on a look of a worried father, trying to understand his daughter going on a date with a young male, covered in tattoos, with no job.

'One would question the point as to why the Entity was even bothering with us… Only one possible reason comes to my mind and that is. We can possibly prevent something from happening the Entity cannot change or stop.

That can only be about one thing, a matter which the Entity fears most (assuming it can express fear.) This is an early breach into their world of "dark energy," carried out by ignorant, aggressive, and damaging humans. Possibly forcing a change in our universe, and altering the Entities universal purpose.'

Everybody was quiet while Tom's words sank in. Only the rapid key clicks of Tim's computer keyboard heard. Then the added gentle tinkling of Max's ice in his scotch tumbler. This drew attention to him, as such, he felt compelled to speak.

'Well then mates, are we not wasting our time in trying to stop this cold dark matter from being produced? Will our human race still be destroyed?' Then pausing to take another large swig of his new scotch.

'Something else bothers me. Why can't this Entity confirm who is brewing up this cold dark matter, especially now we have just about proved where it will be created... in the Large Hadron Collider.

This Entity must be listening in, and know what we are up to. Anyway, how does the Entity know that this CDM creation is about to happen... can it see into the bloody future? If this Entity can crash Doc Dave's Cessna 402 at a precise location, it can do just about anything.'

Emma gave a gentle cough, took a sip of her wine, and then with a serious studious look, answered Max's question.

'Remember, the Entity has no emotions, conscience, or scruples, it functions on pure logic. Its decisions are simple and it normally plans, and works in hundreds of millions of year time-spans. On our planet, the Entity has its best short-time-span power at any of the gravity ring sites, the Veevers site being the prime and most powerful.

If the Entity did not want our help to stop the creation of cold dark matter on earth, then it would have said and done nothing to contact us. It would have simply erased all the biological beings off the face of our planet, then start the whole planet life process all over again. As the Entity has previously advised, it has done this many times in our past. The Entity has already told us it will do this again if we do not succeed.

We must accept that the Entity is a master at planning. Dave. Tom and I now believe that our personal lives have been shaped and directed over the last twenty years or more, to converge on this single point in time.

This would include the Entity having been involved in Dave's failed marriages and his business. Tom's chair at Princeton becoming available because of the sudden death of a colleague. Then there was the subsequent loss of his position at Princeton, and possibly his mentor and friend Professor Ben to lung cancer. Then again, there was also the sudden cancer-death of Tom's wife.

As for me, both my parents killed in an unusual road accident, and my brother murdered in odd circumstances in Cambodia, leaving me with no close dependents

It now appears to us in hindsight that each of us have been carefully prepared. Stripped of all our immediate dependencies, diversions, or any personal obstacles, we are now ready. The strategy behind all of this biological and psychological cleansing is that we are now, I believe; ready to give our total effort to the Entities small problem... and our large problem.'

Emma took another sip of her drink, then scanning the faces of her attentive audience, she then continued in her quaint Scottish brogue.

'As for what is known, I am certain the Entity would know the LHC is the most likely place on this planet that could produce CDM. However, I also believe the Entity has no problem with humans creating CDM.

After all, they did tolerate the Martians being in possession of CDM on their planet Mars. We believe the Entity is only concerned with what this CDM will eventually be used, and what damage it may cause to its long-term universal plan. The people who will ultimately have control of this CDM on Earth is the Entities main concern, and more importantly, what they will use it for...

In short, the Entity is the only singularity who will have the power to move, remove, or plan new planets in our solar system, not us humans, or any other biological life form. It is the Entities job to maintain the universe in balance and order, also to develop higher intelligence.

To the Entity, we are playing with powers and forces that at our stage in evolution well beyond our full understanding. It would be like giving a hand grenade to a three-year-old toddler who will eventually find a way to remove the pin. The end result is not a desired out-come. However, by then a resolve to the problem would be far too late... a matter of irreversible damage.'

With deep concern, Randall butted into Emma's mini lecture with a flurry of questions.

'What about Max and I, do you think that we were also manipulated by this Entity in the same callous way?' and Tim, surely not young Timothy.'

Emma sounded humble and reserved in her reply.

'From what we have managed to understand from the Entity, the entire human race is influenced by the omniscient presence of the Entity. However, only certain chosen humans are; as you say, manipulated. You and Max, along with Professor Reg, Sally, Chirpy, and Jan are obviously chosen ones, chosen to carry out an important mission to try to save this our planet.'

Randall would not give in easily and wanted a full answer to his question.

'And Tim, what of Tim.' All turned to look at Tim who was not in the least distracted from his computer work. Fingers clicking away like a mad knitter. Entirely focused on working the Internet, oblivious to all. Emma's voice dropped to almost a whisper.

'The Entity has already described autistic humans as special... just as we do. Though some prodding the Entity eventually revealed that autistic-savant humans were an attempt by the Entity to produce an enlightened human to further bridge the gap between a human being and the Entities universal understanding.'

Randall was still looking at Tim who was diligently working away without any expression on his face. Thinking yes, this Entity has passed on a portion of its self. Like the Entity, Tim has no a social skills or emotions, and has no detectable conscience. Tim has a brilliant mind for detail, memory, and numbers. Computers were a natural progression, yet Tim has difficulty in getting his pants on the right way around, and needs help tying his shoelaces... no doubt just like the Entity.

Randal noticed the wide smile spread across Emma and Tom's faces they had read his innermost and innocent thoughts. Randall took the opportunity to get in another urgent question,

'These Martian chaps, they must have had some tremendously advanced technology when they first set-up camp on our planet at the Veevers crater site some 15,000 or so years ago. It would appear the Martians built the massive gravity antenna system. What did these chaps know about cold dark matter, or for that... matter, about the Entity?'

Tom decided to answer Randall's probing question.

'Without doubt the Martians were considerably more advanced than us. We must accept the fact that it was only a comparatively short 10,400 years ago when all Martians evicted from this planet by the Entity. It would appear the Martians had previously been busy colonising our planet for several thousand years.

I guess during that time we were still hunters and gatherers. We were at a very immature Mesolithic stage of our early development cycle. This was a strange time for our planet earth, a time of great climatic instability.

Apparently, long before the Martian decision to colonise Earth, for them a known close life-planet. The Martians were busy working on an alternative plan. This was to slip into another dimension to resolve their dying planets problems, and their future existence. It looks like they were still hell-bent on working on this fourth dimension idea, when the Entity resolved the problem for them. All in the blink of a Martian eye. They were exterminated.'

We would guess that the Martins knew all about the Entity, and its work in maintaining balance within the universe. Then they made a terminal mistake in trying to outwit the Entity. I reckon the Martians had miscalculated the Entity, in not considering the universal actions the Entity can, and would normally take.'

Tom paused, was he going too fast. Did they understand this critical information? His decision was to continue.

'Now this is the terrifying part folks. We have since figured out the Entity did not intend to allow the Martians to become the master race of our planet Earth; apparently this is not the true evolutionary way.

The Entity only wanted a little Martian DNA introduced to strengthen the human gene pool, thus creating the now-recognised "modern Homo sapiens." At the same time, basic levels of technology eventually passed on to the new breed of human. These new Martian hybrids encouraged humans to think of them as Gods.

After only some 4,800 years of earth occupation. The last of the hundred per cent DNA Martians were finally extinguished at around 10,400 years ago, having unwittingly completed their useful task. By the Entity standards of value, the Martian life cycle and functional use had travelled its path to a pre-determined conclusion.

The remains of their vast underground colony still exists today, some five miles below ground, close to Veevers crater. We now know, a crater caused by the impact of their last space shuttle from Mars. My guess would be the Entity caused this shuttle crash.

This was indeed an interesting period for our planet and species. I can tell you now as an Anthropologist; this new information fills in the missing years. Clearly answering the old question of how the human race made the jump from Neanderthal to Homo sapiens, and then to modern Homo sapiens.

Emma took up the story again in her tilting Scottish accent...

'Randall, we now have the facts. The Martians did not build the earth antenna system, no the poor wee things were just trying to find a new home. By all accounts, the Entity created the Earth gravity-ring antenna system. However, the Martians most certainly used the system when they first occupied our planet earth.

This antenna originally built some billions of years before. Apparently, this system of complex graviton pipes through the centre of our planet is the normal and natural way the Entity identifies likely life planets. The carefully chosen young life-planet, with a small orbiting moon. This planet accurately placed at just the right distance, to orbit around a quiet star for the development of new life.

All of this agrees with Tim's theory of early life bearing meteorites and asteroids, containing the basic live bacteria. Life ingredients, having been attracted to our planet by this powerful gravity device. The odd asteroid sent along to add the much needed water mass, and create weather change.

The stockpot of life was now complete, and then left tenderly simmering away for a few billion years. It was now a quiet period on Earth. Except for the occasional Entity tweaking needed to balance things up a bit. Such as a huge asteroid hit causing a twenty-degree pole shift to resolve a small error in the rapid growth of a large hungry species, the Dinosaurs... And then the Martians arrived.'

The Martians knew all about this natural life-planet development cycle, and had planned to arrive on Earth a few hundred years before the antenna system drifted out of alignment around 10,000 years ago. They calculated the planned switch-off time caused by the Earth's crust (tectonic plates) moving, thus breaking the receiving signal, all but halting the massive bombardment of the Earth with millions of large meteorites and asteroids. The Martian timing was perfect.'

Tom gave Emma a rest and continued this interesting story to his fascinated, but shocked eager listeners.

'The planet Mars was quickly losing its life sustaining protective atmosphere, and the great Martian oceans were rapidly evaporating into space. Life on the planet's surface was progressively dying, as the Martians buried deeper into the crust of their planet Mars. This to avoid the punishing UV rays, and electromagnetic radiation from the once life-giving Sun.

Three thousand Mars years, of living underground had created a new breed of genetically changed Martians. Martians who could no longer tolerate even our low-level of Earth Sun radiation, the very reason why they still needed to remain underground on colonising our planet Earth. To the Martians, our Earth was a hostile planet.

Martian DNA and genetic manipulation produced some strange, odd-looking crossbreed human and Martian beings. Some of which are well documented in Greek, Roman, Mayan, Inca, and Egyptian mythology.

These strange looking Martian hybrids had powerful tools that could cut through hard stone like hot butter, and could lift massive stone blocks into the air. They went about erecting great buildings, many of which are still standing to this day.

These new breeds of humans were eventually worshipped as living Gods, who then went on to colonise other parts of our world using the ten gravity ring sites, these sites being places of significance for the first Martian settlements.

Overtime the new Martian Gods passed on the valuable knowledge of astronomy, mathematics, irrigation, also the mining and use of metals. Plus many other skills we now take for granted in this modern world.'

Tom slipped into a philosophical mood, looking sadly out of the penthouse window at the beautiful panoramic view of the Swan River, and then continued the story.

'You know my new friends. I regret that my old friend and mentor Professor Ben Lock did not live long enough to hear that his theory of an omnipresent metaphysical intelligence, existing throughout the universe is now a fact. At my last meeting with Ben when he gave me the Martian bone, he said these words as part of his current theory.

"Is there a plan to this continuing evolutional change to all life forms on the planet earth? I am sure that this must be part of a greater universal plan controlled by some form of advanced intelligence. If there were such a form of universal intelligence, was it known to exist in our distant past? As such, then locally accepted, being worshipped as an all-powerful compliant God."

Tom took on a new rejuvenated thrust with his lecture.

'Why even Spinoza's philosophy way back in 1656 was all but correct, he did not believe that a God ruled over the universe. However, he did believe in cause and effect, as such, any God must surely be the natural world, having no personality.

Spinoza believed that everything that happens occurs through the operation of necessity. I ask you all to consider this now... Was Professor Ben correct in his theory of a universal intelligence, and how close is that description of Spinoza to this Entity we have now come to know?'

Everyone except Tim fell into silent in deep thoughts to consider this weird Spinoza theory, written over 356 years ago. This fact, plus all the new information and recent experiences, creating many questions in their minds. Following Tom's gaze out of the penthouse window... Max thought what would be next, what can we do, we are nothing to this Entity. They all heard the voice in their heads at the same time, just as there came a loud knock on the penthouse door. Doc Dave advised...

'Your buffet lunch is here mate's, it's a pity I can't join you as it looks damn good, but alas I've already eaten, having just been fed through a little bloody tube at Royal Perth Hospital.'

Dave the ghost and the Entity had announced their presence.

Tom raised his hand and put his finger to his lips in a gesture of silence as Randall opened the door to the waiter. The same waiter that served them dinner last night entered the room pushing a long trolley, followed by two helpers. He displayed a surprised look as he recognised the familiar faces.

Everyone looked on in utter silence, eyes watching the waiters every move as they nervously set-up the buffet table. Dave had decided there was no reason for him or the Entity to remain quiet, as nobody could hear him, except... well those chosen ones in the room… Dave continued...

'We were listening into your interesting conversation. I think the Entity is impressed at your new understanding of how it carries out its work, and how we have all arrived at this particular point in time.

You will no doubt be happy to hear that the Entity has stopped talking about killing us all... well for the time being. Then again, I have managed to gather a swag of information on the LHC in Geneva, but I will need some help from Emma on all the technical bits. I don't mind admitting it's all beyond me chum, give me a lump of rock anytime and I will tell you everything about it but...'

Suddenly Max blurted out in a loud bewildered voice.

'Shit Doc, stop crapping on, bloody-well tell us, is this CERN crowd making this bloody cold dark matter stuff at the LHC in Geneva or not?'

The waiter froze and the two helpers looked on in surprise. Everyone else in the room remained silent, with the two waiters sporting the standard Hotel trained neutral look. Tim carried on tapping away on his computer.

'Oh hell Max, now look what you have done, you've frightened the bloody hell out of him. Tell the waiter that you want that almost full bottle of Penfolds 1992 Grange wine he swiped of those pissed business blokes table last night.'

The waiter coughed, regaining his slipped composure remembering his odd dinner guests from the previous night, then raising a confident voice.

'Will your invisible friend who went to France last night be joining you for lunch sir, and should I bring a little extra food?' the curl of a smart mocking smile appeared on the waiter's thin lips.

'No waiter that won't be necessary, he says he is not hungry at the moment as he has just been fed through a tube. On the other hand, he did say he would like that bottle of 1992 Penfolds Grange wine that you nicked from the table next to us last night. If you like I can give you the bottling number mate...'

The shocked look on the waiters face would have been worth bottling. Max was enjoying this new power. The waiter with a trembling voice replied.

'No, no that won't be necessary sir, I will have the Grange sent up to you right away; please sir I mean no harm, I need my job...'

With a smile, Max waved the waiter out. The waiter and helpers scurried out of the penthouse as Doc Dave gave out a long ghostly laugh, advising all he was leaving them to go crook hunting, starting with Tim's list of bad blokes.

Three days later Doc Dave was still in his deep coma. The Doctors were requesting to bring Dave around; however, Max and Mary refused until Tom's neurosurgeon son had cleared Dave. The Hospital advised that Doctor Luke was due back in Perth soon.

Dave had been busy. With the help of Randall and Tim, he had managed to view and log many offshore and BVI client account details. It had been an easy task. Tim had already setup a client activity alarm for each of Randall's Uncle Jeremy bad guy accounts. When the account was attempting a logon Tim advised Dave and he was there looking over the bad guys shoulder as he entered the account details.

Dave was amazed, he had never seen, or thought that amount of money ever existed... stolen money, misappropriated, or ripped off the tax system. Dave was now having second thoughts about the Australian Tax Office. The poor bastards were losing out badly to these smart crooks. No wonder they grabbed every cent they could get off easy tax targets like him... Dave considered it was time for a progress report.

'If this was not such a serious matter we are involved in, I could have heaps of fun ghosting around. You would be surprised what some people get up to, we humans are a bloody funny lot. I can understand now why the Entity most of the time remains as just an observer.

Our human impulsiveness is bloody frustrating; it is just as well the Entity has no emotions or anger. Because if it did, we would have been swatted dead, like a swarm of annoying flies.

As for the Large Hadron Collider tests, well my friends, the main players who are carrying out the most expensive and complex collider research work are just about every major world power.

They all have a piece of the action. I think Emma has the right idea, we really do need to acquire a seat at the CERN events planning committee table. After all, these people do ultimately approve and coordinate all of the projects and experiments.

Another thing, I would like to hear if my efforts were successful. How are Randall and Tim going with all those account numbers and passwords I gave them?'

Just then Tom gave out a surprised "what-the hell" and Emma gave out a loud "WOW"... all but halting the intense conversation with Dave. At the same time, Max and Randall turned to see what was going on.

Tom and Emma were looking over Tim's shoulder peering at his laptop computer screen, which was now forming a rolling list, made-up of BVI, Cayman, Lichtenstein, Latvia, and Isle of Man banking accounts.

'Are those figures in millions?' Emma nudged Tim for an answer without reply. Tim just kept on rapidly tapping away at the keyboard.

Randall leaned over and took a close look at the screen, and with an evil smile confirmed the figures were in fact... billions of dollars, adding...

'By Jove young chap what a smashing idea, do you see chaps, Tim has created a second safe-haven account in the same name however, with a new account number. No money has yet changed hands or banks but we now have password control over the second account.

Brilliant work, only one small thing comes to mind, the account holder will soon discover that his normal account balance will have a massive decrease of funds. We must work quickly to prepare one huge transfer of funds into our own offshore safe-haven accounts.

Then there is the other problem my fellow thieves. These crooked chaps will not take this stealing matter lightly. They will without doubt launch a full investigation at any cost to discover who has pinched their ill-gotten gains.'

Max let out a loud gasp and looked at the others with wide-eyed surprise...

'If all the bloody zeros are in the right place, that total figure is just a few million under seventeen billion US dollars. For Christ sake, this bloke,' pointing to Tim, 'has only been at it for five hours... How much more money is out there to pinch?'

Doc Dave's ghostly voice softly invaded their heads offering both an answer and a grim warning.

'I would guess many billions more Max. Nevertheless, just as Randall has rightly pointed out, these are very nasty people we are about to divert this money from. I hope that Randall knows his stuff when it comes to shifting this massive amount of money... and how to cover his tracks.

Don't ask me for any ideas on money matters; my poor and present financial state, confirms me as totally unqualified for this money business.'

Tom and Emma were having a discreet chat together about the most recent turn of events. All were concerned at being caught with their fingers in the illegal money till. Max, Randall, and Dave were debating how to transfer this huge pool of money… without leaving a snail back-trace.

Meanwhile Tom and Emma had identified another emerging problem. This being that Dave will need to remain in his coma for at least another three weeks, possibly a month.

They would need Dave as a ghost to spy on both the money-crooks reaction to their missing funds, also the people who were involved in creating CDM. Their lives may well depend on knowing what these people were up to; firstly, they had to resolve another urgent developing problem.

Doctors at Royal Perth Hospital were becoming suspicious, and were about to bring Dave out of his coma regardless of Doctor Luke's diagnosis. Dave had figured the main reason for this was they wanted him out of their care, and well... they needed the bed.

In their qualified opinion, there was nothing they could see wrong with him. Everybody agreed from their position, the Doctors were absolutely correct in their diagnosis.

Tom came up with what he thought to be a practical plan. When his son Luke flew back into Perth on his way back from his Hong

Kong medical seminar. Luke should suggest moving Dave to a private hospital.

Max could see that Tom's plan was flawed. His son Luke would not fall for this weak reason to keep Dave in his coma. They were about to lose their resident ghost, he immediately got on to the phone calling Mary. Then using his best Max charm, and caring concern, finally got Mary to agree to sign Dave out as a patient, and moving him into a private hospital.

The cost and problem quickly resolved by Randall paying a substantial fee to the private hospital to collect Dave, with Max and Mary going along in the ambulance.

Emma went on and explained they had other developing problems. Dave had recently discovered in Geneva, most of the world powers had research-time booked on the LHC to carry out experiments.

Then Emma remembered the Russians, British, Chinese and the Americans were all interested in what her little chaos group were up to. There must be a lead, or connection in this somewhere. Someone knows something that has meaning to all this interest and mystery.

Emma's emotions had overwhelmed her, as all had noticed she was now crying.

'I don't mind admitting it boys, I am frightened. As I see current matters, we have around four major world powers and their government security people looking at what we are researching. Why are we of such interest to them?

I for one have absolutely no idea at this time, and then to find out that we have been all lured into some elaborate trap. Recruited against our will to resolve a world problem. A mission given by a universal Entity, with failure not an option, as with failure we will all surely die.

I know it was my idea, but now we are about to steal vast amounts of money from some of the most brutal, vicious, and dangerous people on the face of this planet.

I have to remind you boys we are all scientists, gentle people who only seek the truth in the form of proof. Scientists who research sometimes obscure scientific theories, turning those theories into fact.

We are no match for the cunning challenges or the desperate depths these ugly people will go to, to recover their lost money. I am afraid for us all, these people have access to privileged information and powerful people, and we will all be at enormous risk.... Is there no other way?'

A clear and familiar voice rang out in all their minds...

'And whom do you fear the most? Be advised, we do know what fear is. Next to love, it is a human's greatest emotion. In your world, fear has been the cause of many wrong decisions and much human loss. Then again, fear has been a motivator, a driving force, and the path to many of your greatest achievements.

In this your time of fear... what would be your choice to achieve the best possible outcome for your world? We watch and wait with great interest.'

Everybody in the room knew who was speaking. For the first time the Entity had spoken directly to them all. It had applied pure logic without human emotion to the situation. In doing so, had brought all the many problems down to a simple matter of choice.

However, it was obvious to all in the room except Tim that this was not just a simple choice in which way they should go. All in the room now understood the numerous difficulties and threats to their future existence, although only one of the threats confirmed as actual.

This was a threat that also offered a slim chance of hope, and that was the Entity. The best way and choice was obvious, and Max had a neat plan to resolve part of this.

'We need a good place to hide so we can work without interruption. A place the crooks and government spies would never think of as a possible operations centre. A place that can reach the world yet is also close enough to an Entity gravity-ring to offer maximum support when needed... We must go back to Sandfire.'

Max was right, Sandfire was the obvious choice, however; they needed an undetectable fool proof plan of operation. First, they would need to split-up into two groups.

When they became fully funded Tom and Emma, with Doc Dave as their invisible man, would go to Geneva and negotiate with big dollars to buy access to the CERN board. They must find out about all the projects scheduled for tests and experiments, especially those that might offer a path to develop CDM. The other group, Randall, Tim, and Max would provide all the funding to run the master plan from a safe remote distance at Sandfire.

Randall had taken to comforting Emma in his own crisp British way.

'Please don't cry my dear; we are all be here to protect you. Do believe me, I promise you that we will resolve this CDM problem and the Entity will let us all live, I am sure of it, especially now that we have a sound plan.'

Emma did not look convinced at Randall's soothing words; she had other concerns about Randall. Mainly how quickly he had accepted her very unprofessional and risky funding plan, and how did he manage to implement it so quickly? Emma politely listened.

'You are of course quite correct Emma; we are not of the criminal bent. However, I have often thought that had I decided to try my hand at the occupation of devious and crooked things. Being absolutely sure I would have made a jolly excellent criminal.'

Emma could sense that Randall was about to add some much needed humour to the tense debate.

'Did I ever tell you that my Uncle Jeremy was a career criminal?'

Emma looked up at Randall with the beginnings of a smile.

'Oh yes indeed, on my last visit to Brixton prison, Uncle told me why he always went back to corporate theft each time he got out of prison.

Uncle said pinching the money was always the easy part. Covering your tracks, and storing the loot in a safe place, then spending it. Those were by far the hardest parts to deal with in the criminal misappropriation of funds business. I must say, he should know, after all he has spent enough of his time residing at Her Majesty's pleasure learning to perfect his trade.'

Tom and Dave found Randall's story amusing. On the other hand, Max thought Randall had little in the way of a full understanding or appreciation for the grim task that lay ahead, or for that matter their serious situation. However only Emma knew what Randall was capable off...

Max had unwittingly stepped into Randall's playful "must know" spider web. Emma's face went from tears to a wide smile as she had seen this comedy-wit ambush, many times before. Randall was ready like a spider waiting on the first vibration of his web to signal a pending victim.

Max mimicked Randall's posh English accent, with a few obvious errors.

'Well do tell old chap, and just what-the-hell did you bloody learn from your crooked uncle Jeremy... sport?'

All eyes and ears were turned and tuned to hear Randall's reply.

'I do hope the Entity is listening in chaps, as this information if carried out with accuracy, will provide us with all the funds and tools needed to fight this nasty problem. Well at the very least deliver a satisfactory financial conclusion.'

Randall raised his nose to an aristocratic angle, while pouting his lips and pointing his chin in stately repose.

'I detect a measure of scepticism coming from our bearded, bonked on the head pilot friend. Be advised Max, my uncle has since left Her Majesty's free accommodation.

In the two short years since his eviction, Uncle Jeremy has bought a large castle in Germany, and now owns a multi-million dollar business empire throughout the world. Therefore, a well thought-out crime does indeed pay old man.

We should follow Uncle Jeremy's fine example and only pinch from those who have come by their money dishonestly and those who we consider can afford to lose some. Uncle Jeremy's money pinching business presented me with a huge, but interesting challenge.

Several years ago, using uncle's new offshore banking information, I put together a computer program, expressly for exercising Tim's agile mind. The data is still in my laptop... actually the very same data Tim is now using.

Tomorrow at one minute to midnight British UTC-time, we will launch our own concerted attack on twenty of the most notorious tax safe-haven countries around the world.

You see chaps; we have written a computer program to enable a series of fast computer account swaps. Then with the help of Dave's ghostly acquired information, Tim's mighty computer skills, and of course my cunning, devious mind, we will steal some money, correction, a great deal of money. Tim is entering all the account numbers and details as we speak.'

Randall paused, looking over Tim's shoulder at the laptop screen.

'The program has been locked at 432 notoriously bad people's safe-haven accounts with a total transfer of some 23 billion US dollars.'

All let-out a gasp of awe, Max interrupted Randall's aloof speech, waving a small calculator in his hand.

'This calculator doesn't have enough zeros, but I calculate that it is close to around fifty-three million nicked from each account, you'll never get away with it mate.'

Max then furrowed his brow with concern, again mimicking Randall's posh English accent.

'Another thing old chap, to have this computer program ready so soon you must have been thinking about ripping off this loot for some time.'

Randall was angry at this sudden attack on his character, and glared into Max's bloodshot eyes. Emma quickly came to Randall's rescue before they came to blows.

'Max, be assured; Randall has no need to steal money as he will never be short of a pound or two. He is a multi-millionaire in his own right without his Daddy's money, and I am talking about British pounds not those colonial dollars.

Max please listen to what Randal has to say... He likes wee games and large challenges; this is just a game to him. Go on Randal tell us how the program of yours will work.'

'Well my dear, prior to being interrupted by our rotund pessimistic Jewish friend here,' nodding in Max's direction. 'I was about to say that I am expecting news shortly from my Melbourne, London, and Hong Kong offices, giving us the details on a number of new shelf companies that we now own.

All of these companies now registered with a number of offshore tax haven accounts, ' then glancing at his Rolex. 'We have only fourteen hours, one minute and fifty-eight seconds London time to get this show on the road, and there is still much to do.'

Being a pilot, Max had calculated what that time was. Not yet ready to concede to Randall's hair-brained money scheme.

'So what happens at one minute to midnight GMT London-time? How do you know that all this account stuff will work? We should be worrying about the worlds Mafia and a dozen military despots calling on us for their bloody money back, all ending up in our slaughter?'

Max paused, holding a long hard stare at Randall without blinking.

'Then there is my main question. How the bloody hell did your uncle, get all the account numbers and passwords to make his swindle work. After all we did have a ghost helping us with that side of things... mate?'

Everyone waited quietly for the answer; they had all formed the same urgent concern. Randal was still watching the laptop screen, casually adding a few keystrokes to Tim's computer work, and then replied in his matter-of-fact way...

'Well if you really must know old man, Uncle Jeremy did receive most of his account access data from me. He had well over two thousand account numbers to choose from, and I enjoyed hacking into every one of them.

Uncle Jeremy may have used some of my incomplete data, I do not rightly know. At that time, the risk of detection would have been quite high. However, this time, any risk of detection will be quite low.

In this present safe-haven account money-raid, we shall have a superb and unique advantage. With the help of our handy resident ghost Doctor Dave, I have picked out from my original two thousand accounts, only those accounts with a balance of more than seven hundred million dollars...'

Sensing the shock of this bold statement, Randall drove home his reasoning into a firm prospective.

'My dear friends we should all consider this. Without these huge funds at our disposal, we will never have a chance to buy our way into what is going on at the Large Hadron Collider.

We need to know what all the major players are up to, and those booked to use the collider. Without this information, in short, we will have failed in our world saving mission... The end result is not at all appealing to ponder over.'

Randall lit a cigarette while all waited for his ending, then in a quiet voice.

'If we should fail to stop the creation of CDM, my guess is chaps that all of us will be exterminated by some catastrophic world event, created by the Entity... as it has promised.'

Randall paused to let this grim vision of events sink-in, and then changed subject by continuing with his money plan.

'At one minute to midnight UTC, trillions of dollars are moved regularly by secure EFT's (electronic fund transfers) around the world each day to play the overnight world money markets, and to execute equity settlements.

These senior tranche sweeps, and transfers happen every single day, because at sixty-one seconds it is all another day's interest gained or lost on world money markets.

We will piggyback on to this mass of money movement. Our transfers of around twenty billion dollars or so should pass un-noticed in the massive world money frenzy.

The first five triple-A money moves will be within the existing 432 accounts. That is, we will move 432 varying amounts of funds five times into each of the other's accounts bounced from mirror ISP servers all around the world.

With each transfer, we will siphon off a few hundred million dollars here and there. Then we will finally transfer all the remaining funds held in the duplicate accounts into our twenty new shelf company tax haven accounts. Then close the duplicate accounts.

Can you imagine the account owner's first reaction chaps, with the realisation, confusion, and suspicion? What will all these nasty corrupt people be thinking, and the poor blighters they will blame within their own ranks?

I would guess that a few drug-lord wars would erupt into outright slaughter, accusing each other of pilfering their offshore accounts. My guess is a few despots will go broke with no money to pay their army or buy weapons,'

Then Randall brightened up a little, attempting a dash of British humour.

'You know my dear friends, Max did mention the word; and strange as it may seem, you cannot spell the word "slaughter" without considering that this word without an "s" would spell laughter...

Chapter Nineteen

They are looking for the God particle

Dave thought the money plan was sound; giving it his full verbal support, he could not fault it. The others had remembered Dave's earlier admission about his lack of talent with money matters and were tending to follow Max's pessimistic view.

It was both a complicated and a risky plan. However, Randall did point out that they had no other choice if they wanted a chance at getting a look into what was going on within the LHC. Big money will without doubt open big doors.

Tom suggested it was about time they all stopped planning. They must now move forward with some firm action to their agreed plan. He considered the first smart move would be to get out of Perth, suggesting the Randal Falcon jet made ready to fly them all out of Perth.

They should leave immediately after Randall had pushed the computer button at the start of the money-grabbing program tomorrow morning. Tom did not know much about computers but felt it best that they should all get out of town, and soon.

Randall and Max had tried to convince Tom that Randall's laptop was safe and completely untraceable. Dave having seen some of the powerful names on the plundered bank account lists agreed with Tom, they should reduce their risk of exposure and leave Perth as soon as possible.

337

It was a busy afternoon and an even busier night. Soon after his dinner in the penthouse suite, Tim put to bed at 7:30pm. It was a gruelling day for Tim's extraordinary brain being totally exhausted by the day's effort.

Doc Dave flitted about between Geneva and Perth having long chats with Emma about technical matters he had difficulty in understanding. Dave assured them all he was safe, and the Entity, represented by Einstein and Darwin were alongside him at all times observing everything being said and done.

Everyone had noticed over the last few days the Entity becoming increasingly withdrawn, having little to say about anything currently being planned. All were frustrated in that the Entity would not respond to any of their direct questions.

It was as the Entity had said many times previously; it was an observer of the human race, planning changes only for the long-term. To the Entity, the cycle of our future existence in this solar system was now well advanced, and our predestined ending already written in time.

Tom was becoming a bit paranoid after hearing Emma and Randall casually admit the British MI6 and the Russian FSO were watching them, not to mention the Chinese CSS. He was now concerned about possible spying by the CIA and others who were interested in what these people were researching in the UK.

Listening to Tom, a thought had occurred to Max, what if they were followed back to Sandfire, a prospect that was worrying him. After all, it would be an easy task to track the whereabouts of the Randall Corporation jet.

Max had a simple answer flash through his mind to resolve this problem; they should fly directly to Sydney. Then buy another aircraft with their new funds; the Falcon jet should then fly on to the UK via America, with the named passengers still on the original flight plan.

Randall thought this was a jolly good idea, adding a better way. They should fly the Falcon to Melbourne first, and then they should head to Sydney by train to pick-up the new aircraft, just to confuse any nosey spy people.

Max rolled his eyeballs at Randall's cloak-and-dagger antics, pointing out; if there movements closely watched, then they should all try to act normal. The Sandfire Air Charter Company had lost an aircraft that needed replacing, the Randall jet was in Australia on business and had simply offered them a lift over to Melbourne.

Randall quickly caught Max's drift, further suggesting that Emma and Tom should remain in Melbourne for a few days to complete the business documents for the newly created companies Then fly on to the UK with the Falcon, and then to Geneva. Tim, Max, and he, would then fly their newly purchased aircraft, loaded with a range of smart electronic and computer goodies, up to this hidey-hole place on the edge of a desert called Sandfire.

It was a plan, not a complete plan, but a workable start. Randall looked around; it was obvious everyone was tired. At two in the morning, they all decided they could do no more and should attempt to get some sleep.

The enter button on Randall's laptop pushed at exactly 7:58am, just as Randall took a large bite of his French toast. This being two minutes before midnight London UTC, allowing a few seconds delay for the ISP server connections to put the data traffic through the servers.

The computer screen instantly filled with row after row of the download instruction data, ticking off the handshake encryption lock-keys one after the other. All eyes firmly glued to the laptop computer screen, as the seconds ticked by without a word spoken. Then the screen went blank followed by a black screen displaying a revolving blue circle in the middle.

Everyone turned their attention to look at Randall, who was in the middle of applying a thick layer of marmalade on his English muffin. Then noticing the look of concern on his friend's faces, Randall proceeded to explain the situation between large bites of his jam muffin.

'Nothing here to worry about chaps, the request has been completed before the midnight closing deadline. You see; the various banking institutions are now thinking about our instructions, the next stage will be checking our authority to access the accounts, and well... do the accounts have enough funds in them. Then the final stage will be the paying out the tranches as instructed. This part could take a few hours; we should get out to the airport, anyone for a muffin egg Benedict?'

The Randall Falcon jet made a fast departure from Perth International airport, climbing steeply to the programmed 45,000-foot cruise altitude. No sooner had the jet levelled out; Tim had the laptop ready and plugged into the Falcons direct satellite internet link.

Everyone watched him in childlike expectation as Tim established the computer uplink and locked on to the World Wide Web. The only sound was the subdued whine of the jet engines and Tim's computer keyboard clicking away with the long strings of address code entered.

As the pages of code rolled down the small screen, Tim leant back, eyes still riveted to the laptop screen with a blank look on his face. The scrolling stopped displaying a blue screen with a picture of a bank vault in the centre. Randall casually leant forward and with a long index finger pushed the enter key. Immediately the screen lit-up with row after row of banking transactions, the first being...

Global EFT, request accepted... Instruction carried out...
Transfer complete to account. #XXX+++ US$34,000,000
"Thirty-four million US Dollars" Transaction carried out.

As each instruction-line went down through the pages, the total sum flicked over registering an ever-increasing dollar total like a crazy one-armed-bandit in the granny snug of an English pub. Randall gave out a low whistle.

'By Jove, not bad old boy, to the minute we have netted just over seven billion US dollars. Max old chap, I think we now have enough money to go shopping for a nice aeroplane when we get to Sydney, what, what.'

Everyone gave out a nervous laugh except Tim. Dave's voice burst into their heads with a ghostly laugh adding...

'Well friends, I hope the baddies can't find out who has pinched their money, because within the next day or two they will for sure start shooting one another to get some answers.

From what I have seen in the movies, these real-life guys are by far meaner and more determined blokes. These guys will cut-off bankers fingers in the Cayman Islands, BVI, and Lichtenstein, and then threaten their wives, kids, and family to get the details of all these dodgy account transfers.'

Tim stopped staring at the screen then looked over at a vacant seat. All followed his gaze looking in suspense that someone, or something would appear in the seat; Tim talked to the empty seat...

'Doctor Sharp, most of the new money transfers will be recovered by the present account holders. I have arranged that some of the moved money end-up in another drug Lords account, and then partially returned by some way or means. The money transfers that we have chosen to keep are now untraceable. The previous owners of these funds will soon regard these small fund problems as an acceptable collateral loss.'

'Call those a small bloody fund problems.'
Max blurted out, he was having some difficulty with this statement by the most times silent Tim.
'For crying out loud... Jesus mate, we've just gone past ten billion bloody US dollars, and the counter is still clicking over like a mad poker machine.'
No one said a word; Emma got out a large notepad and started working with Tom looking over her shoulder. Randall and Tim resumed their business of stealing the world's illegal drug money.
Max lay-down on the thick luxurious leather lounge, he had calmed down, accepting the deed as done. Nobody could change things now. He was staring up at the ceiling of the jet, dreaming of the aircraft he would buy as the Falcon quietly whined on its way across the sky at 515Kts, cruising at 45,000 feet towards Melbourne. A thought occurred to Max, he should borrow Tom's laptop and checkout what aircraft are for sale on the east coast of Australia.
'Sorry Max, all I have in my baggage now is a few changes of gear, and some technical documents. My laptop computer, camera, cell phone, and my ancient Martian femur bone all left at the Veevers plane-crash site.
You know, I do have my suspicions the Entity had planned it to be like this; well they did want their bone back. The way I figure things are, if this all goes wrong, we will have no material evidence to back-up any of our incredible stories.'
Max gave Tom a quizzical look, followed by a cheeky smile.
'We will still have over ten billion US dollars to spend Tom, that's not such a bad effort mate; crikey, we will all be bloody rich.'

'Something to cling-on to I guess Max, but where would you spend all this money my Aussie friend. There will be no shops if the Entity carries out its threat, and sends us all back to the Stone Age.

Anyway, how long would it take the Entity to fix that... just a few well-placed clues to the Mafia drug Lords and we would all be victims of unfortunate accidents? One thing I have learnt about the Entity in my short experience in its presence. They make a neat job of cleaning up, and we are not important to them at all, in a natural universal sort of way.'

Max just kept staring up at the ceiling, he then sat-up, blurting out as if he never heard a word Tom had spoken...

'I will go and ask the captain if we can borrow his laptop to go online shopping for an airplane. We must all try to enjoy this unusual experience while we can. Think positive mate. We will find these bastards, and another thing Tom, I am convinced that we will save the world. Just as the superheroes would do in the movies, except we'll be drinking premium malt scotch while we fight for the future existence of mankind.'

Tom smiled, and then Max noticed the others had also heard him… they were not smiling. This was serious business.

Everything started happening quickly from that time on. A secret base was quickly set-up in Melbourne to crank things into gear. In just eleven hectic days, Emma and Tom became the CEO and Chairman of their new company, Quantum Universal NL.

The new company directors then made a generous donation of forty million dollars each, to both Princeton and Oxford Universities. This money was to help establish a new Quantum Physics research lab facility.

The next smart move designed by Randal and Max, was to offer both Universities a seat on the new company Quantum Universal NL's research and projects board. A few more million dollars and a large new building grant got them the immediate access to lease a private company office system at Oxford University.

These extensive rambling offices were in the old Particle Physics wing, just a short walk from Professor Reg, Sally, Chirpy, and Jan's normal working areas. The old chaos group were beside themselves, delighted by the exciting new developments... and overwhelmed with the vast amounts of money available to them.

They were all told to say nothing, to stay low and let the University bask in all the glory. Jan explained, apparently some wealthy American Professor of Anthropology who had befriended Emma on her recent lecture tour visit to Russia, had decided to become a philanthropist.

This Professor bloke had stumped-up all the funding for the whole bleeding development programme. Emma and this Professor would meet them soon in Oxford, she needed them all to remain calm and say nothing.

The Oxford Vice Chancellor was pleased with the large donations, which apparently more than covered the government-funding shortfall, and had to ask the Dean of Physics, Professor Roger Walker, who was this Quantum Universal NL. Apparently, a senior director of this new company was in fact one of his regular staff, a quantum physics lecturer by the name of Doctor Emma Archer. All were smiles at the vast money donation, and the academic exposure gained from the unexpected windfall.

At Princeton University, Vice Chancellor Professor George Gamble could hardly contain his enthusiasm, keen to get his hands-on the forty million dollar cash research grant.

George proudly told the financial board that he always had every confidence in his old friend Professor Harold. Reporting that he was pleased to meet his new business associate Mr Randall, a well-known eccentric, English philanthropist. Chancellor George suggested that his friend Professor Harold be recognised for his fine work. Deserving a place in the hall of fame in the Princeton cloisters... All of the board agreed, much to the amusement of Tom.

Randall's next strategic move was to win over the co-operation of the twenty members on the board of CERN in Geneva. Achieved, by simply offering them two-billion US dollars, a mind-bending amount of cash for research funding.

The funds were in consideration that his company Quantum Universal NL acquired a seat on the board requiring an active and leading role in the LHC project. Randall then advising that his company wished only to be involved in the continuing experiments, and the scheduling of events during the next eighteen to twenty-four months. A time over which the board had total control of the LHC project.

Half the board objected to this pushy offer, citing their cautious reason to be "Why would this new research company want a say in what we do, what's in it for them." More importantly. "Who were these people?"

The Director of finance stood up and advised the shocked board. One billion in refundable US dollars had already been deposited into the CERN bank accounts. A further deposit of one billion dollars was ready on acceptance of Quantum Universal NL's business terms.

These dollars would fund the running costs of the collider facility for three years. The director of finance added his background checks proved this new research company had the funds and being extremely well connected, this was a take-it or leave-it deal, open for only two days.

Another director stood up and added that this company, Quantum Universal NL may well be a new organisation, however, it was supported and backed by two of the world's most prestigious academic institutions. Namely, Oxford University England and Princeton University America, and that some of their brightest and most respected academics were on its governing board.

Of the twenty major European and world organisations that made-up the CERN control board, a vote was carried; eighteen to two in favour of Quantum Universal NL becoming a controlling member of the CERN board.

Dave discovered that the two votes against them were "observer nations" the Russian "Quantum Depth Research Group" funded by the University of St Petersburg, and strangely enough the Iranian "Particle Research Institution." The CERN control board now consisted of twenty-one executive members.

The new research company Quantum Universal NL was now an official member of the exclusive CERN board. With full access to the CERN advanced revolutionary computer network known as "The Grid."

This new computer operating system had its own ISP network being the next powerful step beyond the current World Wide Web. Randall and Max were like little boys in a free candy shop studying the many project files on the Grid. Meanwhile Tim just went about finding ways to get around all the private encryption lockouts and passwords.

Emma and Tom were never followers of world political events however, a new strange and unusual set of events were currently taking place in the Middle East. The world media were reporting good news for a change.

The world powers had stepped back from the brink of military action, welcoming with huge relief at Iran abandoning their nuclear weapons programme.

In a show of commitment, Iran had extended an invitation for the world major powers to observe the dismantling of their uranium enrichment processing plants, ending the fear of Iran becoming a nuclear-armed power.

Dave had discovered that shortly after the decision to abandon their nuclear programme, Iran had suddenly become heavily involved with the Large Hadron Collider project. They were very active and had managed to gain a full seat on the CERN governing board. As a spooky afterthought, Dave felt compelled that he should mention this unusual, odd, and sudden Iranian interest to the others.

The move to Sandfire over a month ago was low-key with Tony still trying to figure out why this posh pommy Randall bloke would invest heaps of money in Doc Dave's little air charter business... and who was the young bloke who most times looked up to the sky and never talked?

Tony's suspicions were increasing; being told that Doc Dave was in London with those two people that were with him in the Cessna plane crash. It all sounded a bit weird to him... still their money problem was gone. Then there was the other strange thing, this weird lot hardly ever came out of Max's bloody caravan... what the bleeding hell did they do in there all day?

Tim and Randall were busy as ever using their new superfast computers, working with the now available CERN Grid data. Max, with the help of his new computer nerd friends, being elevated to super hacker of satellite snooping equipment.

Max was never that interested in the endless streams of encrypted data that he knew always imbedded in all the general communication traffic. This data included geophysical data, and spy pictures collected by the world's orbiting spy satellites.

That was a job for Pine Gap, the not so secret Australian, American, and British satellite spying facility. A facility firmly established in the Northern Territory, being not far from the town of Alice Springs.

Randall had briefly stopped complaining about his regular eviction from Max's caravan to smoke his cigarettes outside. Nobody cared or listened about his complaints about the poor standard of food, plus the crude accommodation at Sandfire, Max could shut out his pleas with apparent ease.

Max was sitting back in his chair in a daydream looking at his computer screen decorated with a length of green Christmas tinsel and a little white angle on top. Outside a video camera gave him a commanding view of his almost new Cessna Caravan turbine aircraft, posing in the bright sun on the hardstand.

Alongside was a proud Tony, busy with his Christmas present, a new Toyota Landcruiser cleaned for the second time that day. Tony was still sporting a big ear-to-ear grin. Doc Dave had paid him in full, saving him from bankruptcy again, just as the Doc had promised. The world was not such a bad place after all, as the Doc said, "Just think positive mate."

A voice filtered through, disturbing Max's tranquil thoughts.

'I say old boy, is that chap Tony the full quid. I mean to say, it must be over 45 degrees out there in the sun, and he is washing his clean vehicle again. I am starting to think that all the Australians in these parts are a little sun damaged, or possibly worse old chap.'

Max switched the big computer monitor screen back to the streams of satellite-imbedded data he was downloading for Tim to check over.

Max realised that to Randall, things at Sandfire must look a little odd.

'Sorry old sport, I'm still coming to terms with the fact that we have a new current model aircraft, and that we own the bloody thing.'

'Well, take your last look at your flying beauty pilot Max, because we have some interesting and new situations to look into. Tim and I have been going over all the old data the chaos group has sent us from Oxford.

The group still thinks we are just researching the Veevers crater phenomena, but we do feel certain there must be a common link to connecting all our bits of information together.

Two of our group, Chirpy and Jan have pointed out that the four governments snooping around our research work being, the Americans, British, Chinese and the Russians have mostly lost interest in us. It would now appear that they already knew all about the odd gravity clusters around the world, and had for some time… On the other hand, was it something else that caused them to lose interest?

346

Chirpy and Jan have concluded that these people just wanted to know more about Emma's work with gravitons and the Higgs boson particle, how we got involved, and well... Did we know any more than they did about the string theory of the standard model? Jolly interesting, don't you think?'

Randall noticed that Max had become disturbed at this casual news from Oxford. He had tensed his lower jaw, changed expression, and switched back on to hard rational thinking.

Max knew little about string theory and physics but had a good sensitive Jewish nose and a gut feeling when it came to nosey, snooping people. These people were from the big end of town... world government, security agencies. He knew these kinds of people only spied around for a damn good reason.

Meeting Randall eye-to-eye, he began to express his unusual and odd analysis of the chaos group's recent big brother surveillance. Max then added his reasoning and observations; applying some standard Max logic.

'This lot tells me one thing mate; something is going on around this world. Something that is much bigger than we have going on right now... These nosey world governments are up to something fishy. I get the feeling these blokes thought your chaos group was on to them, poking around in their business; whatever that might be.'

Max stroked his ragged black beard, and then scratched his face, then announced his odd thoughts.

'Randall mate, I think someone has a much more important and bigger agenda than we have... and we are trying to save this bloody world. I ask you this mate; what the hell could be more important than that?'

Max was still looking into Randall's confused face, when a clear but quiet voice rang out from the normally silent Tim.

'They are simply looking for the God particle; it has to do with faith. Only faith installed from birth, and the dedicated belief by fear of an all-powerful personal God can have this effect on a human mind... or sanity. We know insanity is also a personal matter, together they are dangerous.

We must find out what would cause these four major world powers to conspire in this way, in a matter dealing with faith... The world's largest and newest religion Islam has now fallen quiet to the world, and the world's oldest religions are watching and waiting in bewilderment... and fear.'

Max spun around in his chair staring at Tim who just continued to click away on his computer. Tim had spoken his first words in nearly two weeks and that was it, he then relapsed into silence... Max blurted out.

'What the hell is Tim on about, that's crazy talk man. What has all this government interest got to do with bloody faith, religion and a God? We have the closest thing to a God on our side mate, the bloody Entity...'

Randall raised a scholarly finger interrupting Max in his full swing rant.

'You know what old chap; I think some of this stuff is starting to make sense now, let's see. Tim has mentioned the God particle now that is the name given to the elusive Higgs boson particle.

This is one of the expected results of exploring the Terascale in particle physics, using the Large Hadron Collider at CERN in Geneva. This Higgs boson particle is by theory what keeps the universe together and stops all mass objects like planets from flying apart at the speed of light, hence the nickname God particle.'

Now, if the gauge-Higgs unification could produce a stable pair in a Higgs-boson nucleon collider-collision then... bingo... they have a way to produce both mini black holes and possibly cold dark matter.'

Max was not convinced about the Higgs boson particle idea. Mainly because he knew little or nothing about quantum theory, or for that matter the reference to a God particle. In a face-saving move, he just continued his ranting on, mimicking Randall's posh accent.

'I still don't follow this; my dear old mate. As Emma has said, we already know the LHC can create both harmless mini black holes and a few particles of CDM. I thought we were all looking for those bastards at the LHC, who are the idiots about to create huge amounts of this cold dark matter stuff.

We should be concentrating all our efforts on stopping the bastards before they eventually turn this planet earth into a black hole. We need to stop to them, and soon, or the Entity will bloody stop them with their well-proven extermination methods. The most likely way, by smashing us lot back to the Stone Age, with a massive earthquake, pole tilt, or some such thing.'

Max stopped ranting, eyes bulging, staring at Randall then waited. Randall was deep in thought, hardly listening to a word of Max and his explosive views, he then announced in his aloof English accent.

'That's another thing that has crossed my mind old boy, just how, and in which way would the Entity carry out its nasty threat. After all one must remember, the Entity did say it planned for events well into the future.

That being the case, it must have already decided on the way we are to be disposed of. Well chaps, if we are to believe the Entity, and remember the Entity does not tell fibs, a date and time must have already been set. Has anyone ever thought to ask the Entity the date of this event; that is assuming we should fail in our mission?'

Tim stopped rattling his computer keyboard, a sign he might again say something. Max and Randall turned in silence, and then Tim slowly spoke.

'This cataclysmic event has been recorded for many thousands of years. The Mayan calendar and other ancient writings have the date well documented as the northern hemisphere midwinter's solstice, being the 21st day of December 2012...

Logic and timing suggests the possibility, that those who do not follow the cross would have created cold dark matter on the 22nd of December 2012. We can see this as the end-of-mankind, as in the Mayan calendar prediction. This date being the same date as the saviour's true birth date. The end-days will be three days before the biblical scriptures listing of the wrong birthday date of Jesus Christ, as the 25th December, when using the Gregorian calendar.'

Randall and Max were both staring at Tim. Both responded in loud unison...

'Would have created.'

Max continued, as Randall froze terrified, his mouth moving but words failing to form, drying up in a sea of fear. Realising the link to Islam, "Those who do not follow the cross" They both suddenly realised that this matter most certainly had a connection to religious beliefs... Did the pending discovery of the God particle with the LHC in Geneva have anything to do with this CDM event?

'If Tim is right mate, then we only have some ten days left to stop this all happening... Shit we need to let the others know about this, and get the date confirmed by the Entity.'

Max was now terrified, mainly at Randall's reaction.to this bad news. This display of fear was completely unexpected, and out of character from this cool, always in control person. He was seriously considering offering Randall a shot of his hidden stash of scotch

'Randall for fucks sake mate, snap out of it, we've got a lot of bloody work to do. If Tim is correct, then we must tell the others about this link with religion.'

Tom had never been to Europe in the winter. They had both just returned from Geneva only two hours ago where the outside temperature was a cold minus four degrees. Tom assured that this is normal weather for 10th of December.

Tom looked at his watch, it was 7:50pm, and looked up just as Emma came over to the table with a beaming smile and sat down for dinner. The atmosphere inside the warm restaurant was very much a Christmas scene, with all the usual decorations. Although, the Christmas cheer had not reached any of the close group of people he was now involved with... Christmas was the last thing on their minds.

'Emma, at what time is our meeting with Professor Reg and the others as we will need to set-up some sort of phone conference call with Randall, Max, and Tim at Sandfire.'

'Professor Reg suggested we should hold the meeting in his secret dungeon office at 9:30. He thought that our new Quantum Universal NL Oxford office might have surveillance, if not bugged. Tom we should head over there after we have finished dinner as we have a lot to discuss.'

Tom had briefly met-up with Professor Reg, Sally, Chirpy, and Jan only eight days ago at their stopover in Oxford on the way to Geneva. He was impressed with this knowledgeable and talented odd group of scientists, and looking forward to meeting up with them again.

Tom had immediately bonded with the chaos group as genuine people, people that he liked and could work with. Another thought had occurred to him, did the Entity have a hand in this bonding process, maybe a part of some plan.

As they finished their quick meal, Tom was thinking ahead. There was the other major unresolved problem to address; they were yet to tell Professor Reg and Sally, Chirpy and Jan about this all powerful Entity.

Emma sensed the uncertainty, bringing Tom back to reality.

'Come on laddie, let's go, we have important work to do tonight.' reading Tom's thoughts. 'Yes Tom, I too am worried, that we have to tell some nice people in Oxford that their world may be about to end. We need their help to assist in some way to discover who on this planet is messing around with cold dark matter, and help us put a stop to it.'

An excited Professor Reg met them at the door with a well-lit pipe; he had and a warm handshake for Tom, and a big hug for Emma. Professor Reg and the others led to believe Tom was an enormously rich philanthropist, if only they knew. Randall and Emma had made Tom promise not to tell them anything about the money stealing part of their project.

This was going to be hard... hard to tell the story and hard for them to understand. These people think we have come here to Oxford to educate them about an exclusive world discovery. I guess there was some truth in that.

Also that we are about to publish a scientific research paper, confirming the significance of a number of the world's oldest buildings, with a phenomenon known as gravity ring clusters, with the prime site being at the Veevers meteorite crater. Then confirming how life first brought to this planet earth in some sort of controlled meteorite showers... oh boy, are they due for an almighty shock.

'Quickly now, the others are waiting, we have so much to discuss.'

Professor Reg scurried off down the steps leading to the bunker, closely followed by Emma and Tom who were finding it hard to keep up with the excited 81-year-old Professor of Astrophysics.

There were genuine smiles, hugs, and handshakes all-round then Chirpy quickly got down to business. Then standing on her plastic milk-crate in front of the well-filled chalkboard. She was ready to start. The group suddenly silenced by Chirpy's, squeaky high-pitched voice, abruptly piercing the air.

'You're late... We have been waiting over an hour for you people. Let me begin. The wine is a nice Merlot; I have brought three bottles to celebrate our involvement in the new company Quantum Universal NL, and the proposed publishing of our research.

We also welcome Professor Thomas Harold as a member of our fine chaos group. Please join me in a glass accepting Professor Harold as a member. Professor, as an indorsed member of the chaos group, you may now call me Chirpy to my face.'

Chirpy held her glass in a salute and took a sip, just as Dave gave a gentle ghostly chuckle startling both Emma and Tom. Tom looked at Emma; yes, she had also heard Dave... Dave launched into his report.

'We have some very interesting and urgent problems brewing, which add yet another strange angle and dimension to what is going on. Randall, Max, and Tim have just identified a firm link between this CDM stuff and religion, and not all religion's, just Islam. Firstly, do you think it is a good idea to tell these nice people about the Entity, and me being a ghost?

I think we could get this job done without the added complication. These good people think this is all about some newly found scientific phenomenon, why don't you try telling them about Veevers and the visiting Martians first, see if they will accept that bit for a start.'

Emma and Tom agreed with Dave, chatting to him in their heads. They would discuss this new CDM and religion angle later. Things were going to be difficult enough without adding religion into the equation.

It would take some effort and time just to cover the extraterrestrial colonisation of earth, and now there was this imminent threat to the survival of all humans on planet earth.

'Professor Harold... hello Professor... are you okay,' Chirpy was busy waving her hand at Tom. 'You appear to have gone into some sort of trance sir... are you okay?'

'Please accept my apologies Chirpy, I was in deep thought about what Emma, and I are about to tell the chaos group, oh and please call me Tom. I think it might be better if I come over and spoke from the rostrum?'

Chirpy with a quizzical look stepped down from her milk crate and poured Tom a glass of wine holding it out to him as she neatly kicked the plastic milk crate aside.

Tom looked out at his small audience who were no longer smiling; they had all anticipated and sensed that something was not right. Tom attempted to lighten up the gloomy mood in the room.

'Thank you all for accepting me as a member of your chaos group. Emma has told me a great deal about your research.' Then noticing the minor shock on the faces of all four, quickly moved into reassurance mode. 'Please be assured that Emma has not breached the confidence of your chaos group research work.

Within the next hour or so, you will learn that we are all in some way connected to the same field and research project. Our paths have crossed in what Emma and your chaos group had found out about the Veevers crater and gravity cluster-rings, and what I was about to discover in my own academic research field as an anthropologist.

I guess you are all wondering why Randall and Tim are still in Australia, well I can tell you they are doing important work on this... our project. They are both well and staying in a place called Sandfire, a roadside diner outpost with just a small airstrip on the edge of the Great Sandy Desert in Western Australia.

Jan stood up to speak but Tom answered his question. 'And might I add quite close to the Veevers crater.'

Tom paused to take a drink of his wine in the now silent room when Sally in scarcely a whisper added sadly.

'We miss them all dearly. Tom, what is it they are doing that cannot be carried out here in Oxford, will Tim and Randall come home now?'

Tom felt that Sally was speaking for them all, and with the deep concerns of a mother. Tom looked out at his small, but confused meeting, and continued.

'Randall and Tim are working with two other guys we have met in Western Australia. These two people, just like me are very much involved with events at the Veevers crater site, and therefore again connected with your chaos research project.

These people are Doctor David Sharp a Geophysicist, who also owns Sandfire Air Charter, and yes my new friends; this is the same charter company whose airplane crashed in the desert... with us in it. The other guy is his chief pilot Max Zusman, who also happens to be a smart satellite systems computer hacker. Together with Tim, these four guys have a great amount in common, and are working well together in finding out answers to our problem of...'

This was too much for Jan to hear and hold, then in a bursting interjection.

'Yo you're telling us th that those bleeders are still at it in Australia, hacking into bloody gov government secret info. We will all end up in bloody ja jail. Anyway the government blokes are not interested in us any more, looks like no nobody is, so wh what's this problem then.'

Tom took another sip of his wine, while considering a believable answer.

'There is a very good reason for their hacking, and also why the Feds are no longer interested in this group Jan, We now think these nosey government guys have decided that this group is not looking at, or into what they themselves are doing.

We now believe we know what they are involved with whom they are involved with, and what they are about to do. Randall, Tim, and Max are helping us stop these people in their mission.

We, that is Emma and I are about to ask you all to help us in resolving this grim problem. A situation that we now know is a matter of life and death, for... well to be blunt, most of the species on this planet.'

That did it; Tom now had their full attention, all leaning forward with worried looks to hear his every word.

'We know there is a concentrated effort by a number of high profile organisations from around the world, to create for the first time on this planet a black hole. Yes, that is correct, Cold Dark Matter. The intension, we now believe, is to produce CDM in large enough quantities that can with the smallest error, most certainly cause irreversible damage to our planet.

We must stop this from happening.' Tom paused for effect looking over at the stunned faces, now full of questions.

'That my new friends is the reason, and the only reason that we have paid the hefty price of two-billion US dollars to acquire a seat on the board of the CERN. We would then know when, and who is scheduled to carry out this research test project in the LHC program.'

Jan butted in with a surprised stutter.

'You paid two billion yank dollars to fi find out what's going o on at the LHC in Geneva. Christ mate, you gotta be f fucking bonkers.' Waving a thick file in front of his face, Jan pushed on with his point.

'It's an open bleeding science grid project Tom, you could have got your ha hands on all that info f for a pint or two at the local pub.'

Tom had a thought-word with Emma and Dave.

'This might be a little harder to get over than we first thought... anybody got a better idea?'

Emma returned the thought.

'Give me a go Tom, they are all my good friends, and I know them well.

Just as the Entity has warned us, this truth business from a secret source mixed with the unbelievable can be tricky.'

Emma stood up speaking from her seat and called for the floor.

'You do not know Tom well, but you all know me. Believe us, this is a world survival crisis.' Then turning to face Jan. 'We know what is in the standard LHC programme file that you are holding, and I can assure you all, there is another agenda to the published research test listings...'

Chirpy stood up demanding the floor, although no one would have ever noticed her profile, and interrupted Emma in her abrupt manner and squeaky voice.

'Emma, how did you come to meet Professor Tom, and this other man, this Doctor Sharp? Something has happened in Australia that has us all a little baffled and worried. You were a predictable and dedicated scientist, but now...' Chirpy paused, 'I would say we are much concerned about you.'

Dave could see a looming problem; they needed to move things along.

'Crikey mate, this little bird is smart. You are going to have a battle on your hand's convincing her about all this CDM stuff. Emma, why don't you just tell them the truth, but I think you should try to leave out the bit about the Entity for now.'

Emma responded to Tom and Dave by thought, she was both surprised and concerned at what Chirpy had said. "You were a predictable and dedicated scientist." Was this the view her chaos group now had?

'Dave may be right, but it's still my go Tom,' and walked down to the front as Tom took his seat. This sudden action without a word spoken made the group suspicious.

'Yes Chirpy, something did indeed happen in Australia. I will explain the circumstances and tell you all a most interesting, yet terrifying story. A story that decides our future existence with every second we go forward in time from events that have happened and are entrenched in our past.'

Emma told them about Tom's ancient bone with a metal prosthesis given to him by his mentor and friend Professor Ben. Who in turn received this bone from an old Australian prospector, previously the property of an old Gadichi man called Munyo.

Tom had agreed to return this special bone to the original find site in Australia, and recommended to use Sandfire Air Charter, which was how Tom met Dave. Doctor Dave Sharp knew this Munyo, being an odd coincidence in itself. Apparently, for some time Doc Dave and his pilot Max had been experiencing strange things happening to their aircraft instruments out and around the Veevers crater area.

Emma continued telling the story for the next hour and a half while they all listened on in fascination. Emma left out the part about meeting the Entity and substituted Dave and Max's satellite data showing a vast underground cave complex just north-east of the Veevers site. This being in the exact same position where Randall and Jan had plotted the odd gravity cluster ring. It was about then she felt her story begin to rapidly fall apart and paused for a thought-chat with Tom and Dave.

'This story is going all wrong Tom; I have a problem in telling fibs, this will not hold together without telling them something about the Entity. Another thing is we need to talk urgently with Randall, Max, and Tim.

We could really do with the help of the Entity at this time, to convince them that the Entity does in fact exist. To see the Entity represented as Einstein and Darwin, they would all have to meet at a gravity ring site, the nearest being Stonehenge.'

Dave suggested they should all try linking up for a thought transfer, a sort of teleporting. 'Well it worked with Randall and Max at the restaurant.'

A sharp clicking stopped the three-way thought chat. Professor Reg was tapping his pipe on his large glass ashtray, politely asking for attention.

'You seem to be a little distracted, are you all right my dear, is there something wrong, might I ask a few points about your bizarre story?

What evidence do you have that this ancient bone and the underground city at Veevers, are actually Martian remains? In addition, who told you there is a world threat from the creation of CDM?

We agree it does appear there is a small connection on this point, as our own, and recent LHC information has brought this fact to our attention. Nevertheless, the search for CDM is now a formal listed item on the LHC research schedule. Where in the first place did you get the idea that this CDM research project was now a threat to our planet?'

Tom and Emma looked at each other; it was time to tell the truth, to advise them all there was much more to tell. Although he added cautiously, that the truth would without doubt challenge their levels of the believable... to extraordinary limits.

Tom then went on to tell them about the plane crash being a planned event by a universal power known as the Entity. This universal omnipresent Entity, whose short time energy better concentrated at a gravity ring site. Then about the Entity taking on the forms of Einstein and Darwin to reduce their fear levels.

The look on their faces just confirmed what they had already expected. None of their stories were being accepted or remotely believed. Doctor Sharp agreeing to remain in a coma to perform some ghostly duties almost laughed at by the Oxford chaos group... scepticism was rife, and sarcasm would surly follow.

This next part would be especially difficult. Tom asked them to give him time to explain, asking them to all sit in a circle facing one another. Chairs and desks moved out of the way; looking at the circle of confused faces, Tom realised that he had one hell-of-an almighty task ahead of him.

'Okay, who of you hold firm religious beliefs? Who of you believe in spirits and ghosts, a planned destiny, or a universal intelligence? Moreover, who of you can have an open mind to try understanding, or accepting the slightest possibility of a new truth about our

357

evolution. With this new understanding, bringing the answer to. Why do we exist, and why are we here.

We now have this knowledge, and can provide that answer. An answer that is both terrifying as it is wonderful. Ladies and gentlemen you are all going to be, well I guess... enlightened. We are all going to have a chat with Randall, Tim, Dave, and Max in Australia by a form of mind teleportation. You are going to experience this by hearing all their voices inside your heads.

They all stared in silence at Tom. Jan was about to snigger a smart comment about this un-scientific claim, but Tom had read his mind giving Jan a hard serious look of I dare you to speak.

Jan noticing Toms look deciding to follow the chaos group and remain silent. Tom continued with his planned séance.

By my time, it is around 7am in Australia so let us hope they have all finished their breakfast. This demonstration is possibly the true meaning of a séance, or the unification of science and I suppose good old metaphysics'

Chirpy mumbled something about a load of old mumbo-jumbo crap, while Jan said they were all bleeding mad. Sally reminded them all they were scientists and work on supported theory and confirmed facts, not spiritual fantasy. Professor Reg smiled at Chirpy and relit his pipe. Nevertheless, they all finally agreed to hold hands with much mockery.

Dave made a ghostly trip over to Sandfire and got Randall, Max and Tim ready as Dave would be the only means to connect them all to Emma and Tom.

The first words in his head made Professor Reg jump with fright and disbelief, all were concerned he may have a heart attack. Dave casually introduced himself and Max to the others in Oxford.

Randall butted in with a cheery hello chaps, all recognising Randall's posh English voice. Chirpy was amazed, stating that she never believed in ghosts and séances but was terrified that if this was indeed happening, adding in her squeaky voice that Randall and Tim must be dead.

Randall declared he was far from dead, and that this is the best experience he has ever had in his life, total secure wireless communications, far better than a mobile phone... and cheaper. He was then abruptly requested by all to shut-up as it looked like Tim was about to speak.

The seconds ticked away and then in an emotionless flat toned voice Tim announced his presence.

'I am not dead, my life cycle has long to run, should our planet and our species survives beyond the next Entity correction. This is the way of the universe, and has always been so.

Test number 175 at the LHC is in progress with proton particle beams having once reached the power of 9TeV. They have already been accelerated in the main ring of the LHC loop, to soon collide at the detector site CMS. But detector site ALICE has the Bose-Einstein Condensate unit, and this will be the only means to capture CDM for the client.'

The short silence confirmed that Tim had completed his message, this opportunity taken by Emma adding more information.

'When Tom and I were in Geneva, we inspected this Bose-Einstein Condensate unit. As Tim has said, this unit fully installed at the ALICE detector site. We had guessed then, this could possibly be the final holding point for any created CDM. Then surprised who is running that experiment, and even more surprised at who was funding it. These people must be the ones who Tim calls the client.'

Max had no idea what a BEC, Bose-Einstein Condensate unit was, and asked what this gear does. He had come across a few references to the building and installation of BEC units in his satellite data hacking, especially in the Saudi Arabian data reports to British, Chinese, and Russian universities.

Professor Reg had quickly recovered from his health threatening shock, accepting this frightening spiritual experience as fact. He decided to answer Max's question trying out his newly established metaphysical communication link.

'Basically without getting into too much detail a BEC unit will produce the coldest ever, recorded temperature known, plus 100pK or in Celsius, minus 273°C almost absolute zero. At those super low temperatures, atoms will slow down to a crawl and settle occupying the lowest quantum state... particles will slow down to a stop.

In comparison, the lowest natural temperature recorded in deep space is minus 271°C or plus one Kelvin, interestingly enough found in the Boomerang Nebula. Therefore, we have discovered a way on earth to produce a colder temperature than can ever be achieved in deep space.

The Large Hadron Collider superconducting beam magnets use liquid helium producing a temperature of minus 271°C. One would then ask why such a low temperature created by a BEC unit would be required at the LHC in Geneva. What would it be used for?'

A well-known squeaky voice burst into the spooky conversation.

'I can answer that, but I think most of you would have already guessed the answer,' Chirpy's squeaky voice cut through everyone's mind.

'CDM is in theory non-baryonic, for example consisting of matter other than protons and neutrons. Dark Matter particles interact with one another while other particles do so only through gravity... raw gravity. CDM is therefore pure gravity particles.

The new research at the LHC will provide us with the answer to this theory; however, we should all acknowledge that without CDM our galaxy and the solar system would never have formed.

Super low temperatures will hold, and suspend the captured CDM particles. Just as well, since without this super low temperature the particles would represent the heaviest mass ever known on earth. It has been calculated a mass of CDM particles the size of a grain of rice, would weigh in excess of 200,000 tons. The most likely other reason for using the Bose-Einstein Condensate unit is that it is small, and possibly transportable.

With the CDM held captive and suspended in the BEC unit with laser beams, there would only be the BEC unit weight itself to consider. And that could only be a few hundred kilos at most.'

They all thought through this new information for a few seconds, then Chirpy came alive again with a piercing voice to ask the obvious questions.

'What danger is there in the LHC creating minuscule black holes and CDM particles? If produced, they will just simply evaporate. Why is this Entity so concerned, and who would want to attempt to create a large amount of CDM... Agreeing with what Professor Reg has said for what use, and for what possible purpose?'

Randall thought he had a good and likely answer to those questions, as he and Tim had put some time into researching the properties and the power of CDM.

'Tim and I do believe we have sorted out the answer to those questions my dear. You see it is all to do with cycles of celestial events, biological life development cycles, the big bang theory, and yes God... oh and a fair few big sums thrown in.'

Jan added his two bobs worth... 'You've g gone bonkers Randall. The bleeding Australian sun has g got to you, better come back mate.'

Randall was quick to reply. 'No, please listen to me old chap. This all makes complete sense now. Consider if this 200,000-ton grain of CDM were to lose its super cold suspension environment. The first thing to happen would be for it to seek gravity, our earth's gravity.

Something the size of a grain of rice weighing 200,000 tons would fall quickly to the centre of our planet. As for the danger, well my friends, most of us know what would happen to this small grain of CDM when eventually subjected to our earth's high core temperatures.

The little chap would expand at the speed of light. In the same way as the big bang, then we would be no more. Eventually I suppose over a few million years, collapsing into the most likely event, a small black hole... This CDM is pretty powerful stuff chaps.

The Entity obviously takes a very dim view of us lowly biological life forms messing around in their business of arranging, relocation, and removal of planets in its universe, as the Martians were quick to find out.

The good news is chaps we now believe we have all the knowledge, and information we need to put a stop to this CDM creation. Just as well, because we have just figured out when we are all about to die if we fail, we calculate this event will take place in exactly eleven day's time'.

Sally, Chirpy, Jan, and Professor Reg chorused. 'How do you know that?' Followed by Emma and Tom 'Has the Entity confirmed this?'

Randall continued with his pleasant mater-of-fact chat.

'Not yet old boy, however, we are sure that it will. We know this Entity works in event cycles, apparently so does everything else in the universe, and has done so since the beginning of time... or, as one would say, since the big bang.

Once you get your head around the fact that everything has a beginning and ultimately an end, and then apply that to your everyday universal thinking it all falls neatly into place.

Bear in mind chaps that most events can be rescheduled, providing that they still fall into an acceptable order. We will be rescheduling things by ending the creation of CDM on earth, we would hope within the next eleven days. The Entity has left a small window of opportunity open for us to choose a few options to fix, or change things.

If we are not successful, then my friends the present planned cycle will complete its course, as advised by the Entity, and our fate... Apparently, the Earth will suffer a cataclysmic event, blasted back to the Stone Age, might I add yet again.

The date is easy to work out; it has after all been available to us for many thousands of years. Just follow the ancient writings; Nostradamus, or the cycles of the Mayan and Hindu calendars. All of which have time span cycles of 5200 years, and of course the same time cycle also applies to the Egyptian stone calendar.'

Randall sounded like he was enjoying his doomsday lecture ending with.

'I can advise you now folks that our time on this world is up on the 21st day of December 2012, which happens to be the end of the fourth world. This is a significant date being the end of two complete ancient 5200-year calendar cycles, or Mayan "Tuns" from the last major world event.

The last event was the birth of the modern Homo sapiens by genetic modelling and DNA cross breeding of Martian DNA. Ending with the final extermination of the Martians by the Entity some 10,400 years ago. This dual cycle ends on this same predicted date... the 21st December 2012. Winter solstice, our very own Ouroboros... we will devour ourselves... again.'

Everyone remained stunned by this casual statement from Randall; Tom then said aloud what all thinking.

'That is the old prophesy for Armageddon, the end of the world, could there be some truth in these ancient calendar events and writings.'

Tom added, as more in thought than in conversation.

'Well I guess this would have been end of the world as the ancients would have known it. However, as Randall has said, everything does fit. This is all about timed cycles for both present and future events; as such we should still have an opportunity to change the future by changing the present event.'

Chirpy was not convinced and snapped back...

'Do you really believe in this Armageddon rubbish, and that it is about to happen in eleven days. My God Tom, you are an educated man, a scientist, the same as we all are.'

Chirpy then sprung to her feet in the form of a small, vertical person of angry denial, and then continued her broadside on the matter of disbelief.

'What evidence is there that any of this will ever happen? The LHC equipment in Geneva fires minutely small beams of protons in opposite directions then guides them into a head-on collision.

The impact may be superfast, but the results are minuscule. Only a few bunches of the billions of proton particles in the beam would ever collide and split, as viewed in a detection unit. To generate 200,000 tons of super compressed CDM material would take thousands, if not millions of years. This huge CDM collection event is unachievable.'

They all looked at Tom, but Emma answered in a nervous Scottish lilt.

'Last month I would have agree with you Chirpy, but today with what I have learnt and experienced with my own eyes and ears, I must disagree.

Several points you have raised, I know would normally require proof by evidence, but along with Randall, Tim, Dave, Max and Tom I do believe our world will suffer a catastrophic event in eleven days. My dear friends at this moment you have all been personally experiencing very strange and very un-scientific phenomena. Mind teleportation of our thought-words across the world.'

Emma did not receive the expected immediate reply, then looking down.

'Chirpy, I notice that you have just broken the ring. The other half of our group in Australia can no longer hear you. If you want to hear more about this pending disaster, then we must all join hands again.'

Chirpy was quick to take Emma and Jan's hands completing the circle once again... Emma then continued.

'As for the huge detector mass required to achieve this amount of CDM, I can only assume that they. The ones who are creating this CDM, have found a way to increase the mass exponentially...'

Randall burst back into the conversation.

'By Jove chaps, I do believe we may have lost you there for a minute. Maybe the Entity has connection problems similar to British Telecom...'

Nobody laughed at Randall's corny joke. This was a serious matter. Randall uttered a small embarrassing cough and continued.

'Now that we are all here together again, Tim, Max, and I believe we have come up with what we think is an excellent logical conclusion. Moreover, a possible fix to this pending catastrophe. A fix, which we would like to pass on to you, chaps for your learned judgment and hopefully your approval.'

All at the Oxford end were surprised, and braced for this supposition.

'Firstly, we must confirm the exact timing of this event. We have all given a great deal of thought as to what we have learnt about the Entity. The Entity has advised us on a number of occasions that it can only work in long universal time cycles, thousands, millions, or billions of years.

Whereas we, and our solar system, by the Entities time frames, unfortunately survive and live in extremely short time cycles of a few million years. That is possibly why my fellow chaos group, the Entity is seeking our help to resolve this short time event problem.

Having considered all of this; we have with certainty, deduced the exact date the Entity has already planned to snuff us out. On the other hand, by golly, at this very moment we have no idea in which way.

Our sniffing around the Russian and Chinese government satellite traffic has uncovered a fair bit of talk about Iran. We also think something is going on in the Middle East. Whatever it is chaps, we in the west would have been horrified if the truth had finally came out.

I say would have. As by then, the western world, and us, may never know if this lot ever happens... as we will all be dead. However, I do think we should accept that the calculated world end date is to be the 21st of December 2012. By the elimination, and consideration of likely human calculation errors, Tim has, as close as possible determined the first CDM being planned for creation on the day after. This being 22nd of December, so there we are... everything fits... do you not agree.

We are now certain this pending event is linked to the Middle Eastern LHC experiments, which are about to be conducted in Geneva. Oh by the way, are any of you religious people aware, the true birth date of Jesus Christ was in fact calculated to be 22nd of December, year zero of the Christian calendar... not year one on the 25th December... interesting eh.'

Chapter Twenty

Your planet will attract a dark asteroid

Day Ten to impact

Doc Dave cut Randall's cheery lecture short, interjecting with some basic ghostly logic.

'One-way for a quick answer mate is to ask the Entity, if the Entity is willing respond. Einstein and Darwin are standing right beside me watching and listening to our debate.'

The response to Dave's suggestion was swift. Einstein provided the answer in a clear voice...

'Will knowledge of our presence confirm anything, or resolve this situation for the human race... no it will not. Only you the chosen ones can do that. For you time never stops and now becomes your most urgent concern.

Cycle twenty-four has now passed, being in the mid-year 2006 of your calendar. Your galactic equinox is almost complete. With the removal of this present situation, your planet and galaxy will enter into what you call "the age of Aquarius." This would also be our preference. However... only time will provide an answer.

If you should fail in your mission. Then in eleven earth days from now your planet will attract a dark asteroid catapulted from behind your star. The consequences for all the biological life forms on your planet earth will be that of almost total extinction.

365

However, the planet earth will remain in its planned balanced orbit around your star for the next forty million earth years... This will be the end cycle for your planet, and begin the planned ending of your solar system.'

Tom glanced around the circle of scientists holding hands. Conformation brought with it horrendous shock at the Entities emotionless words. Dave looked at Randall staring blankly at Max, while Tim displaying an expressionless face, with Randall's hand on his shoulder continued working on his computer.

This was no longer a theory, or a good guess... this was all going to happen. A dark asteroid will strike the earth a week next Friday on the 21st day of December 2012, just as the ancients had predicted... fulfilling the prophesy of Armageddon.

Professor Reg was first to speak, with a surprisingly firm voice,

'We had better get on with it then, putting a stop to this making of CDM. We are now sure where it's going to be created; and we have only a few days left.'

Taking a powerful suck on his pipe, held firm by clenched teeth, he then blew out a large cloud of smoke for effect, adding in a humble tone.

'What I would like to know is, if we are indeed successful at stopping the creation of this CDM... how then would this Entity stop our exceptionally long, and well-planned extinction?'

There was no reply from the Entity, but Chirpy had a question to ask, delivered in a shaky voice. Out of fear, she could not stand up.

'Randall, you only answered two parts of my question. The third part was who would want to create such a massive amount of CDM... and for what reason?'

Randall replied softly with unease.

'I thought you had already worked that one out my dear when you said, "My God Tom, you are an educated man, we are all scientists here."

Tim, Max, and I now believe that this is indeed all about possessing a part of God. With some sort of powerful deal cut by the world's superpowers to satisfy one particular religion...Islam. Tom did say this would shake anyone's faith.

Apparently, the Entity is not religious in any way. Those of us who hold firm religious beliefs should at least try to approach this with an open mind. We atheists and agnostics are all included in this one... There is no escape from this planned catastrophic world disaster, whatever your religious beliefs may be.'

Randall paused, thinking, who would have thought only ten months ago that he would be discussing the end of the world with his friends... the chaos group. He quickly snapped out of his grim thoughts. Thoughts that Emma, Tom, Dave and the Entity could read with clarity... pressing on, he broke the moment of silence.

'Emma, Dave, and Tom have explained the Entities position. It firmly denies that it is a deity or a God, and has never been a God. However, it freely admits to using the fear and power of religion to bond people of differing tribes, nations, and countries together.

The Entity sees this bonding as a united effort in the cause to develop a greater human intelligence. When asked about God, the Entities view is firm. They are the keepers of time and order, and the developers of universal intelligence; they are the natural Universe and not a judge of good or evil.

They plan universal events, firmly denying they create. The Entity has also advised that religion and God is a creation; devised and developed by humans... man-made, for man's supreme and personal use. It points out that no other biological being on this planet. Other than us humans has accepted, or acknowledge the existence of a personal super being, deity, or God.

We do all agree chaps; the big bang was indeed the start to the creation of the universe, and all known life. This will soon become a fact confirmed by modern quantum physics. The God particle will in due course exist with the help of the LHC in Geneva. All of which will become a reality within the next few weeks... if we survive.

Consider what this vast power on earth would mean to all the devout believers... capture your God in a box. One would have to admit to it chaps, you could not have a more personal God than that.'

Max politely cut into Randall's powerful unfolding story.

'We know that Saudi Arabia has one of these BEC units installed in the Kaaba in Mecca. They have also funded another BEC unit setup at the LHC in Geneva, or at least the data streaming from the satellite traffic says so.

You know mates, I think they want to take God home to Mecca... and who is to say they are wrong. After all, they would then have a part of what caused the beginning and creation of all known things. The very accepted meaning of a God.

At the same time, they would also have the power and means to destroy any opposition to their religious beliefs. Including our planet, if not our entire solar system. This is a far greater threat than any nuclear-armed Islamic Nation. It is no bloody wonder the Entity is a bit pissed-off mate. Those Iranian blokes are playing around in the Entity's back-yard, with the Entities tools.'

Emma came out of her shock mode with frightening speed demanding...

'What would the major world powers be thinking of in aiding this to happen? They have been spying around our chaos group for over a year now, yet they must have been involved in this BEC project for years.

We know from our recent visit to CERN in Geneva that it was the British, who designed and built the Bose-Einstein Condensate unit installed at the LHC. Therefore, we must assume that we British also built the BEC unit installed at Mecca.... No doubt, there will be another BEC unit somewhere in Iran.

The Americans have also been busy; they have built as part of the collider experiments a massive generator and stripping unit at the PS (proton synchrotron) station loop.

Typical of the US they always do things over the top, but this generator is huge, way beyond all expectation. Tom and I have found the Iranians, who have a seat on the CERN board, actually supervises both of these projects. Through the Azad University in Tehran.

The odd thing is we know the funding for both of these projects is coming from all the Asian and Middle Eastern bloc countries, but managed by Saudi Arabia.'

There was a short pause and then...

'So what are the Russians and the Chinese playing around with at the LHC in Geneva?' Dave's ghostly voice was asking a question they all wanted to know. *'What say we go have a look over the next few days and sort out what they are doing? Then we should have the complete picture, and with a bit of luck a way to stop these bastards creating CDM.'*

Chirpy retorted in her squeaky voice.

'We should examine all possible ways to sabotage this CDM project right now. To my understanding, we have a big problem... this is obviously a huge world political situation.

The major world governments involved have obviously approved of this project. They have all traded peace and stability in the Middle East for a far worse world outcome... The total extinction of the human race and most biological life forms on the surface of this planet.'

Tom decided to add his views on the problem.

'Ah ha but do these western governments know what they have approved, and ultimately agreed to? We know what is being planned and what the conclusion will be, only because we have had some powerful inside universal help.

I see another possibility, one in which all the government powers involved are close to being innocent. They just see this CDM event as an opportunity to resolve, and remove one of the major world-threatening nuclear armament problems. At the same time, the west would be conciliatory to Islamic religious beliefs by helping Muslims acquire some God particles.

Friends, we have almost assembled all the pieces together to fully understand this unfolding disaster, simply because we now have the money to open the many doors that look into the right places.

I believe I have figured out what is about to happen, and I guess the reason why. If I am right in my assessment of this pending world bureaucratic catastrophe, then we will need to be very careful. Especially in which way we bring the creation of cold dark matter at the LHC in Geneva to an end.'

Tom could see and feel that his argument was being accepted and continued.

'My friends reflect on this possible theory to this grim situation. Consider this. If the British, Chinese, Russian, and American governments have come to some sort of an agreement with most of the world's Islamic nations.

Part of this agreement might be to assist these nations through Saudi Arabia, as the central negotiator, to helping bring God to Mecca in the form of a few suspended God particles. After all, we do know there are plenty of excellent scientists that are also devout Muslims.

These Muslim scientists fully understand quantum mechanics and all about the big bang theory. A theory now almost a fact, and will be, when the LHC conducts the Higgs Boson field test.

Being in possession of a few particles of the beginning of the Universe would be a matter of exceptional and great religious significance to all the world religions. However, Muslims would now have their true faith and the evidence, for all their followers to witness in the Kaaba at Mecca.

Let us assume the USA and UK governments have settled some sort of deal with the east. A deal, whereby Iran and Pakistan, and a number of other Islamic countries agreed to disband their nuclear defence programmes, in exchange for some CDM God particles.

This would be a world first in peace negotiations between Islam extremists and the western world. A peace plan that a few eccentric scientists in Oxford University England, calling themselves the chaos group, were about to derail. This chaos group, about to expose their secret deal by snooping around graviton particles, gravity waves, string theory, and CDM... How am I doing so far?'

Max gave Tom a quick answer... and a question.

'You are doing great mate. Okay Tom, let's say we accept your theory for now, but as Doc Dave has mentioned earlier. Where do the Russians and the Chinese fit into all this weird religious stuff in Geneva?'

'I can answer that Max,' Emma butted in. 'Tom and I have discovered from our recent visit to Geneva, and reading the CERN business records. They are both funding Middle Eastern nations, Iran by China, and Saudi Arabia by Russia. The odd thing is we don't think these superpowers know the real purpose behind their contracted research and development projects.'

Chirpy snapped. 'And what are these projects about then?'

Emma continued by answering the Chirpy question first.

'China is about to test a newly developed way to carry a far greater and thicker beam of protons around the 27-kilometre collider loop. The theory being that with the increased mass, more particle collisions will take place, offering a greater and faster detector result.

Meanwhile, the Russians are working on the final assembly of a Proton Synchrotron enhancer. This is a special machine designed to load massive amounts of lead-ion material into the SPS (Super Proton Synchrotron,) which will spin-up the lead protons before releasing into the main 27-kilometre accelerator loop.

The end result will be a huge collision of lead-ion proton particles travelling in a much larger modified beam. These powerful beams will arrive at the ALICE detector site, smashing head-on at almost the speed of light. This is the same site having the new BEC Bose-Einstein Condenser installed, as such, would obviously be where the CDM... God particles will eventually be collected.'

Nobody said a word, so Tom and Jan released hands to take a drink of their wine while the others looked on in silence. This matter needed some well thought-out planning and some urgent decisions made. The circle resumed just as Randall spoke.

'I say chaps this drama has taken on a whole new direction. Not only are we about to be smashed into global oblivion, but the very people who will be responsible for this apocalyptic disaster are really nice chaps who are trying to do jolly good things for the world.

On the one hand, we have the righteous western-world powers trying to patch-up their differences with the militant Islamic nations. Then on the other hand, we have the Islamic nations trying to get closer to the divine point of all their religious beliefs and creator... Allah... God.'

Randall paused, but nobody wished to comment on his odd observation, as such he continued with his theory.

'To me it all sounds quite innocent and harmless, except for three things, two being "belief," and "faith." The western-world powers think that by helping these Islamic nations in collecting and holding a few particles of CDM being the God particle. This was obviously an acceptable risk in satisfying the Islamic "belief."

Then we have the central Islamic negotiator Saudi Arabia. All Saudi Arabia wanted to do was obtain a few CDM, Allah particles as proof to the world of nonbelievers in the Muslim "faith."

One would then ask the relevant question. Why then is Iran running an advanced LHC project to create massive amounts of CDM? Might I add chaps, it would appear that Iran is set to harvest a much larger amount of CDM, Allah particles. An amount Iran knows is capable of destroying this planet, if not our solar system.'

A frightened Jan took the opportunity to ask a question.
'You said th three things Randall, what's the th third thing?'
Randall resumed in his aloof manner…
'Well Jan old chap, since you were the only one to ask, the third thing is ultimate world "power." I for one would doubt the Saudi theocracy knows little or nothing at all of what the Iranians are jolly well up to with all of this.

Let us face it chaps, we in the west have been conned yet again. The Iranians have traded their advanced nuclear weapons technology for something far more powerful. An inside access to the unique power of the Universe, and a possible way to bring an end our world the earth, as we know it.'

There was a murmur of unease from the group, yet still no questions. Randal needed to drive his theory home, deciding on a few examples.

'Fellow scientists, we are aware that a few particles of CDM reaching ambient room temperature would expand in an explosion equal to five tons of C4 explosive. One cannot imagine what half a gram of this CDM would do. Then again, when we know what cataclysmic damage something the size of a grain of rice will cause... I totally agree with Chirpy and Dave, we must move fast to stop this world catastrophe happening.

Is it not a strange paradox chaps; the Entity has driven home the point many times that everything within the Universe works in cycles. Well as it happens, so does the Large Hadron Collider.'

All agreed they should engineer a plan immediately to permanently derail the BEC and CDM projects. However, they must make every effort to avoid any death or injury. If possible, they should try to find a way to involve and connect the Iranians as being the people answerable in any future accusations. Ultimately the people responsible for any injury or damage sustained by a failed LHC project.

Dave pointed out to the group that being a ghost had been useful, having its advantages in that he was able to go instantly to just about anywhere at any time. The disadvantage that soon became obvious was everything at the location being in real-time.

He would have to wait for someone to say or do something that was of interest to the group, even then all he could do was observe. The greatest advantage of all was being the only member of the group, who could see and talk to the Entity. Now as the time was drawing near, the Entity had little or nothing to say. This was un-nerving and stressful for them all.

Dave advised Mary had been visiting him almost every day at the private Perth Hospital. Considering the few days that remained he would like to spend some time with Mary, she at least deserved that.

Dave suggested that he should gather what useful information he could in the next few days at CERN in Geneva to help come up with a plan to end the CDM project. He should then come out of his coma and into the real world.

All agreed this would complete his mission. Emma and Sally were in tears at Dave's tender consideration, and Chirpy sniffed loudly into a large white handkerchief.

Randall, Tim, and Max were to remain at Sandfire and continue as the group's bankers and fund managers. They must continue gathering all available information on what was happening in Geneva and the Middle East.

Chirpy and Jan agreed to join Tom and Emma along with three other Oxford scientists to take-up their positions on the CERN board in Geneva, as this was to be expected.

Professor Reg and Sally would hold a low profile, and let the Oxford University run everything at the new offices of Quantum Universal NL. Professor Reg and Sally now had other matters on their minds. Tomorrow they would both go directly to Jodrell Bank to plot the pending arrival and orbit of the incoming dark asteroid.

They all agreed to meet back in Oxford in two days, hopefully with a workable plan. Christmas was not far-off so staff and other people would most likely start to move into holiday mode at the LHC in Geneva. Jan made a useful observation.

'Well a Christmas holiday for all the b bleeding Christians working at the c collider. What about the bleeding n non-Christians, and what about the la large Muslim workforce who will r remain at the LHC over t the Christmas period?'

Day Nine to asteroid impact.

The other members of the CERN board were not impressed with the four new well-funded board directors. The Iranians were suspicious from the start, as they had thought that the new directors would have taken up their new positions, after their Christmas celebration break.

This was obviously not going to be the case as they had also brought with them three Oxford scientists, determined to re-establish their Oxford University research programme.

At the CERN meetings, which also included various LHC research project groups. Some well-placed questions soon revealed odd anomalies in the normal published test programme.

It became obvious with a little additional thought reading that the Iranians were well ahead in all four parts of their CDM God particle project. With frightening realisation, the group learned the Iranians intended to commence the first high mass lead-ion collisions tests within the week.

Jan and Chirpy concluded they must be almost ready in setting up their main CDM programme. The Entity had confirmed the event would stay within the ancient time prediction.

It now appeared obvious that the Iranian plan was to create CDM on the infidel prophet's true birthday, 22nd December. They must all stay focused on finding a workable plan to destroy these projects. One advantage was their encrypted security cards now gave them unrestricted access to all areas of the LHC, getting them into the most sensitive parts of the LHC project.

Jan had opened a port on the CERN grid computer giving Randall, Max and Tim direct access to all the security and safety control settings. Who would know, or guess that people from halfway around the world could have access to change and manipulate the computer control systems of such a large and well-protected project in Geneva?

Everything at the LHC in Geneva suddenly went quiet. Jan and Chirpy were convinced that the Iranians were on to them. Randall said neither he nor Max had detected any move to change the Grid encryption codes, adding that the level of technical notes was high. They had the impression that something important was going down. Assuring them it was nothing to do with their snooping around.

Dave later confirmed that a large Iranian workforce was pulling to bits part of the ALICE detector port. Because of this work going on, everything was at a standstill. Dave had no idea what they were doing. Emma noted a small work-order in the collider service logs… apparently, they were installing a new port window; this would take about two days. No reason given as to why this expensive change deemed necessary, or required. Emma was suspicious.

Day Seven to asteroid impact.

The meeting in the warm cafe in Geneva was as cold as the weather outside. The mood of grim reality had chilled the atmosphere.

Today would be their last day in Geneva, seven days before the Entity intended following through with ending the human race by means of a dark asteroid. They had only seven more days left to resolve the CDM problem.

Tom, Emma, Chirpy, and Jan were busy over a cup of coffee; discussing an unthinkable plan. How they would end the creation of CDM.

Destroying the whole LHC project in normal circumstances would be impossible, the project having too many rigid safety lockouts in place. However, they all knew that with their unique access, specialist skills, and inside knowledge. They could if need be, easily evade the many safety lockout systems and launch a runaway helium-proton fusion process.

This was an unbelievable matter to discuss over a cup of coffee, but considered. Depending on the amount of fusion material available, they could cause a thermonuclear detonation. The result would cause a vaporisation of the whole project, and unfortunately most of Geneva... Was this really an option; one they should actually consider? They must find another way.

Being scientists, they all wanted this magnificent LHC project to continue. All knew that this experimental particle collider operating within its designed operating parameters was without doubt completely safe. The new information recently gained from the LHC about matter, energy, space and time was opening new doors to the unexplored areas of particle physics.

The Entity approved of such discoveries as part of the human evolutionary development process. A necessary path and means to gain higher intelligence, thus opening a way to eventually discovering what the Entity ultimately made of. Clearly, the early creation of CDM was not on the Entities approval list.

In the next few days many plans meticulously considered and rejected on which might be the best way to sabotage the LHC. It was a difficult task. They should consider some method that would cause the least amount of damage, or loss of life. Yet permanently end the Iranian CDM God particle research programme, within the limited time available. All but two plans rejected. Tom grimly reminded them of what was a stake.

Plan "A" was the preferred choice, but needed some further detail for this plan to work. Reluctantly plan "B" was included as the last resort... a forced helium proton fusion bomb. Then if all failed plan "C" was the last choice, as suggested by the Entity. This plan was to occupy the Martian subterranean city near Veevers, a place in which some humans could still survive.

By Emma's observation, this confirmed to her that the Entity was not confident of their success. In Tom's view, this part of the catastrophe was most likely an exact and planned event to save some humans from the extermination... was this intentional?

The return journey to the UK and Oxford was by fast train, the Eurostar. The channel crossing spent in one of the two rarely used private VIP cabins. Pleasant though it may have been, but the subject of conversation was not. Nobody could bring themselves around to discuss death and destruction. They felt and sounded like a terrorist group, planning a deadly bombing... and they were.

Day Six to asteroid impact.

'Can you see it now?' Sally was pointing out the small, scarcely visible, dark half circle crescent on the high definition photo. Everyone crowded over the viewing table to look through the tripod magnifying glass at this object.

'The high resolution photo was taken 182 days ago, when the earth was on the other side of the sun. This picture recorded at 2am in the morning facing out into space. We can see this photo now confirms the presence of a huge dark iron and rock asteroid hurtling through space towards our sun.

We have managed to find three other successive night photos that show this asteroid just before the object was lost from the viewing frame. The differing time shifts and angle, gives us all the information we need to calculate speed, distance, time, and size.

As we speak, this seven kilometre-wide dark asteroid is well hidden behind the sun, and invisible to all those on earth. This asteroid mass is now only some three days out from a boost into a powerful slingshot towards our planet earth. We have calculated this huge impact will cause a crater of some fifteen-hundred kilometres across, with an estimated depth of some twelve kilometres. The composition, velocity, angle, and the mass are more than sufficient to extinguish all life on this planet.

Sally and I are sorry to advise that a near-future earth asteroid collision has now been fully confirmed.'

Jan gave out a low whistle. 'So th the Entity was not bullshitting us w we really are going to be clobbered by a bl bloody great asteroid.'

Professor Reg pulled his pipe from his mouth, blew some smoke and then added...

'The Entity is also good at sums. Sally and I have calculated the speed and the angle of the sling mass. It will take a little over three days, exactly seventy-six hours and three minutes for the asteroid to travel from the sun to the impact site on earth.

We have also calculated the impact point to be in the Syrian Desert. The impact rim will include Israel, Damascus, Lebanon, Iraq, and all of the ancient religious areas in the east. This event will take place at 11:20am local standard time on 22nd December 2012. Just as the Entity, and might I add ancient history has predicted.

Interestingly enough, the Entity has made the choice to vaporise first. The part of our planet earth it has determined as being the cause of this earth problem. These areas are strangely the birthplace of both Christianity and Islam.'

Professor Reg fell silent, as there was no need for further words. He clamped his pipe hard between his teeth and joined the others holding hands in the circle as they were about to begin another séance meeting. This would most likely their last séance, as Dave had planned to come out of his coma within the next few hours.

Sally looked up at her circle of friends noticing the fear on everyone's face, hesitated then added in a quiet voice.

'For those of us too frightened to ask, this dark asteroid could not have been seen as an incoming threat. Dark asteroids are usually made-up of solid iron and nickel with an outer shell of burnt-out carbon and dust.

The black carbon outer shell absorbs most of the light making this type of asteroid almost invisible to detect in space. An astrophysicist would need to know the approximate location where to find them, even when using infrared imaging. We suspect that this asteroid has come in from the lesser-known asteroid group of the Oort cloud.

On its close pass by our sun, this asteroid will heat-up like a bar-b-cue heat bead. The asteroid will glow white-hot displaying in our sky as an ever increasing ball of white fire on its way to a collision with earth.'

Randall's crisp English voice cut through their minds like a knife.

'Come, come now my friends that will do for now with all this doomsday talk, we must be positive. This is not going to happen chaps. We must trust the Entity to follow through exactly as it has promised.

I will remind you all of what that promise is. If we can stop the creation of CDM before the 21st being next Friday, then the chaos group and the whole world spared. Now do listen closely my friends. We three brilliant computer whiz kids think we have sorted out a fix for this mess. We have now come close to perfecting an answer. However, will still require to do one little bit of special twiddling, also gather some additional data.

The three of us smart chaps here have been sniffing around in the CERN grid computer. We have come up with a set of Iranian equations that relate to the maximum safe operating limits for the four parts of their CDM project.

We can tell you now chaps the Iranian LHC operating limits are well outside the CERN approved limits, actually on the upper edge of the large twenty per cent safety limit.

We believe that we can change the project computer safety limits. Offsetting the feed instruction by increasing the beam capacity, then adding a delay to hide our handiwork. Then bingo, an aperture meltdown. Or maybe we could just mess around with the beam tunnel vacuum, now that's a thought?'

Tom was not so sure, computers not being his strong point. Although some of the words used were frightening, like a thermonuclear detonation and meltdown. He was a scientist, an anthropologist not an anarchist... Tom was worried. Had we come down to this?

'Meltdown, we don't want to cause an atomic reaction leading to an explosion. Anyway, I cannot see how this CDM project, which is only one of many hundreds of research projects conducted at the LHC, has such a priority.

This is a huge project needing so many equipment changes, how could this work continue without somebody becoming suspicious. Another thing, how could anybody manipulate the safety limits on a ten billion dollar piece of complex research equipment like the LHC, without the safety officers finding out, and shutting the goddamn test-shot down?'

Max was quick with the answer to Tom's worrying question.

'They will fool the safety systems in the same way that we are going to, by carefully changing the bloody safety limits. However, we will use our knowledge to stop this bloody project in its tracks, by smart computer hacking.

The comforting thing is mate, we are much better at it than they are. Tom you should understand this mate, we're talking about an ion beam aperture meltdown mate, not a bloody nuclear meltdown.'

Randall added in a sober voice...

'Mind you, Tom is not far-off the mark old boy. If we get the timing wrong, a proton fireball could rupture a helium line causing a leakage into the tunnel. This would then feed a runaway proton-helium nuclear explosion. Not a nice thought chaps.'

Randall's voice tapered off into silence as everyone digested this horrendous possibility, Max continued talking about the plan.

'These blokes are shit cunning bastards. They are keeping their heavy lead-ion collision run at a low profile. Today is the15th December, everything is going into hold and holiday mode at the CERN in Geneva.

The small skeleton staffs attending over the Christmas period are all volunteers. You can guess who make up the largest numbers of Christmas volunteers; yes, you guessed it, nearly all are Muslims, with a few non-Christians. These blokes will have the run of the bloody place from about now until early January.'

Chirpy's high-pitched voice had an added tremor leaving everybody in no doubt that she was very frightened.

'Friends, I have calculated we now have even less time than we thought. We must address the fact that when this asteroid becomes visible in just three day's time, the whole world will go into uncontrollable panic. As a result, millions of innocent people killed before the asteroid impact.

How can we avoid this world panic? The only possibility I can see is we must bring our sabotage plan forward. We must halt the creation of the CDM within the next three days, before the incoming asteroid can be seen from earth.'

Then as an afterthought clearly heard by all.

'Should we advise the authorities, they might have some sort of contingency plan for an earth impact?' Then screeched a frightened question.

'Randall, how faraway are you from implementing your plan to ending this CDM creation project?'

'Not far away chaps, maybe a few days. We do know as a last resort that we can always blow the place to Kingdom-come with a massive helium leak creating a proton fusion reaction.'

Everyone was shocked at this blunt statement… Randall defended his brutal words.

'You must try to understand good people. A terrible loss of life action would, without a doubt be a far better alternative than our present position. Well better than allowing the Entity to end all human civilisation with an asteroid impact. I do suspect the Entity already knows this will be our choice, and that we now have only three days left to stop the creation of CDM.

As I see the situation, we have but one choice left within these next three days. That being we must attempt to melt the beam apertures of all 7000 helium cooled superconducting electromagnets in the LHC loop. We can do this by simply dumping the vacuum in the guide rings causing the lead-ion particles to heat-up like billions of micrometeorites entering our atmosphere.

As previously discussed, this action would need implementing at precisely the right time. This precise timing is the tricky bit for which we will need some additional info.

If we are successful, then our two billion US dollars paid to the CERN might just be enough loot to cover the cost of repairing all the massive damage we will have caused.

With my careful planning, the Iranians will without doubt get the blame for this. The Saudi's will point the evil finger at the Iranians for sabotaging their God project. When the dust settles and the blaming sorted, the west will ultimately smell of sweet innocence, and we will have saved the human race from extinction in the process.

All we have to do now is hope that nobody changes the CDM God programme at the last minute. Not a bad plan eh chaps what, what.'

Nobody laughed at Randall's attempt at humour, Dave's voice came into their heads. He had other problems they should all know about.

'Max and Randall have asked me to get that last one bit of data to make their plan work. The password to the CDM project sequence file. The bloody password will be in Arabic, it will no doubt give young

Tim a few headaches in trying to hack into their CDM grid program file.

The problem for me is; I can't pick-up a pen to write anything down. I can only observe things happen. Unless the technician says the password, or access code in his thoughts, I have no idea what they are saying. Our best chance is to let Tim know which room the control-system client laptop is in, with luck he can find a way to hack into the data port via the router.

Talk about having a ghost of a chance, my stress level is so sky-high. I feel like I have the world on my shoulders.'

Talking with his pipe clenched firmly between his teeth Professor Reg offered comfort.

'You do have the world on your shoulders young man.'

Professor Reg was a man not known for pulling his punches. This was serious business. He could see that some senior confidence building was urgently needed.

'Sally and I look forward to meeting with you and your wife Mary when this CDM problem has been sorted out. I expect to smoke many pipes and drink much fine red wine. All while listening to you and Max talk about your flying exploits in the Australian outback... You will find a way Dave, just like we did, when we were confronted with enormous odds fighting world war two.'

Those were comforting thoughts from Professor Reg, Emma's were not.

'I know some of you are thinking why not just let the world know about this disaster. The American government could possibly send a missile to destroy this asteroid.

Three years ago, I went to a world disaster conference in the USA. One of the subjects covered was what could we do in the event of a pending large comet or asteroid hit. The experts in the field of missile platforms and nuclear warheads were not very assuring. To hit an object of just five hundred metres across at a safe distance from earth was all but impossible.

In our situation, I remind you this hard asteroid is seven kilometre wide and made up of mostly iron and nickel. Even if a direct hit achieved, then most of the blasted parts would continue towards earth.

An asteroid made of nickel iron blasted into say four or five pieces would be just as devastating for our planet as the direct hit. Attempting an early shot would compound the accuracy error, also bringing the missile too close to the sun resulting in a meltdown or pre-detonation.

The effect would be much like throwing an unlit match into a blast furnace, and hoping it would not ignite. This large asteroid arriving via our sun would appear to be the worst possible situation imaginable.'

Emma had said what Reg and Sally could not bring themselves to say. There was no chance or hope in avoiding this catastrophic disaster. The only glimmer of a chance lay with believing in the deal set by the Entity, and stopping the creation of CDM on earth.

The discussions and planning continued well into the small hours of the morning. Plan "A" was simple, the plan was to sabotage the LHC during this next Iranian research experiment, number 176, which was currently being set-up. As Randall commented, "it would be like watching a 27-kilometre fuse blow... twice."

They had all agreed the tricky part would be in timing their move for when the collider was running at full capacity. Max was still not sure, that even if they were successful in destroying this means for creating CDM. Would the Entity keep its word and save the earth from this asteroid impact.

Time was running out... it was now another new day.

Chapter Twenty-one

Stop the creation of Cold Dark Matter

Day Five to impact.

Test project number 176 was now up and running in the collider with a CERN work slot of six days. The sixth day would be the 22nd of December 2012. A day that the chaos group were planning should never arrive for this particular LHC research test. For if, it did then they would have failed.

The plan was simple enough, when the collider beam-pipes were running at full speed and close to full capacity. The beam-pipe vacuum valves were to be cracked open by a hacked instruction from Randall's computer. This dramatic action causing a slow vacuum loss, allowing standard atmosphere to enter the main beam loops.

The big problem was judging when the collider was running at full speed. Much like a train crash, a derailment at slow speed is a huge inconvenience but at a high-speed is an absolute catastrophe... they had planned for a full-on catastrophe.

Knowing when all the LHC systems were at the best state to create the maximum damage was very difficult. Randall, Max, and Tim had everything ready, but needed the operator client system-plan for when the Iranians intended to run the system beyond the CERN design safety limits.

With Doc Dave's help and a current Arabic language converter Tim now had access to the client controller's project computer. It was now a matter of waiting on how the project scientists wanted to conduct their LHC test. The nail-biting problem was the Iranians appeared to be in no hurry to spin-up their project to full power.

Max was in a high stress state. Randall was putting on a brave face, but worried he was beginning to crack under the immense pressure. Corny jokes only hid the truth for a while.

'For fucks sake Randall what's up with this lot. We only have two days left before the whole world will know about this bloody asteroid heading our way. Have you given it some thought we could override their control locks and initiate a full power run-up of the LHC program? Then we could crash the system and put an end to all of this.'

'I do hear you old man. However, a runaway power-up will just cause the Iranians and the CERN safety chaps to panic closing the whole project down. Starting all over again in a few weeks. Not such a good idea Max. Nevertheless, I do understand your frustration, another scotch old boy. By the way have you heard anything from Tony and his family?'

Max did not notice Randall's neat diversion from his poor idea.

'I had a quick chat with him on the HF radio this morning as his satellite phone can't get a satellite. The reception was very poor with all this weird solar activity building up. Tony reckons he has just about finished the new airstrip at the Veevers site.

I sure hope he has read my map okay, and he is grading the right bloody place. Because I know, there is only one bit of hard desert land out there close to Veevers mate. He tells me the new grader is going well and his missus is now a gun front-end-loader operator, but he still thinks we have all gone troppo.

I don't think that story about a new mining geological survey camp out there was very believable at all. Tony is a loyal bloke, and he is not stupid. I really feel bad about all of this; we should tell him what is going on. After all he does have a right to know the world as he knows it is about to end.'

Randall was in dream thinking, I wonder what the Martians have down there. Then realising Max had asked a question…

'I do agree with you old man, then again you could say the same for the rest of the world's population. Tony will soon find out what is going on tomorrow evening, when we tell him the location of the entrance to the Martian subterranean city.

How long do you think it will take to dig out the entry? I rather imagine that it would be some sort of grand affair, somewhat akin to the Parthenon in Athens Greece.'

Max looked at Randall who was gazing out of the caravan window, lost in a dream of ancient times. He could never quite understand if Randall had a full grip on the enormity of their problems.

To Randall, everything was like some challenging game that he delighted in a chance to win.

'I don't think so mate, logic would tell me that the more advanced people become the less fancy they are. My guess is it will look something like one of those new frigging stainless steel fridge doors stuck in some rock face, or like the stainless steel lift doors in the Australian Tax Office building.

Let's all hope that Doc Dave has got the info from the Entity right, since I can't see anything that looks like an entrance from any of my InSAR satellite EMR data.

We have another almighty problem to climb over mate. We have to get the rest of the chaos group, and their immediate family over to Western Australia before the panic starts to set in. Time is running out fast, I think that would be a job for you. Being better qualified at jet transport than me old mate.'

Randall was still looking out of the caravan window in half a dream when he casually informed Max.

'All has been resolved Max; I chartered a Boeing B737 in London two days ago as a private charter flight under the guise of a special holiday package called "Escape the winter for Christmas in Australia." This was part of my devious plan to maintain total secrecy in this dreadful matter.'

Randall slowly turned to face Max showing his tears, then adding.

'For a few extra million pounds the aircraft owners have given my pilots a quick refresher course on the B737 to get them current. We were damn lucky old chap, as the Boeing built to a special client order with extra long-range fuel tanks. This will give the aircraft a range of a little over 11,000 nautical miles needing only one fuel stop on the way to Australia.'

Randall paused in his casual delivery of this magnificent effort, wiping a solitary tear with a tissue, and then continued in a sad voice.

'I am sorry to say, Professor Reg and Sally have chosen not to come along. They consider themselves as too old to start a new life in a new world, offering others a chance to survive. They wished us well, saying they could never live five miles below the surface, without a view of the sky and stars.'

Max was getting cranky at this sad and tearful situation frustration had set in... are we all starting to give up, is this how it will all end.

'Can't you use your smart pommy education to change their minds? Randall, I was forming the firm opinion that you were some sort of an unstoppable bloke. Having the means to resolve every bloody situation.'

Max stared at Randall, he had put so much trust and hope in what this man could do. That much trust from him was normally only reserved for Doc Dave.

'Alas my good Aussie friend, the Boeing B737 with all 62 passengers and crew is in the air as we speak. Professor Reg and Sally are not on-board... they called to tell me after the jet departed. They are both happy that Tim will have a chance to survive into the new world.

They both believe they may be of some assistance should the world governments decide on a possible plan of action to stop this incoming asteroid. After all, they do have the most current data on this catastrophe. Hopefully we can help them from our new position of relative safety.'

During this exchange of serious conversation, no one had noticed that Tim had stopped clicking away on his computer. When Max and Randall stopped talking there was just the hum of the air conditioning, they both swivelled around in their chairs to see why.

Tim was sitting back in his office chair. Randall gently turned him around to face them... he was crying. Then in a quiet whisper...

'What is this,' touching his tears, 'what is happening to me?'

Randall quickly came alongside Tim's chair; it was obvious Tim had heard Professor Reg and Sally were not on the Boeing jet he had helped to charter. Then in sudden act of affection, Randall gave Tim a big comforting hug.

'This is a good thing young chap; you are experiencing sadness and fear at the possible loss of your loved ones. This is a time when we must all draw strength from one another... just remember Tim, it is not over yet. We are after all the best jolly computer hackers in the world... We can still beat this huge challenge that we have before us.'

Randall was looking over Tim's shoulder and caught sight of Tim's computer screen at about the same time as Max. Big bold letters displayed...

Action alarm... section 43AL coolant leak at SCM No.3056 safety level 4... Hold status for investigation and rectification... calculated project delay... 8 to 20 hours.

This was a demoralising blow, reducing further the chance to end the creation of CDM prior to the asteroid becoming visible from behind the sun. Max gave a polite cough sounding more like a gulp.

'Shit, it looks like they have sprung a small helium gas leak at a superconducting electromagnet, close to the ALICE detector. This delay could lose us a full day, that's going to cut things very bloody fine mate.'

Randall was still hugging Tim who was crying freely now with rivers of tears running down his face, Max went to find some tissues. Randall thought this was a remarkable...

Tim the prodigious savant was showing emotions, emotions that he was never born with. What did the Entity say, "Tim is an enlightened human who can feel our presence." Could the Entity, just like Tim suddenly gain some human emotions... a mind to change our planned ending?

Max broke the spell of thought, handing Randall a box of tissues to dry Tim's tears, and then seeking a change of direction.

'I have been following the Doc's flight from Perth, with his planned stopover. The Doc and Mary will be in Newman by now, this is all starting to get to me; I must be getting soft but I do miss the Doc, you know, he's all I have as family in this world. Is that a normal feeling for a bloke Randall?'

Randall hesitated as he was about to hand a few tissues back to Max... remembering this was not the macho thing to do in the Australian male culture.

'I must say Max that Doc Dave of yours must be one hell of a tough, as you say bloke. After almost four months in bed in a coma, he reluctantly took part in half a day of physiotherapy, and discharged himself from hospital.

He then took delivery of his new Cessna Caravan 208 and departed Perth. Heading for this mighty fine airport of Sandfire. You know old chap, I have only ever seen Dave in real-life flat on his back in a hospital bed. I must say I am looking forward to meeting this chap. With his body fully connected to his spirit and of course the lovely Mary again.'

Max had lapsed into deep thought again. Dave and Mary will arrive around 8:30am tomorrow morning after a matrimonial stopover in Newman. Apparently the Boeing 737 will be arriving at around midday tomorrow landing at Port Hedland, glancing at the status clock now showing 1:15am, or is it now already today… yes time never stops.

'Come' on you blokes, we need to get some sleep. The shit is going to hit the fan thick and fast in around eight hours; we are all going to need our wits about us to sort out this bloody mess. Let's try and get some sleep.'

Day four to asteroid impact

'You look fucked Doc. I reckon you must have lost about ten kilos while you were having a nice sleep, and we were all working our butts-off.' Walking past Dave to give Mary a big hug and a kiss.

'Never thought you'd ever see this bloody place again eh Mary.' Then out of urgent curiosity, nodding at Dave 'What's this skinny guy been telling you?'

Mary radiated a beautiful smile of utter innocence that immediately fired a dozen warning shots of terrifying concern. The bastard has not told her… Max hoping his shock did not expose his concern. Mary then launched into a delightful chatter of questions.

'Dave tells me that he has a new English business partner who has more money than good sense and has fallen in love with our wonderful Australian bush.'

Randall gracefully moved forward quickly shaking hands with Doc Dave, commenting Dave looked far better asleep in his hospital bed. Then gracefully dropping on to one knee, he promptly kissed Mary on the back of her hand in a right royal manner. Randall had assessed the critical situation in an instant.

'Yes my dear, I must confess that I do indeed have more than a few screws loose up-top, and also more than a few million pounds to spend. Nonetheless, I do know a good deal when I see one.

I have assumed that Dave has informed you that we have embarked on a little tourist project.'

This was a first for Dave; he had no idea what Randall was talking about. Deciding to say nothing, and look intelligent with a smile on his face. Randall droned on with confidence.

'One in which we are bringing a jet-load of frozen pommes out to sunny Australia to enjoy a hot Christmas in the bush. Well by all accounts, our first jet-load of British tourists arrive here today.

Mary dear, being a director of our new company. Might I ask if you would be so kind as to perform some tour-guide duties to our new

388

guests? Max will be happy to fly you out to meet our guests arriving by chartered jet into Port Hedland later today.'

The look on Mary's face was one of both confusion and surprise. Randall had hit all the right spots. Mary could be part of all what was going on, she liked the idea, and now totally hooked. Max and Dave sighed in relief. Randall's smooth tongue had resolved a potential disaster yet again, well for the time being.

Max and Mary were waiting on the tarmac as the Boeing 737 landed at Port Hedland. It would take another two hours to clear customs; this was a most unusual event for the town, a direct flight in from the UK, this never before attempted.

Reporters from the local newspaper, The Pilbara Echo were asking some awkward questions like. "Why in the hell would anybody in their right mind want to fly halfway around the world to have Christmas in an iron-ore, dust covered, dirty Australian mining town?" Nobody could provide a convincing answer, and just continued smiling into the crowd of inquiring faces.

Randall a few days previously had done a special deal with the South Hedland Motel. He had reserved all forty rooms for an extraordinary amount of money. Paying cash in advance... money really talks.

The new British guests were to have every available convenience at whatever the cost. The Motel manager thought Randall was a mad pommy but still took his money. Now all he had to do was find the existing guests some alternative accommodation.

Mary was a bit suspicious about this odd tourist business. Nevertheless, with a little prompting from Max, went about organising all the transport and guest accommodation. This leaving Max free to separate and contact Emma, chirpy, Jan, and Tom for the flight back to Sandfire.

Just before spinning-up the Cessna Caravan turbine engine, Max had a question that needed an urgent answer

'Please tell me guys that all those happy people on the Boeing flight have no idea what the real situation is. Do they still think that this is all about a free Christmas holiday in the Australian bush?'

Jan looked up, but Tom answered Max's question.

'That was one of the most difficult things I have ever done in my life. Eighteen hours of trying to keep-up an appearance to all those nice happy people. All looking forward to a company paid holiday in

Australia; a few innocent people, who in a year or so from now may ultimately be the only surviving humans on this planet.

Believe me Max; they have no idea what has to come; and Mary, what of Dave's Mary. How did she accept this catastrophic news?'

The five of them were all watching from a distance as the happy smiling Mary went about helping the excited passengers. Max experienced a small-uncontrolled shiver and replied.

'Doc Dave in a six-hour flight from Perth couldn't bring himself to tell Mary what was going on. Randall had smartly thought-up a plan to leave her behind in Port Headland to look after the other passengers... She knows nothing. What about your family Tom?'

'With more help from Randall we have chartered a small private jet in the US, promising a magnificent all expenses paid Christmas holiday in Australia. When we get to Sandfire, I will find out if they have taken up my offer... I certainly hope so.'

Tom was not his usual pillar of confidence.

'This power over who should live or die does not sit well with me; I am but a simple academic. As an Anthropologist, I study human remains to learn from and to preserve our human past. I find it extremely difficult to make decisions that will ultimately preserve our human future.'

Emma and Chirpy had a little cry while telling Max about Professor Reg and Sally refusing to come with them to Australia.

'Their last words were that we are the only hope to put a stop to all of this. Sadly adding "God be with you." Emma's whisper was lost in the whine of the jet engine starting and the futile meaning of those last words.

'Is it not ironic, that when faced with both the truth and the end. That people still have some hope in religion. In that it may somehow save them.'

Chirpy in her typical and blunt manner reminded them all of what would happen. If known, a possible refuge from this catastrophe was available in a remote Australian desert.

Chirpy went on to explain her point. All the powerful world governments with certainty would immediately commandeer the Veevers crater area, securing it with a heavy military presence. The world population would arrive in droves in the hope of finding a place for survival. Ultimately, the whole area would quickly descend into uncontrolled anarchy.

Tom quickly moved away from this accurate but grim description, enquiring if there was any good news from the LHC in Geneva.

On the forty-minute flight out to Sandfire, Max was cross-examined on the present CDM situation. The mood shifted further, when Max told them about the CERN collider project being on hold because of a possible helium gas leak. The atmosphere in the aircraft slipped into that of almost accepted defeat.

Emma and Tom clearly hearing the deep thoughts and concerns of the silent Chirpy, Jan, and Max; concerns on what might happen next. Terrible thoughts, the possibility of avoiding a world catastrophe was to them, now all but lost.

On arrival at Sandfire, Emma, Chirpy, and Jan were quite surprised at receiving the big hug from Tim. This being a display of affection they had never seen or experienced before. The personal stress was now apparent. Everything the chaos group had known about one another was now quite different... including Tim.

At the Sandfire Fort, Jan threw a number of newspapers down on the large alfresco table. Then in his stuttering Midlands accent, added his view on the current world news.

'You lot think it's hot ear in Australia, well av a lo-look at that lot.'

The London Guardian inside page had a half page article "Drug cartels fight it out on the streets in a bloodbath over lost millions." The LA Daily News front page said it all "Tax havens no longer Heaven," then an interesting article on page four of the British Scientific Journal.

"Unusual and enormous solar flare activity reported in the seventh year of the normal eleven year cycle. Communications and satellite systems are experiencing odd and significant disruptive interference from a number of unusual powerful sun-solar flares.

Experts say we should expect a solar tsunami. The flare trend is still increasing, as many of the older and less RFI protected satellite systems fail under the relentless barrage of Radio frequency interference from the Sun."

The Business Observer carried a front-page story that told all.

"World communication business giants watch as stocks tumble and data satellite systems fail with increasing solar sun activity. This solar activity could eclipse the 1859 perfect solar storm." Then a second huge heading, "Gold stock prices spike forty per cent to $2496 an ounce as money moves in a flood out of un-safe BVI banks and other tax havens into gold stocks."

'Ow long do you th think we av before they fi figure out who pinched their bleeding money then eh. Just as w well we're hiding in a bleeding desert in Australia.'

Chirpy picked up the newspaper having heard little of Jan's ranting concerns about the stolen drug millions. She had focused her attention on the many solar flare articles. After reading, she then opened up her mind.

'The Entity was correct. We should all remember that it is a far smarter intelligence than we will ever be. My suspicions are that all these events are somehow connected. I think we...'

Just then, Chirpy's vocal thoughts rudely interrupted by a sudden outburst of verbal enthusiasm from Randall. Thumping his beer can hard on the table then letting fly with his newly discovered conclusions.

'By Jove chaps I do believe that I have the answer to this rather odd and unusual happening at the Large Hadron Collider.'

Chirpy was not amused at this sudden interruption and by the looks on Emma and Tom's faces, they agreed. They both wanted to hear what Chirpy was about to say however, Randall pressed on in his excitement.

'Do you not see it chaps, this delay is just a cunning Iranian diversion to give them time to change, or add something to the LHC loop system? No doubt this was needed to make their CDM God particle plan work'

Emma, Chirpy, Tom, and Jan remained puzzled as Dave, Max, and Tim jumped to their feet. Then without a word, smartly walked off in the direction of Max's well-equipped satellite tracking caravan.

'What the fu fuck was that all about Randall,' everyone staring after the trio now climbing into Max's caravan.

'Well it suddenly occurred to me old chap that at the slightest hint of a helium gas leak at the LHC. This would have caused the automatic safety control systems to immediately suspend and close the entire research facility.

The CERN would have no if's or butts about it old man... safety is their main concern. Being so, one would wonder why they had not done so. My guess is chaps they do not have any emergency at all, and the CERN safety board know all about it.

I think that this was a well-planned excuse for the Iranians to fiddle around with some of the collider system controls, most probably disguised as some sort of scheduled safety drill... Now all we need to know is why.'

Day three to asteroid impact
Six hours to the asteroid visibility.

Everybody was crammed inside Max's large forty-five foot caravan. Large as this caravan was; eight people had very little room to move, let alone sit-down as every spare inch of space fitted-out with electronic equipment.

Emma and Chirpy sat on Max's single bed watching his smaller 32-inch TV monitor, following the rapid screen changes as Tim, Max, and Randall went about hacking into the CERN Grid computer in Geneva.

This time they did not bother covering their hacking tracks, as time was fast running out. Emma on the flight from England had recalculated the solar event time on earth. Calculated for when the asteroid would first become visual from behind the sun.

The event would first appear as a visual shortly after 1:16 pm GMT. Seen first, on the small central Pacific Island of Kiribati, to those observers with a means to view the solar flare activity.

However, the asteroids actual minimum distance from the sun would be at 9:12pm Sandfire local time. This would be in five hours forty-three minutes from now. The first asteroid exposure removed the last possible chance to hide this cataclysmic event. That was assuming the Entity had no means to stop the flight of this asteroid. Max let out a loud remark, pointing at his monitor.

'Would you look at that, Randall was bloody right.'

Everybody crowded around Max's massive fifty-inch central monitor that was plainly suffering from signal loss due to the sun's heavy solar activity.

'The smart-arse Iranians have used the bloody safety drill and lock-down time to hook-up some sort of access port at the ALICE detector site. Doc, can you try to get into their CCTV system. It does not matter much anymore if the security blokes suspect any hitchhiker's playing around. If we can get a picture it could give us a few visual clues on what's going on over there in Geneva.'

393

Randall came into Max's tiny bedroom and handed Chirpy a notebook computer, and Emma a scientific calculator.

'Chirpy, this notebook is on Wi-Fi linked into our main computer router so you can work online in real-time. What I have in mind girls is; I need to know when they start to run-up the collider. I must have their approximate proton mass to do a nice job in melting all of the 7000 super conducting magnets.

Remember ladies, too early and well you know the answer, they will just shut things down over Christmas, to reprogram a start all over again in a few months. We know that restart will not happen. If we leave it too late, then my dear they will have created CDM to which, the Entity has a solution. The total extermination of the human race.

It will be the end of all human earth-surface civilisations. And for us surviving humans, the start of a very long period of hibernation underground, we must get this right.'

As Randall turned and walked the few steps back to join the others in the main part of the large caravan. Emma thought that Randall was losing his humour. This was a bad sign, Randall was at the most serious she had ever known him to be, and she needed his strength to carry on... they all did.

Two hours and six minutes
To asteroid visibility

The satellite phone in Dave's caravan was full of static and almost impossible to hear. Tom had managed to reach his son Luke in LA who it would appear required some heavy convincing to get on the private chartered jet.

His daughter Lisa refused to change her planned Christmas arrangements. Luke promised his father he would try to change her mind when Tom told him it was now a matter of life and death, persuading him that all his family must come to Australia immediately, insisting Luke write down the private jet company name, and the Sandfire airstrip coordinates.

He would explain everything in detail when they arrived. Tom felt a bit left out now, and wanted something to do to keep himself busy. Also to divert his mind from his family worries.

Emma and Chirpy were crunching collider loop mass equations. While Max and Jan were monitoring all the LHC control and safety lockouts. Both were ready to disable, or switch on a CERN system as needed, with Randall and Tim running the main grid hacking system-attack as their central control.

Max briefly stopped working on his computer and turned to face Tom. He was responding to Tom's request for a job, then with a firm voice and a respectful smile.

'Professor Thomas, you would have be one of the coolest blokes I have ever known. Looking back over all the things we have been through over the past few months, you have never once panicked. We have all drawn strength, watching as you quietly accepted this pending world catastrophe. Nor have you shown any doubt that we can win this huge battle.

Mate, I have this gut feeling the Entity chose you for your knowledge of religion, and not just old bones. The way I see things is the Muslim God particle thing may all about a battle for world power and dominance. Using religion as some sort of front to achieve that power.

You are a respected authority on the world religions there must be something we have all missed. What I am going to suggest to you, me being a simple dumb pilot. You should go over everything leading up to this pending world disaster, especially from the religious angle. Try looking a bit deeper at what Randall and I figured out about this God particle stuff.

You never know Tom, if we can figure out the true purpose behind all of this. Religious or otherwise, we might just gain a few minutes of advantage. At this late stage that might be all we will need.'

Tim had stopped working and turned to face Max, Randall, and Tom, he had the beginnings of a real smile on his face. At the same time, Jan gave out a whoop of excitement, pointing to Tim's computer monitor.

'Look th they've started to run-up the bleeding collider, which was marking time at a possible hit of 23 TeV... but why so b bloody high?'

Then a squeaky Chirpy yell rang out from Max's bedroom.

'Run that security frame again Dave okay, hold it, back a frame, and another, that's it.

Look at the Arabic script on the clipboard that man is holding. That says "thahab" that is the Arabic word for gold. You know, I think these Arab scientists may have discovered a way to add the needed mass to make the huge amounts of CDM, by using gold-ions instead of lead. What do you think?'

Randall was in a deep binding thought mood again. Dave, Emma, and Tom had easily read his thoughts, and then Emma provided a possible answer.

'It could be the answer Randall. Nobody to my knowledge has ever put this theory to the test. We know on the periodic table that lead has a proton number of 82 and gold is 79. Although only gold is the primordial transition metal. However, the proton mass numbers for both are very close... could this be the CDM mass builder?

Well I suppose we are about to find out, when the LHC has been run-up with lead-ions in one 27 kilometre beam pipe, and gold-ions running opposite in the other. They will circulate for a short time, when they have both reached the maximum speed and beam load; directed to smash head on.

Then both of the aligned beams will smash into each other at almost the speed of light, releasing massive energy in the collision. The BEC unit will be set to collect,' Emma shouted out... 'Look at that mass build up. They may be about to create some CDM right now... but it is too early.'

Chirpy then put everything into crystal clear perspective.

'Yes and three days too early, this must surely be just a full test-run. We were all working on the 22nd of December as the true CDM creation date. Well at the least, they have begun running up the LHC system,

I had assumed that it may take a few days to reach the critical speed and mass for the main event. However, a good test run and a high TeV is all we need to do our sabotage damage.

When the gold-ions enter the system, we can measure the amount of proton mass build-up. However, with two differing ion streams this may be difficult, it's new technology, we do not know what to expect.'

Tom casually filled up everyone's glass, those that were drinking scotch and wine and finally Randall's beer. Then taking a long sip of his scotch sat back and glanced at the big countdown clock above Max's head, forty-seven minutes to asteroid visibility, he then sat down and opened his mind.

'We still have three days one hour and forty-seven minutes left to Armageddon. We should remember the Entity has no concern about the world population knowing that an asteroid will strike the earth in three days.

Trying to end this apocalyptic disaster before this asteroid becomes visible from earth was our idea. We know, and are aware the

Entity has no emotions, or consideration. It's only us, we humans that are concerned about the mass hysteria this asteroid will cause in those final horrific three days.'

Then taking another sip of scotch, the tumbler firmly clutched in both hands like an old man, he continued exploring his known understanding and view of this rapidly closing world.

'Gold has been a mystery to us for many thousands of years. We know what the periodic properties and elements are, but we do not know everything about gold. Such as why was gold so special to the ancients.

Gold has little practical use; it is too soft and scarce for making into anything useful such as a cutting blade, body armour, or a drinking vessel. So why was it so important to own this metal over ten thousand years ago, especially being such a rare metal to find, and yet so highly valued by all who seek and hold it.

This metal gold, first discovered sought and collected by man in every part of our inhabited world, and well before any transoceanic travel was possible. How did the ancients all around the world arrive at this same conclusion, at about the same time. What was so important about this rare yellow metal gold?

Looking at gold from an anthropologist point of view, this metal is uncovered and found at many of the ancient locations and dig-sites worked around the world.

The Aztecs and Mayans collected gold to adorn their Gods. The Spanish Conquistadores came from the other side of the world to invade the Aztec and Inca Empires to get their hands-on gold, and then take it back to Spain to adorn their Christian Churches.

Egyptian Gods being mostly clad with gold. King Tutankhamen's death mask was of solid gold, he being considered as a living God. Who knows maybe he was part Martian. I now believe that it is the very element itself, which has the unique value, and not just for making shiny ornaments.

It must have another use. A use that we are yet to discover, or are possibly soon to find out about. This curious matter will no doubt become clear when we enter the Martian underground city in the next few days,' then Tom thinking aloud. 'I would like to offer my theory.'

Tom glanced around the caravan, nearly all were engrossed in what they doing to save this world. Only Jan was listening, giving Tom his full attention.

Jan was fascinated by what Tom was saying… was there some connection between gold and the Entity? Chirpy paused, and started to listen. Tom continued with his view.

'We must consider, the alternative and ancient use for gold might have already been rediscovered by the Iranians. A new, or was it an ancient method to create huge amounts of CDM, using gold ions.

Did the Martians come here to earth just to mine for gold? After all, they had the technology to go anywhere. Apparently, they were considering moving into another dimension. Was our gold needed to make this jump?'

Staring into his now empty whisky tumbler Tom again continued.

'The Entity has revealed and confirmed over the past ten months valuable information, much of, which was only previously ever suspected. One such admission being the pyramids built on the many different continents around the world, such as the Egyptian and South American pyramids, and others, were all built for a special purpose. Strangely, it would seem all at about the same time.

We have known for some time that all pyramids around this world are constructed to a specific, conscious design. They use a form of advanced mathematical equal constant.

The two-point-seven tetrahedral geometry, also they are perfectly aligned to the Orion star belt. All face the same way, built without the use of a magnetic compass, yet pointing to true north, not magnetic north.

We are amazed at how they were built, using massive stone blocks cut to such an exacting size. We now know how these achievements carried out, and why... by extra-terrestrials possibly from Mars. My guess is the entrance to the Martian subterranean city at the Veevers crater will be via a pyramid.'

Jan added, 'Yeah built by those little green men fr from bloody Mars, with metal leg joints.'

Tom's quiet reminiscing, suddenly shattered by a loud interjection from a bewildered Max.

'SHIT we have just lost two of our five satellite systems, this space storm is bad new mates. These bloody solar corona ejections could wipe us out.'

Randall asked if he was on one of the failing satellites systems and was advised not yet, indicating that not all of the communication satellites were going down at the same time.

Panic started to set-in. Without these satellites, communication to the CREN grid computer in Geneva would be lost. Dave yelled out in utter disbelief realising the grim consequences.

'Randall we've got to pull the vacuum plug on the collider circulating rings now before we lose all the bloody satellite links and any possible systems control. Emma what-the-hell is the current proton mass status in the collider?'

Emma came back immediately reporting the energy level was not anywhere near high enough to do any severe and permanent damage to the LHC system.

Then her attention suddenly drawn to Tim pointing at his computer monitor, and they all turned to look. Randall explained for those who could not get close enough to see Tim's screen.

'Something has spooked these Iranian chaps. They have just opened up their new ALICE gold-ion port and are flooding the loops both ways with lead and gold ion particles...

Well really, would you just look at that; they have also put the BEC unit into the detector window. I think Emma was right, these blighters are about to start harvesting a sample of Cold Dark Matter,' then with a serious face. 'We will have to put a stop to this chaps.'

Before Randall could say another word Max quickly reached out and pushed the enter key to start the standby computer program. A program set to open all ten of the collider loop vacuum dump valves. These valves take about ten minutes to motor fully open. The slow response designed to stop the inrush shock-affect from damaging the 27 kilometre long beam pipes.

Eighteen minutes
To asteroid visual

Everybody had eyes glued firmly on to the main control-centre computer monitor. All were amazed at the speed of the proton particle build-up. They were even more amazed at the level of scientific knowledge and the skills of the Iranian scientists who had pioneered this new gold mass proton project.

The two remaining satellite links were dropping in and out with the computer buffers filled to their maximum with correction errors. It was difficult to find out if a computer instruction had been accepted, locked and confirmed... or not.

Chirpy was concerned. Had the computer dump-valve instruction finally remained received and now being implemented? Then there were the CERN alarms, and all the automatic shutdown safety systems. Max did not sound very confident as he provided the answer to the waiting chaos group.

'Don't panic friends, we have changed all the dump-valve alarm levels, but that will not bloody help us much when the temperature starts rising in the guide rings. This will happen the instant the first valve cracks open in the vacuum pipe.

As for, has our computer instruction worked, well mates. All I can tell you is we have an eighty-five per cent conformation that our instruction received by the CERN grid. On the other hand, at this stage we only have a 20 percent indication of a conformation handshake in that the instruction actually carried out.

All this sun activity and solar flare storms are gradually knocking out the world satellite communications. This is the most likely reason why the Iranians were spooked into suddenly starting to move their programme forward again. I would bet that it was a direct order, sent to them directly from Tehran… via a dodgy satellite link.'

A solid silence fell over the caravan with everyone staring at a screen while various computers crashed and then rebooted again. All they could do now was to wait until some sort of positive indication confirmed a result.

Max switched one of the remaining satellites over to BBC world. Between the many picture dropouts and pixel disintegrations, the story was clear enough. The world was experiencing one of the heaviest ever recorded sun-solar storms.

Apparently, smaller ionised plasma eruptions were taking place all over the Sun's surface, with massive X7.8 eruptions mainly at the Sun's South Pole. The end result was in blasting the Earth with huge coronal mass ejections, creating a geomagnetic storm. The patchy news pictures were showing the Sun's activity. As all power-utilities and satellite systems failed, causing billions of dollars damage around the world.

'By Jove chaps that was fast. The CERN status has just confirmed that our dump taps have just started to open, and the ten vacuum pumps have automatically activated, trying to offset the leak.

It must be an ear-splitting experience in the LHC with all the alarm sirens blaring away. Look, we have another success. The beam pipes are starting to heat up, now that's encouraging, I believe the plan may be jolly-well working chaps.'

All noticed that Tim had stopped entering data and was glaring at his computer screen. Both Randall and Max switched over their screens to see the detail. Soon noticing what Tim was concerned about. The Iranians were busy shutting down the slowly opening dump valves. They had already reversed and shut four of the ten vacuum valves. It was now a race against time.

The third satellite link suddenly dropped out un-noticed by the others. In all the confusion, only Tim appeared to have noticed this grim loss... how long before this last two remaining satellite links went offline...

Suddenly Max had it all figured out.

'Those bastards are shutting the bloody vacuum valves manually... they must have somebody at every dump-valve site... We're fucked; it's just a matter of time, it's all over for us now mates.'

Seven minutes to asteroid visibility

Jan yelled out in panic. 'You don't bloody know that Max, force a fucking computer override command right now you shitheads. Put the computer request into an endless loop... don't hang about.

Listen mates, we can open-up the fucking valves faster than they can shut them down. We only need a few more minutes and the bloody beam magnets will melt their beam apertures.

Then with some luck, the safety abort valves will automatically dump the 290 tons of super conducting electromagnet helium gas into the safety reservoirs. Quick, repeat the CERN grid valve instruction over and over... jam up their bloody computer system with input instructions.'

Only Tim's computer was still holding online, with Randall's computer all but a total loss dropping in and out. They both knew what was required as they went at their keyboards like maniacs with their fingers a blur of movement.

Everyone was shocked at Jan's brilliant outburst of strategy although, more so at the strange fact that he never once stuttered throughout the entire screaming episode.

The chaos group all looked on in expectation, as there was nothing any of them could do now to help at this critical time. Emma and

Chirpy were hugging each other and crying openly... this was their last chance to hide from the world this impending world misfortune.

Four minutes to the asteroid visibility

The CERN grid computers were being bombarded in-between massive data dropouts with request after request to open the vacuum dump-valves. The dump-valves were motorised and designed with flameproof metal boxes and cable protection.

The chaos group were visualising the Iranians in a panic trying to close or jam the valves with the motors repeatedly instructed to open them again. They would without doubt, as a last resort try cutting through the cables, which were protected in metal conduits... it was a mad race against time, and time was running out by the second.

Everyone on both sides of the world knew the LHC Grid computer must remain on line and functioning. A full mainframe computer crash would be fatal as this also controlled all of the other CERN safety shutdown systems. For the Iranians the Grid must be on line to complete their mission, and for the chaos group the Grid must be on line to stop them.

It was just about then that both Randall and Tim's computers dropped out to display blank blue screens, and never to reboot. The last satellite had finally gone down... they were now totally isolated from the rest of the world on a dusty airstrip at the edge of the Great Sandy Desert in Western Australia.

The big digital time laps clock above Max's head displayed the countdown at "zero" the earth asteroid visibility will be from now.

Earth impact three days
One hour and zero minutes

It was now 9:12 pm local time, asteroid show time. Tom asked quietly.

'What now my friends, what happens next... If this plan "A" has failed, you say that plan "B" will happen automatically in two days with the imbedded computer sleeper instruction.

Then again, this may never happen. Even with my limited understanding of computers, the huge CERN Grid computers would have been completely isolated in the LHC safety shutdown procedure. Then I guess it is now the last resort... plan "C."

Nobody wanted to say anything as Randall filled everybody's drink except young Tim who had fallen asleep at his computer workstation. The group had all been working for nearly thirty hours straight... it was all too much for Tim.

Randall stepped outside to catch a breath of fresh, but still extremely hot air. The others slowly followed Randall outside and all sat down around the alfresco table again. Jan had remained in the caravan to put Tim to bed.

Nobody spoke a word as they all looked up to the sky. Watching the flashing and glowing balls of light bouncing about in the deep black velvet night sky. What would tomorrow bring when the CNN, BBC, and the other world media released the details of this impending catastrophic asteroid event. Ten long minutes passed as Doc Dave decided someone must say something, then in a soft voice.

'My friends we have no other choice, we must follow through with our plan "C" as we are now responsible for around seventy people's lives. Max and I will fly into Port Hedland in a few hours and bring out all the people from the motel in three trips each back to Sandfire. Then we will fly them all-out to the new Veevers airstrip.

I will try to call the Hedland motel in about half an hour's time for them to get ready. With a bit of luck we might get through to Port Hedland from the Sandfire Roadhouse.

The Sandfire Roadhouse satellite phone will be out for sure, although with some luck the old original phone system may still be working okay to Hedland. I know that particular phone is still on the old buried landline; being fibre, it should not be affected by all this heavy solar activity.

Max and Randall's heads both shot-up at the same time, eyes wide... Dave was surprised at this sudden unusual reaction... he had read nothing in their minds.

'Has something happened mate, what's going on, did I say something wrong?'

Dave all but knocked from his chair as Max and Randall rushed past him towards Max's caravan. Max yelled back to the confused group from the caravan door...

'Bring a vehicle up to the caravan Doc; we need to get over to the Sandfire pub with some computer gear.'

Everyone looked on in interest as Max and Randall quickly loaded up some computer equipment into the back of the Mini Moke. Then without a word took off into the black night, leaving them all in a swirl of red dust. Jan tumbled out of the caravan followed by a sleepy and confused Tim standing at the caravan door...

'What the hell was all that noise about, Tim needs his sleep?'

Dave smiled a crooked smile he had just figured it all-out.

'Those two smart-arse computer hackers are going to try to hook-up a computer modem to the old roadside buried phone cable over at the Sandfire pub. There will be a good chance that the old fibre cable system is still working.

The computer speed will only be slow but good enough to get in touch with the world again. With luck, we should get some current world news, hopefully before everyone wakes up in Western Australia.

If they can get the phone modem working into a major city. We will know within the next hour if this world is preparing for an asteroid strike. Or the LHC in Geneva has suffered a massive melt down.'

Chirpy was certain this was the end, being totally resigned to a pending world catastrophe. Although, Chirpy had some other important doubts on her mind to resolve. She had decided this was about the right time to ask her questions, then in a shaky high-pitched voice.

'As I understand you Doctor Sharp, your man at the Veevers site has not yet found the entry to the Martian underground city. We could be out there looking for weeks. What about life-support, we will all need basic provisions. Medical supplies, food, water, shelter, clothing and so on?

We have put our total trust in the Entity. An Entity who we have come to know as having no compassion or consideration for humans, or any other biological life form. We might be better off taking our chances close to the government support centres.'

Dave replied to Chirpy in a slow and confident voice.

'Yes you are correct; we have put our total trust in the Entity. Although not in how the bugger goes about callously and relentlessly in its cyclic business of universal events. We have put our trust only in its truthful and vast knowledge of the past. Also in what it knows will eventually come around again in our future.'

Then Dave shocked everyone to the core with his next disclosure...

'I do know the exact location of the Martian city entrance as I have already been there with the Entity. The city has an entire ecosystem designed to support earth humans. If required for many thousands of years. We will also have access to all the Martian areas that contain many advanced technologies.

With these new technologies, we can help repair our damaged world from our new safe position.' Then looking around at the surprised faces. 'From the safety of this underground city, we could do a great deal of good in helping our old-world. With the advanced technology, we can also help to create a new world.

Every known plant species on this earth hydroponically preserved, along with every seed. It is a research scientists dream.'

There was a low gasp of surprise from Chirpy, Max, and Jan at Dave's extremely confident; yet outrageous statement. Tom and Emma had not read any of this critical survival information in any of Dave's thoughts. Tom was forming a new suspicion, and Emma agreed.

Tom's chair squeaked as he reached forward to recover the bottle of scotch on the table. The others turned to hear him thinking he had something to say, so Tom politely obliged.

'I believe entirely in what the Entity represents within this universe. It might not be a God, but in our limited and primitive knowledge, it is probably the closest thing to a God that we will ever come to know.

As far as I can figure things out, everything the Entity has decided to tell us has come true. The attempted or actual creation of CDM, the arrival of a dark asteroid, the actual date for the impending earth impact, even this Martian underground city. To me, it is all true.

If the Entity has said we can survive in the old Martian city then I believe that we can, and I think that Dave is right. We will most certainly be of great use in helping our planet earth recover from this catastrophic disaster from this safe position. I am cynical enough to think that this may well be what the Entity had planned for us all along.

Consider the facts now before us. The Entity is a precise planner, it would have known all about the enormous panic created with a three-day impact warning. We had a much longer warning of this event. Time to prepare a few planning options... including this one skilfully supplied by the Entity.

I did have my doubts about all of this.

405

How would the Entity, being involved only in long-time universal planning cycles. Have developed a means to stop this seven-kilometre wide asteroid from completing its orbit to collide with the Earth?

The Entity has said this threat to our planet could be avoided, only if we could stop the creation of Cold Dark Matter on earth. Did the Entity know all along that we would fail?

There is after all another three days and one hour left to impact. We may still have one last horrendous option left to stop the creation CDM. That is assuming that we have already failed in this attempt, and that plan "B" will still work.'

Tom scanned the terrified faces, now hanging on to his every word.

My friends, a frightening thought has come to my mind. Have any of you ever considered this could be a carefully planned final solution by the Entity, unwittingly led into an ultimate end situation. One whereby we few humans being the only survivors of this planet earth are predestined to start a new world. I guess we will all know the truth tomorrow if we are to be the survivors of a new world... aboard the Entities Noah's Ark.'

The shock of this new possibility now evident on all their faces. Nobody could think of a suitable reply. Just then, a familiar voice came from the shadows. Everyone was listening so intensely to Tom that no one had heard Randall and Max return. The whites of their teeth showing that they were smiling seconds before the group could see their faces. Randall spoke first.

'I can jolly-well answer that question for you old chap. You know, I do think that Chirpy was right on the ball with this very possibility earlier, when she so rudely interrupted by me.

We know that this incoming asteroid was about to be catapulted towards earth from directly over the Sun's South Pole. You will no doubt be pleased to hear, that with the help of Max and his box of electronic tricks. In addition, might I add his little black book of unlisted emergency phone codes? We have just been speaking directly to no other than Professor Reg and Sally in Oxford. Yes chaps in Oxford England by means of the good old reliable marine fibre-optic cable, you know, under the ocean.'

Chirpy had enough of Randall's ramblings and snapped a razor cutting response, obviously agreed by all.

'Well get on with it boy, we are all educated people here and know that a marine cable goes under the ocean. What we urgently want to know, are we all condemned to be moles living five miles beneath the Australian desert. Or has our sabotage plan in Geneva worked.'

Randall's jaw dropped, as he was briefly stunned into silence by Chirpy's cutting tongue. On the other hand, did he detect a hint of humour in her voice, thinking how remarkable. Max took this brief opportunity to continue the story.

'Professor Reg and his missus sound like a really nice old couple. They were at the famous Jodrell Bank Observatory, and witnessed the entire bloody solar event from start to finish.

Apparently, they were with a bunch of other scientists watching and recording this unusual Sun storm phenomena, when a gigantic plasma ball suddenly rose above the Sun's South Pole at exactly 1:11 GMT. This occurrence then followed by the largest coronal mass ejection ever recorded in one solar event.

This huge solar mass ejected out of the Sun's South Pole, directly into the path of the large plasma ball, totally vaporising it. That ball of plasma we know was in fact a seven-kilometre wide dark asteroid on its way to earth. How close was that mates.' then with a beaming grin and cheerful chuckle. 'So you see the Entity did have a way of stopping this bloody great asteroid.'

The whole table struck dumb at the magnitude of this good news and information. Could this be true, did they actually succeed in sabotaging the LHC in Geneva, was it now over?

Randall had recovered from Chirpy's cutting interjection adding.

'Professor Reg received a secure landline call from one of our on-site scientists at the CERN in Geneva. Seemingly, chaps, the LHC has gone into a full safety lock-down, because of suspected computer failures caused by the massive sun solar storm.

The solar storms have been knocking out the power generation grids, and communication systems all over Europe. Creating huge power spikes and jumping equipment pulse protectors. They confirm that substantial damage was caused to the Hadron collider-beam guidance system and it may take years to repair, and many millions of dollars to fix.'

Max reached out and grabbed for the bottle of whisky on the table, as everybody jumped to their feet hugging one another shouting and whooping for joy. All the noise awoke Tim again, and he came over to join them with a big smile on his face.

Emma was thinking this was the first time she had ever seen Tim really smile. He had a beautiful warming smile that matched his big brown eyes, and then waving her arms for attention.

'My good friends and members of the chaos group, as Tom had asked about an hour ago. 'What should we do now my friends, what happens next?'

Max stood up, a little unsteady now but still firmly gripping the neck of Tom's third bottle of scotch. Then butting into Emma's happy speech,

'I can answer that; I can tell you all what we are going to do.' Max then took a long satisfying swig direct from the bottle of whisky.

'When we are all sober again, especially me and the Doc here,' waving the bottle of scotch in Dave's general direction.

'We are going to fly out to our new Veevers airstrip to pick-up Tony and his lovely family. Then the lot of us are going to fly over to Port Hedland. Then we are all going to jump on that bloody big Boeing 737 with all of our sixty-odd happy people. Then we are going to fly that jet up to Darwin for the biggest and booziest Christmas anyone has ever seen or had. What do you lot say to my great plan eh, mates?'

Smiling like a Cheshire cat with a grin from ear to ear, Randall retrieved the bottle from Max, taking a quick swig.

'I must say Max, that all sounds like an excellent idea to me. To remain within your strict Australian drink-flying rules, we think you and Dave had better get off to bed now.'

Randall then waving the half-full bottle of Tom's fine whisky high for all to see.

Tom and Dave had easily read Randall's pissed brain, he was attempting to reduce the number of whisky consumers for the remains of Tom's scotch. Tom and Dave thought Randall and Max made a fine sparring pair for available whisky consumption. Randall finished with…

'Meanwhile, I will with great care, look after what remains of Tom's scotch.'

All were laughing at Randall's corny joke when Tom nudged Emma, drawing her attention to Tim, who was now staring ahead in some sort of a trance. Soon all the others noticed the strange change in Tim and became silent watching and wondering. Tim spread out both his arms, palms facing upwards, smiled, and then in a happy voice called out.

'The Entity is here... we should all listen this last time.'

They all looked at one another knowing exactly what was required, and then joined hands around the table closing the ring and waited... The voice heard within their heads was Albert Einstein.

'Please try to understand our simple message. We are the keepers of time and order and the developers of universal intelligence... that is all we do, that is all we have ever done. We are the natural universe, an omnipresent entity throughout this challenging universe. Biological creation is evolution by natural selection over universal time. An existence created only by necessity within an environment.'

"We are planners in time and space, we do not create."
"We are not alien to this or any other planet we are universal."
"Everything has a beginning and everything has an ending."
"Everything has a purpose and everything has a reason to be."
"Everything with a biological life cycle has a life force."
"Every life force is always a part of us... the Entity."

There was a brief pause, as Emma bravely took the opportunity to ask the Entity what could well be the groups last few questions.

'Can you tell us what the future will now hold for our planet, and our stupid aggressive human species? In addition, what would have been the result if we had not destroyed the collider? After all, and as agreed, we still had another three days and one hour to impact. After the dark asteroid became visible from behind the Sun. During this time, we then had one last option to stop the creation of CDM before 21 December 2012. By causing a helium fusion reaction at the LHC in Geneva. Had we succeeded with the helium solution, how would you have then stopped this large dark asteroid from continuing on its path to collide with our planet Earth?'

'Emma, we can only plan for an event in your future. You have been advised what is planned for your planets time cycle. A future is what you humans must create. We only know of the plans we have made. The future is not ours to know.

Any future only achieved after a period in time. We do not share, or indulge in human speculation.

You are correct, a small amount of Cold Dark Matter may have been created on your planet before the calculated impact time, however not enough to be of concern.

This was a situation changed with an instant human decision that we cannot see or control. However, as you have witnessed this possible variation ultimately planned for, thus considered in our infinite calculations for what may happen.

A greater, and planet destructive quantity of CDM was being processed for creation on the fourth day. The dark asteroid would have struck your planet one day before... as was planned.

Take notice and remember; this present time was once your future... a future planned in time from your recent past to now.

Aggression on your planet is your natural way forward through evolution to further your technical development and on to a greater intelligence. In the following, we share these same limitations with all biological life force beings.

"We cannot visit the past, however we can with great accuracy, remember, record, and learn from the past. A past within a cycle of planned time will again become the new future, somewhere at some time."

"We cannot visit the future. However, we can see where we want to go and plan with infinite accuracy to arrive at that point in time. A future where we have once visited in the past, in another time and place."

"The past is now your history and the future is what you now expect to achieve. We differ only in the way, and length of time it will take to accomplish these natural and necessary tasks in this our universe."

The intelligent beings on this small planet may never be masters of universal time, gravity, mass, and light, within their planets planned short life cycle. However, they will indeed gain a great knowledge and understanding about these universal matters, and there ultimate use.

To accomplish this knowledge. Your world will need to revisit and revise old paradigms that have now become entrenched in your planets early education, and continuing to the present. We advise many of these beliefs are wrong, diverting the human mind from the truth; a truth needed to understand this, your present universe. With the truth, you can accomplish that which we cannot... You can create the actual future.'

There was another long haunting pause, leaving the group in awe at the Entities moving words, and then the Entity continued...

'Emma you are expressing a doubt, for what can be planned and ultimately accomplished by the Entity. You must accept the fact; we do not make mistakes... ever. Time and intelligence will provide an answer to resolve all future universal challenges.

Intelligence raises curiosity, which drives ignorance into learning with an inspired understanding and a newfound knowledge. Retained knowledge through evolution is intelligence. Universal intelligence is the ultimate supreme purpose of this... and every other universe.

Randall was quick to see this was all about another end cycle, one in which the Entity would end all contact with the group as this CDM threat situation now resolved.

He must ask one last burning question, knowing it would most likely not be fully answered, however even a good clue would be a worthwhile fragment of information.

'I sense that you are about to leave us old chap, would you be so kind as to answer me one last question. As I understand from our past conversations, the Entity has admitted a few useful clues here and there about the way the universe works.

You mentioned that you had given guiding advice to a number of chaps from Socrates to Adolf Hitler and from Jesus Christ to good old Winston Churchill. Out of all the names mentioned only one of these brilliant men is alive at this time... Hawking... is he by chance on the right track with his theories on black holes. Is all information and matter lost at the event horizon entering a black hole?'

'The time is almost with you for your planet to have this knowledge; an answer is within his mind and life cycle. Only two symbols of the equation need resolve, one added and one changed, he has no other distractions.

There is no paradox as space and time are as one, when viewed from your point in this universe. Nothing is ever lost, only changed in

411

state, and moved in time... Consider what a black hole would represent at the other end and he will have his answer... the answer to this universe and the next...This knowledge will resolve for your world, what is time.

Within our plan, your earth cycle is not yet complete. Other challenging events will follow within your short biological life cycles. You must be ready for when we return. This present earth cycle and event is resolved... for now.'

Those last words contained a number of intriguing clues together with a strong message. All had a lingering suspicion that this may not be the last time they would hear from the Entity. Randall let go his hands, grabbed his can of beer raised it and said...

'We should all drink a toast to that last moving speech from the Entity,' then taking a large gulp of his beer.

'Chaps I say to you all, a Merry Christmas and a safe planet earth, might I also add congratulations to us all on our fine work in preventing a world catastrophe. Here we are, now left with this amazing story, sadly a story that unfortunately cannot be told.'

Then looking piously at the dark sky of flashing lights.

'All of us having survived this experience, I believe this old world will continue along its miserable selfish way. We should remember, we still have Quantum Universal to manage, and might I add my friends, a rather large bank account. After all, we did agree to do some good with all this money. Meanwhile, let us all drink and be merry, after all it is the time of the year they call Christmas.'

The group talked for many hours going over the events of the last ten months. Then Jan amazed the group in a clear and stutter-free voice, putting forward an interesting theory, or was it now an observation.

'I've been thinking. Was all of our worlds recorded past, and known near catastrophes, avoided in this same bloody way? The Entity had made mention of how it tipped off Einstein about Hitler being close to completing an atom bomb. If the Entity had not got involved at that point, what would have been the result for our world?'

Jan paused as he thought to add a little more...

'Then there was the back-down of the cold war, did the Entity have a hand in that. We were on the brink of world bleeding nuclear annihilation. What about the Cuban crisis, the Vietnam War, and

President Kennedy's assassination. Then in recent times the Chernobyl, Three Mile Island, and the Fukushima nuclear power plant disasters. Did the Entity have a hand in planning all of those world disasters, and then again... in the eventual resolve and planned outcome.'

All agreed it now appeared that Jan was correct, it was a brutal way for the Entity to achieve its mission. We are all continually in danger if we fail to meet the Entity's planned development programme.

Then in a voice not much more than a sad whisper, Emma added her view...

'The Entity has also admitted that it helped in creating many other world disasters, including most wars. In addition, the spread of deadly disease, the Black Death plague in 1348. Then there was the Spanish flue pandemic in 1918, killing millions, around five percent of the world's population... and now we have AIDS. Was this in part just fulfilling its mission to rid this world of excess resource dependant, non-productive human beings? In a similar way we would with excess animal stock, this being just a sort of destocking of humans... a regular cull.

War, in aggression or defence, used to accelerate resourcefulness and technical development. Just look at the technical achievements we have gained during the last two world wars.

Most of our current aircraft, shipbuilding, and electronics technology all originally developed for a war effort. We civilians only get to see and use the new technology developments for war, if a possibility exists to extract a commercial profit.

We are all still very much part of the basic planet earth evolutionary process... the strongest and smartest will ultimately survive. The day we stop developing intelligence on this planet, is the day we humans are no longer needed.

Extermination, death by event, or end-of-cycle we must accept as the natural and progressive ending to all life within the universe. Old life must make way for the new. Just like on earth, your achievements; no matter how small, are more important than your very existence. However, one must first exist to achieve. This simple paradox is conclusive proof that all life is meaningless in this universe, without advancement and progress. Intelligence and development is the licence to survival.

I have arrived at the conclusion that this is how the universe works. It is an enormous numbers game, with the added advantage of almost infinite time... Something will happen sometime, somewhere... out there.'

Tom stirred from his deep thoughts on Emma's observation, and the subject debated saying...

'What should we do with all this new and proven knowledge? We now have the facts and answers to many of the world's greatest mysteries.'

A hint of dawn was showing as a large curve of light. The sun was giving off a magnificent display of power and energy. Chirpy was admiring this new dawn... the creation of a new day. Now just a flickering solar glow at the edge of the vast star-studded Australian sky. She knew the answer to Tom's question.

'Tom, the Entity has said that too much knowledge too soon will create a great imbalance. However, knowledge gained too late can be fatal. Technology must be in balance with intelligence, passed on slowly in small increments. We have just witnessed the best of all insider information... the knowledge to why we exist.

** THE END **

"It's being here now that's important. There's no past and there's no future. Time is a very misleading thing. All there is ever, is the now.

We can gain experience from the past, but we can't relive it; and we can hope for the future, but we don't know if there is one."

(George Harrison) The Beatles
B25/2/43 to D29/11/01

Did George know of the Entity?

Introduction: About the Author

I was born in Edinburgh Scotland, this making me a true Scotsman with rights to wear the Dallas Clan tartan.

My working background covers a number of trades and disciplines, with many years based in the north west of Australia. There I worked and operated as the owner and founder of a number of small, but varying types of business ventures. These included a long career in RF communication systems, mine claim pegging, contracting to the mining industry, computers, aviation air charter, vehicle hire, and automotive engineering.

After many years, the family and I moved down to Perth Western Australia, there becoming the owner of another radio communications company. This new venture promptly followed by a classic and vintage vehicles sales business. I then for some unknown reason, drifted into the herbs and spice wholesale business, and then into owning a Mexican restaurant... Why, I really do not know.

I am very much married with beautiful children, who have now given us beautiful grandchildren.

My hands-on diverse business background has provided me with a long list of interesting true-life experiences to write this, and other novels.

I am fortunate in having a wide range of odd life experiences, together with my sound technical input, and a wild and cynical imagination. This combination offers me endless material to write convincing, modern, realistic fiction.

Website: www.nivendallas.com

417